PUMPING IRON

"Joe, you can't rush weight training," Chet said as Joe continued to bench press two hundred pounds.

"Don't tell me what to do," Joe wheezed. He launched into another set of repetitions, struggling not to let the weight drop down on his chest. Chet reached for the barbell. Furious, Joe lowered the weight and pressed it up again. "Back off, Morton. You're making me look bad."

As the muscles in Joe's arms started to shake, the barbell wobbled. Then the weights on one side slid to the end of the bar, and the unbalanced bar tipped under Joe's trembling grasp.

Lunging forward, Chet managed to get hold of the bar but with only one hand. He tried to wrestle the bar up by himself as Joe's strength gave way, but he couldn't get control of it.

Now the bar was swinging in a horrible parody of a cheerleader's baton twirl. But in this case the "baton" was moving with more than a hundred pounds of force on its weighted side—straight at Chet Morton's head!

Books in THE HARDY BOYS CASEFILES™ Series

Available from ARCHWAY Paperbacks

THE HARDY BOYS CASEFILES NO. 63

COLD SWEAT

FRANKLIN W. DIXON

AN ARCHWAY PAPERBACK
Published by POCKET BOOKS
New York   London   Toronto   Sydney   Tokyo   Singapore

AN ARCHWAY PAPERBACK *Original*

An Archway Paperback published by
POCKET BOOKS, a division of Simon & Schuster Inc.
1230 Avenue of the Americas, New York, NY 10020

Copyright © 1992 by Simon & Schuster Inc.
Produced by Mega-Books of New York, Inc.

ISBN: 0-671-73099-1

First Archway Paperback printing May 1992

10 9 8 7 6 5 4 3 2 1

Cover art by Brian Kotzky

Printed in the U.S.A.

IL 6+

COLD SWEAT

Chapter

1

"YOU DID *WHAT?*" Frank Hardy stared at his younger brother in disbelief.

Joe Hardy's smug grin didn't disappear, nor did the devilish glint in his blue eyes. "I signed us up for memberships in the Harbor Health Club. That's where we're heading right now." He steered the Hardys' van toward Bayport's newly renovated dockside area. "They were running a two-for-one deal."

"I heard that the first time you told me," Frank said. "This time around, I was hoping to hear *why* you'd sign me up for something I hadn't okayed."

"I did it *for* you, Frank." Joe reached out and squeezed one of his brother's lean arms. "You could use a little chunking up, you know, and

1

we have a few days off from school to concentrate on it."

Frank shook his arm free. "Okay. Give me the whole story. How did you find out about this big bargain?"

"It was a miracle," Joe explained. "I was just checking the place out and saw Chet Morton there, signing up."

"Chet?" Frank shook his head. "If you'd said he was trying a new fast-food joint, I could buy that. But Chet Morton at a gym?"

"After he signed up he went to talk with this gorgeous blond girl," Joe went on. "I think she must teach an aerobics class—she was wearing these purple tights, a high-cut blue-and-purple leotard, and an instructor's T-shirt—"

"*Now* I understand why you joined," Frank said. "You've found a new place to chase girls— or one girl at least. And you expect me to help you do it."

"Hey, I only expect a little financial help— like paying half my expenses." Joe was smiling as he pulled into the club's parking lot and brought the van to a stop. "Trust me, Frank, I won't need help with the girl."

"You're a real case." Frank rolled his eyes as they walked toward the gym.

Joe shrugged. "You found me useful enough when we tangled with those crooks in Las Vegas."

Silently Frank had to admit the truth of that.

Both he and Joe had pushed themselves to the limit on the *Final Gambit* case. So why did his brother have to be a pain now? Couldn't he just ease up?

Joe tugged on Frank's arm. "Come on, let's hustle. We've got to get to our first training session."

Shaking his head, Frank followed. "I suppose somebody has to be around to catch you when you fall on your face."

Besides, Frank was interested in seeing the new Harbor Health Club. Five years before, it had been the Dockside Gym, located in the basement of an old warehouse. Frank remembered the place as a sweat-and-strain shop where aspiring boxers worked out.

The neighborhood had changed, and the old warehouses were turned into condominiums. The owners of the gym had bought the whole warehouse, renovating it into an upscale health club. The poor boxers stopped coming, and the rich newcomers didn't pour in, so the Harbor Health Club went broke.

Frank remembered when Pete Vanbricken, a football star, bought the club. Was it doing better now, he wondered?

It looked pretty ritzy, Frank had to admit. The grimy old redbrick building had been sandblasted clean, and new windows had been installed. He could see beach umbrellas scattered on the roof. Frank was willing to bet there was a pool up there, too.

Joe led the way past the reception desk and down one flight of stairs to the locker room. Inside the room a tall man with dark, slicked-back hair glanced up at them and grunted. He shoved a long black gym bag into his locker, slammed the door shut, and strode off. Huge muscles, straining against a skimpy athletic shirt and shorts, rolled and bunched as he moved.

Another locker door was slammed shut, and Chet Morton was revealed in slightly tight sweats stretched over his bulk. His greeting was almost as cold as the stranger's. "What are *you* two doing here?" he demanded.

"We signed on for a little toning up," Joe explained as he stripped off his clothes and pulled on a pair of shorts and a T-shirt. "We're supposed to be training with somebody named Jan." He glanced at Chet. "Do you know her?"

Chet just gave him a dirty look and stomped off upstairs to the gym.

Shaking his head, Frank finished changing into the workout clothes Joe had brought for him. Then he and Joe followed Chet upstairs to the gym.

Frank was a little surprised by the large and airy gym. Years ago, as a kid, he'd sneaked a peek through a basement window into the Dockside Gym. Subconsciously, he'd expected to see the same cramped, badly ventilated room. But instead of rough concrete floors and cracked, yellowing plaster, he found thick carpeting and cool gray walls. The double-height room was lit from a rooftop skylight and high windows.

The people were different, too. Instead of the hopeful boxers and the old pugs training them, now well-built trainers supervised the workouts of people in expensive exercise clothes. Frank saw the guy with slicked-back hair from the locker room. He was working out with a huge barbell in an area with rubber tiles on the floor. Frank watched the impressive play of muscles in the man's back as he curled the barbell up to his chest.

Around the room potted plants had been placed for decoration, and enormous mirrors stretched along all the walls. Frank knew that the mirrors were supposed to help people check their form as they exercised, but he suspected that vanity was involved as well.

Frank noticed Chet Morton standing in front of a mirror. Chet's gaze moved around the room and back to his own reflection. Instinctively, he threw back his shoulders and sucked in his gut.

As the Hardys moved behind his mirror image, Chet turned to them. "You guys really going through with this?"

"I'm looking forward to working out," Joe said, grinning. "Not to mention meeting Jan."

"It's pronounced *Yonn*," a deep voice rumbled from behind them.

5

Joe's smile slipped a little when he turned to see the owner of the voice.

Just call him Jan the man, Frank thought, taking in a tall character whose chest pulled against the instructor's T-shirt he wore. Tall, mean, and muscles on top of muscles.

"Jan Cole," the man identified himself. "You three must be Hardy, Hardy, and Morton." He squeezed Joe's arm muscles as if they were so much meat. "Good."

Then casting a careful eye over Frank's physique, Jan Cole said, "You have potential."

Looking at Chet, however, he frowned. "Maybe we can shape you up—after we get rid of this lard." His slap to Chet's stomach echoed like a cannon shot.

Chet winced. But Jan Cole had already turned away to talk to a muscular young instructor who was showing one of the club members how to use an exercise machine. "Hey, Penman," Cole said, "work up an exercise routine for these guys."

The younger man nodded, annoyance creeping over his dark features. Cole didn't notice. He had turned back to the Hardys and Chet. "You"—he pointed at Joe—"know how a lat machine works?"

Joe glanced over at a machine that vaguely resembled a gallows. A crossbeam rose slightly over Joe's head, and weight plates were set into the bottom of the riser. A wide handle on a cable dangled from the crossbeam. The cable ran through a pulley system and attached to the weights.

Cole led Joe over, sat him in a seat in front of the machine, and adjusted a padded clamp that rested over his thighs. "I'll give you a low weight—just so we can see what this will do for those latissimus dorsi muscles." He slapped the muscle group just below and behind Joe's underarm.

Cole then led Frank over to a cable rowing machine. "You can try this out," he said, and helped Frank to get started.

Then he turned back to Chet and frowned. "And *you* can drop to the floor and give me fifty—or as many as you can manage."

Frank didn't like the way Cole spoke to Chet—or the way Joe was grinning over at the resistance machine.

"Don't sweat it," Joe said, watching Chet puff through his first push-ups. "I mean, a little exercise never killed any—"

His words were interrupted by a moan over at the treadmills. Joe turned to see a young man in a sweat-stained running suit wobbling on the moving belt. The runner's face went from red to white. His eyes rolled up in his head, but he didn't drop. Instead, he was flung off at the same speed the track was moving.

Both Frank and Joe dropped their cables. Before they could get up, though, the man had dropped—right on top of Chet.

Penman, the young trainer, rushed over from the desk where he'd been working on the boys' exercise program. He helped the runner up onto wobbly feet.

"I warned you, Mr. Laufner." Penman shook his head. "Overextending yourself is not the way to go."

Jan Cole swaggered over, giving the runner a slap on the back. The poor man nearly collapsed again. "Either a guy wants to get strong, or he's not good enough." Cole looked down at Chet. "You should remember that, Morton."

Penman sent the runner off to the showers. "I've got a program set up for you," he said to the boys, handing them each a piece of paper. "It's a six-day schedule. Mondays and Thursdays, you'll tone up your legs. Tuesdays and Fridays, you work on your chests and backs. Wednesdays and Saturdays, it's time for your shoulders and arms."

"And on Sundays we pray for strength to live through this," Frank added, glaring at his kid brother.

"Every day you'll work on your abs—those are your abdominal muscles—and you'll get some cardiovascular exercise—treadmill, stationary cycles, maybe some aerobics."

"Really?" Chet brightened at that thought.

His expression changed when Penman handed

him another paper. "This is a diet plan," Penman explained. "I'm afraid that you'll need a little more than exercise to get into top shape."

Turning from the crestfallen Chet to the Hardys, the instructor said, "Okay, you've had a quick orientation. You can stay and work out a little more or you can come back tomorrow, rested and ready to work."

The boys headed back down to the locker room and took showers and changed. Laufner, the runner who had collapsed, was still sitting on a bench resting as they tied their shoes. Frank noticed that the color had returned to his slightly flabby face.

"Hey, Cosgrove," Laufner called to a man who was just finishing dressing. He slid his arms into an expensive-looking black satin bomber jacket. Cosgrove was the muscle man they'd seen earlier. Frank wondered why he'd had such a short workout.

The big man spoke as he slipped his shoes on. "Well, Laufner. Glad to see you got your breath back."

Laufner flushed. "Has your gambling luck gotten any better, Big Walt?" he asked nastily.

Cosgrove whipped around, hauled Laufner off the bench, and slammed him into the wall of lockers.

"Little man," he said grimly, "watch your mouth. It might start a fight the rest of you can't finish."

9

Laufner slid to the floor. Before Frank or Joe could move, Cosgrove grabbed his gym bag and started from the room.

Laufner scrambled to his feet, and Frank Hardy blocked him from taking off after Cosgrove. "Take it easy," he advised. "That guy could finish you."

Frank had noticed two things about the mysterious Mr. Cosgrove. His big black gym bag had turned into a small red one, and the red bag hadn't been zipped closed. Frank spotted something sticking out of it. What he saw made him stop Laufner. The runner didn't have the muscle to take Cosgrove on.

He'd have even less chance against the pistol Frank had seen in Cosgrove's bag.

Chapter

2

JOE STARED in surprise when Frank suddenly grabbed his arm.

"Come on," Frank said. "We're getting out of here."

"What's the big idea?" Joe wanted to know as his brother steered him up the stairs to the main entrance and foyer.

"Something weird is going on. That Cosgrove was carrying a gun." Frank quickly clued Joe in on what he'd noticed about Cosgrove's bag.

"From the way he treated Laufner, Cosgrove doesn't seem to be wrapped too tightly," Frank said. "And when you add a gun—well, let's just say I'd like to keep an eye on him."

They were in the parking lot, opening the doors to their van, when Chet Morton came running up. His hair was wet, and the tail of his shirt hung out over his jeans. "What's with you guys?" Chet demanded. "First you push in where you're not wanted, then you run off without even saying goodbye. I want—"

The mysterious Mr. Cosgrove roared past in a low-slung red Porsche right then. "Some car," Chet said appreciatively.

"I'd be more impressed if it weren't rented," Joe cut in. "You can always tell by the first three letters on the license plate."

Frank and Joe realized that they wouldn't have a chance of following the Porsche, so they stood talking with Chet. The front door of the health club swung open, and Jan Cole came swaggering out. Before the door had time to shut, it was pushed open again, and another man stepped out.

Joe recognized him immediately—Pete Vanbricken. He'd seen Vanbricken's face on the sports pages often enough, first as a local football hero—Bayport High's star quarterback. Then there were Vanbricken's triumphs in college games, the trophies and awards he'd won. Most recently Vanbricken's victories had been in pro ball. He'd been the first-string quarterback for the Midland Foxes, leading them to the play-offs at the top of their division for three straight seasons.

Too bad about last season, Joe thought. He'd been watching the game on TV and knew there'd be trouble when those two linebackers hit "Pistol Pete" both high and low. Not only had he gotten sacked, he'd wound up with a separated shoulder. End of career.

Pete Vanbricken had come back to Bayport and bought the Harbor Health Club. Almost every local TV show had an ad featuring a smiling Pistol Pete inviting people down to his club.

Pistol Pete wasn't smiling now, however. As the ex-quarterback stalked out of the club, his face showed nothing but rage. "Cole!" he yelled.

Jan Cole glanced almost languidly over one shoulder. "Whatsamatter, boss?"

Even from a distance the boys could see a vein stand out on Vanbricken's temple. "Where do you think you're going?" he demanded. "This isn't your break time. You're supposed—"

"I don't see any time clock in there," Cole interrupted. "And I'm not just one of the employees around here."

"That's another problem," Vanbricken said. "I've been getting complaints from club members and the staff—complaints that you've been harassing them."

"Yeah, yeah," Cole scoffed. "We've been through this already."

Joe was surprised. This didn't sound like an employee talking to his boss. Cole was nose to nose with Vanbricken, sneering at him.

13

Cole's next words were even more surprising. "Look, Vanbricken, you need me. So you should learn to cut me a little slack. You couldn't keep this place going without the help I give your cash flow."

Pete Vanbricken completely lost it. His fist whipped around to crash into Jan Cole's stomach. Joe could hear the force of the blow, but Cole stood unmoved, his face still in the club owner's.

Vanbricken was not a small guy. He was an athlete, and even at thirty, he had a quarterback's physique. But the hulking Cole had five years and at least fifty pounds on Vanbricken.

Cole raised a fist as if he were pleased with what was about to happen. Joe took a step forward. He had to stop this slaughter!

Behind him, Frank never moved. He just leaned back against the van and cleared his throat very loudly.

It was as if he had blown a trumpet. Both men stepped back from their confrontation. Cole glared at the audience, while Vanbricken just stared blankly at the boys. Turning, Vanbricken stalked back into the club.

Cole hesitated for a second, almost as if he were about to speak. Then he glared once more at Chet and headed back inside, too.

"Wherever he was going," Joe said softly, "he changed his mind in a hurry."

He was about to say more when a yellow car,

a small but sporty model, rolled into the parking lot.

The car pulled up near the Hardys' van, and a very pretty young woman jumped out, already dressed in a leotard and tights. She had a perfect figure for the workout clothes, shoulder-length blond hair, and the faintest sprinkling of freckles across her high cheekbones and snub nose.

Joe recognized her immediately as the girl he had seen Chet speaking with when he'd checked out the gym. Seeing her up close confirmed Joe's initial impression. She *is* gorgeous, he thought.

"Chet!" the girl said, smiling as she walked over to them. "I see you've started your training. Great!"

"Uh—yuh," Chet managed, staring at her, his heart in his eyes. One hand went to tuck in his shirttail, the other to straighten out his tousled, still-damp hair.

"So, Chet"—Joe moved in smoothly—"aren't you going to introduce us to your friend?"

Judging from the look he got, Joe thought Chet would have been more willing to introduce him to a passing steamroller.

"Dawn Reynolds, this mental misfit is Joe Hardy," Chet finally said. "And this is his older brother, Frank."

"Nice to meet you, guys," Dawn said. She smiled again at Chet. "Guess I'll see you around."

"Every day," Chet promised fervently.

15

Dawn glanced at her watch. "Yow! Got a class to start. I'm going to be late."

Her hand went to her forehead. "Oh, great. I forgot my sweatband." Dawn dashed back to her car, rummaging around on the front seat.

At the same time, Chet rushed over to his car. He came back a moment later, a dark blue terry-cloth band in his hand.

"Can't find it?" he asked. "Here, use one of mine. It's clean," he hurriedly assured her. "Never even been used."

"That's so sweet," Dawn said, taking the band from him. One end fell from her hand, exposing the length of the band. In brilliant yellow letters, the name *Chet* had been embroidered onto the toweling material.

Chet blushed. "My mom made it," he quickly explained. "But you can wear it so your hair hides the name."

"It was nice of her to do that—and nice of you to lend it to me," Dawn said with a smile.

Chet's face grew even pinker as she raised her arms, slipped the band on, and fluffed her hair over his name.

"How do I look?" Dawn asked.

"G-great," Chet assured her.

"Very nice," Frank said.

"Yeah—really hot," Joe added.

"Well, I will be, after a few minutes," Dawn assured them. She ran for the entrance.

"Dawn seems nice," Frank said to Chet, who was grinning broadly.

"Yeah," Joe added. "I look forward to getting to know her better."

His comment earned him another black look from Chet. "I'll tell you right now," he said, "I don't want you bothering—"

"Hey," Frank spoke hurriedly to cut off an argument, "let's head to the mall to Mr. Pizza."

That put Chet in a good mood. Soon they were seated in a booth at their favorite pizza joint. Chet had a faraway look in his eyes and a silly grin on his face even as he ordered a pie with the works.

"How soon they forget," Joe teased him, shaking his head in mock sadness.

"What are you talking about?" Chet asked.

"I'm talking about those diet sheets, all crumpled up and stuck in your shirt pocket." Joe pointed to the bent papers curling out from Chet's breast pocket. "I'll bet monster pies aren't on that list. Tsk-tsk. What would Dawn say?"

Chet bit his lip and Joe laughed. His laughter quickly ended when Chet pushed the pie away. "Here," Chet said, "you guys can have this, too. My treat."

He turned to their pal Tony Prito, who ran the place. "Hey, Tony," Chet called. "Give me a salad. No oil, just vinegar."

The Hardys watched Chet attack the green

salad in grim silence. "Hey, it was just a joke," Joe said a little lamely.

"No, you were right," Chet told him. "I ought to get used to eating like this." He finished the last forkful, then stood up. "I've got to train myself to stay away from temptation. See you guys tomorrow."

Joe stared openmouthed as Chet walked away. "I never thought I'd see the day."

"What day?" Callie Shaw asked as she walked up to their table. Frank's girlfriend carried several shopping bags of various sizes, which she dumped on the seat beside Joe. Then she slid in beside Frank, a smile on her cute face as her sharp brown eyes took in Joe's expression.

"You look as though you've heard they repealed the law of gravity," she said.

"No, it's something weirder than that," Joe told her. "Chet Morton just turned down a pizza—he paid for it and gave it away." He pointed to the pie, which still sat in the middle of the table. "Help yourself."

"And get my arm broken when Chet comes back from the men's room or something?" Callie asked suspiciously.

"No, Joe's telling the truth," Frank assured her.

"It may be true, but I don't believe it," Callie said.

"From now on, call Chet Mr. Willpower."

Joe told Callie the whole story, making it as humorous as possible.

Frank Hardy didn't laugh, though. "I don't think this is so funny," he said. "I mean, we all know about Chet and pizza. If he's willing to give it up for this Dawn Reynolds, he must feel pretty strongly about her. I don't know if it's a good idea, you pushing in and competing for her."

"Competition is the American way," Joe assured him. "Chet wouldn't appreciate it if he had too easy a time. What's that line from school? The one about the bumpy road to love?"

" 'The course of true love never did run smooth,' " Callie quoted. "That's Shakespeare, from *A Midsummer Night's Dream*."

"Exactly!" Joe nodded energetically. "If Chet's truly in love, it shouldn't run smooth. Otherwise, 'May the best man win' as someone else said."

Frank shook his head. "Let's head home," he said to Callie, "before he quotes himself to death."

The next morning Joe was seated at the breakfast table when Frank walked into the kitchen. Frank clung theatrically to the door frame and stared at him. "The world must really be upside down if you're up and ready before me."

"Let's cut the comedy," Joe said, smothering

a yawn. "We need a healthy breakfast if we're going to survive the workout planned for us this afternoon. Did you see the weights those sadists expect us to lift?"

"I hope you're satisfied," Frank said, heading for the refrigerator. "If you ask me, we should leave Chet to suffer alone."

"If there were a mystery behind this, you'd happily take on the torture," Joe kidded. He reached over to turn on the kitchen radio, hoping to catch the weather report.

Instead, he got a special bulletin.

"The police have identified the body found this morning floating in Barmet Bay," the announcer said. "The man, who was not a resident of Bayport, was tentatively identified as Walter Cosgrove. . . ."

Chapter

3

JOE NEARLY SPEWED cornflakes across the kitchen table. "That couldn't be—I mean, it has to be a coincidence. The Cosgrove we met at the health club yesterday doesn't have to be *this* Walter Cosgrove."

Frank's eyes narrowed in thought. "That runner who nearly passed out—Laufner—called Cosgrove Big Walt. So it would seem that he is or was a Walter Cosgrove."

"So maybe he *was* up to something weird with that gun, the way you figured." Joe shrugged. "I guess we'll find out today at the club."

The locker room at the Harbor Health Club was buzzing. Members who never spoke to one another were talking together, all about Walt Cosgrove.

"It *has* to be our Cosgrove," Laufner, the runner who'd almost passed out the day before, said as he shut his locker. "The newspaper described him as dark-haired, muscular, and in his middle thirties. That fits Big Walt to a T."

"If he walks in and hears you talking that way, he's not going to like it," a heavyset member said, pulling on his sweatpants. "He'd think you were wishing him dead."

Laufner snorted. "And what if I did?" he asked. "Cosgrove thinks he can push anybody around. He's the biggest pain in the club." His voice dropped. "If you don't count Cole."

After pulling his T-shirt on, the heavyset man shook his head. "You really like to live dangerously, don't you? If Cole heard you talking like that, *you* could end up floating in the bay."

Laufner brayed a laugh. "The only thing he can do is exercise us to death—and I think he's already doing that."

The two men headed up the stairs to the gym.

Joe turned to Frank. "Looks like our friend Cosgrove was loved by all," he said in a low voice.

"We still don't know if he's the Cosgrove from the news reports," Frank said.

Dressed and ready, they went up to the gym, where they found Chet Morton talking with Terrance Penman. "Hey, guys," the young trainer said. "We've got a couple of people using the

22

free weights, so start with some warm-up exercises.''

Joe glanced over at the lightly tinted glass wall that separated the gym from the aerobics studio. He saw a leotard-clad female figure in there. "How about some aerobics?" he asked.

Chet noticed Dawn and nodded. "Sounds fine to me," he said.

Dawn Reynolds grinned at the three boys as they opened the glass door and stepped into the studio. A small group of men and women had already congregated there, forming into ranks.

"Hi," Dawn said, "and welcome to the wonderful world of aerobics. This is a basic class—just the thing to get you warmed up for your work out there." She nodded toward the gym.

"I hear it's just like dancing," Joe said, needling Chet. Joe was a good dancer, but Chet tended to stay off the dance floor.

"Let's start with some leg lifts," Dawn said. Rock music with a heavy beat started playing as she took her place at the front of the group. "A hundred!" Dawn called, starting the exercise. As the pretty instructor counted down, they all performed the exercise. By the time they reached fifty, Joe's leg was beginning to get tired. It wasn't exactly like dancing, and his muscles were protesting at the unfamiliar exercise.

Joe glanced over at Chet. Face red and panting a little, Joe's friend grimly tried to keep pace.

"Yeah, that's the way to do it!" Joe called to him. Joe worked hard to eliminate any trace of being out of breath and tried to lift his leg even higher.

For a second Chet took his eyes off Dawn to glare at Joe, and his face went even redder. Then he continued with the exercise.

For the next half hour the class continued. Joe felt sweat trickling down his back. Chet had big wet blotches appearing on his T-shirt.

Dawn continued leading the exercises, her voice normal, hardly a blond hair out of place. Joe began thinking of a cartoon he'd seen once. The caption had read "Aerobics in Hell." It had featured a devil leading a bunch of sinners in an apparently endless workout session.

At last the music ended and Dawn said, "That's it—very good, everybody!"

As soon as he could trust himself to speak normally, Joe walked over to Dawn. "That was a great starter," he said, pumping his arms a little. "It really gets the blood moving. Right, Chet?"

Chet only nodded, apparently not trusting himself to speak without panting.

Frank Hardy joined them, letting out a deep breath. "The only thing is, I feel as if my session has just ended, instead of just begun."

Dawn's laugh was bright and bubbly. "No goofing off, now," she said in a mock-stern voice. "Terrance is ready for you. And remember—I can see everything that goes on out there." She laughed, indicating the glass wall.

"We'll do our best to give you a show," Joe promised. He could feel Chet's eyes burning into his back.

"Why don't you cool it a little?" Frank whispered as they headed out. "You're going to push Chet into hurting himself or something."

"I just want Dawn to know how fit I am," Joe whispered back. "Besides, all's fair in love and war."

"You're just full of quotations lately," Frank said, shaking his head.

Terrance Penman set Joe up at a rowing machine, showing him how to set the weight resistance for ninety pounds. Joe leaned back against the weight, pulling on a bar and cable that was almost like the attachment for waterskiing.

Instead of skimming along the water, he had to haul against the weight. Now I know how galley slaves must have felt, rowing those big boats around, Joe thought.

He had three sets of exercises to do, repeating his hauling motions first ten times, then eight, then six. By the time he finished, the ninety-pound weight he was trying to move felt more like a ton and a half.

Straining, Joe finished the last set of repetitions. Chet Morton came over, wiping sweat from his face. "Finished with your reps?"

Joe nodded.

"Penman said you could show me how to change the weights."

"You want them lighter?" Joe asked.

Chet glanced from the weight setup to the list in his hand. "No—more. I'm supposed to be pulling one hundred sixty pounds."

Joe stared. "You're pulling seventy pounds more than I am?"

His only response was a shrug from Chet. "It's because of my build—and because I've worked out with weights before."

Joe remembered Chet's weight room, set up in the old barn near his house. Sure, Chet had worked out in there, but Joe had never taken it seriously—until now.

As Joe rearranged the weight plates, Chet said sweetly, "I wonder if Dawn can see *this*."

Joe jerked upright, stung. "There. I've reset the pin for one hundred sixty pounds. Did you see how I did it?"

Chet nodded. "Thanks. Well, I might as well get down to it."

"Yeah. Good luck on finishing it."

Glancing upward, Chet only smiled. "Oh, I'll finish it, all right. See, this *isn't* like dancing."

He leaned back and pulled with an even, steady stroke. Joe watched as the stack of weight plates rose at the end of the cable.

A little farther along on the rubber-matted surface, Frank was lifting a barbell weighted at one end while bending over. "Six," he grunted, letting the barbell down and releasing his two-handed hold. "Wait till you try this one, Joe. It's a real killer."

Joe checked the weight on the barbell. "That's one hundred thirty-five pounds, the same as I have to do," he said. "Okay, I might as well do it now."

"Could be worse," Frank said, toweling off. "When I took these from Chet, he was pulling fifty pounds more."

"What is this guy, Superman?" Joe grumbled as he took over the barbell.

By the time he finished his sets, Joe was beginning to feel a sensation of heat in the muscles over his upper ribs and at the rear of his shoulders. This must be what iron-pumpers call "feeling the burn," he thought.

His next exercises were with dumbbells. First came the flat fly, where he lay on a bench, raising the dumbbells straight-armed until they met over his chest. Then he did dumbbell pullovers, lying with his hands clasped together holding the dumbbell behind his head, then bringing it over his chest.

Joe glanced over at the bench beside him, where Chet was lying down, pressing a barbell straight over himself. Judging from the plates on the bar, he was pressing more than two hundred pounds! Man, if his arms give out, that thing will land right on his throat, Joe thought.

27

Then he noticed that Frank was standing at the head of Chet's bench, ready to take the weight if needed—"spotting" it was called. A much lighter barbell stood off to one side. That must be the one Frank had used, Joe decided.

Finishing his last set, Joe sat up. "How did your bench pressing go?" he asked Frank, who was still spotting Chet.

"Okay," Frank said. "I managed to get through it all." He stared at Chet, silently counting his reps. "That's it."

Chet let Frank take the weight over his head. "I'm beginning to get back into this," he said happily. "Bet I could do another set of six before my muscles maxed out."

" 'Maxed out'?" Joe repeated.

"When your muscles have done the maximum amount of work they can, they just give out," Chet explained. "It can be scary. One second you're doing the exercise, the next, your arms or legs are like rubber."

"Nice time to tell me," Joe said, glancing at the barbell Frank was lowering to the floor.

"Hey, you get the light one that Frank used. It weighs only one hundred seventy-five pounds," Chet said.

Joe rolled his eyes. "Great. That's like picking up Frank and doing bench presses with him."

Chet shrugged. "Hey, iron man, your brother could do it."

"Then get off that bench and let me get to work."

Frank stepped away. "I'll let you guys sort this out while I get some water."

Chet walked over to the smaller barbell. "Okay, hotshot, I'll spot for you."

Joe positioned himself on the bench, and Chet carefully lowered the barbell over Joe's chest. He didn't let go until Joe had a steady grip.

"Okay," Joe said. "Here we go."

He bombed his way through the first set of ten repetitions. "Take it easy with those reps," Chet warned. "There's no reward for speed."

"Sez you." Joe went into the second set, eight reps this time, but he didn't do them as quickly.

"Joe, I mean it," Chet said. "You can't rush weight training. If your muscles aren't ready—"

Teeth gritted, Joe performed the third set, eight more repetitions. He was gulping for air by the time he'd finished. It felt as if he were trying to push a mountain up off his chest.

"Joe—" Chet began.

"Don't tell me what to do," Joe wheezed. He launched into the final set, only six reps this time. Three times Joe raised the bar, more slowly with each repetition.

Halfway, he thought. Again, he pressed the bar upward until his arms locked. Four. It was a struggle not to let the weight drop down on his chest.

Chet started to reach for the barbell. Furious,

Joe lowered the weight and pressed it up again. "Back off, Morton." His words emerged as gasps. "You're making me look bad!"

Joe's spurt of anger-induced strength wore off halfway through his final rep. Now he knew what maxing out meant. His right arm felt as if it were going to crumple.

The barbell wobbled, and Chet moved forward again, leaning over Joe to grab for the bar.

But the barbell wobbled more, the weights on the right-hand side sliding right to the end! The grip that was supposed to hold them in place fell to the floor as the unbalanced bar tipped under Joe's waning strength.

Chet managed to get hold, but only with one hand. He tried to wrestle the bar up by himself—Joe was no help at all. Weight plates clattered on the floor as the unbalanced bar tore loose. Neither of them could exert control as the bar swung in a horrible parody of a cheerleader's baton twirl.

In this case, though, the "baton" was moving with more than one hundred pounds of force on its weighted side—and the open end of the barbell was heading right for the side of Chet Morton's head!

Chapter

4

FRANK HARDY was stepping back to the weight section, sipping water from a paper cup, when he saw things going wrong for Joe and Chet.

He dropped the cup, splashing water on the carpet as he flung himself forward. Frank barely beat the swing of the barbell. His open palm caught Chet in the chest with a hearty slap. Chet bounced back, his head moving away from the deadly arc the barbell was following.

Frank's impact also made Chet lose his grip on the flying bar. It spun round till it crashed into the floor, bounced, then flew off to smash against one of the mirrors lining the walls.

Shards of glass filled the air, and everyone dove for cover. A young woman working out with dumbbells dropped them and yelled as a

31

piece of glass caught her in the leg. Blood ran down over her knee, the red in sharp contrast to her green workout clothes.

Joe was up and off the bench, miraculously unhurt. He caught the young woman before she fell. "Wha-what happened?" she asked. Her big brown eyes, wide with pain, stood out from her pale face.

"I'll tell you what happened," an angry voice loudly announced. Jan Cole stomped over and pushed his face into Chet Morton's. "Stupidity happened."

Chet was so shaken up from the disaster that he couldn't even answer. "What's the matter with you, kid?" he demanded. "You said you knew your way around weights. Don't you understand what a spotter's job is supposed to be? The minute Hardy began to have trouble, you should have taken that weight from him."

"I—I tried—" Chet began, licking his parched lips.

" 'I tried,' " Cole mimicked him bitterly. "Well, *I* don't think you were even paying attention. You were probably too busy checking out the girl exercising next to you to take care of your buddy. So she's hurt, and you and Hardy nearly got killed. Too bad that bar *didn't* hit you in the head—maybe it would have knocked some sense into you!"

Chet stood frozen, white-faced, as Cole turned

from him to the injured girl. "You okay, Linda?"

She nodded, her short dark hair bobbing. "I think so," she answered in a faint voice. "The glass—it's still in my leg."

Lips pressed tightly together, Linda looked down at the wound in her leg. A long, sharp piece of glass gleamed in her outer thigh.

"Oh, gross," a member of the gathered crowd—Frank thought it was Laufner—muttered. As far as Frank could see, it hadn't gone in too deep or cut any major blood vessels.

Still, the sight was enough to make Linda squeeze her eyes shut and turn her head away.

"We'd better get someone to take a look at that," Cole said. He glanced around at the collection of glass shards on the floor. "And I'll have someone clean up this mess—not you, Morton."

Cole's voice rose, and Chet stopped as he was bending over to pick up one of the pieces. "You'd probably break something else." His voice dripped with sarcasm.

"It's not Chet's fault," Joe spoke up. "He told me to stop, and I didn't listen to him." He took a deep breath. "If anybody's responsible for this, it's me."

"He should have done more than talk—he should have acted," Cole said. "And how come those weights slipped off? Morton, did you check that barbell before you gave it to Hardy?"

Chet opened his mouth. For a moment no

words came out. "Well, no," he finally said. "But Frank had just used—"

"You were supposed to check it." Cole turned away, dismissing him.

Boy, this guy is a real sweetheart, Frank thought.

As Cole led Linda carefully toward the exit, the glass doors of the aerobics studio swung open. Dawn Reynolds rushed to the scene of the disaster, her face pale.

"What happened, Chet?" she asked. "I had my back to the glass wall, but I knew something had gone wrong when my class stopped dancing. That girl—was she bleeding?"

Chet could barely speak. He stepped away from them, so Joe got the job of telling Dawn what had happened.

As Dawn listened to the story, her face grew even paler. She rushed over to Chet, who stood with round blank eyes, turned on the damage surrounding him.

"Chet." It was nearly a whisper, but Frank could hear her clearly. Dawn's voice shook as if she were on the verge of tears. With a stifled gulp, she went on. "Maybe—maybe I did the wrong thing, encouraging you to join the club and work out. I know you want to get healthy. But I would never forgive myself if you got hurt."

"It wasn't his fault," Frank spoke up. "Joe even said so."

"That's not the point," Dawn said in a constricted voice. "You can do a job on muscles—and even bones—if you push yourself too hard. I wouldn't want to be responsible for your getting hurt."

Chet stared at Dawn, wide-eyed. From the look on Chet's face, Frank knew Dawn had already hurt him pretty badly.

"You think I can't handle myself?" Chet asked in a low, hoarse voice. "Or maybe, maybe this is a brush-off." Chet's voice became louder and higher as his facial muscles grew hard. " 'Hey, Chet, it was nice, but now, bug off. I've found a more *interesting* member at the club.' "

The glare Chet shot at Joe Hardy sizzled with hate. "I saw him showing off for you. But he can't pump as much iron as I can—or as much as his brother can!"

"Chet, I was wrong," Joe began.

Chet cut him off. "Big deal. You spoke up kind of late. I'll never get an exercise partner around this place."

He checked out the gym, his lips in a straight, tense line. "I've paid for my membership, and I'm staying in the club, no matter how anyone tries to get me out."

Dawn stepped back as if Chet had slapped her in the face. She opened her mouth as if to speak, then turned and ran—not to the aerobics studio, but to the main exit and out of the club. Chet had obviously hurt her.

Chet turned to Joe, his voice poisonous. "Well, go on, lover boy. I'm sure she's ready to cry on your manly shoulder. Or maybe you can go the pity route. You know, 'That maniac almost killed me!' "

Chet's face twisted, and for a second Frank thought his friend was going to spit on Joe. Chet spat words instead. "Well, all I can say is too bad!"

He kicked at a pile of glass fragments and stormed off to the locker room. The maintenance man who had appeared shook his head and began to sweep up the debris.

Laufner and the other bystanders in the gym quickly resumed their exercises, careful not to make eye contact with Frank or Joe. To Frank it seemed as if he and Joe had become surrounded by a bubble of silence. I don't think Chet's the only one who'll have a hard time getting exercise partners, Frank thought.

Joe Hardy stood stock-still for a moment longer before turning to Frank. He seemed greatly troubled.

Frank almost didn't have the heart to say "I told you so"—almost.

"Well, Mr. True-love-never-did-run-smooth, are you happy with your little competition with Chet now?" he finally asked.

Joe couldn't meet his eyes, and Frank felt a twinge of regret. His comment had been a cheap shot.

"It couldn't have happened on purpose, could it?" Joe finally asked in a quiet voice.

The question was so out of left field that Frank didn't understand it at first. "What are you talking about?" he demanded.

"I mean, it was an accident, right? Chet's been my friend—well, as long as I can remember."

Frank could do nothing but stare.

"He just about laid it out, in front of everyone," Joe said, still bewildered. "He talked about how he almost killed me."

Frank felt a chill run down his back as he stared at his brother. "You can't believe that Chet—" he began.

"If you had asked me yesterday, I *wouldn't* have believed it," Joe said. "But then, I wouldn't have believed Chet could ever act the way he just did. I still want to believe that what happened was plain bad luck."

His voice faltered as he raised his eyes to Frank's. "The question is, what if Chet *made* it happen?"

Chapter

5

THE HARDY BROTHERS waited in uncomfortable silence to go down to the locker room until they thought Chet Morton would have left the club. Even then, they didn't speak until they were in their van, out of everyone's earshot.

Joe saw that Frank's first reaction to his suggestion had been disbelief. But Joe knew his brother and believed that even now he was examining the situation from every angle, tearing it apart as logically as possible.

Frank got behind the wheel of the van, started the engine, and pulled out of the lot. "Let's go over the whole chain of events, step by step. We got to the club, heard rumors about Cosgrove, then went upstairs and met Penman."

"Who sent us off to warm up with some aerobics," Joe said.

"Where you goofed on Chet and tried to turn the class into an exercise in one-upmanship," Frank said, accusing him.

"Then we went on to hit the weights," Joe said, accepting what Frank had said. "I started with the cable rowing machine."

"I worked out with the dumbbells—flat flys," Frank said. "I also saw Chet working on the dumbbell pullovers."

They worked their way through all the exercises until they reached the bench press. "I did my presses with Terrance Penman spotting," Frank said. "He showed me how the set screw works on the collar that restrains the weight plates. I did my four sets, no problem. By then, Chet had finished with the lat machine. Because there was another barbell available, he loaded it up, saying we'd save the one I'd used for you."

"So it sat around waiting for me after you finished." Joe frowned. "Did Chet go over to it at all?"

Frank shook his head. "He couldn't—he was lying on the bench. As far as I know, he never went near your barbell."

"Until he picked it up for me." Joe frowned. "He couldn't do anything. He'd know he'd be suspected right away. Who else could have done it? Cole? Penman? What reason would they have, though?"

"So Chet's got a bit of a motive and not much

opportunity. That's if you can possibly suspect one of your best friends."

Joe gave his brother an uncomfortable smile. "I don't have much of a case, do I?" They drove home the rest of the way in silence. Joe couldn't erase Chet Morton's angry face from his memory.

The Walter Cosgrove case was getting lots of media attention. As the boys walked into the kitchen, the hourly radio news was giving more details on the mystery man.

"Cosgrove was a traveling salesman who often visited Bayport," the announcer said. "When he was found in the bay, he was wearing an expensive black silk bomber jacket and a gold chain. His car, a late-model red Porsche, was found abandoned on Millman's Pier."

"That's definitely our Cosgrove," Joe said. "Black jacket, red Porsche."

Frank nodded. "And they found the car not far from the Harbor Health Club."

The radio report continued. "Chief Ezra Collig said that at this time the police are treating the case as one of suspicious death."

Turning from her place at the kitchen stove, where she'd been listening, the boys' aunt Gertrude shook her head. "It's just as I always say," she said. "That dockside neighborhood is an awful area. I read that it's trendy to move down there. Although why anyone would want to live in an old warehouse is beyond me.''

''They renovate them first, Aunt Gertrude,'' Frank said.

''But people get murdered down there all the time,'' his aunt said, as if that would settle the argument. ''You wouldn't find me dead down there.''

''I certainly hope not,'' Joe said, stifling a chuckle.

Aunt Gertrude's face went red. ''You know what I mean. Why do you boys have to go to a dangerous area to visit a health spa or whatever it is? If you need exercise, you could always help with the housework.''

The boys disappeared before she could discover any chores to back up her theory.

By the time the evening TV news was on, the police had released the coroner's report.

''At the top of the news tonight, more about the death of Walter Cosgrove,'' WBPT's anchorman announced. ''According to the coroner's report, Cosgrove did not die by drowning in Barmet Bay. There was no water found in the dead man's lungs. The medical examiner has pinpointed the cause of death as a brain aneurysm, a blood vessel bursting in the brain. Here with us tonight is our science correspondent, Dr. Burl Alpert, to explain the phenomenon of—''

With animated graphics and simple words,

41

the science reporter explained what a brain aneurysm was. "Not an everyday way to die," he ended, "but not suspicious, either. Apparently, Mr. Cosgrove had parked on an old pier. We'll never know why for sure. The quick onset of an aneurysm could have killed him instantly, and his dead body could have fallen into the bay."

The camera pulled in for a close-up on the science reporter. "There was no sign of violence on the body—unless you count the odd condition of the deceased's feet. According to the coroner, the skin of the soles was bleached white in several spots with frills of dead skin at the edges. That's a sign that Cosgrove must have suffered from blisters before he died."

Burl Alpert paused with a puzzled look. "But the violence there, I'm afraid, would have to be self-inflicted. Over to you, Scott."

Frank went to bed after the report on Cosgrove. Joe stayed up for the sports scores, but hit the sheets soon as well.

The Harbor Health Club was not its usual well-run self when the boys visited it late the next morning. They found a rather harassed-looking female staff member behind the reception desk, her instructor's T-shirt plastered to her leotard top with sweat. She passed them through with only a quick look at their membership cards.

"You may not find your usual trainer available today," the woman warned them.

"Why?" Joe asked.

The woman was obviously too tired to do anything but tell the truth. "They're giving statements to the police about Walter Cosgrove. Even Mr. Vanbricken is down at headquarters." She glanced at her watch. "And so is the person who was supposed to be relieving me."

The locker room attendant was full of his experiences "down at the precinct," as he put it. He also had some colorful theories about what had happened to Cosgrove, but Joe wasn't interested. He had promised himself, he would be all business and concentrate on exercising.

That promise was broken the moment he walked up the stairs.

Dawn Reynolds was hovering by the entrance to the gym. She had lost a lot of perkiness in one day. There were dark shadows under her eyes, and even her blond hair seemed to hang limply.

"Joe, I need to talk to you," she said, the words coming out in a rush. "I've got this problem, this, uh, situation . . ."

She spent another moment fumbling for words before falling into a painful silence.

Joe immediately understood why, as he heard Chet come stomping up the stairs behind him.

He neither looked at nor spoke to either of them.

Dawn squeezed her hands together and watched Chet move off.

"Dawn!" An instructor rushed up, grabbing the girl's arm. "I've been looking all over for you. Barbara's supposed to be teaching an aerobics class, but she's still with the police. We need you to fill in."

Staring helplessly at Joe, Dawn let herself be pulled into the aerobics studio. Joe shrugged and decided to hit an exercise bike for his warm-up, staying far away from Dawn—and temptation. After a few miles of pedaling and fifty stomach crunches, he was ready to face the iron again.

That day's target was his shoulders and arms. Joe began with four sets of military presses, raising a ninety-five-pound barbell behind his neck. Then came the front presses, using a seventy-five-pound bar.

As he worked out, he was joined by a dark-haired young woman, also using a barbell. Joe didn't need to see the bandage wrapped around her leg to identify the girl who'd been injured the previous day. "You're Linda, aren't you?" he asked.

"And you're Joe." She grinned. "I thought you might need an exercise partner."

"You're on," Joe said.

As they worked together, Joe felt a warmth beyond the burning of his muscles. Linda was a very committed bodybuilder. It showed in the definition of muscle under her skin, and in the serious way she pushed herself to the limit in her exercises.

"I thought you'd be home after what happened yesterday," Joe said between sets of barbell curls. His upper arms ached slightly as he pumped them up.

"No pain, no gain," Linda said with a grin. "I don't want to fall behind on my training. The injury wasn't bad. If I'm careful, my body can handle it."

Joe glanced over to where Chet Morton stood at the pressdown machine, working on his triceps. In between straining against the machine's resistance, he kept peeking over at Joe.

Good, Joe thought. Maybe he'll lighten up a little if he sees me paying attention to another girl.

Joe was working on consecutive curls when Chet came over and picked up a barbell. There wasn't much room in the weight area, so he set up the bar in front of the power rack. The rack was a sort of mechanical spotter. Struts placed in the back of the rack ensured that the bar couldn't fall below a given height.

Whoever had used the cage last must have been doing squats—the struts were at waist level. Joe continued his curls as Chet assembled a one-hundred-forty-five-pound barbell.

Picking up the weight, Chet began front military presses as Jan Cole came by.

"Know what you need, Morton? You need to use *all* of your body. Ever done any power movements?"

"A few," Chet cautiously admitted.

"Well, you ought to do more. Put that thing down."

Chet carefully lowered the barbell.

"See, *this* is what you need." Cole squatted down, grabbing the barbell in an overhand grip. In an explosive movement he brought the weight up, straightening his legs, then his back, which brought the barbell to hip level. In a smooth continuation of the movement, he flexed his arms at the elbows. The weight rested on the heels of his palms, at shoulder level. "Now you try it," Cole said, pushing the weight up and over to Chet.

Chet wasn't ready for it. He stumbled back, hands up, trying to wave Cole back. But Cole couldn't stop. Nearly one hundred and fifty pounds were rushing straight at Chet!

Joe's friend did his best. He grabbed the barbell, staggering into the power cage.

"Drop!" Joe yelled. "Let the cage catch the weight!"

Chet must have heard him. He let his feet fall out from under him.

Too late, Joe realized that Chet was falling at an angle—the bar wasn't going to catch!

"Get out from under there!" he yelled to Chet in horror.

Chet was on the ground, unable to move. Above him, the left-hand side of the barbell had caught on the protective strut.

But the right side hadn't. The heavy weight smashed to the floor, right where Chet lay!

Chapter

6

FRANK HARDY had come out of the locker room a bit later than his brother. He was only warming up on a stationary bike when he heard the commotion behind him.

Turning, Frank was just in time to see Chet Morton go down. Frank leapt from the cycle and sprinted over to the power cage, joining Joe and Linda, the female bodybuilder.

Jan Cole stood horrified in front of the cage, staring down at Chet's still form. The barbell lay half across the stocky teenager's chest.

Cole licked his lips. "Chet, you're not—?" he began in a hoarse voice.

As if in answer, Chet gave a low groan.

Terrance Penman came rushing up. "What happened?" he demanded.

"It was an accident," Cole said rapidly. "I handed him a weight, but I guess he wasn't ready for it."

"You *handed* him a weight?" Joe said incredulously. "You nearly shoved that barbell down his throat."

"Let's not talk about that now," Frank said, kneeling by the side of the power cage. "Chet is our only concern." He looked worriedly at the heavy barbell, resting across the left half of Chet's chest. That could mean danger not only to his left lung, but also to his heart.

Frank glanced up at Terrance Penman, who stood beside Linda on the right-hand side of the cage. "We'd better get this weight out of the way first."

Penman grasped the barbell to take some of the weight. Still on his knees, Frank took hold of the bar as well, shifting it gingerly. He was in a clumsy position, though, and couldn't use his full strength to move the bar.

Realizing this, Joe pushed past Jan Cole to add his muscle to the effort. With the three of them, moving the barbell was easier. As soon as the bar was off Chet, Frank left the weight to Joe and Penman and turned back to his friend.

"Chet?" he said in a low voice.

Chet's eyes fluttered open, and his right hand moved to his left side. "Hurts," he muttered, and his face contracted in a spasm of pain.

"Don't talk," Frank said quickly. "Don't do

anything.'' He looked up at Cole. ''Is there a phone around here?''

The big man stared dumbly down at him.

Frank felt a surge of impatience. ''Look, we have to call an ambulance and get him to a hospital. We've got to do it as fast as possible.''

Chet could have broken ribs, Frank realized. One of those broken bones could slide into his lung and puncture it. Frank replayed the fall in his mind. It didn't seem likely that Chet would have damaged his spine, though.

Penman pushed past Cole, who still stood unmoving. ''The closest phone is in the hall on the way to the locker room. I'll go.'' He headed off.

Cole seemed to snap out of his trance. ''What do we need an ambulance for?'' He stepped forward, reaching toward Chet. ''I'll help him up and take him in my car.''

Frank rose to his feet, blocking Cole's way. ''We don't know how badly off Chet is. A slightly wrong move and we could kill him.''

A shadow of scorn passed over Cole's face. ''He's probably faking it.''

Joe Hardy leaned into Cole's face. ''Let's see how *you'd* look if some creep tossed a barbell at you.''

Frank gave his brother an elbow in the ribs. ''Cool it, Joe. We've got other things to worry about.''

Penman ran back. "The phone's dead and so's the one in the locker room. We've had lots of trouble with the service here—they can't seem to get it right. I should stay with Chet. Will one of you run to the main office and try to call?"

"I'll go," Frank said.

Frank took off and pushed through the knot of onlookers who had stopped exercising to stare at Chet. "That guy must be jinxed," Frank heard Laufner mutter.

On the way to the exit, Frank passed the glass wall that separated the aerobics studio from the gym. He could just make out the pounding beat of music, but nobody was dancing inside. They were all clustered against the glass, staring out at Chet.

Frank saw Dawn Reynolds, her hands clutched together, her eyes staring fixed and unfocused. She seemed to be viewing the most terrible thing she'd ever seen in her life. Frank watched as a tear trickled out from the corner of one eye and down her cheek.

Seems as if she was right, Frank thought grimly. Chet stayed at the club, and he did get hurt.

The more he thought about it, the angrier Frank became. This whole situation was Jan Cole's fault. Where did he come off, tossing a heavy barbell like that at anyone?

Frank reached the reception desk, which was

still empty. That phone wasn't working either. Behind the desk was a door marked with the word *Office*.

Pete Vanbricken's office. Frank decided to see if he had a working phone. Also the sooner Vanbricken heard about Chet's accident, the better. Especially if he heard about it before Jan Cole had time to concoct a story for him.

Frank walked up to the office door, rapped sharply, and said, "Mr. Vanbricken?"

There was no answer, but the door swung slightly open at his knock.

Frank pushed the door open wider and stepped inside. The lights were off, and the office was empty.

It was a spacious room, carpeted in the same industrial gray tweed carpeting that covered most of the floors in the club. The walls were painted Harbor Health Club gray. Even the plants in front of the windows were indistinguishable from the greenery decorating the main room of the gym.

The only nonstandard items in the room were the framed photographs on the walls—mementos of Vanbricken's glory days—and the big teak desk by the window. In the pictures, a very young Pete Vanbricken grinned shyly while holding aloft a college championship trophy. An older, more confident Vanbricken slapped a high-five with his teammates as the Midland Foxes won a final play-off game.

For a moment Frank wondered where Vanbricken was. Then he shook his head. The shock of Chet's injury must have addled his wits. Hadn't somebody mentioned that Vanbricken was away from the club, down at police headquarters?

Frank tried the phone. It worked and he stood glancing out the window as he relayed the information to 911.

Frank's gaze dropped and passed over the top of the desk. Abruptly, he zeroed in on a piece of paper. He'd spotted his name on the sheet. It seemed to be a list of new members of the Harbor Health Club. Chet, Frank, and Joe were listed, with their membership fees beside their names.

Frank frowned when he saw the figure. He and Joe had gotten a two-for-one membership deal. Yet the dollar amounts beside their names were much larger than what they'd actually paid.

Scanning the list, Frank noticed that almost all of the new members were paying hefty sums. His eyes stopped again on another name he recognized—Hurd Applegate.

Something wasn't right. Hurd Applegate could certainly afford the amount listed by his name, but he was an old man, almost a recluse. Why would he enroll himself in a health club?

Frowning, Frank turned to the door as it was pushed open. Jan Cole stepped in, his shoulders almost brushing the door frame. When he saw Frank, he stopped in his tracks and glared.

Muscles bunched and grew in the man's shoulders and biceps as he clenched his hands into fists.

"What are you doing in here?" Cole growled.

54

Chapter

7

FRANK WATCHED AS JAN Cole's suspicious eyes moved to the papers on Pete Vanbricken's desk. Then they went back to Frank's face, filled with worry as well as suspicion.

Whatever's going on, he knows about it, Frank thought. And now he's afraid I know about it, too.

Out loud, he said, "What am I doing here? I'm using the phone. Also I'm looking for your boss, to tell him about that stunt you just pulled with the barbell."

Frank walked toward the door, and Cole reluctantly gave way. "You're just lucky that Mr. Vanbricken's not here and that I have to go with my friend to the hospital," Frank went on.

Frank stepped past the reception desk and

started back to the gym. He met Joe halfway back.

"At last!" Joe said. "I thought maybe there wasn't a working phone in this whole place."

Frank and he ran back to the gym and got there just as the ambulance pulled up. Two paramedics tore inside to Chet. After a quick examination, they lifted Chet onto a gurney and wheeled him back out to the ambulance.

Penman rode with Chet, and Joe and Frank followed in their van to Bayport General Hospital.

Frank explained what had happened to the Emergency Room doctor.

"Possible chest trauma," the woman said, writing on a clipboard. "And you say he was out. Do you mean unconscious?"

Frank shrugged. "I don't know. His eyes were closed, and he didn't seem aware of where he was."

"He's been awake since then," Joe put in.

"Right," Penman agreed. "I talked to him on the way here, and he made sense."

Chet was rolled into an examination cubicle, while the Hardys and Terrance Penman were left to take seats in the waiting room.

"This has been some week," Penman said, shaking his head. "First Cosgrove dies, then Joe nearly gets nailed on the bench press, and now this." He managed a weak smile. "Well, you know what they say—bad luck always comes in threes.''

Silence fell as they waited for news on Chet's condition. After a while Penman rose to his feet. "I guess I should check back with the club.''

He stepped toward the pay phone, then came back a second later, looking a little embarrassed. "Uh, guys, all my money's back at the club.''

Grinning, Joe and Frank shrugged. They were in their gym clothes, too.

Penman went to the nurse in charge and asked to use the phone. Moments later, he was back. "Word of the accident got to Mr. Vanbricken. He's coming over. As soon as he arrives, I'm supposed to head back to the club. They're still understaffed, and the place is a madhouse. I hope I can get cab fare from the boss.''

A few minutes later the Emergency Room door opened, and Pete Vanbricken strode inside. He was still a young man and moved with the confidence of someone who'd been named all-pro quarterback before he was twenty-five. Frank had always thought Vanbricken's face would have made a perfect logo for the Midland Foxes. He looked like a fox, with bright red hair and handsome, yet pointed, features.

Right now, as he motioned to Terrance Penman, an anxious frown creased his handsome face.

Watching the two men confer, Joe gave a sour chuckle. "He's probably worried sick about a lawsuit.''

"I think he's got more than that to be concerned about," Frank said. "There's some funny business going on at that club, and old Pistol Pete is right in the middle of it."

He quickly explained about the list he'd noticed on Vanbricken's desk, with the inflated payments noted beside their names and the odd additional members.

"Old Man Applegate a member of a health club?" Joe said in disbelief. "Stamp collecting would be more his speed."

"That's right," Frank agreed. "So something has to be—Uh-oh, later for that."

Pete Vanbricken came over to the boys. "I'd have been here earlier, but it took a while for the message to get to me at police headquarters." He shook his head, a little exasperated. "If I'd only known the trouble I'd let myself in for by going to the police."

"You contacted them?" Frank asked.

Vanbricken nodded. "When I heard that a Walter Cosgrove had died, I figured I ought to tell them that he was a member of my club. So the cops were all over me. They even made me identify the body."

"They needed *you* to do that?" Joe looked confused. "Why?"

"The police are having a hard time getting a line on him," Vanbricken explained. "And I can understand why. The guy's not married, and he listed no family on his application form. The company he works for, Interstate Sales, is supposed to be sending their regional manager, but he can't fly in from Detroit until sometime tomorrow. So all the police have are a name, a driver's license, and some other paper ID. It seems that Cosgrove moved away from the address in his license, and there are enough Walter Cosgroves in the United States to make checking into his background a real chore."

Vanbricken sighed. "Answering the cops' questions was a real chore, too. They even had me go through Cosgrove's personal effects over at headquarters."

He gave them a strained smile. "But I'm sure you don't want to hear about that. Right now, all I want to know is that your friend is all right."

The door to the examination area opened, and the ER doctor came out. "Frank and Joe Hardy?" he called.

"Right here," Frank said. He and Joe stepped forward, followed by Pete Vanbricken.

"Your friend was very lucky," the doctor said as she led them through the door, then down a hallway lined with small cubicles. "If that weight had landed an inch or two farther to the right, it would have crushed his chest."

Vanbricken breathed very hard through his nose.

"We've taken X-rays, and they show no broken bones or internal damage," the doctor went on. "Your friend is in here." She pushed aside the curtain on one of the cubicles, and there was Chet.

At first Frank thought he was sitting up, but then he realized Chet was actually lying back against the raised top half of a mechanized hospital bed. Chet's T-shirt had disappeared, and a heavy swath of taping ran around his midsection. But his color was back, and he smiled when he saw the Hardys.

"That tape job makes you look like the mummy's brother-in-law," Joe said, grinning with relief that his friend looked so well.

"Don't make me laugh," Chet said, his right arm going over to his left side. "They taped my ribs, even though they think they're only bruised." He glared at Frank. "And what's the big idea of telling them that I passed out? Now they're afraid I might have landed on my head and gotten a concussion."

"If they'd only asked me, Chet, I'd have told them that landing on your head couldn't hurt *you*," Joe said.

"Chet, I told them everything that happened to make sure they'd give you the right treatment," Frank said.

"Sure! And now they want to keep me overnight for observation," Chet said in disgust.

"And what's so bad about that?" Frank wanted to know.

"Have you ever eaten hospital food?" Chet asked.

In spite of himself, Frank had to laugh.

Pete Vanbricken stepped up to the bed. "Chet, I'm glad to see you looking so well."

Chet was surprised. "Mr. Vanbricken! What are you doing here?"

"Call me Pete," Vanbricken said. "As soon as I heard there'd been a little accident at the club, I came right over." He tried to give Chet a smile. "Boy, talk about beginner's bad luck—"

"Chet's only bad luck was having that clown Cole as an instructor," Joe interrupted. "I don't know what Cole told you, but Frank and I both saw what went on. Cole pushed a one-hundred-forty-five-pound barbell onto Chet before he was ready. If Chet had been anywhere else instead of in front of the power cage, we wouldn't be talking about this here. We'd be talking in the morgue."

"I *thought* I'd find you here," a voice said from the doorway.

Joe, Frank, and Vanbricken turned to find Con Riley leaning against the door frame, arms crossed over the chest of his blue uniform jacket.

"Officer Riley! What a surprise to see you!"

From the tone of Vanbricken's voice, Frank suspected it wasn't a pleasant surprise.

"Do the police need me for something else?" the club owner asked.

"Actually, Mr. Vanbricken, you aren't the

one I was looking for. It's these two young men." Con smiled at the Hardys.

Vanbricken stared in surprise. "What?"

"I heard the Hardy brothers had come with Chet to the hospital." Con Riley gave the boys a long, appraising look. "I didn't know that they were members of your health club. But when I mentioned it to the chief, he thought we should talk to them."

Vanbricken stared at the Hardys as if they'd suddenly sprouted feathers. "The chief wants to speak to these kids? But they only became members the day Cosgrove died.

Con Riley shrugged. "What can I say, Mr. Vanbricken? Orders is orders."

"No need for handcuffs, Con," Frank said. "Joe and I would *love* to talk to you about this case."

Chapter

8

"WELL, I'D BETTER get back to the club and see what's going on." Pete Vanbricken glanced uncomfortably around the hospital cubicle. He left with a halfhearted wave to Chet, looking even more worried than when he'd come in.

The boys watched him go in silence. Then Chet managed a grin. "Well, he certainly went in a hurry." He glanced at the police officer in the doorway. "I guess you guys have to be going, as well."

"We'll come back to visit," Frank promised.

"Yeah, just as soon as we find out where they've put you," Joe said with a grin.

"Just do me a favor," Chet begged. "Bring me a decent burger when you come."

Laughing, the Hardys said goodbye to Chet and went with Con Riley down the hallway.

"Con, can we ask a favor?" Frank asked.

Riley seemed dubious. "And what might that be?"

Frank gestured at the workout clothes he and Joe were still wearing. "We came here straight from the gym. Our street clothes are back there. Could we change before we see the chief?"

"Yeah," Joe said, looking down at his shorts. "I always prefer to wear long pants when I tangle with Chief Collig."

Laughing, Con Riley promised them changing time.

The Hardys returned to the club and changed into their street clothes. Back in their van, Joe wanted to know, "So what are we going to tell the cops?" He got behind the wheel and started the drive to headquarters.

"We'll tell them about what we saw in the locker room the first time we came," Frank said. "Including the gun."

"I didn't see any gun," Joe objected. "Although I did see Cosgrove acting like a gorilla."

"Well, I guess that's about all we can say about Cosgrove." Frank shook his head. "Too bad we never got to follow him."

He thought back to the near-fight between Vanbricken and Cole, then Dawn's showing up, and the caveman competition between Joe and Chet.

Maybe if all that whole nonsense hadn't happened, they might have had time to observe Cosgrove before he died. Of course, then there were all the accidents. What had Penman said? Bad luck comes in threes?

The glimmer of an idea passed through Frank's mind. Two of those accidents involved one person. Joe was acting as if the slipping weight had endangered him. But in reality, *Chet* was the one who had had to be rescued from that swinging barbell.

Frank tried to concoct a scenario where Cosgrove's death, the strange list on Vanbricken's desk, and the attempts on Chet were somehow tied together. He gave up with a frustrated sigh. If there was a common thread, he couldn't find it.

At headquarters Con Riley brought the boys to the detective squad room. Spread over several desks were clothing, a toiletries kit, luggage, and other personal belongings.

Staring down at the collection was Chief Ezra Collig. Sitting at a typewriter was a detective Frank had met a couple of times before. What was the guy's name? Owens? Nevins? Something like that, Frank knew.

The man had a hunt-and-peck style of typing, hitting the keys only with his forefingers. He looked up as the Hardys entered. So did the chief, who frowned a greeting.

"Frank and Joe Hardy," Collig said grimly. "We were just about to finish up this case when we heard that you may have known the deceased.''

"Just for a few minutes," Frank said. "We joined the health club he belonged to and met him in the locker room twice.''

"And that's it?" Collig asked. His eyes were suspicious as he looked at the Hardys. "I've known you guys too long. You have a very bad habit of upsetting my cases after I think they're finished. So I figured I'd check with you this time.''

Joe shrugged and Frank seemed to be studying the dingy tile floor.

Collig sighed. "As far as we can find out, this Cosgrove guy was a loner with no home, no family, no life. We don't even know where to ship his personal effects. He's a nothing, a zero, who happened to drop dead and fall in the bay.''

"Well, he was a gambler, and not a very lucky one, from what I overheard," Frank said.

Collig nodded. "We heard about that.''

"He had a nasty temper," Joe put in. "We saw him nearly deck someone in the locker room.''

"Yeah, the guy seemed like a bundle of laughs," the detective said. "Everybody at the health club mentioned that.''

"Did anyone mention his gun?" Frank asked.

The three police officers glanced at one another, then at Frank.

"What gun?" Collig wanted to know.

"The last time we saw Cosgrove in the locker room at the Harbor Health Club," Frank said, "he nearly decked a guy named Laufner. After that he grabbed his gym bag and left. The zipper on the bag happened to be open, and I saw a gun inside it."

The police officer's eyes shifted to Joe. "You saw this, too?" Con asked.

Joe shrugged. "I saw Cosgrove nearly deck Laufner. I didn't see the gun."

The detective frowned. "Frank, are you sure you saw a gun? By your own admission, you only got a quick glimpse. Maybe you saw something that *looked* like a gun—the handle of a portable hair drier, for example."

"Cosgrove wore his hair slicked back. Was a hair drier found in his luggage?" Frank asked.

Now it was Collig's turn to frown. "No. But neither was a gun."

Frank stepped to the desk with the little red gym bag on it. A pair of sweatpants, a black athletic shirt, an athletic supporter, and a towel were piled beside it. "This is the bag I saw. There was a gun in it. What more can I say?"

"I think you've said enough already." The detective pushed back his chair and bitterly pointed a finger at the typewriter. " 'Go ahead and write up the report,' the chief said. 'We'll just ask these kids on the off chance they know something.' "

He gave the Hardys a black look. "I was on

67

the last page of a fifteen-page report. And you see the way I type.''

Even Con Riley had to laugh at that complaint.

"So, is it a case of the Hardy boys strike again?'' Collig asked. "Have you sent us professionals back to square one?''

Frank wasn't about to answer. When the chief sounded nice and quiet, almost friendly, that was the time to watch out for an explosion.

Collig's expression darkened. "We thought we'd covered this guy as well as we were able to. We got the boss of the health club to identify the body. And, of course, we filled a lot of notebooks with statements about Cosgrove from the people who worked there.''

"About nine million useless questions and answers,'' the detective at the typewriter griped.

"We even identified that stupid red bag you were pointing at,'' Con Riley added. "Vanbricken knew it right away—he said it was like Cosgrove's trademark.''

"Right,'' the annoyed detective chimed in. "We even got a confirmation on that from the head trainer over at the club. What was his name? Cole?''

"What about the big black bag Cosgrove carried?'' Frank asked.

The police looked at one another again. "What bag is that?'' Collig asked with a resigned air.

"It was another weird thing I noticed,'' Frank

said. "When he was changing into his workout clothes, he had a large black bag. When he left, he had that red one."

Frank frowned. With everything else that had happened, he'd almost forgotten that fact.

What *had* happened to that big black bag? he wondered.

"So this is what it comes down to," Collig said quietly. "You saw a gun, which no one else did, and also saw another bag. None of this is supported, of course."

"That's just about it." Frank gave an embarrassed little shrug.

Collig looked at the evidence spread out around the squad room, his face twisting into a scowl. As far as they knew, this was everything Walter Cosgrove owned in the world. "Con, you arranged for copies of this guy's fingerprints to be sent to the feds in Washington. I know you can't speed up their computers, but see if you can move us ahead in the line."

Collig then glanced at the fourteen pages of the report his detective had prepared. Frank understood the timing. It was supposed to have gone out to the media the next morning.

The chief clasped his hands behind his back, set his teeth, and gave a low growl from the back of his throat. "I hate to tell you this, Nevins, but it looks like this investigation isn't over yet."

Chapter

9

AS THE HARDYS WALKED down the steps of police headquarters, Joe shook his head. "You know, Frank, I expected Chief Collig to kill you."

"He shouldn't have," Frank protested. "I just raised some questions. And I think that the chief is cop enough to want answers to them."

Joe glanced at his brother. "Frank, are you *sure* about this? Maybe the black bag was Cosgrove's sample case. I mean, he was a salesman, after all."

"Do you know what he sold?" Frank suddenly asked.

Joe stared at him blankly for a moment, then shrugged. "I don't know," he admitted. "What would a company called Interstate Sales sell?"

"Sounds like something the Gray Man would set up to use as a spy cover."

That got a laugh out of Joe. "Yeah, I can see it now—Walt Cosgrove, Secret Agent. So who do you think got him, Frank? The Purple Claw? The Yellow Fang?"

Frank gave him a look. "I'm just suggesting that the company name sounds like a phony," he said. "My interest is in what happened to that bag and gun."

Joe shrugged again. "Well, he was a salesman and obviously traveled. Maybe he had the gun for protection."

"So what happened? The minute he dropped dead, his gun and his sample case disappeared?" Frank shook his head. "There's something screwy there."

"Looks like you're finding something screwy everywhere," Joe countered. "The only fact we've got is that Cosgrove is dead. There's not even any sign of foul play. Hey, maybe we should face it—we might never know what happened."

Frank stopped in his tracks. "No, but we can try to find out more about that black bag—ask some questions around the club, maybe. It strikes me that there's one person who might be able to tell us something."

Joe stared. "Who?"

"Pete Vanbricken," Frank replied. "He was able to tell the cops all sorts of stuff about Cosgrove's red bag. Maybe he'd have something to say about the other one.''

Joe thought for a minute. "We've even got something to sweat him with," he said. "What about those records with the fake fee payments you saw in his desk?"

"Right. If he's got one thing to hide, maybe he's got more. Let's see if we can find anything more about him." Frank climbed into the van, and Joe followed.

They didn't drive very far until Frank found a parking spot near the offices of the Bayport *Times*.

"This may not be the right place to start researching," Joe warned. "The *Gazette* is much more of a scandal sheet. If any paper's going to have dirt on Vanbricken, that would be the place to look."

"But we don't have a friend at the *Gazette*," Frank pointed out. "With luck, we'll find Liz Webling in the office."

Liz Webling's father was editor of the Bayport *Times*. A budding reporter herself, she was often found around the offices of the paper, doing odd jobs.

That day she was at the front counter, taking classified ads. As far as Joe could figure, she seemed pretty disgusted with her assignment.

"Hi, guys." Liz looked up from the pad where she was writing down information. "So what's the story on this fancy health club you joined?'' She leaned over the counter, toward Frank. "I've got a scoop for you," she said. "Callie Shaw is pretty p.o.'ed that you haven't invited her to the club as your guest. She's bought a leotard just for the occasion.''

"Boy, Frank," Joe said. "You're in major trouble.''

"I've been hoping that Chet would give me a guest pass to check out the place," Liz said a little wistfully.

So, Joe thought, Liz hadn't heard about two things: Dawn Reynolds and Chet's injury.

"I don't know if Chet's going to be around the club much for a while," Frank began. "He's in the—''

He was interrupted by a ringing telephone. Liz picked up the receiver and began frantically scribbling. "What model car, sir? Right. What year?''

She finished the call and tore another sheet off her pad, adding it to the pile at her elbow.

"What's the matter with Chet?" Liz asked.

"He's in the hospital," Frank began again, only to be interrupted by another call.

"Chet hurt himself working out, but he's really okay," Joe quickly said when Liz hung up. "They're only keeping him for observation. He'll be fine. We'll explain more about it later. Right now, though, we need to look in your morgue.''

"Nobody's back there now," Liz said, turning

toward the rear of the offices. "Does this have something to do with a case you're working on?"

The boys were saved from answering her question when a man walked in to place a classified ad in person. Hurriedly stepping past Liz, Joe said, "We know how the system works. You can trust us. We won't mess anything up."

With Liz trapped by her client, they managed to make it back to the morgue. Frank immediately went to the clipping files, searching for a folder with Pete Vanbricken's name on it.

The file turned out to be a heavy manila envelope about four inches thick. Frank and Joe split the folders inside into two sets and began riffling through them.

Joe wound up with clippings from Vanbricken's high school days up to his first play-off victory for the Midland Foxes.

"How's it going?" Frank asked as he scanned his set of clips.

"Well, a movie titled *Vanbricken—the Early Days* would probably be rated G," Joe said dispiritedly. "He was a very good boy."

"His later life looks much the same," Frank said, riffling on. "There's a whole lot of stuff here about fame not spoiling him. Here's an article about him visiting an orphanage, another about him dedicating a youth center, and still another about him running a booth at a street fair to raise money for a community group."

Joe finished with his files. "So maybe we were wrong, thinking he's got things to hide?"

Adding Joe's files to his, Frank replaced them in the envelope, refiled the whole thing, and closed the cabinet with a thump. "Maybe we're wrong to depend on reporters and press agents for our information," he said, rising from his seat.

With the telephone still attached to her ear, Liz turned pleading eyes on them as they started out the front door. "Come on, guys," she said, placing a hand over the receiver. "Tell me what's going on."

"We'll be back with the story," Frank promised.

"*If* there's a story," Joe added.

Outside, Joe asked, "Okay. Now do we check the scandal sheet?"

"We do better than that," Frank told him with a grin. "We'll check in with the one person who probably knows the most dirt in this town."

Joe looked at his brother, his eyebrows raised. "And who's that?"

Frank's grin got broader. "Dad."

Fenton Hardy was in his office when the boys got home. The door was open, and Fenton was sitting at his desk.

"Dad?" Frank said. "Are we interrupting anything?"

Fenton raised his eyes from the papers he was

reading. "Nothing important. What's up, boys?"

"We were wondering what you could tell us about Pete Vanbricken," Joe said.

"Football hero at Bayport High, some years before you went there," their father said. "He was a college all-star, went pro, played for some team out in the Midwest, got injured, and returned to Bayport. He also happens to own the health club you two joined."

Fenton gave them a keen glance. "My turn. Why are you asking?"

Frank leaned against the wall. "We were wondering if you knew anything about him having trouble with the law."

"Or getting into any other kind of trouble," Joe added.

Fenton was interested. "So, you suspect that our local hero has feet of clay?"

"We're just wondering," Frank said. "Can you tell us anything?"

"Only that as a kid—and even as a celebrity—Pete Vanbricken seemed to be a real straight arrow," Fenton said. "Whenever there was a good cause, you could depend on him supporting it, even if it wasn't always convenient. He always volunteered for police anticrime programs. He used to go into tough neighborhoods and talk to the kids."

"Not even a breath of scandal around him?"

Joe asked. "Gambling, fighting, chasing women?"

"Vanbricken dated a lot of glamorous women when he was riding high—right up to the time his shoulder got injured," Fenton said. "But I wouldn't say he chased them. He didn't bet on anything, and he didn't get into fights. As far as I know, he's got the best-polished halo in town."

The boys thanked their father and went out.

"So much for getting any dirt." Joe sighed.

"We still have one other source," Frank said, frowning. "The man himself."

Joe stared at his brother. "What do you expect him to do? Come up to us and say, 'Oh, by the way, fellas, have you noticed that I've become a crook lately?' "

"No," Frank admitted. "But there are a few questions I'd like to ask him." The expression in his eyes became remote and thoughtful. "And I'd be real interested to see how he answers them."

Supper was going to be late that night, so the boys got into their van and headed back to the Harbor Health Club. The place was a lot livelier than it was when they had worked out earlier.

"Looks like the joint is jumping," Joe said, staring at the crowded parking lot. "How come it's not like this during the day?"

"I guess after work is the time when the condo owners come in to sweat." Frank gave his brother a grin. "Here's your choice, Joe.

Quick access to everything but no company during the day, or lots of babes on exercise bikes and a long line for all the equipment you want to use at night."

Joe sat silently behind the wheel, a frown on his face.

"Well?" Frank asked.

"I'm thinking, I'm thinking."

Laughing, Frank opened his door and headed toward the club.

They were in luck. The young woman behind the reception desk told them that Mr. Vanbricken was still in his office.

Moments later Frank and Joe were inside the spacious room. This time, Pete Vanbricken sat behind his desk. There were papers spread all over it, but Frank didn't see that interesting list.

"Hello again, guys," Vanbricken said. "Normally, I wouldn't be here, but I had a lot of catching up to do after losing most of the day." He gestured at the piles of paper on his desk. "What can I do for you?" A look of concern came over his face. "There's no problem with your friend Chet, is there?"

"No," Frank replied. "We're just puzzled by some things the police told us about Walter Cosgrove."

"Or rather," Joe said, "what you told the police about Walter Cosgrove."

"Cosgrove?" Pete Vanbricken sat straighter in his seat, his face a blank mask now.

"Yes," Frank went on. "I'm a little confused. You told the police that he always carried a little red gym bag. But when I saw him, the afternoon before he died, he had a big black bag."

Vanbricken's eyes narrowed. "Wait a second," he said. "You're Frank Hardy, aren't you? Jan Cole told me he'd found you in this office unauthorized and unaccompanied. That's trespassing."

"I came in to use the phone and to tell you what happened to Chet," Frank said. "Unfortunately, you weren't here."

"Yes," Vanbricken said. "Unfortunately. Everyone in the club knew I was speaking with the police."

He opened a desk drawer and took out a large binder. When Vanbricken opened it, Joe realized the binder was actually a large checkbook, the kind that businesses used.

Vanbricken took up a pen and scribbled rapidly across two checks. Then he tore them out and handed one each to Frank and Joe.

"What's this for?" Joe stared suspiciously at the piece of paper in his hand.

"It's a refund on your membership fee," Vanbricken told him.

He rose from his chair and leaned across the desk. "I want both of you out of this club—and don't come back!"

Chapter

10

FRANK HARDY threw his check down on Vanbricken's desk. "You don't understand," he told the health club owner. "Maybe you think you can stonewall us, but the police know about Cosgrove's black bag—and also about the gun he carried in the red one."

"Apparently, *you* don't understand," Vanbricken said. "I just asked you to leave these premises. You have no right to be here." He stabbed a finger onto his desk intercom. "Rosalie," he said, "get Jan Cole in here, please."

A moment later the door opened, and Jan Cole stood in the doorway. As he saw Frank and Joe, his eyes hardened. "The Hardys, huh? In here shooting off their mouths?"

Vanbricken folded his arms across his chest.

"Jan, these gentlemen are no longer members of the club. They will not be allowed back on the premises, and you will escort them out now."

Frank glared at Vanbricken. "This isn't going to work, you know."

Vanbricken scooped up Frank's check from his desk. "Don't forget your refund. Now—out!"

"Listen," Frank began again.

Cole shrugged his massive shoulders, bringing his brawny arms up. "You heard the man—out!"

With Jan Cole looming over them like an unfriendly thundercloud, Frank and Joe left the office.

"Hey, don't I at least get a chance to say goodbye to the friends I made around here?" Joe asked as Cole marched them around the reception desk. "What about Dawn Reynolds?"

"She's gone," Cole said. "And you're history. Out the door."

A moment later the boys were standing in the parking lot. Joe gave Frank a look. "Here's another fine mess you've gotten us into," he said, quoting Oliver Hardy. "I was just beginning to get into this club stuff. *And* I was about to ask Dawn out."

He shook his head. "But I'm not in as much trouble as you are."

Frank looked at his brother in puzzlement. "What are you talking about?"

Joe grinned. "How do you think Callie's going to take it when she discovers she's bought a new leotard for nothing? No membership, no guest passes."

Frank shook his head. "That's the least of my worries," he said. "What's eating me is that something wrong is so obviously going on in that club and we don't have a clue as to what it is."

Joe had to nod. "Maybe Vanbricken didn't tell us anything, but he did give away how he felt about Cosgrove. As soon as you mentioned him and his black bag, Vanbricken acted scared to death."

"He certainly did," Frank agreed. "But over what?"

Joe glanced at his watch. "I don't know about you, but I do my best thinking on a full stomach. We're late for supper."

Frank only picked at his food, his mind obviously miles away.

As they cleared the table, Joe shook his head. "You're still a growing boy, you know. Thinking so hard is making you lose your appetite."

"I'm only trying to apply a little logic." He grimaced. "The only problem is, all my thinking isn't working."

"Do you want to run what we know by me?" Joe asked.

"Okay. Let's think of it this way. Walt Cosgrove was a member of the Harbor Health Club.

Walt Cosgrove got killed. Chet Morton is a member of the Harbor Health Club. Twice, Chet Morton almost got killed."

"Hey," Joe objected. "I was a member of the Harbor Health Club, too, and one of those accidents nearly got me."

"I've thought about that," Frank said. "And it seems to me that Chet was the one in more serious danger."

Joe shrugged. "Then I guess it's a case of pure logic not being able to conquer the real world."

Frank nodded. "But we do know something funny is going on at that club."

Joe grinned. "Frank Hardy sees Cosgrove with a black bag and a gun at the Harbor Health Club. Frank Hardy mentions those facts to the owner and gets thrown out of the club."

"At least it beats being almost killed," Frank said.

"Chet was in the locker room with Cosgrove, too. You noticed the gun and bag, so suppose Chet noticed something else."

"Ergo," Frank said in his most professorial tone, "logically, we should talk to Chet Morton."

He looked at his watch. "The hospital visiting hours are on. Let's get moving."

At the hospital, the boys found that Chet was in Room 318. They rode the elevator up to the third floor, Joe carrying a light jacket over one arm.

After the elevator doors opened, they made their way down the hallway to Chet. "Nice," Frank said, walking in. "Your own private room—as long as they don't bring somebody in for the other bed."

Chet was sitting up, dressed in his own pajamas. He looked pretty much like his usual self, except for the wince of pain when he raised his arm to wave hello. "How's it going, guys?" he asked.

Joe advanced to the bed, keeping his face very serious. "We bring you gifts, O Mighty One." He whipped the jacket off his arm, revealing the fast-food burger and fries hidden underneath.

Chet's eyes glowed. "Great!" he said. "You wouldn't believe what they tried to feed me. Meat loaf, creamed spinach, and mashed potatoes like setting plaster."

Frank glanced over at the empty dinner tray at the end of the bed. "I see you managed to choke it down, though."

Chet opened the burger box and took a bite of the quarter-pounder inside. "Yeah," he said, his mouth full. "But man does not live by creamed spinach alone."

"Anyway, now that we've bribed you, we want to grill you," Joe said.

Chet paused in midchew. "About what?"

"About Walt Cosgrove," Frank said. "You

were down in the locker room before us, that first day in the gym. Did you notice him?"

"The big guy, slicked-back hair, black jacket?" Chet said. "Yeah. I noticed him. He was opening a combination lock when I came in. He had a black bag on the bench behind him, and he was opening the locker." He frowned. "Funny how the dumbest things stick in your brain. I recall clearly that it was locker thirteen. The lock had a smear or a rust mark on the U-shaped piece that locks in—"

"The shank," Frank said.

"Whatever." Chet shrugged. He squinted, trying to think back. "Funny thing is, I saw the same lock the next day—on the same locker." He looked at the Hardys. "I remember thinking there weren't supposed to be permanent lockers. Doesn't the club have a rule about emptying lockers every day?"

Frank frowned. "It does look like Cosgrove kept his own personal storage space there."

"Maybe he greased the palm of the locker room attendant," Joe suggested.

"I don't care about that." Frank had a curious glint in his eye. "I wonder if Cosgrove's locker is still there, untouched."

"Yeah," Joe said. "It's too bad some idiot got us thrown out of the club."

"What?" Chet sat straight up, then winced again at the pain in his side.

Frank explained about their brief interview with Pete Vanbricken.

Chet suddenly grinned. "Well, I've got the perfect reason for you to return to the Harbor Health Club," he said. "And I even have the tickets to get you through the front door."

Early the next morning Frank and Joe were heading down to the Harbor Health Club's locker room when a voice roared from the top of the stairs.

"Hey! What are you two doing here?" They turned to see Jan Cole glowering down at them.

"We're guests of Chet Morton," Joe said airily. "He got two free passes with his membership, after all."

"But don't worry," Frank told the trainer. "We won't sully your precious gym. We're just here to pick up Chet's things."

"Oh." Cole thought for a moment but didn't come up with any reason to stop them. "Just be quick about it."

"We will," Frank said. He and Joe continued down the stairs.

"Well, you guessed right," Joe said as they stepped into the empty locker room. "There's no attendant here."

"I saw him wheeling a big load of laundry around the back of the club." Frank hurried over to the lockers. The attendant might be gone, but how soon before he'd be back?

Chet's locker had been number seventeen, in the same bank as thirteen. There was a lock still on thirteen. Frank grinned. He'd counted on the confusion at the club the day before, and it looked as if the lockers hadn't been cleaned out.

He glanced into the showers. Nobody was around. "Keep watch," he whispered to Joe.

"I hope you know what you're doing." Joe stepped over to the locker room door, keeping a nervous eye on the stairway.

"That's two of us," Frank muttered. He reached under his shirt and removed the stethoscope he had tucked into the waistband of his jeans.

It's good that Dad has such a large collection of useful tools, he thought, inserting the earpieces. Where else could I find a safecracker's best friend?

Moving to locker thirteen, Frank set the disk of the stethoscope to the back of the lock with the streaked shank.

As he slowly turned the dial on the combination lock, amplified clicks resounded in his ears. Then came a loud clunk as the first tumbler set. Frank immediately started turning the dial in the opposite direction. At last, he got another clunk.

Just one more to go, he told himself, carefully spinning the dial again.

The final clunk sounded in his ears, and he pulled down on the lock. It slid open.

Leaving the stethoscope looped round his

neck, Frank removed the lock and eased the door open. The space was empty, except for a large leather duffel bag standing up in the bottom.

Frank reached for the zipper that fastened the bag and tugged it down. It would be just my luck to find a month's worth of stinky sweat socks in here, he told himself.

As the bag opened, the hiss of Frank's indrawn breath echoed off the tiled locker room walls. He hadn't found sweat socks.

Instead, the bag was stuffed with bundles of hundred-dollar bills!

Chapter

11

JOE HARDY turned at his brother's involuntary gasp. What he saw caused his eyes to grow round. Frank was jamming his arm as far as it would go down between the packaged bills.

"There's nothing underneath. The whole bag is packed with money!" Frank whispered.

Quickly he stuffed the bills back into the bag and zipped it closed again. "Let's get out of here," Frank said quietly. "There may be lots of legit reasons for keeping a fortune in cash hidden in your gym bag. But this bag combined with a dead man—"

"And the best bet is that this is dirty money." Joe rushed over to Chet's locker while Frank closed locker thirteen. "Let's not forget why we came in the first place."

Using the combination Chet had given them, Joe undid Chet's lock and opened the door. He pulled out Chet's gym bag and began stuffing the contents of the locker into it. "Shoes, socks, pants, shirt, undershirt—what's this?"

Caught in a seam between metal pieces, an envelope fluttered against the inside of the locker door from the breeze Joe made packing.

Joe pried the envelope free. On the front, in scrawled handwriting, he made out the name of Walt Cosgrove and a midwestern post office box address.

Inside the envelope were ten hundred-dollar bills.

Whistling silently, Joe stuck the envelope on top of Chet's things, zipped up the bag, and slammed Chet's locker shut. He turned to Frank, who had closed and locked locker thirteen.

"*Now* let's get out of here," Joe said.

They went up the stairs and out of the club with only a friendly smile from the receptionist. The boys crossed the parking lot in silence, not talking until they were in the privacy of their van.

"Well, what do you make of that?" Frank asked when they were inside.

"If Cosgrove was a salesman, I wonder what kind of commissions he made!" Joe exclaimed. "This is beginning to look fishier and fishier,

Frank. We've got a guy who can't be traced and a bag full of money in his locker."

Frank nodded. "If Cosgrove had been murdered, I'd say we had a strong motive—in fact, a lot of them."

Joe unzipped Chet's bag, showing him the envelope with the bills in it. "This was in Chet's locker, stuck on the back of his door."

"Very interesting," Frank said, checking the envelope over carefully. "Seems like Cosgrove lived out of a post office box in Midland, Iowa."

"Skip that for a minute. An envelope like this is just the right size to slip through the ventilation slits on a locker door." Joe frowned thoughtfully. "It must have been dropped in through the locker door and got stuck there."

"Maybe the money in Cosgrove's bag didn't belong to Cosgrove," Frank said, still staring at the envelope. "Maybe Cosgrove made an unauthorized withdrawal from that mother lode of cash. Then he found out he was going to be discovered and had to hide it."

"And we know why he'd steal some of those hundreds," Joe added. "Cosgrove didn't have just a gambling problem—he had a losing problem. He took some cash, then heard someone and had to hide it quickly. So he just stuck it in the nearest locker at hand. But he probably got killed for stealing anyway."

He frowned. "That would make perfect sense,

except for one thing. There's no indication of foul play in Cosgrove's death.''

"Unless you count the blistered feet,'' Frank pointed out.

Joe gave him an impatient head-shake. "They printed the whole coroner's report in the *Times,* and we both went over it. The blisters on Cosgrove's feet weren't from burns. They were contact blisters.''

Frank was silent for a moment. "Do you remember what Cosgrove wore on his feet?'' he suddenly asked.

Joe stared at him but answered. "A pair of flashy black Italian loafers.''

"Was he wearing socks?''

Closing his eyes, Joe tried to visualize the scene. "No!'' he finally said. "He wasn't wearing socks.'' His eyes opened—wide. "I remember now how odd I thought it was that he put his jacket on before slipping into his shoes. Hey, I saw his bare feet for a second, and I don't remember seeing any blisters on his soles.''

"And he didn't walk as if he had blisters when he left the locker room,'' Frank said.

"So he had to get the blisters after he left the health club,'' Joe said. "But how?''

"Tight shoes, no socks. Maybe he walked for a few miles. That could raise blisters.'' Frank shrugged. "Running would raise them even faster.''

"But he left in a car—that red Porsche the

cops found abandoned on the pier," Joe pointed out. "Maybe he was running from someone."

"A big, muscular guy with a gun?" Frank seemed dubious. "Why would he have to run?"

"As long as we're at it, who was he running from? To where? *From* where?" Joe slumped back in his seat, reclosing Chet's bag with the envelope inside. "Right now, our questions seem to outnumber our answers by about ten to one."

Behind the steering wheel, Frank slipped the key into the ignition. "Well, we won't find out anything more around here."

As the engine turned over, he heard a voice call, "Hey! Hardys!" Frank saw Terrance Penman waving from the entrance of the club. The instructor, dressed in a warm-up suit, ran over to the van.

Frank killed the engine and Joe rolled down his window.

Penman leaned in. "Just wanted to say goodbye to you guys, since I heard you canceled your memberships."

Joe and Frank glanced at each other, but neither of them corrected Penman's mistaken idea. "You were a good trainer, Terrance," Frank said. "We'll miss you."

Penman's voice got lower. "I can understand why you'd want to bail out of this place." The hand he'd rested on the door tightened into a fist. "It's so frustrating! The Harbor Health Club could be a gold mine. But the way the place is mismanaged is criminal."

"What do you mean?" Joe asked.

"For starters, why did Vanbricken hire Jan Cole as head trainer?" Penman shook his head. "I've watched him work. He's not qualified. And as far as I've been able to find out, he's not certified. He's like a guy who bulled himself into shape by lifting weights like crazy, and who thinks that's the only way to get fit."

The young man's dark face twisted. "Cole finally got smart and asked me to design the training programs, before he killed a member. But—well, you've seen him out on the floor. That caveman style of his doesn't work. It turns people off. They don't renew their memberships—or like you, they get out. All the sane people, at least."

"So nobody at the club likes Cole?" Frank asked.

"He pals around with the out-of-towners, the traveling salesmen, those kinds of people. Cole's the one who set up the special visitor's rate that lets them use the club facilities. But compared to the people he turns off, there's a net loss. A *big* loss. How can the club keep going if it loses more members than it takes in?"

"How, indeed?" Frank said.

Penman lowered his voice again. "So I just wanted to tell you you're doing the right thing, leaving. Look, here's my card."

The card showed the outline of a muscular man. Underneath ran the caption "Bodybuilding by Penman—call 555-0909."

"I train people on the side," Penman explained. "If you want to continue training, give me a call. I'll probably be at a new club soon."

"You're going to quit?" Joe asked, surprised.

Penman shrugged. "A lot of staffers have, since I came on board. You know who left yesterday? Dawn Reynolds."

He looked at his watch. "My break's going to be over before I get any breakfast. Take it easy, guys. Maybe I'll see you again."

"Maybe," Joe said, watching the young man dash off.

His expression was skeptical as he glanced across Frank. "If Dawn quit yesterday, what's her car doing over there in the lot?"

Frank followed Joe's pointing finger. From their higher vantage point in the van, they could see over the other cars parked in the lot. They had a clear glimpse of the distinctive little sports model that Dawn drove sitting off in one corner.

"Let's move it," Frank said, hitting the ignition again. As they started out of the lot, Joe reached out to flick the radio on.

"The news at this hour." An announcer's voice came out of the speakers. "Police have found a strange new wrinkle in the Barmet Bay drowning. Walter Cosgrove was merely an alias of the man who died in the bay. Police announced this morning that a fingerprint check has positively identified the dead man as Walter Ostrowski, a convict released three months ago from Midland Penitentiary in Mid—"

Joe turned off the radio. "This is getting weirder and weirder. We not only have dirty money, but a dirty dead guy."

"And the connection seems to be the Harbor Health Club," Frank said. He cast a worried glance over to Joe. "You know something else? Those 'accidents' that kept happening around Chet now seem less and less accidental."

"But who would be after Chet?" Joe asked. "And why?"

"Maybe he saw something he wasn't supposed to see," Frank suggested. "Something he doesn't even remember, but if he did—"

"Somebody would be in trouble." Joe pulled on his seat belt. "Well, what are you hanging around for? Chet was supposed to be sprung from the hospital this morning. Let's go out to his house."

The Morton farm was on the outskirts of Bayport. The road Frank and Joe took to get out there was more like a country lane.

Mrs. Morton was out in the yard, and she waved to the boys.

"We stopped by to see how Chet's doing," Frank called.

"Well, the invalid isn't acting very sick," Mrs. Morton said with a smile. "Believe it or not, he's off for a run. I can't believe the good that health club has done for him."

Joe and Frank glanced at each other. "Maybe we'll go out and join him," Joe said. "Which way did he go?"

Mrs. Morton pointed to the far end of the yard. "That trail goes through the forest, then loops around back to the main road," she said. "You might be able to catch up with him."

Getting out of the van, Frank and Joe set off at a brisk pace. The trail curved its way around the trees, so they couldn't see very far ahead.

Only when they reached the main road did they finally catch sight of Chet. He was in his slightly tight sweat suit, jogging determinedly along.

Joe grinned. "I'll bet he's regretting this," he said.

"I don't know," Frank said. "It beats aerobics." He gestured after Chet. "Let's pick it up until we get close enough to call to him."

The Hardys had pretty much used up their first wind by the time they got within calling distance. Chet had reached the foot of a low hill. Faced with the prospect of running to the top before catching Chet, Joe decided it would be easier to use his voice. Even so, he puffed for a moment before yelling Chet's name.

Chet turned. Waving them on, he stayed where he was, running in place.

"He's serious about this." Frank's voice had a slight wheeze.

"At least we can take it easier catching up to him." Joe set a decidedly less brisk pace as they jogged toward their friend.

They were still a good fifty feet away when a car came over the crest of the hill. Joe immediately recognized the trim yellow vehicle. "Hey! That's Dawn Reynolds's little buzz bomb," he said.

Checking back over his shoulder at the engine noise, Chet must have recognized the car, too. He stood at the side of the road, waving.

Then he stopped waving and froze for a moment as the car swerved and aimed straight for him. From where they were, both Hardys could hear the engine's whine of increased acceleration.

The car was almost on top of Chet before he moved. He did move with surprising agility and vaulted over a fence at the roadside, landing in the drainage ditch on the other side.

Perhaps Dawn Reynolds had missed Chet, but she wasn't finished. The yellow car raced on, engine roaring, racing down the wrong side of the road.

Now it was headed straight at Frank and Joe.

Chapter

12

THE YELLOW CAR continued down the road, bearing down on the Hardys, moving at top speed. Frank and Joe had a few seconds' more warning than Chet had gotten. The only problem was they had no convenient fence to jump over.

The boys did the best they could, though. When the car was right on top of them, they leapt in opposite directions. Frank dove left, Joe jumped right, and the car roared through the spot where they'd been. The Hardys rolled ungracefully to the pavement.

Frank scrambled to his feet, staring down the road to see if the car was coming back for another try at them. All he saw was a rapidly disappearing yellow blur heading back toward Bayport. "You okay, Joe?" he asked.

Joe rose slowly to his feet, rubbing his knee. "I'd ask if anybody got the license plate number, but in this case, we know that car—and who drives it."

"Did you see Dawn behind the wheel?" Frank asked.

Joe looked up from examining the hole in the knee of his jeans—and the scraped flesh under it. "We saw her car, isn't that enough?"

He shook his head. "To think I wanted to get into competition over her! Now I see she really wanted to get close to poor Chet." Joe frowned. "Close enough to put the imprint of her front bumper on his head."

Frank, however, wasn't convinced. "I didn't see the driver, either. Come on, let's help Chet," he said.

They ran over to the fence in time to see Chet climb stiffly back over it. He favored his left side as he climbed up to the road and winced as he bent to swing a leg over the fence. But Chet had the oddest expression on his face. "You know," he said, "I don't know if I'd have been able to do that if I hadn't been working out."

"Did you get a look at who was driving that car?" Frank asked.

"I'm afraid Frank and I were too busy jumping to get a decent ID," Joe said. "You sort of froze there for a moment, so we were hoping that maybe you got a glimpse of who was behind the wheel."

Chet shrugged, a little embarrassed. "At first when I recognized the car, I was happy. Then I saw the person driving—and, well, it didn't look right."

"You mean it wasn't Dawn?" Joe asked.

"The person behind the wheel was wearing a broad-brimmed hat, pulled low, and sunglasses." Chet frowned. "It didn't look like Dawn. At least I don't think it did."

Frank frowned, too. "What you mean is, it didn't *not* look like Dawn, either. In that getup, the driver could have been anybody, including her."

Chet nodded uneasily, giving the Hardys a wary look. "So what brings you guys to this neck of the woods?" he asked.

"We wanted to see how you were doing," Joe said.

"And it looks like we came along at just the right time." Frank hesitated for a second. "As I'm sure you've begun to suspect, those accidents at the health club may not have been accidents. It seems as if someone's out to get you. And we think those attacks on you may tie in with Walt Cosgrove's death."

"There was a report on the radio about him," Chet said. "It turns out he's a crook or something. But what does he have to do with me?"

"I don't know, and it sounds like you don't know," Frank said. "But somebody thinks you know something about Cosgrove that you shouldn't. And that's what we've got to find out, if we have to go over every second you spent with him."

"Even if we did, we wouldn't waste much time." Chet rolled his eyes. "I only saw him twice, for about five minutes in all."

"But you must have noticed something," Joe insisted. "Maybe it didn't seem important at the time, but it means something now that he's dead."

"Was there anything out of the ordinary?" Frank asked. "Was there anything peculiar about the bag Cosgrove was carrying? Did he talk with anyone?"

"He didn't talk, he just grunted," Chet told them.

"Take it right from the top," Joe suggested. "From the moment you entered the locker room."

Chet shrugged, but began to recite the facts. "I came through the door, and the locker room was empty except for this big guy. He looked up, grunted at me, and opened the locker."

"We remember this part," Joe said. "He opened the lock with the streak on the shank. What happened then?"

"What else? He began changing out of his street clothes and putting on his workout gear."

"You didn't notice *anything* else?" Frank asked.

"I noticed the guy had a great build, but that's

about it." Chet looked down at his still-ample stomach and gave the Hardys a rueful smile. "You know, if I had a bod like that, I wouldn't mind advertising my name on a sweatband."

"What?" Frank looked puzzled.

"My sweatband. Remember? The one with my name on it? You were there when I gave it to Dawn." Chet sighed. "You know, I never got that back."

Joe gave him an uneasy glance. "If Terrance Penman is right, you may never get the sweatband back. He claims that Dawn quit the Harbor Health Club."

Chet gave them a goofy smile. "Well, even if she *is* gone, she'll have my sweatband to remember me by." He sighed. "Too bad I never got her number."

Frank and Joe exchanged glances. She may be trying to kill him, Frank thought.

"Look, Chet," he said. "Right now, you should be thinking about your safety, not your sweatband. You had two close calls at the gym, not to mention this last little brush with Dawn's car. Be careful, okay?"

"Okay, sure," Chet said.

"We'll walk you back to your house, and please don't go out unless you absolutely have to."

At least our words are finally sinking in, Frank thought as he watched Chet's expression go from goofy to worried.

"We're on this now," Frank said. "We'll find out who's after you."

"And then we'll put 'em out of business," Joe promised. "But till then, watch it, will you?"

Chet was silent all the way back to his house.

When Frank got home he read the newspaper reports on Cosgrove/Ostrowski's criminal record.

His reading gave him an idea. He led Joe to their father's office.

"Dad, we need help, and we're hoping you can give it to us," Frank said.

Fenton Hardy looked up from his desk. "What kind of help?"

"If I remember, you've got a police friend who's an assistant warden at the Midland Penitentiary."

Frank's father nodded warily. "Does this have something to do with the fact that the guy who was found in the bay served time there?"

"Guilty as charged," Frank admitted. "We'd like a copy of his record."

"I think I'll need a few more reasons," Fenton told his sons.

"We've gotten some indications that Ostrowski's death ties into the Harbor Health Club in some way," Frank said. "Maybe it's a long shot, but now it turns out that Ostrowski and Pete Vanbricken were both in Midland a few years ago."

"One in the football stadium, the other in the pen," Fenton pointed out.

Frank shrugged. "I said it was a long shot, Dad. But maybe they had associates in common. That's what I really want. A list of Ostrowski's known criminal associates."

Fenton Hardy looked at his sons for a long moment. "A shot that long needs a moon rocket, not a cannon." Then he grinned. "But maybe it's worthwhile."

He reached for his phone. "Let me talk to my contact, and we'll see."

Frank and Joe headed into the kitchen.

By late afternoon their father caught up to them, a sheaf of flimsy, curling papers in his hand. "The wonders of modern technology," he said. "Walt Ostrowski's entire prison record, fresh off the fax machine."

He spread the papers across the kitchen table, and the boys began to read. Joe's eyebrows rose as he scanned the arrest record. "This guy's life story reads like a bad gangster movie. Six months for assault and battery. Two years suspended sentence for weapons possession."

The more Joe read on, the more his eyebrows rose. "Assault with a dangerous weapon, case dismissed. Assault with intent to kill, also dismissed. Attempted arson, dismissed for lack of evidence. Then they finally arrested him for assault with intent to kill, and it got plea-bargained down to reckless endangerment."

He shook his head. "Ostrowski certainly wasn't a saint, but he must have had a tremendous lawyer."

"The real story isn't there, but my friend told it to me," Fenton Hardy said. "Ostrowski was connected—he was a low-level thug in the Stanek crime organization based in Midland. Notice all those assault arrests? Ostrowski was a legbreaker for one of Stanek's most lucrative operations—loan-sharking."

"Stanek lent people money at a ridiculously high rate of interest," Frank said.

Fenton nodded. "In the business, that interest is called the vig—vigorish. Under the classic form of the racket, the loan would be compounded weekly, with large unpleasant types like Ostrowski sent around to collect the payments. The catch was that most of the payment only covered the vig. Victims could never pay off the basic amount of the loan, and wound up eternally in debt."

"And if they couldn't make the weekly payment, Ostrowski would play rough," Joe said.

"More recently, crime types have used loansharking as a wedge to get control of legitimate businesses," Fenton went on. "A company would get a desperately needed loan from Stanek, then discover the loan could never be paid off. But Stanek would forgive the debt for a partnership. Not only would he get a share of the company's profits, he could use his influence to steer business toward other companies he controlled."

"Sounds like a sweet deal," Frank said. "Get money from lots of small people, then use it to build yourself a business empire."

Fenton shook his head. "A closer description is 'extort money from lots of people.' Remember, the source of Stanek's cash flow is thugs like the late, unlamented Mr. Ostrowski." He frowned. "Big guys with guns who beat people up for a living. Of course, that's how Stanek started out himself. His nickname is Big Ed, and he's famous for forcing money out of deadbeats with a baseball bat."

"I don't think I want to hear any more," Joe said, putting his hands up.

"Here's something you might be interested in hearing." Frank looked up from the fax sheet he was reading, a triumphant glitter in his eyes. "Here's the long-awaited list of known associates. The third guy down on the list is a man named Jan Kolachev."

Joe frowned. "So?"

"Think about it for a second," Frank said. "Walter Ostrowski changes his name to Walt Cosgrove, a nice, WASPy, white-bread last name. One of his associates is named Jan, J-A-N, pronounced 'Yonn' Kolachev. And here in town we've got a Jan Cole. The last name is nice and white bread, but that Jan belongs with names like Ostrowski, Stanek—"

"And Kolachev." Joe began nodding. "Cole—Kolachev. I get what you mean."

"My friend at the prison had one other piece of information that's not on the record," Fenton added. "When Ostrowski was released from prison, he apparently got a promotion. The rumor is that he's now working as a courier for the Stanek organization."

"And he visits Bayport—where perhaps an old buddy just happens to be working," Joe said.

Frank got to his feet. "Come on, Joe. I think we've got some good reasons to chat with the bully of the Harbor Health Club."

Chapter

13

FRANK AND JOE climbed into their van in the early evening twilight. Frank got behind the wheel, started the engine, and headed for the Harbor Health Club.

"I think the pieces are beginning to come together now," Frank said. "Walt Cosgrove, actually Walter Ostrowski, is a low-level thug in a criminal organization. He's a courier—"

"And we know what he's delivering," Joe cut in. "We saw it in his locker at the Harbor Health Club. Cosgrove delivers money—by the big, black bagful. And if my guess is right, he delivers it to Jan Cole, a.k.a. Jan Kolachev. What bothers me is why."

"Oh, it's strictly business. The money comes from the Stanek loan-sharking operation." Frank gave his brother a grim smile. "You see, the big problem with making illegal money is that you're still expected to pay taxes on it."

"Or you go to jail," Joe said. "That's how the feds nailed a lot of gangsters, like Al Capone."

Frank nodded. "And the feds start asking embarrassing questions when you obviously have a lot of income and a lavish life-style and can't explain where your money comes from. What's going on here is obvious. Stanek is taking dirty money extorted through his loan-sharking racket and turning it into clean money here in Bayport. It's called money laundering."

"So the Harbor Health Club isn't just a gym, it's also a laundry," Joe said. "But I don't see how sending it here makes the money clean."

"Remember that list I found on Vanbricken's desk? The one that showed us paying an incredible amount for a membership? The one that showed Hurd Applegate as a member? That's how they do it."

The light bulb appeared over Joe's head. "We paid a rock-bottom membership rate. But on their records, they pad that amount out with dirty money."

Frank nodded. "Not only that, but they must add names at random to their membership records—also at inflated rates."

Joe grinned. "They must have picked Hurd Applegate out of the A's in the telephone book.

Anybody who actually saw him would know he wasn't gym material."

"It's actually a clever scam," Frank said. "A gym's financial success is marked by having lots of members who never come in."

Joe looked puzzled again.

"The idea is to have people pay for memberships, but not increase the demand for more machines or more trainers. Health clubs make the most profit out of people who sign up in a burst of enthusiasm, then give up exercising. The club still keeps the person's money but doesn't have to provide any services."

"That's a very nasty way of looking at the situation," Joe said.

"No, it's just a very clear way," Frank responded. "Now look at the Harbor Health Club. Not only do they inflate the amount of membership dollars coming in, but a lot—maybe most—of their members don't even know they belong to the club. The result is a very tidy profit."

"And that probably goes back to one of Stanek's front companies, which is an investor in the club." Joe nodded, impressed. "Very slick. The club pays taxes, and the dirty money becomes all legal and legit."

He looked at Frank. "No wonder Cole doesn't care how he treats people at the club. As long as they keep them on the books, the place looks like it's making money like crazy."

Frank nodded. "It's just like he told Vanbricken when they argued out in the parking lot. He's responsible for the club's cash flow, because a lot of it is actually coming from Midland.''

He frowned. "The big question is, how does Vanbricken fit in?"

"You mean, is he really the boss of the operation?" Joe asked. "After all, he is supposed to be the owner of the club. He was on the Midland expansion team—right in Big Ed Stanek's backyard. And didn't you say that those phony records were on his desk?" From Joe's expression, he obviously thought the question was answered.

"But what about the way Vanbricken and Cole fought that first day we came to the club?" Frank said. "Pistol Pete wasn't acting like the boss. He sounded as if he couldn't keep Cole under control."

"What's that old saying about a falling-out among thieves?" Joe shrugged. "I mean, these guys are crooks, Frank. You can't expect them to act like honest people."

He turned to Frank, eagerly going on. "In fact, that explains what happened to Cosgrove—"

"Ostrowski," Frank said.

"Whoever," Joe said impatiently. "He was a crook, too, and he was stealing from the money he was delivering for Stanek. He was found out and got killed. End of questions."

"End of one set of questions," Frank said, bursting Joe's smug bubble. "But it's the beginning of a bunch of new ones. How come the money is still in the locker?"

"Whoever killed Ostrowski didn't have time to move it," Joe said. "The killer probably didn't expect Ostrowski's body to be found and thought there'd be lots of time to take care of the cash. Instead, the police declared it a suspicious death and then started questioning everybody who worked at the health club. Not a good time to be moving the money—or to be caught with it. So it was left."

"I'll buy that," Frank said. "But tell us, Mr. Wizard, how did Ostrowski get killed without leaving traces of foul play?" His tone grew serious. "More importantly, where does Chet fit into all this nonsense? And let's not forget Dawn Reynolds. Why was it her car that nearly ran the three of us down?"

They rounded a corner, rolling toward the parking lot entrance for the Harbor Health Club. An older compact car, white with a black roof, pulled in ahead of them. But the small car didn't stay. It veered to a corner of the lot, screeched into a U-turn, and tore back to the entrance, engine roaring.

Frank stared, annoyed. His eyes went wide when he recognized the person in the passenger seat. "We may get the answer to one of our questions," he said. "That's Dawn Reynolds!"

Whipping the wheel around, he took the van into a tight turn and set off in pursuit.

The driver of the compact car must have noticed them, because the car suddenly accelerated, half-skidding into a turn.

Both Hardys were rocked in their seats as Frank took the van through the same maneuver. "Of all the lousy spots for a car chase," he complained between his teeth.

Bayport's waterfront had always been considered picturesque, in a decrepit sort of way. It was the oldest part of town, with streets that twisted like snake tracks, joined up at odd angles, and in some cases extended only for a block or two.

The van's brakes and tires shrieked protests as Frank attempted a high-speed chase through this winding course. He muttered under his breath as the little white car consistently eluded him. His van was much more powerful than the smaller car he was pursuing. On a straightaway, he'd have been right on his quarry's back bumper.

There were no straightaways here. Thanks to its size, the compact was more maneuverable.

For about the fifteenth time, Frank brought the van slewing around a sharp turn. The usual view appeared in his windshield—a vista of red-brick buildings, stretching about half the length of a normal block. Some of the buildings were run-down, dingy, and dark—those were the abandoned warehouses, leftovers from the old dockside neighborhood.

Some other buildings were sandblasted and had lights blazing in all the windows. These were the newly renovated condos.

Ahead of them, the little white car fishtailed down the block, skidding off to the left as the road took another winding turn.

Frank goosed the gas pedal down, sending them rushing forward, then feathered the brakes to send them shuddering through the turn.

The far end of the curved road came to an intersection. It also showed something a little different—a condo under construction. Half the street had been torn up by a combination backhoe and earthmover.

Probably digging to set up new plumbing or cable TV, Frank thought. His attention was focused on the fleeing compact car, which screeched around the work area and made a hard right onto the intersecting street.

But when he tried to follow, a loud, bleating tweet echoed off the brick walls on the block. The earthmover was working overtime. It was backing up, blocking the remaining strip of street!

Sweating, Frank tromped on the brakes. A quick look told him that at the speed they were going, they wouldn't be able to stop in time. He turned the wheel, aiming for the sidewalk. Not the best choice, he realized, but it beat smashing into the construction machine or the hole in the ground.

The van overreacted, swerving instead toward the brick wall of the empty warehouse across the street from the construction zone. In the passenger seat, Joe braced himself for a crash.

Frank gripped the wheel so tightly, his knuckles went white. He'd have to steer into the skid, hoping he'd have enough maneuvering room to regain control of the van before it impacted.

He fought the steering system in a desperate struggle to keep the wheels from locking. By cutting the wheel farther and farther to the left, it might just be possible to spin the van around. Of course, he might also send them broadside into the wall, or just overturn the van.

Momentum had them lurching onto only two wheels. Frank kept feathering the brakes, still guiding them into a turn.

The van spun out, coming to a stop with its rear wheels on the sidewalk and its front wheels pointing back the way they had come.

Inside, Frank and Joe Hardy let out shaky sighs of relief.

"Next time I want that feeling, I'll go on an amusement park ride." As Joe unclenched his grip on the dashboard, his hands still trembled.

"Hey, I'll even pay for your ticket. But I *never* want to feel like that again," Frank said.

A gloved fist thumped on the driver-side window. It was the worker who'd been operating the earthmover. "You guys crazy?" he asked in the furious voice of a man who's nearly been scared to death. "You could have gotten killed driving like that."

Frank glanced over at the construction site. The driver had obviously shifted gears when he saw them flying at him. The big mechanical digger now teetered on the lip of the pit it had dug.

"Hey, mister," Frank quickly said. "Isn't your machine about to fall into that hole?"

As the man turned to look, Frank whipped the van into another tight turn. They bumped off the curb, swung around the construction worker, roared down the open stretch of street, and duplicated the turn the little white car had taken.

The street ahead of them was empty.

"Now what do we do?" Joe wanted to know. "We've lost them."

Frank cut back on their speed. "Check every cross street as we pass," he said. "Maybe we can get some clue as to the way the car went."

The Hardys did even better than that. As Frank drove past an alley mouth, Joe yelled, "Hold it!"

Frank brought the van around to block the alley. It was a skinny dead-end street, and at the brick wall that marked the end of the alley, a small white car with a black top straddled the curb at a weird angle.

The Hardys got out of their van and cautiously approached the other car. No one was inside, and the trunk was open. Several pieces of luggage were scattered around on the street and sidewalk.

"Looks like we interrupted somebody's getaway." Frank turned on his heel and started back to the van. "They can't have gotten far on foot. We'll split up and search. You take the cross streets on the right-hand side, I'll take the ones on the left. Meet you back here in five minutes."

He reached the intersection of the street they'd driven down, turned, and vanished behind dingy brick walls.

A moment later Joe followed. When he reached the street, it was empty again. Frank had already disappeared into the maze of side streets that branched off.

Walking along, Joe noticed several things. For one, this part of the dockside area hadn't been touched by urban renewal yet. The buildings were dirty brick, with heavily padlocked doors. The streets were cobblestoned, probably untouched in the last hundred years. And there was nobody around. He felt all alone in the gloomy shadows cast by the pale twilight glow.

Or was he alone?

In the distance Joe could hear scuttling

sounds. For a second he thought of rats. Then he recognized what it had to be—the scuff of athletic shoes on cobblestones.

Zeroing in on the faint noise, Joe turned a corner, ran down another curving street, took another turn, and found himself surrounded by the blank brick rear walls of a bunch of warehouses. No doors or windows broke the expanse. But about halfway down the block was the black entrance to an alley.

Joe started forward, then stopped. The noises ahead of him had ceased. He picked up his pace, running for the alley.

He whipped around the corner and was surprised to see Dawn Reynolds hunched against the wall, a wild light in her eyes.

Since she'd left the abandoned car, Joe had expected to find her carrying a piece of luggage. Now, he discovered, that wasn't why she'd opened the trunk.

Dawn was carrying something, all right—the heavy metal tire iron from the car's repair kit.

Joe saw it clutched in her hand as she swung it straight at his head!

Chapter

14

JOE HAD NO CHOICE as the deadly length of metal swept toward the side of his head. He could only throw himself backward.

Landing flat on the cobblestoned street was a nasty jolt to his body. But it beat having his brains knocked out.

The tire iron swept through the space his head had occupied a moment before to smash with a dull clang into the brick wall. Dawn was strong, and she hadn't held back on her swing. Chips of broken brick flew from the point of impact.

Dawn's weapon rebounded from the wall, but she still held on to it as she turned to Joe, who had managed to rise only to a sitting position. With a wordless cry, the young woman charged forward, tire iron held high.

If I try to get up, I'll only be up to her waist before she starts hammering me, Joe realized. I've got to bring her down.

So, Joe made no effort to rise. He waited until Dawn had almost reached him, then pushed off from the ground, swinging his feet in a wide arc.

Joe's low-level roundhouse kick caught Dawn right behind the knees. She dropped like a felled tree, throwing one hand out to break her fall. Still on the ground, Joe dodged desperately to avoid Dawn's other hand. Even so, the tire iron clanged onto the cobblestones mere inches from his ear.

Both of Joe's hands shot out to seize the wrist of Dawn's club-wielding hand. That was the immediate danger to him. He had to disarm her.

She yelled wildly, punching at him, kicking at him, as he increased his grip. Dawn's free fist smashed into the side of his head, her knee hit his ribs with bruising force. But she didn't distract Joe from what he had to do.

A click came from the compressed cartilage under his fingers, then a grinding sound as he squeezed wrist bones together.

Dawn's yells changed to screams, and Joe could feel the play of muscles in her imprisoned wrist. Now, he thought, shaking her arm violently. Dawn's fingers lost their grasp on the tire iron. It clattered to the ground.

Joe let go with one hand and loosened his grip

with the other. He didn't really want to hurt her, after all.

The girl's only reaction was an attempt to pull loose. She was still screaming, and now she was scratching at Joe's fingers with her free hand.

Surprised, Joe slackened his hold, and Dawn tore free. She was halfway to her feet before Joe threw a tackle into her. Dawn dropped facedown to the cobblestones. The second impact seemed to knock the fight out of her. She lay where she fell, unmoving, sobbing.

For the first time, Joe could make out what she was saying.

"Don't kill me," Dawn pleaded in a low, hoarse voice. "Please, don't kill me."

"Dawn," Joe said.

The girl didn't even raise her head to look at him. She remained turned away, one cheek resting against the cobblestones.

"Dawn, listen to me." Joe put a hand on her shoulder, about to shake her.

The moment he touched her, however, it was as if every muscle in her body went rigid. *"Please!"* she screamed.

As gently as he could, Joe turned her resisting body toward him. "Look at me—look!" he insisted. Dawn's eyes held no trace of recognition.

"My name is Joe Hardy. We met out in the parking lot at the health club, remember? I even took an aerobics class with you."

Dawn remained frozen.

How do I get through to her? Joe wondered. "C'mon, Dawn. You've got to remember me. I'm a friend of Chet Morton's."

"Ch-Chet," she stuttered through clenched teeth. "Joe. Joe Hardy."

It was like watching a computer turn on, Joe thought. At first, it processes data very slowly.

"You're Joe Hardy, Chet's friend," Dawn finally said, the fear partly leaving her eyes. "You're not a hit man."

"A hit man?" Joe repeated, surprised. "People have called me a lot of things, but never that." He stared at Dawn curiously. "Why would you think I was a hit man?"

"Because I'm sure there's one after me," Dawn spoke rapidly, the words tumbling out. "That's why I quit my job, why I'm leaving Bayport. They want to kill me, as soon as they figure it out."

"Figure what out?" Joe asked. "And who are 'they'?"

But Dawn wasn't listening. She pulled herself to a sitting position in the middle of the alley and clung to Joe, trembling.

"My friend Monica helped clean out my apartment, then we were going to pick up my car. But when we got to the club parking lot, it was gone! I—I guess we sort of lost it. Monica whipped her car around and sped out of—"

"Dawn," Joe began, but the girl's story kept tumbling out.

123

"I guess she was right because this big black van started chasing us. Monica tried to lose them, driving through Dockside, but she didn't know the neighborhood and got us cut off in a blind alley. So we decided to split up and run for it. I took the tire iron—"

Dawn's eyes seemed finally to focus as she looked at Joe in horror. "I could have killed you! Just because I thought you were chasing me."

Joe looked closely at the young woman. At least she didn't seem crazed anymore. Still, he'd have to proceed carefully.

"To tell you the truth, I *was* chasing you," he said quietly. "My brother, Frank, and I were in the black van."

Dawn's face tightened, and every muscle went rigid again. "Why?" she whispered.

"To ask you some questions," Joe said as gently as he could. "You said your car was gone, but we saw it this morning. It nearly ran down Chet Morton."

"Chet," she said. A tear ran down her cheek. "It's my fault. I'm going to get him killed!"

"Whoa," Joe said. "Hold on. I want you to tell me everything. But I also want my brother to hear."

Joe helped Dawn to her feet, and together they retraced their steps back to the abandoned car. Frank was standing alone beside the Hardys' van. "I came up empty," he said with a nod at Dawn. "But I see you had better luck."

"Just listen," Joe said. "I think she's got something very important to say to us."

"Everything's my fault," Dawn said miserably. "And I didn't know what to do."

"Start from the beginning, Dawn," Joe said in a calm voice. "How did it all start?"

"It was Monday." Dawn blinked in surprise. "The day I met you. Or rather, Monday night. I take the afternoon through evening shift on Mondays. After my classes, I was in my car heading home when I remembered I had some paperwork to take care of. I turned around and drove back to the club. It wasn't locked up, so I figured somebody was still working."

A shadow came over Dawn's face. "When I went to get my papers, I heard noises coming from the gym. I checked it out, and—" She gulped and began shivering.

"Just take it easy," Joe crooned.

"I saw Jan Cole and Walt Cosgrove. Walt was on the treadmill, which was kind of funny. He only worked out with weights. Then I saw the gun in Jan's hand."

"He was going to shoot Cosgrove?" Frank said.

Dawn shook her head. "He was just threatening Walt. Jan kept pushing up the speed and the incline on the treadmill, making Walt work harder and harder. Walt kept pleading with Jan to stop. I guess he wasn't used to running. He kept saying his feet were getting all cut up, but Jan paid no attention."

While Dawn shuddered at the image, the Hardys exchanged a triumphant glance. So *that's* how Ostrowski's feet got all blistered, Joe thought.

Dawn continued with her unpleasant memories. "It was so weird. Jan kept hollering, 'Why are you short?' It doesn't make any sense. Walt was taller than Jan."

"Was that all Cole said?" Frank asked.

"No. He also asked, 'Where is it?' He sounded so angry, so scary, I couldn't figure it out."

"What happened then?" Joe asked.

"Jan upped the speed again, and all of a sudden, Walt let out a yell and grabbed his head. He wasn't running anymore, and he got thrown from the track of the treadmill." Dawn shuddered again. "He landed like—like a sack of potatoes. I thought I was going to be sick. Somehow, I don't know—the look on Walt's face, the way he fell—"

She looked at the Hardys. "I've seen lots of people pass out. But this was worse. I knew Walt Cosgrove was dead."

"What happened then?" Frank asked.

"I got out of there," Dawn said. "But Cole must have heard me. He came after me, I heard him running. I knew he'd catch me if I headed for the parking lot. So I went upstairs to the pool. It sounded like he was right behind me. But I managed to jump off the tanning deck—I used to do gymnastics—and I got away.''

Her lips trembled. "It was only when I got home that I realized I'd dropped something in the chase. I'd left the sweatband I was wearing.''

Joe stared at her. "The sweatband with Chet's name on it.''

Dawn nodded. "I didn't think Cole would find it. The lights were off in the stairwells, and it was dark up on the roof.''

Frank's eyes narrowed. "So he didn't get a look at the person who saw Cosgrove die. Chet's headband would be his only clue.''

"I came back the next morning to look for it,'' Dawn said. "But it was gone. The news talked about how Cosgrove's body had been found, but there was nothing about him being killed. Maybe I'd been wrong. So I didn't say anything.'' She looked at the boys. "I was scared—afraid of Jan Cole.'' She shivered. "I saw him in a fight once. He was—bad.'' Her voice ran out.

"And then?'' Frank pressed.

"That day, Chet nearly got his head smashed in by a barbell.'' Dawn bit her lip. "I tried to tell myself that it was just an accident. Then, the next day Jan dumped the barbell on him and nearly killed him again. And all of a sudden, the news was saying Walt Cosgrove was actually some gangster named Ostrowski. I—I decided to get away and fast.''

"And just leave Chet to be taken care of by Cole?'' Joe felt the anger igniting in his chest. "That was real nice. Especially since you're the one who got him into the club in the first place.''

Dawn shrank back, staring at the ground. "I tried to get him to leave the club,'' she said. "But he wouldn't listen to me. And I couldn't tell him why I was afraid for him. Jan Cole would be after us both.''

She looked at Joe. "I tried to talk to you about it, the day after the first accident, but you acted so weird, and I got called away—''

"Oh.'' Joe could feel his face turning bright red. "I didn't know what was going on. I thought that you—''

"Forget about what you thought,'' Frank cut in. "Now we know the whole chain of events. Cosgrove/Ostrowski was bringing dirty money to Cole, so he could turn it into clean investment money. Ostrowski was stealing from his shipments and kept coming up short. Cole tried to sweat the money out of him but accidentally killed him instead.''

He glanced at the young woman. "Dawn saw that, but because of the sweatband, Cole thinks Chet is the mystery witness. So Cole tried to arrange accidents at the club for Chet. When that didn't work, he must have stolen Dawn's

128

car to try to run him down. It was available, Dawn wasn't around—and Cole probably knew that in that car he could get real close to Chet."

"It all holds together," Joe said.

"We've got one witness here, but we'd better get Chet to explain about the accidents to the police."

Frank dug into his pockets and came out with some coins. "I noticed a pay phone on the next corner over," he said, "the only one for blocks. How's that for a good omen?"

"And because we told Chet to stick tight at home, he should be easy to catch. As soon as he gets down to headquarters, this whole thing will be tied up." Joe grinned. "Well, what are you waiting for? Start dialing."

Dawn didn't say anything. She kept looking down at the pavement. A tear fell from her eye to the cobblestone. "That's what I should have done," she said in a strangled voice. "I should have gone straight to the police, instead of wimping out."

Frank started off for the pay phone. Behind him, he could hear Joe trying to soothe the young woman.

"Okay, you didn't do it right away, but you're doing it now. And you'll have us to help you. Chet, too. You should have seen how he handled that hit-and-run attempt. Maybe he's not an aerobics whiz, but he sure can pump iron— and jump out of the path of speeding cars."

Too bad Chet isn't around to hear Joe acting as his fan club, Frank thought, heading around the corner. Looks like Joe is over Dawn Reynolds. I wish I knew where Chet stands.

Night had come, and the pay phone's light was on. Frank picked up the receiver, happy to get a dial tone. Quickly, he punched in Chet's number on the keypad.

Mrs. Morton answered.

"Hi, it's Frank Hardy," Frank said with a grin. "Could I talk to your invalid, please?"

"I'm afraid he's not here," Mrs. Morton said.

The grin erased itself from Frank's face as he listened.

"That Mr. Vanbricken from the health club called. I didn't quite understand what got Chet so excited." Mrs. Morton sounded puzzled.

"But it had something to do with one of the aerobics instructors—Dawn Somebody."

Chapter

15

"WELL, UH, OKAY, Mrs. Morton. Just let him know I called."

Frank Hardy didn't know how he managed to sound natural as he got off the phone with Chet's mother. Inside he felt numb.

Sure, the way Chet felt about Dawn, he'd go running if there were something he could do for her. The call had come from Pete Vanbricken. Maybe if Jan Cole had been on the line, Chet might have hesitated.

Frank broke into a run, heading back to the van.

Joe and Dawn had been working on Dawn's abandoned getaway car, locking the doors, putting the luggage back in the trunk. Dawn was slipping a piece of paper under the windshield wiper.

"It's a note to my friend Monica, telling her everything's okay." Dawn's smile faded when she saw Frank's face.

"Bad news," Frank announced. "The money launderers must be getting desperate. They've decoyed Chet down to the club—"

"That doesn't sound good," Joe said, throwing his door open. "But how did they get him out so easily?"

"They used his weak spot—Dawn."

Dawn Reynolds gasped as she realized what Frank meant. "Then I'm coming, too," she said.

Frank got behind the wheel, started the engine, and pulled out of the alley.

"Shouldn't we call the police?" Dawn asked.

Frank sighed. "If we try to present our case, they'll have to check things out. And while they do that—"

"Who knows what will happen to Chet?" she finished in a faint voice.

"On the other hand . . ." Joe said. "Hey, Frank. Stop at that pay phone, and I'll make the call."

Frank pulled over to the curb, and Joe hopped out. He picked up the phone and dialed the emergency number.

"Hello? I'd like the police, please." He spoke in a nasal tone, more high-pitched than his usual voice. "Yes. I want to report suspicious characters hanging around the Harbor Health Club."

Joe hung up with a grin and got back in the van.

"What 'suspicious characters'?" Dawn wanted to know.

Frank took the van around a turn. "In about five minutes, us."

The parking lot for the club was surprisingly empty as they pulled in. "I don't get it," Dawn said. "This is yuppie hour—our busiest time."

"Not this evening," Joe said, pointing to the glass double doors. A hand-lettered sign announced that the club was closed because of plumbing difficulties.

"That would turn *me* off," Frank admitted. He pressed against the door handle. The door didn't move. "Locked," he announced. "This may be a problem."

Frank turned to Dawn. "Unless—did you turn in your keys when you left?"

Dawn nodded. "Yeah, I turned them in."

She suddenly glanced up, frowning in thought. "But there might be another way in—the opposite route to the one I took to get out that night."

Leaving the van parked at a slant in front of the entrance, the Hardys followed Dawn around the side of the building.

In its past life as a warehouse, this single-story section must have been a loading dock. Obviously some deliveries were still made to this area. But the rooftop above had been fenced in with an elaborate trellis.

"This is the tanning deck," Dawn said, looking upward. "There's a rooftop stairway leading up to the second-story roof. The pool's up there—and that's where I got out. There's a sliding glass door that doesn't lock correctly."

"So our only problem is getting up there," Frank said.

"Just get *me* up there," Dawn said. "I can take care of the rest."

Joe laced his fingers together, and Dawn placed her foot in the improvised stirrup as Joe crouched. "One, two—three!"

Grunting, Joe straightened his legs and back, throwing his arms up as Dawn leapt. The girl used Joe's impetus to send herself even higher. Her fingers caught in the trellis work fence, and she scrambled over.

A moment or two later, a long strip of heavy canvas came rippling down from the top of the fence.

"What's this?" Frank called up.

"It used to be part of the canvas awning from our snack bar," Dawn whispered back. "I think it will hold you."

The Hardys quickly scaled the improvised rope until they were on top of the roof.

"Nice setup," Joe muttered, looking around. "Too bad I never got the chance to use it."

Frank tried to relate the rooftop layout to the facilities below. "There's the skylight for the gym," he said, pointing.

They set off, moving as quietly as they could. "The bad guys might be right under us," Frank warned in a whisper. "Let's not warn them by clomping around up here."

He carefully set a course to pass the skylight. With luck, they might get a glimpse of what was waiting for them down on the ground floor.

Crouched down, Frank peered through the glass—and froze. After hearing Dawn's story, the scene he was witnessing seemed all too familiar—horribly familiar.

Jan Cole was standing beside a treadmill. Now, instead of Walt Cosgrove, Chet Morton was running for his life.

A hiss of indrawn breath beside him made Frank turn. Dawn and Joe were also taking in the same view.

"We'd better get in there—and fast," Joe said.

The rest of Dawn's route worked perfectly. The glass door slid open, and they crept quickly down the darkened stairwells.

As Frank eased the ground-floor stairwell door open, they were just around a corner from the entrance to the gym.

"You can't do this, Cole," a voice pleaded over the hum of the moving treadmill. "It's not going to work."

Frank recognized the speaker. It was Pete Vanbricken. He hadn't seen him from the skylight, but Frank knew the club owner must be in the gym. And he seemed to be arguing for Chet's life.

"Shut up, Vanbricken." Jan Cole's voice was hoarse and cold. "I've heard enough of this whining from you. The kid has to die, and this time I'm making sure you're in on it, right down to getting rid of the stiff."

Cole gave a chilling laugh. "I don't want you getting any attacks of conscience later. I mean, a guy can't afford a conscience when he's taking money from Big Ed Stanek."

"I don't care about the money," Vanbricken said desperately.

Frank crept to the doors, peering into the room through the thin space by the hinges. He could see Chet's running figure from behind, and Cole, but Vanbricken was still invisible.

"Hey, what more does a washed-up football player need?" Cole asked sarcastically. "You've got a pretty little health club, everybody looks up to you, you're a regular hometown hero. And nobody has to know how lousy your business really is, because Big Ed keeps your cash flow going. Of course, he cleans up his own, too. But one hand washes the other."

"Money laundering is one thing," Vanbricken said. "And, yes, I let that slide. But

136

can't let this get completely out of hand. We can't have a murder—"

"Get it through your head, chump!" Cole's yell was like an animal's cry. The mask was off, Frank realized. Cole had given up trying to act civilized. Now he was just a desperate, sweating thug, winning arguments with the loudest voice—and a ready gun.

"We already *got* a murder," Cole went on a little more quietly. "I croaked Ostrowski—Cosgrove, to you. And this kid knows about it. He saw me. I found his dopey sweatband, and I knew I had to shut him up—permanently. Otherwise, he'll end up putting the bite on me."

"You never told me any of this!" Vanbricken's voice was anguished. "I'd never allow—"

"That's why I didn't tell you." Cole cut him off. "You still have this stupid idea that your loan deal left you and Stanek partners. It ain't that way, stupid. That's why I'm here, to run things. You sure couldn't do it."

"I put every penny of my own money into this place!" From his hiding place, Frank could hear the despair in Pete Vanbricken's voice. "I figured it was my last chance—coming home where I belonged. What else could I do? I came out of college knowing only one thing—how to throw a football. Then those big gorillas wrecked my arm in a game. I bought this place and watched it sink week by week.

Then some friends back in Midland said they knew a guy who would give me a bridging loan.''

Vanbricken laughed bitterly. "And Big Ed Stanek winds up as my partner. Then this whole money laundering thing starts. Now I find out you've been going around killing people.''

"Just one.'' Jan Cole sounded almost offended, as if Vanbricken had attacked his professionalism. "And I tried to off the Morton kid here. My first shot would have been a perfect accident. Everyone was too busy pumping their pecs to notice me loosening the grip on the barbell. But it didn't work,'' he growled.

"So I tried a little harder. And *that* didn't work. Finally I decided on a hit-and-run bit, nice and far away from the club. I even stole that dizzy Reynolds kid's car, because I know this jerk is hot for her.''

Chet's shoulders pulled in when he heard Cole's words. Then he winced and grabbed for his taped ribs.

"I figured the dope would just stand there smiling and waving while I ran him down. Instead, somehow he jumps out of the way. So it's time for another accident.''

Cole flung out an arm to point to Chet's wheezing progress. "Why do you think I got the kid on the treadmill? Maybe he'll go the way Ostrowski did. Then everybody will say it was natural causes.''

For a moment the two men stared at each other. The big room was silent except for Chet's gasping breaths.

"Cole, Cosgrove died from a brain aneurysm—he had a weak blood vessel inside his skull. He died by accident." Vanbricken tried hard to persuade the thug. "It's not murder."

"That's not the way the cops would see it—not with my record," Cole objected. "Besides, they'd start asking questions about why I was sweating Ostrowski. And Big Ed wouldn't like it if word of his little operation here got out."

"And what if the treadmill doesn't kill this boy?" Vanbricken asked.

"Then I blow him away." Cole's voice was casual, as if he were discussing swatting a fly. Then a note of ice entered his words. "That's what happens to anybody who gets in my way."

Joe and Dawn joined Frank behind the angle of the door. "We've heard enough," Joe whispered. "We've got to get in there and stop that maniac."

"Cole is facing away from these open doors. Let's try a straight rush—we don't have time to do anything fancy. From the way Vanbricken's talking, he may even help us."

They crept around the door, then ran flat out into the room. The carpeting and noise of the treadmill would hide their footfalls. Frank now saw where Pete Vanbricken was standing, beyond the treadmill, out of Frank's line of vision, but in Cole's line of fire.

There was just one thing Frank hadn't calculated on—the decor of the gym. He'd forgotten that the walls were lined with mirrors.

Cole saw them before they got three strides into the room. But he didn't turn to the Hardys. Cole took care of the nearer danger—Pistol Pete Vanbricken, who had tensed for a lunge.

Before the ex-football star could launch himself, however, Cole's gun went off, deafening even in that large room.

With a hoarse cry, Vanbricken went down. Thick red blood soaked the sweatpants he was wearing and the rug he lay on. He clutched at his leg, trying to slow the flow.

"Keep running, Morton, or you get the next bullet!" Cole shifted his aim to cover the Hardys. Their rush stumbled to a halt, just a yard short of attack range.

"Well, well," Cole said, "the smart guys. Bet you're wishing you did what Pistol Pete said and stayed away from here."

"Not really, Mr. Kolachev." Frank was banking on the chance that using the man's real name might distract him enough to let them try something.

It didn't work. Jan Cole's eyes just got colder, and he moved a step back, the better to cover the two boys. "You really are smart guys," the gunman said, smiling thinly. "Too smart for your own good. Now, back up."

"And who's going to make us?" Joe bluffed. "You may be able to shoot one of us, but the other will be on top of you."

"Kid, I could probably put this gun away and still handle the two of you," Cole said. "But I got an easier way. How you doing back there by the door, Dawn?"

With a sick feeling in his gut, Frank turned to see Dawn Reynolds standing frozen, peering in the doorway. Cole's gun was now centered on her head.

"Curiosity killed the cat," Cole said. "Now, come on, step in. And don't try pulling back. You're not giving me much of a target, and that means I'd have to go for a head shot, which would ruin that pretty face."

The Hardys both watched as Dawn slowly, unwillingly, stepped into the room.

"Now, you were wondering how I could make you back off, I believe," Cole said with an ugly smile. "I'm going to count to three. By then, if you aren't moving back, I'll shoot Dawn in the leg. She's farther away than Vanbricken is, so I can't guarantee hitting a vein. Maybe I'll hit an artery, and she'll bleed to death all over the floor. But it'll be your fault. One . . . two . . ."

The Hardys stepped back.

"See? You guys *are* smart."

"Jan—Jan, look," Dawn began. "Chet didn't

see anything. I did. I was wearing his sweat-band—"

"Too late now, honey," Cole said. "He's heard and seen too much. And with all you witnesses, it looks like I can't hope for an accident. Guess I'll have to shoot you all and make a run for it."

"At least you'll have that bagful of money in locker thirteen," Joe said boldly. "But I don't know how Big Ed will take your using his money as a getaway fund."

Cole froze long enough for the Hardys to step forward again. But he snapped the gun on Dawn. "Back off or the girl gets it!" he screamed.

Defeated, Frank and Joe retreated out of attack range again. Cole calmed down.

"You got a point, kid," he said. "Since you're so good, maybe you can help with one more future plan. Who gets it first, huh?"

Cole shifted over so he could more easily cover the three people standing in front of him. The treadmill was directly behind him, and for a second, Frank thought that maybe Chet could sneak up from the rear.

But, no, he realized, Cole had been checking the mirrors. He was out of Chet's range, too.

"So, smart guy," Cole taunted, "who do I shoot? You? Your brother? Or the pretty blond?"

Cole's smile vanished, and his voice went flat. "I think I've made my choice, Dawn."

Frank tensed himself for a hopeless jump—and stared.

Behind Cole, Chet Morton launched himself up and over the handles and electronic controls of the treadmill. He was propelled by more than just the strength of his muscles or the juice of his emotions.

He had the mechanical assist of a full-speed treadmill!

Chapter

16

CHET FLEW as if he'd been shot from a cannon.

Jan Cole must have caught the movement in the gym mirror. He hesitated an instant and didn't shoot at Dawn.

Cole was just turning his gun to Chet when Chet smashed into him. The impact caught Cole off balance, toppling him to the floor.

The gun went off once, sending a bullet into the ceiling. By then Cole was on the floor with Chet on top of him.

Chet's face tightened with the impact on his bruised ribs. But that didn't stop him. Once again Joe Hardy was reminded that there was muscle under Chet's bulk as his friend aimed a thunderous blow behind Cole's right ear. The thug's whole body shook.

144

"I'll go for the gun," Frank barked, leaping for Cole's outstretched right arm, where the pistol was still clutched in his hand.

Joe decided to come in on Cole's left.

Chet sprawled across Cole's back, a choke hold around his neck, throwing punch after punch into his head.

The big man was in trouble, but he wasn't out for the count. In spite of Chet's weight on him, Cole pushed himself up with his left hand. His right hand started bringing the gun up.

Chet's fist spread into a claw, going for Cole's eyes.

He didn't have to strike.

Joe Hardy was already on hand, kicking Cole's left hand from under him.

As the big man fell, Frank Hardy grabbed Cole's gun hand by the wrist, yanking the arm out straight. He dug his foot into Cole's armpit, putting tension on the gunman's shoulder, and twisted.

Cole yelled, and Joe knew why. That particular move would dislocate the thug's arm if a little more pressure were applied.

The gun dropped from Cole's nerveless fingers.

After this, Joe thought, our only problem is getting Chet to stop beating up on this guy.

The fight officially ended, however, when a small army of police burst into the gym, guns at the ready. "Freeze!" yelled Con Riley.

Chet froze in midpunch, staring at all the weapons aimed at him.

Joe Hardy raised his hands and glanced at his watch. "Does it always take you guys this long to respond to a prowler report?"

"Oh, our first unit was here early enough. They radioed in for reinforcements when they realized who owned the van outside," Con said. "We were working our way in from the roof—some helpful soul had left a rope ladder dangling down—when we heard the shots." He turned to the other officers. "I guess we can put up our guns, people."

"Let's get down to business," Joe said. "We all can testify that the beaten-up character down there attempted to murder us, especially Pete Vanbricken."

Police officers were already moving to give Vanbricken first aid.

"But this lady over here," Joe went on, "can testify that Mr. Cole killed Walt Cosgrove, a.k.a. Walter Ostrowski."

Dawn Reynolds, however, was paying no attention. Her eyes were locked on Chet Morton as she stepped closer to him. "Chet—what you did—that was the bravest thing I ever saw."

Chet stared at Dawn, his face turning bright red as he stammered, "I—uh, well, uh—he was going to kill you, and I couldn't let him do that," Chet finally blurted out.

He didn't have a chance to say any more

Dawn threw her arms around Chet and kissed him.

Joe sighed. "Win a few, lose a few," he muttered.

"Hey, there's always that girl Linda," Frank said with a smile. "Maybe you can work out with her and leave me alone."

Two days later Joe, Frank, and Callie Shaw were walking through the food court of the Bayport Mall.

"So, what's the big deal, guys?" Callie wanted to know. "Why are we expected at Mr. Pizza?"

"I just got the call from Chet," Joe said. "All he told me was that Dawn had a big announcement to make."

"Announcement?" Callie suddenly stopped in her tracks, her eyes wide. "What could that be?"

"The only way we'll find out is by going there," Frank said.

"I'm still not speaking to you," Callie informed him frostily. "After going to the trouble of joining a health club—"

"Actually, Joe signed me up," Frank said.

"You'd think that someone would have the decency to invite his girlfriend to use one of his free guest passes—"

"They threw us out of the club the third day

we were there," Frank continued a little desperately.

"Especially when I went to the expense of buying some new workout clothes," Callie finished.

"Yeah," Joe said. "Liz Webling told us the leotard you bought was pretty hot."

Color crept up Callie's cheeks. "One of these days, I'm going to kill that girl," she muttered.

Then her face brightened. "But now that you're heroes for saving the club, don't you think they'll let you back in again? Maybe I could still use one of your—"

"I hate to break this to you, Callie," Joe said, "but the Harbor Health Club has been closed."

Callie looked as if her whole world had crumbled. "What?"

"The club's accounts were ordered frozen by the feds. They're looking into the Stanek connection. Pete Vanbricken gave the staff two months' wages from what's left of his own money," Joe reported.

"What happens to Vanbricken?" Callie asked.

"He's cooperating in the investigation," Frank said. "From what I understand, he's come completely clean on everything that happened at the club."

"I bet Big Ed Stanek doesn't like that," Callie said.

"I think Big Ed has bigger worries than that," Frank said with a smile. "Almost two hundred thousand dollars was seized in that locker. It looks as if the club wasn't just one of Stanek's money laundries, it was a major distribution center."

"So Cole was a bigger fry than you guys suspected?" Callie said.

"We should have guessed it," Frank admitted. "Terrance Penman mentioned a whole crew of out-of-towners—traveling salesmen."

"They must have been shipping money around like mad," Joe said. "No wonder Ostrowski thought a grand here or there wouldn't be missed."

Callie shook her head. "And Cole could tie the whole network in—if he talked." Her eyes had a faraway look as they continued to walk.

"Look on the bright side," Joe whispered to Frank. "At least she's not mourning her workout clothes anymore."

"I heard that," Callie said.

Frank gave his brother a look. "Well, how about this?" he said to Callie. "The next time we have a mystery in a gym, I promise to send you undercover in your leotard."

"For myself, I can hardly wait," Joe added.

"One day, Joe Hardy," Callie muttered darkly.

Joe pretended not to hear. "We'd better hurry. After all, we don't want to miss Chet and Dawn's announcement."

They walked into Mr. Pizza to find Chet and Dawn seated at a long table. Also sitting beside Dawn was a big middle-aged man in a rumpled suit.

To Joe's eyes, the young couple seemed very quiet and subdued.

Callie busily scanned the whole place. "No sign of Chet's parents," she whispered. "It looks like this big announcement is just for us."

"But who is the mystery man sitting beside Dawn?" Joe whispered back.

As soon as they reached the table, Chet stood up. "Callie, Frank, Joe, this is Mr. Jarvis."

"Are you a relative of Dawn's?" Callie asked.

Frank rolled his eyes. "Ever the investigator," he muttered.

Jarvis stared at Callie as if she'd grown an extra head.

"We haven't told anyone," Dawn quickly explained.

"And I wish you still wouldn't," Jarvis growled.

Dawn seemed determined. "They deserve to know. And I don't want Chet to be the one to explain it."

She looked about to say more, but Tony Prito appeared with his helper. They carried two pies with everything and two salads.

"I figured I'd just order for us," Chet said. Dawn got one of the salads. He got the other.

"I wanted to thank you guys for helping me,"

Dawn said. "You showed me what I should have done. And, Chet, you saved my life."

She took a deep breath. "I also wanted to take this opportunity to say goodbye."

Frank, Joe, and Callie all stared. "Goodbye?" They almost spoke in chorus.

Dawn rested her fingers on Chet's hand. "Chet knows already. I've had a lot of long talks with him. In fact, he's the one who convinced me to testify."

"And go into hiding for a while," Chet added.

"Go into hiding?" The Hardys and Callie exchanged another shocked glance.

"Mr. Jarvis is a federal marshal," Dawn explained. "We're leaving—well, right after this."

"With Miss Reynolds's testimony, we can put Cole away for a long time," Jarvis said. "Unless he rolls over on Big Ed Stanek's whole money-laundering operation."

Joe sat up straighter in his chair. "You mean that if Cole turns informer, you'll let him off?"

"You didn't seem so excited when you suggested Vanbricken might make a deal," Frank said.

"Vanbricken didn't murder anybody!" Joe turned to Chet. "And Cole almost murdered you."

"I thought about that," Chet admitted. "In the end, I decided this was just one battle in a much bigger war." He shook his head. "Sounds pretty overblown when I put it that way. But this is what Dawn and I decided. We were lucky enough to beat the bad guys in Bayport. But Cole can shut Stanek down all across the country."

"Maybe I didn't speak up when Chet needed me," Dawn said. "But I can do some good now." She lowered her gaze to the tabletop. "This is harder than I thought."

Turning abruptly, Dawn kissed Chet. "So long," she said. "I wish I could deserve a guy like you."

"The problems of two people don't amount to a hill of beans in this crazy world," Chet said, managing a smile.

Joe noticed, however, that Chet's eyes never left Dawn as she and Jarvis left the place.

Joe opened his mouth to say something, but Callie was already leaning over, her hand on Chet's shoulder. "I'm sorry, Chet. I wish there was something better I could say."

Chet shrugged and gently removed her hand. "You win a few, you lose a few. . ."

He looked down at the salad in front of him, pushed it aside, and took a piece of pizza.

"I'll tell you one thing," Chet said between bites. "In the future, any weight I lose, I'll do it in the training room in my barn." He sighed. "Those health clubs can be rough on your heart."

Frank and Joe's next case:

The Hardys join their father on an undercover mission into the African wild. On the trail of a multimillion-dollar smuggling operation, they're out to learn the fate of a missing U.S. Customs official. Thrust into a world of poisonous snakes and man-eating lions, the boys soon confront the most dangerous beast of all . . .

Poachers armed with high-powered weapons are devastating herds of endangered species. Shocked by the slaughter, Frank and Joe are dead set on shutting the smugglers down. But they pay a terrible price for the truth: a tragic murder that will lead them out of Africa and to the most painful and perilous investigation of their lives . . . in *Endangered Species,* Case #64 in The Hardy Boys Casefiles™ and the first adventure in the Operation Phoenix Trilogy.

"I need to clear the air."

"Okay," Mark said slowly, as if quite lost. "About what?"

"About this. Us. Our motivations."

"I thought we'd done that already." Mark frowned as he tried to comprehend the situation. "Today's simply about having fun. I've got some great places in mind for tonight."

Lisa crossed her arms over her chest. She and Mark couldn't afford any miscommunication here. "Before I can go anywhere with you, I have to know how tonight is going to end."

Mark shifted, planting his feet on the floor. He straightened but remained seated. The dark blue shirt set off his deep brown eyes, and his troubled gaze locked onto hers. "Tonight ends like any other night. I've already told you to stop worrying. We're friends. I'm not going to seduce you."

Adrenaline unlike any she'd ever experienced pulsed through her. "That's the problem," she said. "I really think you should."

Dear Reader,

I have great friends. Three of them have been friends since high school, while others have been my friends since my college sorority days. All have been with me through thick and thin, good and bad, better and worse. My friends and I chose each other, and I'm a better person for having them in my life. Even though we all live far away from each other and our lives have taken different paths, we are always there for each other.

My AMERICAN BEAUTIES miniseries uses this concept of friendship. Lisa, Cecile and Tori are three single women who have been best friends ever since pledging the same sorority. The fourth sorority sister, Joann, is married with kids. While all are separated geographically, they know that they can always depend on each other. The bonds they have will never be broken.

I hope you enjoy Lisa's story as much as I did writing it, and be sure to watch for Cecile's and Tori's stories in the future. As always, feel free to e-mail me at michele@micheledunaway.com.

Enjoy the romance,

Michele Dunaway

MICHELE DUNAWAY
The Marriage Campaign

HARLEQUIN®

TORONTO • NEW YORK • LONDON
AMSTERDAM • PARIS • SYDNEY • HAMBURG
STOCKHOLM • ATHENS • TOKYO • MILAN • MADRID
PRAGUE • WARSAW • BUDAPEST • AUCKLAND

ISBN-13: 978-0-373-75131-0
ISBN-10:   0-373-75131-1

THE MARRIAGE CAMPAIGN

Copyright © 2006 by Michele Dunaway.

This edition published by arrangement with Harlequin Books S.A.

® and TM are trademarks of the publisher. Trademarks indicated with
® are registered in the United States Patent and Trademark Office, the
Canadian Trade Marks Office and in other countries.

www.eHarlequin.com

Printed in U.S.A.

ABOUT THE AUTHOR

In first grade Michele Dunaway wanted to be a teacher when she grew up, and by second grade she wanted to be an author. By third grade she was determined to be both, and before her high school class reunion, she'd succeeded. In addition to writing romance, Michele is a nationally recognized high school English and journalism educator. Born and raised in a west county suburb of St. Louis, Michele has traveled extensively, with the cities and places she's visited often becoming settings for her stories. Described as a woman who does too much but doesn't know how to stop, Michele gardens five acres in her spare time and shares her life with two young daughters, six lazy house cats, one dwarf rabbit and two tankfuls of fish.

Michele loves to hear from readers, and you can reach her via her Web site, www.micheledunaway.com.

Books by Michele Dunaway

HARLEQUIN AMERICAN ROMANCE

For all the students I have taught over the years,
I hope the friendships you've made and continue
to make last a lifetime.

And to my own friends, thanks again.
You mean the world to me.

Prologue

She shouldn't be kissing him. Not here, not like this. But when he lowered his mouth to hers, no amount of moral fiber could keep her from tasting his forbidden lips.

Mark tasted divine—of wedding cake and champagne.

"We shouldn't be doing this," Lisa Meyer said weakly as, for one moment, they came up for air.

"We should," he said, leaning down again for another kiss.

"You're my best friend's brother," she protested in moth-to-flame futility. "Your date…"

"Is just a friend," he insisted, his dark eyes intense. "It's you I want. Always have. Ever since we first met."

"You're drunk," she said. But weren't they all high on champagne and wedding magic? Joann's parents, Mary Beth and Bud, had thrown quite a bash, and since everyone was staying at the reception hotel, no one had shown much restraint.

She and Mark were young, not quite twenty-two, the world at their feet, and his words made her giddy. Made her forget his playboy reputation now that all that charm was directed at her.

In her wildest dreams she'd never imagined her crush on Mark Smith coming to fruition like this.

"Let's go upstairs," he murmured into her ear. "I want to get you alone."

Oh, she was so tempted, as the heat pooling low attested. But, as wedding party members, they weren't free. Not yet. Not until the bride and her groom said their goodbyes, which was soon. "We still have duties," she managed, her breath a little short.

"A half hour. No more," he said. "I want you, Lisa. I'm not waiting any longer."

"Okay," she heard herself say as she somehow detached herself from his arms. Happiness consumed her and, coupled with all the champagne, she felt as if she were floating as they left the off-the-beaten-path corridor and returned to the hotel ballroom where the two-hundred-plus-person reception was being held.

"Lisa, there you are!" Tori, bridesmaid and another of Lisa's best friends, grabbed her as she entered. "I've been looking for you. It's time to help Joann change. Come on."

And with that, Lisa got sidetracked. Her last glimpse of Mark was him disappearing into the crowd. She sighed and went to help Joann, her body humming with anticipation. She missed catching the bouquet. She tossed some rice. She found her nerves taut as the moment to join him finally came. But the crowd was still thick, and she found herself going in circles.

"Have you seen Mark?" she asked Cecile, another best friend. They were all members of Rho Sigma Gamma—the Roses.

"Nope," Cecile answered. "Why? He's scamming on everyone here tonight. His poor date."

"She's just a friend."

"That's what they all say," Cecile said with a knowing nod. "Wait. There he is. Going out that door. That's not who he came with, is it?"

Lisa glanced over. Mark was leading a tall brunette out a side exit door. He had his arm around her shoulder and was holding her close. "No," Lisa said. "That's not who he came with."

"Well, if you need him, you better hurry up and catch him."

Lisa shook her head. Mark Smith had said he wasn't waiting any longer. How badly she'd misunderstood! "No," she said, plastering a nonchalant expression on her face so Cecile wouldn't suspect anything. "I don't need him. It was nothing important."

At least, not anymore.

Chapter One

Eight years later

That was the thing about funerals. You had to attend, and they were the absolute most inappropriate places to meet men. Which was why Lisa was trying hard to avoid staring at that tall, handsome guy across the way. After all, he'd started staring at her first.

Worse, he hadn't let up.

"Ashes to ashes, dust to dust..." As the chaplain standing by the open grave droned on, Lisa Jean Meyer decided that she hated attending funerals, hated them even more than celebrating birthdays.

Birthdays made you feel old. Funerals made you feel mortal, as if you had too many things left to do and no time in which to do them. It didn't matter if the burial was for someone you really didn't know that well, as this one was, for funerals simply had a way of reminding you that you were about to turn thirty this year—and worse, that you were still single, with nary a promising prospect in sight, including that annoying hot guy standing behind the crowd on the other side of the grave.

He stood taller than those in the four rows in front of him, and his six-foot-plus height gave Lisa an excellent view of a head full of dark, silky hair. His eyes were a deep brown color, and when she glanced at him again, he held her gaze for the tiniest second before blinking and casually looking away. Despite the brevity of the connection, the encounter had left her with the oddest tingle, as if he were somehow familiar to her.

But that was impossible. She didn't know anyone in St. Louis under the age of forty, aside from her co-workers. With her promotion to Herb's lead fund-raiser formalized last week, Lisa had recently transferred from Jefferson City, and as soon as the November election was over, she'd be going back to the state capital. Of course, she hoped that would be with Herb's gubernatorial victory.

Right now family duty called, and Lisa put the handsome mourner and the odd sense of déjà vu out of her mind. Dating and handsome men did not rate a spot in her top five priorities. The funeral had served as an unwelcome reminder that she seriously needed to spend more time with her parents, beyond required family holidays. Unfortunately her career often interfered with any good intentions: even now, her phone vibrated in her right pocket. Her career was priority number one.

Lisa sighed and tightened her arm around her petite mother's shoulders. Funerals, no matter for whom, were depressing. "It's okay," Lisa whispered as her aunt's cousin was lowered into the cold, hard ground.

A sharp wind swirled the leaves at her feet before climbing to toy with Lisa's hair, causing her to shiver. The gust tore some of the blond strands loose from the chignon, and Lisa used her free hand to wipe the wayward locks away from her eyes. Her glove instead further damaged the stylist's updo.

It was hard to believe that Easter had been the previous weekend, for spring had somehow missed St. Louis. Although the April fifteenth final-frost date had also come and gone, this year the trees were late in bringing forth green buds, and a last-minute freeze had decapitated the tulips and crocuses, leaving them wilting around the gray headstones. The north wind again whipped underneath the tent erected for the burial, and the ensuing chill penetrated Lisa's skin despite the heavy black wool coat and tan leather gloves she wore.

"How are you holding up?" her mother asked. Blue eyes, so like Lisa's own, reflected maternal concern.

Lisa stamped her feet slightly to keep the blood circulating. Her designer pumps did little to block the cold. "I'm fine. I'm more worried about you and Dad. I didn't really know the man."

"Well, you haven't seen him since you were five," her mother said as the minister mercifully ended the service. After everyone gave a relieved amen, Lisa's mother added, "I hate that our family is drifting apart. We only seem to get together for weddings and funerals. Hopefully this is the last of the latter."

"A double amen to that. Come on," Lisa said, anxious to escape the cemetery. Now that the event was over and her family duties fulfilled, she had a fundraising dinner that desperately required her attention. She led her mother away from the grave site and toward the line of cars snaking along the crushed gravel lane.

"So, will you be coming to Jud's house?" her mother asked, mentioning Lisa's uncle on her dad's side. "He and Shelia are hosting the family lunch. Everyone would love to see you."

Lisa shook her head. "I can't."

Disappointment etched her mother's features and laced her tone. "Oh. You're working."

"I'm always working," Lisa stressed, for truer words had never been spoken. Because from the very moment she'd stepped into high school and won her campaign for freshman class secretary, Lisa Meyer could be described in one word: *driven*. She'd risen through the popularity ranks, delivered on her campaign promises and exited her senior year as class president and yearbook editor.

She'd had a bit of a rude awakening in college, discovering that she might not have the qualities required to be a big-league politician. Facing failure in the arena she loved, she'd found the next best thing and become a political fund-raiser and campaign coordinator extraordinaire.

After all, someone had to run the behind-the-scenes operations, and there she'd found her niche. Now her goal was seeing Herbert Usher elected the next governor of Missouri.

"You should be at the post-funeral lunch," her mother chided gently. "Your father's side of the family will all be there."

From the corner of her eye Lisa caught a glimpse of the tall, handsome man who'd been staring. He cut an impressive figure as he strode diagonally across the field toward the end of the row of cars. The crowd that had braved the weather had been thick, a solid tribute to her family.

"Mom, I did try to pencil in the family lunch, but I've got some important conference calls to make as soon as I get back to the hotel. Tonight's a major fund-raiser, my first since I've arrived in town. And I'll have to see if someone at the salon has time to fix my hair."

As if proving her point, the wind again tore at her head, loosening more strands. When she'd made the appointment and planned out her day so that she could work in the funeral service, she hadn't factored in the dreary weather Mother Nature might provide. Lisa was at least grateful it wasn't raining, taking more time out of a day she wished had twenty-six hours to it.

"When does your work ever let up?" her mother asked.

"Never," Lisa said honestly, readying herself for the

forthcoming parental dissatisfaction. "Until the August primary, I'll be on call nonstop. And after we win that, I'll be even busier until we win the November election. After that, I might be able to sleep."

Her mother's lips puckered. "We haven't seen you in ages, and seeing you at funerals isn't quality time. You missed celebrating Easter. While I love seeing Andy and the kids, just having your brother's family around isn't enough. Will we at least see you for your birthday?"

"Oh, Mom, please. Of course you'll see me before that," Lisa said, acknowledging her mother's sarcasm. Lisa wasn't turning thirty until early November, right after the national election. "Tell you what—how about I stop by this Saturday? Herb's in Kansas City and Bradley's overseeing."

"That's my daughter, the nonstop career woman." His duties finished, her father came up and embraced her in a warm hug. While her mother didn't like Lisa's long hours, at least her former-military father understood her desire to prove herself. He'd been a dedicated career man himself, often spending long hours away from home and his family.

"I see that Herb's ahead in the polls. How's the campaign going?" her father asked.

"We can always use more money."

Her father laughed, but instead of joining him, Lisa pulled her vibrating BlackBerry from her pocket and accepted the call. "This is Lisa." She listened to Herb for a moment. "I'll be there in forty minutes. I'm leaving now."

"He even phones you at a funeral?" Her mother's censure was evident as Lisa ended the call.

Lisa sighed, the sound lost in the late-April wind. Louise Meyer had stayed home and raised five children, often alone, as Lisa's father had been away on Air Force business. Lisa had never been sure what her father's specific job was, but she'd grown up a military brat whose father often didn't arrive home for dinner and sometimes not even to sleep. Her mother had held down the home front, and having never worked outside of the house, her mother often didn't understand Lisa's lofty ambitions or why, as the baby of the family, Lisa drove herself so hard.

"Mom, I had my phone set on vibrate. My clients must be able to reach me at all times. Tonight's event is the first that I've been responsible for here in St. Louis. Entirely my baby."

Her mother's sour expression didn't change. "I'd rather you have real babies. You're twenty-nine. I'd like some grandchildren before I get too old to play with them."

Lisa gritted her teeth. Three of her siblings had planted themselves between one and two hours away from St. Louis. Andy, the only son who was close—just across the river in Fairview Heights—had wiggled out of the funeral because of a sick child. As for children, her mother was a grandmother ten times over already.

Andy had provided three of those. While children were a someday goal of Lisa's, having a family of her own was not an immediate possibility with her travel schedule. And, of course, she needed a man first. Like that one she'd seen earlier…

Time for a tactical retreat. "I love both of you," Lisa said, hugging each of her parents. "We'll try for this weekend, okay? Right now I have to go."

In fact, all around, car engines had roared to life, the mufflers spewing visible exhaust into the frigid air.

"This weekend," her mother emphasized. "Pencil or type us into that thing, whatever you do with it. Oh, look at that line of cars leaving. Mike, we must get to Jud and Shelia's before everyone else."

Her mother took her husband's arm and faced her daughter once more. "Lisa, I'm serious about this weekend. Don't be a stranger. We left Warrensburg and moved across the state so we could be closer to our family. Now that you're living here until at least November, that includes you."

"I'll try to make more time. I'll see you Saturday. Promise." Lisa hugged her parents again and then headed to her car, a used upscale Lexus that she often chauffeured clients in.

While the car warmed up, she blocked out six hours for her parents on Saturday and entered the information into the BlackBerry's calendar. She placed the device on the passenger seat and shifted the car into drive.

There was a slight gap between a Lincoln Town Car

and the black Porsche following it, and Lisa eased her way into the opening. She glanced in the rearview mirror, and her hand stilled as she began a thank-you wave. Him.

The guy who'd been across the grave site stared back at her, his sunglasses hiding his eyes. His black-gloved fingers drummed rapid-fire on the steering wheel as he waited for her to accelerate. The moment seemed to stretch, and Lisa realized the Town Car had moved.

She turned her gaze forward, took a deep breath and stepped on the gas pedal. She had better things to do than stress over some man she'd never see again, no matter how handsome he was or even if she really did know him somehow. During the funeral, she had missed ten calls, several of which she had to return the minute her family obligations were finished. Other calls were from her best friends, Cecile and Joann. Those could wait, as they often did. Amazing how once you left college, even though you remained friends, you became too busy to see each other as much. What used to be long daily con-versations shifted into weekly ten-minute chats, if that.

The BlackBerry also registered that Lisa had new e-mails, meaning it was going to be a long afternoon. She made a left onto Highway 44, deliberately refusing to watch the Porsche disappear in the opposite direction.

"YOU DO REALIZE THAT if you don't leave, you're going to be late. Oh, and Alanna's called three times now."

The disapproving voice of his fifty-year-old secretary resounded in his executive office, and Mark Smith glanced up from the purchase proposal he'd been reading. Carla stood in the doorway, just as she had any other day during the past five years. The only difference now was that her arms were crossed and she'd lowered her reading glasses so that they hung around her neck by a chain. She arched an eyebrow. "You heard me about Alanna?"

He'd heard her. What bothered him was the first thing she'd said.

"I'm late?" he parroted, running a hand through his dark brown hair as if the motion could make him remember exactly what he was late for. Just because he was turning the ripe age of thirty in June didn't mean his brain cells had already stopped functioning. Thirty was the new twenty, forty the new thirty—or so the ads and magazines claimed.

Heck, he still was height-weight proportional thanks to a healthy diet-and-exercise regime, had a full head of hair thanks to great genetics and had a ninety-nine-percent punctuality record thanks to his meticulousness.

Mark admitted to being anal about little things like timeliness and he'd even managed to arrive at the funeral this morning on time, not that he'd wanted to be there in the first place. With the responsibility of selling his family's die manufacturing company resting solely on his shoulders since his father's heart attack, Mark had a lot of purchase proposals to read and he was falling behind.

"You're going to be late for the fund-raising dinner," his secretary prodded gently, her expression a tad concerned that Mark hadn't clued in yet.

"Oh—" Mark bit off the expletive that threatened.

The dinner! He hated political events. Whereas his father loved politics and once toyed with running for state senate, Mark avoided anything to do with politics like the plague. Like a good citizen, he voted, but that was about it. He'd wiggled out of half a dozen dinners his father had invited him to attend over the years, and finally his father had stopped asking.

But as the new president of Smith Manufacturing— an interim position until the company was sold—Mark knew his responsibilities. He'd fulfill them, as he'd been raised to do and always had—just as he'd done by attending the funeral of one of his father's business associates this morning. This time Mark's mother was sick, and even though the doctor said it was only a spring virus, Mark's dad had felt it best to stay home with her. The conversation this morning had been quick.

Mark stood and grabbed his leather trench coat.

The drive from Chesterfield to the Millennium Hotel wouldn't take but twenty-five minutes, tops. As he accelerated the Porsche onto Highway 40, he glanced at the dashboard.

He'd only be about five minutes late, if at all. The wind blew, beating against the Porsche as the car crept over the posted speed limit. The day seemed as if it belonged more in January than in April, and Mark resented for a moment having to attend. Although, what else did he have to do? His relationship with Alanna was over; he'd broken it off last week. She'd become too clingy, too simpering, as was still evident in her repeated phone calls to his office. Three months of dating did not constitute a relationship. His secretary, Carla, was a saint for putting up with the nonsense.

As for Mark, when a man came within reach of hitting thirty, his thoughts did turn to marriage. He wanted his own Mrs. Right, whoever she might be. Definitely not Alanna. Nor any of the other women he'd dated over the past few years. He'd rather be a bachelor than make "death do us part" vows with the wrong woman.

Maybe that's why he seemed to run through girl-friends like water. Dating was like shopping. When a guy went to the store, he found what he wanted and bought it. If not, he left. Mark wasn't a big believer in wasting time. Wrong woman—nice to meet you, but goodbye.

However, he admitted he was ready to settle down, which was why he was out there searching. His fraternal twin sister Joann had three kids already, and Mark had none. He liked kids and wanted a houseful, but only after marrying the right woman. If he found her. When he did, he wouldn't let her go.

Mark lifted his foot off the accelerator, slowing the expensive sports car to only five miles above the speed limit. Just six more miles and he'd be there, amongst the people jockeying for position, for political favors, for a slice of power that, in the end, was meaningless. Mark shivered despite the climate-controlled air. Joann's friend Lisa had always loved politics.

Lisa. Mark frowned. Joann had attended the University of Missouri and become best friends with her three Rho Sigma Gamma pledge sisters. Nicknamed the Roses, all four had been inseparable until graduation. After that, life had gotten in the way. Oh, they kept in close touch and still maintained confidences, but seeing one another was hard to do when you lived in different towns and had different obligations.

That girl at the funeral today had reminded Mark of Lisa. Same blond hair, same overall build. Attractive. But he hadn't seen Lisa since Joann's wedding eight years ago, when Lisa had disappeared and stood him up. His best friend Caleb's girlfriend had gotten sick, and Mark had walked her outside to get some air. By the time he'd found Caleb and passed off the sick girlfriend, it had been well past the time Mark was to meet Lisa. She hadn't waited, and after a fruitless search, Mark had gone to bed alone.

And since Lisa had been from Warrensburg, on the other side of the state, he doubted that had been her freezing at the cemetery. For a second he wondered if she was married and made a mental note to ask Joann.

Mark whipped the car onto the Broadway exit ramp. Almost there. Mark braked and shook off the melancholy. Duty called.

"LET'S HOPE THERE WILL be some single men here to-night."

Upon hearing Andrea Bentrup's announcement, Lisa looked heavenward, studied the pattern on the hotel ballroom ceiling and mentally counted to ten. Unlike her twenty-two-year-old area assistant whom she'd been working with for the past week, Lisa had been around the political block a dozen more times than the wide-eyed, idealistic, nonstop romantic standing in front of her. Love and politics did not mix. Ever.

Lisa plastered on a businesslike expression and faced Andrea. Hiring her hadn't been Lisa's idea last November; Herb had traded political favors with Andrea's father, a very influential party member. Except for her rabid wishes to settle down and marry, Andrea did a decent job. She was a natural social butterfly who easily made everyone comfortable.

"Well, Andrea, you're free to hope, but don't hold your breath. Political fund-raisers aren't the place to find single men. Besides, our job isn't about finding a husband but helping Herb win the election."

Andrea's skin turned the color of her hair, a light shade of red. "Oh, please don't think I'm saying that I don't want to help Herb win the election. But at least some of these guys have to be going stag and, darn it, I don't want to work all my life."

"No one does. It's called retirement," Lisa said flatly.

"I'm only doing this job until I settle down," Andrea proclaimed. She wobbled a little on the two-inch heels she'd worn to bring her almost to Lisa's five-eight height. Lisa had to admit that Andrea was cute, which hopefully for some man made up for her singular desire to be wed.

"Just make sure you have all the place cards in the correct spots," Lisa said as she turned her attention back to her own tasks. She'd been idealistic once—leave college, find the right job, find the right man and live happily ever after. The day of graduation she'd toasted to her future, sharing a bottle of champagne with her three best friends in the world. They'd held their glasses high, proclaimed they weren't going to settle for anything until they had the proverbial brass ring tight in their grasps.

But life wasn't perfect. Brass rings tarnished.

Tori, the computer-science major in the group, had been ready to make Microsoft worry. She'd joined an upstart St. Louis–based computer company called Wright Solutions, where she'd fallen into a rut.

Cecile Duletsky had been determined to be Norman Lear, Sidney Sheldon or Aaron Spelling and develop television shows. She'd made it as far as working behind the scenes on a talk show.

And Joann, the woman with the promising television news anchor job ahead of her? Less than three months after graduation she'd learned that she was pregnant, married her college sweetheart and become a stay-at-home mom of three with a diploma that collected dust. Lisa had her suspicions that, while Joann was happy, she still had some regrets.

As for Lisa, she finally had the right job but hadn't found the right man. Oh, she'd thought she had, until he'd broken it off and subsequently married. Politics was all about alliances, and Lisa had learned that particular lesson the hard way a little over a year ago.

And Bradley Wayne was still her boss. Although she'd branched out and formed her own company, until Herb's campaign was over, she reported to Bradley.

She surveyed the ballroom again, her radar not sensing any current doom on the horizon. The fact that Professionals for Business Growth had endorsed Herb was excellent. While Herb was a shoo-in for winning the party primary in August, he then would have to defeat Anson Farmer. Even though Herb was ahead in the popularity polls, most analysts predicted that November's gubernatorial election would be close.

But when Herb did win in November, he would become her most successful and highest placed political candidate ever. That feather in her cap would make the endless apartments and lack of permanent furniture worth it. She'd fill a position on his staff. Herb had further ambitions beyond reviving Missouri, and Lisa could picture him in the White House. She planned to do all his campaign fund-raising and ride his coattails all the way there.

"There you are." Mrs. Herbert Usher—or Bunny, as she was known—swept into the hotel ballroom like a woman on a mission. At fifty-seven, Bunny had let her hair turn white and the locks waved around her ears. She reminded Lisa of a younger Barbara Bush. "Lisa, Herb's speechwriter came down with a stomach bug and Herb's not satisfied with tonight's address. He wants you to fix it."

That was Lisa, jack-of-all-trades. "Tell Herb not to panic, and as soon as I finish the final meeting with security, I'll head up to the suite and do a quick rewrite. I also have some thank-you cards Herb needs to sign so that I can pass them out at the end of the evening."

Bunny appeared relieved. "Wonderful. Between us girls, I'm late getting my hair done. Appearance is everything, especially with Anson Farmer's young wife being a former model. The press fawns on her, salivating fools."

"Everything will be fine," Lisa said, touching her own hair to make sure that the redone style hadn't budged. It would crush somewhat when she put the headset on, but that didn't matter; being in touch with her crew was more important. Nothing would go wrong tonight—she wouldn't let it. She'd climbed too far to fail now.

Two years ago, when Lisa had begun working for Bradley, Herb had used multiple political fund-raisers and campaign managers. In the past few weeks Herb had narrowed his focus to one fund-raiser—Lisa—and one campaign manager, Bradley Wayne, her ex. Technically Bradley was the boss, Lisa second in command. Lisa supervised four area assistants who were also technically self-employed: Andrea in St. Louis, Kelsey in Kansas City, Drew in Springfield and Duane in Jefferson City. Duane had taken Lisa's place last week when Herb had promoted Lisa to oversee the entire state, at which time Lisa had relocated to campaign headquarters—St. Louis, Herb's hometown.

"Don't worry, Bunny," Lisa said, concentrating on the task at hand. "We'll have no complications tonight. You'll see."

"That's great," Bunny said as she pulled out her cell phone and prepared to take flight. "I'll see you upstairs in a few minutes."

The first complication Lisa faced came in the afternoon, when the hotel banquet staff made a substitution on the dinner menu. Thankfully she caught the problem early enough and handled the situation easily. The second issue was more difficult.

"Lisa, Larry Smith isn't coming!" Andrea's words blared into Lisa's ear.

"Larry Smith?"

"Yes. I had him scheduled to pass the hat."

"And he's a no-show?" Lisa said into her headset, a twinge of panic constricting her chest. Now five-thirty, people had been entering the ballroom since five for the six o'clock dinner, and Lisa stood near the podium, once again double-checking that everything was ready for Herb's arrival. She'd left this part of the event totally to Andrea.

"Yes, he's a no-show," Andrea repeated, her own panic evident. "He sent his son instead. What are we going to do? When I set this up weeks ago, I didn't think this would happen."

"It did," Lisa said, her mind churning. Unlike Andrea, Lisa wasn't a nervous newbie. Still, Lisa took a moment to berate herself. She'd had to train Duane and his staff or she'd have been in St. Louis earlier to supervise. And Andrea had assured her…. Lisa focused.

All problems had solutions—she just had to find them. She reviewed what she knew. Larry Smith was an old colleague of Herb's and he was to make the first two-thousand-dollar donation and start "Pass the Hat." While the fund-raising dinner brought in soft money from charging exorbitant meal prices, Pass the Hat was a fun event where the hard money was tossed in.

Tonight's event had five hundred people who had spent five hundred per plate. If an average of one thousand dollars per guest was received, Herb would gain five hundred thousand in hard money for his campaign coffers. That had been the goal Lisa had set.

"You said he sent his son instead," Lisa said.

"Yes," Andrea answered. "Larry Smith was going to bring his wife. His son arrived by himself. Now there's an empty space at that table."

Empty spaces were not great but certainly livable.

"Calm down and let me think. Ambruster's out, and so is Bennington," Lisa said, naming some of Herb's friends. They'd agreed to pass the hat at future events that were equally important, so she'd prefer not to use them now. Larry Smith was the vice president of Professionals for Business Growth, hence his suitability tonight. Perhaps all wasn't lost if he'd sent a replacement.

"I want to talk to Larry Smith's son," Lisa said suddenly. "Maybe his father told him what's going on. Where is he?"

"He's the hot one by the door, talking to the woman with the silver hair and glittery red dress. You can't miss him. I told you there'd be single guys here tonight."

Lisa couldn't care less about the younger Smith's marital status. She trained her gaze across the wide expanse of the ballroom. Hot one by the door? Mere seconds elapsed before she located the man to whom Andrea referred. Even from across the room, his magnetism commanded. The guy defined *tall, dark and handsome.*

She could tell he wore custom tailoring, he was at least six feet tall and he had a full head of dark, silky hair. Her breath lodged in her throat as he laughed at something someone in the small circle surrounding him said. He reminded her of the man from the funeral.

No wonder Larry Smith's son had such a multiage group of ladies crowding about. The man knew how to exude sex appeal. But none of that mattered to Lisa, not when her evening, her career and five hundred thousand dollars were at stake.

"I've spotted him," Lisa told Andrea via the headset. "I'm making my way over there now."

"I'll handle him if you'd like," Andrea said hopefully.

"I've got it," Lisa commanded. "Hey, the St. Louis County executive is coming through the doorway."

Andrea sighed her disappointment. "I'm on it."

Lisa wove her way across the ballroom. Her target grew larger than life as she closed in, and she could see his hair wasn't one solid color: the ballroom chandeliers illuminated natural highlights that lacked any hint of early gray.

Close-up, the man was even more impressive, with wide shoulders and narrow hips. Lisa predicted that under his perfectly pressed shirt there was probably a washboard stomach without an ounce of fat. Even from behind she could tell he was the entire package: the gorgeous, moneyed exterior and the type of male physique that, when naked, was every woman's fantasy.

Lisa swallowed and reminded herself that, like this morning, she didn't have time for fantasies or dalliances, even if the man was so gorgeous he made Tom Cruise and Colin Farrell look ugly.

Besides, she hadn't had much appetite for a social life this past year. Concentrating on her career was much smarter than embarking on another futile search for a man. Lisa wasn't a woman who had an issue with sleeping alone. This situation was nothing she couldn't control. "Mr. Smith?"

He turned, leveling a dark brown gaze at her.

Lisa froze as her breath lodged in her throat.

Damn. How dare the fates be unkind? Come on, what were the odds? St. Louis had well over a million people. Smith was a common last name. Everyone called his dad Bud, not Larry. But the memory raced back, proving that eight years was not enough time. How dare it be…him.

Chapter Two

"Lisa?"

She swallowed once and plastered on her most professional and courteous smile. "Hello, Mark."

Those brown bedroom eyes widened at the fact it was her, and Lisa forced herself to act aloof, unaffected. She already knew what he saw: a woman in a demure cocktail dress designed to downplay any sexiness, and sensible designer heels that added only an inch to her height. A thin wire headset with an earpiece wove its way through her blond updo, and she'd lowered the mouthpiece toward her collarbone.

She held her own, refusing to deviate from her mission. "You're here as a stand-in for your father, I believe?"

"Yes," he replied, his intense gaze roving over her as if imprinting this moment onto his memory. Despite her resolve, she flushed slightly as he finished his appraisal. He frowned suddenly. "I saw you at the funeral this morning, didn't I?"

She took a breath and admitted, "Yes. My aunt's cousin."

"Marvin Albertson," Mark said, his tone holding a slight edge of something indecipherable.

"Yes."

His voice dropped. "Well, imagine that. Fate is certainly interesting, isn't she?"

"Very," Lisa said, quite aware that the well-dressed women surrounding him wore intrigued expressions as they listened to the odd conversation.

As if she'd tell them the whole story. That Mark Smith, ultimate playboy, made out with her in a hallway during his sister's wedding reception but then dumped her for someone else. Mark always did run through women like water and he'd proven that Lisa was no exception.

She blinked. She was older and wiser. She met hundreds of people a week and kept copious notes written on the backs of business cards and Rolodex files. Being in town only a week, she hadn't yet looked up Joann's parents, Mary Beth and Bud. Lisa curbed her sigh. Even though she'd given Andrea loose rein, Lisa was ultimately responsible for tonight's dinner. She hadn't double-checked the guest list, a mistake for which she didn't have time to berate herself. Not when she had an evening to salvage.

"Mark, while it's good to see you again, would you mind if we spoke in private for a minute? I'm Herbert Usher's campaign fund-raiser and I need your help."

His shoulders lifted in a slight shrug, indicating he'd

understood that her crisp, professional tone meant she didn't want to reminisce. His navy-blue suit moved effortlessly, indicative of its custom tailoring. This man did not buy off the rack.

"I don't see why not," Mark agreed. He gestured a manicured hand toward the exit door. "Lead the way. Excuse me," he said to the ladies.

"Thank you," Lisa said, ignoring the women's collective exhales of disappointed curiosity. A prickle, however, ran up her spine as she led him out the ballroom doors. She could feel his gaze glued to her backside. "We have a small office set up in here."

She began to open the door that led to a smaller meeting room, but his powerful arm extended past hers and pushed the door inward. His proximity provided a whiff of subtle cologne. He smelled divine—whatever designer brand he wore had blended with the smell of his skin to create a musky, sensual scent all his own.

Whoa. She could not allow herself to be affected. The man was a first-class jerk.

"Thank you," she said politely, stepping past him with an outward composure she'd long mastered and at this moment certainly needed to hide her inner shaking. Mark Smith oozed pheromones or something, for he'd caused her body to react, which hadn't happened since…well, since that night at Joann's wedding. Her only solace was that no one had seen the kiss, and she'd never told a soul of her humiliating moment.

Lisa wasn't one of those people who liked to air her stupidity and failures like dirty laundry.

She maintained her poise, making certain he didn't notice anything out of whack as the door closed behind them. "I appreciate your coming with me."

"You're welcome," Mark said. His eyes narrowed. "No hug for a long-lost friend?"

"I'd rather we keep this professional," Lisa said. She made sure the headset was muted so she wasn't broadcasting the conversation to Andrea or Bradley.

"Have it your way," Mark said, his momentary cheeky grin fading. "What was it you wished to discuss?"

Although his tone never changed, his voice was low and naturally husky, and she concentrated on the challenging task ahead. "Let me be direct. Your father planned to start what we call 'Pass the Hat,' which is the donation part of the evening. It's fun and expected, but the first check has to come from someone enthusiastic about the campaign."

"That person was to be my father."

She nodded, optimistic he understood. "Exactly. Herb can't stand up at the podium and solicit. While he can make phone calls and ask a person directly, to make a blanket request for money during a fund-raising dinner is still considered extremely tacky and in poor taste."

His brows knit closer together as he contemplated this. "My father didn't tell me anything about starting a hat pass when we talked."

Something about his cautious tone put her on the immediate defensive. He could not back out!

"He also didn't tell Herb he wasn't coming," Lisa inserted smoothly. "Anyway, we were depending on him for tonight's campaign jolt."

He took a deep breath, his broad chest expanding and contracting. "My father must have forgotten. You knew he had a heart attack, didn't you?"

"Joann mentioned it," Lisa said, "but she also said he was recovering well."

"He's fine, except that he's pretty much retired and on doctor's orders not to do anything too strenuous as he builds up his strength. Anyway, my mother came down with a cold, and he's home all worried about her."

"Is she okay?"

"It's just a spring virus. But Dad canceled everything. I attended the funeral in his place. Even my standing in for him here was just decided this morning."

Poor Bud. Lisa had always loved Joann's parents. But this conversation wasn't getting her anywhere and she checked her mounting frustration. If Mark wasn't going to help, she had a problem to solve and no more seconds to waste with a man who'd already destroyed her illusions once. "I do understand. I'm sure I can find someone else if you're uncomfortable stepping into his shoes."

"I'm never uncomfortable in my father's shoes."

His sharp and direct retort surprised her, and Lisa's

eyes widened. She'd barely processed his reaction before the door opened and Andrea entered the meeting room. She smiled apologetically.

"I'm sorry to interrupt, but I have your name tag ready, Mr. Smith," Andrea said, handing him the computer-generated "Hello, my name is" sticker. "If you need anything else, don't hesitate to tell me."

"Thanks."

"No problem," Andrea said.

He gave Andrea a cheeky smile, one that Lisa knew worked wonders on women. It had once worked on her. And his grin had the desired effect on Andrea, for she shot Lisa a wistful look as she exited. Lisa kept her lips in a straight line.

"How much was my father going to give?" Mark asked suddenly, his deep voice penetrating her jumbled thoughts. "If he was going to pass the hat, I'm sure you know the exact amount and even had a nice little speech all scripted for him. Now, if you will explain this process to me, I'm sure we can come to some solution that is agreeable to both of us."

"That would be preferred," Lisa admitted as she regained her footing. She never lost her balance in the political arena. There was no reason disequilibrium should be happening now, especially with this man.

He smiled at her, but only in a patronizing way designed to establish that the situation was totally under his firm control. "Of course a solution would be pre-ferred," Mark said. "I'm first and foremost a businessman. I can handle a curve. You've certainly given me those before."

She had? What was he talking about? She didn't have time for this nonsense or digs into her character that she didn't understand. "Your father was going to donate two thousand dollars, the maximum donation he could make."

TWO THOUSAND DOLLARS? Mark froze. The amount of money didn't shock or faze him; his father was extremely generous, and Herb had been a college fraternity brother. Everyone knew how deep those bonds could run. And two thousand dollars was chump change for the wealthy Smith family.

Lisa took a step back. "If that's too much…" she was saying, her concentration fully on the check that was getting away and the problem she had to solve. He found her actions and conundrum slightly irritating.

Eight years had changed her, and at this moment Mark wasn't sure he liked this older and wiser version standing before him. Lisa used to be the one who'd give her shirt right off her back to help her friends. She was the kind who'd take in every stray animal she ran across.

She'd been the one he'd wanted until, instead of meeting him, she'd disappeared into the night without a goodbye. Heck, kissing her in the hallway had made him feel like a superhero. Her disappearance had been a slap in the face.

As for *this* Lisa... The hardened political dynamo standing in front of him was concerned only about her event and his check. He glanced at her hand—surely she should be married by now.

But no, her ring finger was bare.

"Mark, are you okay? As I indicated earlier, I can find someone else if two thousand is too much money."

"The money's fine," he said crisply, poise regained. His gaze roved over her. She was still beautiful. He'd been attracted to her ever since their first meeting years ago, when she'd first become Joann's roommate their freshman year.

And Mark was a firm believer in taking the opportunities that fate granted. He'd seen Lisa twice now in one day. She'd run out on him long ago, but she couldn't run this time. She needed something from him, and he wanted an explanation.

He peered closer, studying the way her blue eyes flickered and the dimple to the left of her mouth twitched. She probably wasn't even aware of that unconscious movement. So she wasn't as composed as she thought, which was good.

He shifted his weight and narrowed his gaze at her. "You know, Lisa, I would have thought you'd be married."

"Well, I'm not."

"Divorced?"

"No." Her voice was frostier now, like the chilly air to which they'd both been exposed this morning. Her posture tensed as she struggled to be polite instead of defensive. Right now she probably wanted to tell him to go to hell, but that two-thousand-dollar check was too important. He felt like Rhett Butler having the upper hand with Scarlett O'Hara.

Lisa Meyer, the woman who was going to change the world one politician at a time, would play by his rules tonight. "I'll help you, but under one condition," he said.

"What?" she eyed him suspiciously.

Mark reached out and grabbed her left hand. Her skin was smooth in his grasp, and her blue eyes widened and her mouth dropped open into a little O shape that he decided he liked. She had kissable lips. But then, she always had. Her mouth had been the first thing he'd noticed about her, back when they'd both been eighteen. And that kiss that night…

"We definitely have to catch up," Mark said, shoving his libido aside as he began his offensive. "My parents will want to hear everything about you, especially since Herb is an old friend. And Joann won't believe that we ran into each other like this."

"That's all?" Lisa stared.

"Well, no," Mark began, his tone foreshadowing the condition he was about to insist on.

"Lisa." A harsh male voice cut sharply through the conversation like a butcher knife. "What exactly are you doing?"

The moment the older man stepped fully into the

hotel meeting room, Mark observed an immediate reaction in Lisa. She jerked her hand from his as the man closed the door behind him and stared through wire-rim glasses down his pointed nose. He had to be in his early forties, but somehow he seemed so much older.

When he spoke again, his voice was clipped. "Lisa, job. Herb trusts you. Tonight is extremely important and—"

"I'm Mark Smith," Mark interrupted, his eyes narrowing at the man's public chastisement. Speaking of politically incorrect behavior, did the man not see Mark's name tag? "I'm Larry Smith's son. You are…?"

"Bradley Wayne. I supervise Herb's campaign."

"He's the campaign manager," Lisa corrected, her tone brutally polite. "I'm the fund-raiser. Together we've partnered to get Herb elected."

Bravo, Mark thought. He'd never known Lisa to be a wimp, which is why it bugged him so much she'd just disappeared that night.

Bradley's lips frowned displeasure. "And, partner, I need for you to pull your weight. I'd expect this type of behavior from marriage-obsessed Andrea but not from you."

Lisa crossed her arms and ramrodded her back. "We were discussing his donation check."

"Which is why you were holding hands." Bradley's reply held just a trace of sarcasm.

Mark stared, his business acumen assessing the man in a nanosecond. Given the undercurrents, there was something more here than met the eye. Had Lisa been interested in the guy once? Surely not, Mark decided.

While Bradley Wayne might be an attractive man on the surface, with his perfect hair and manicured nails, he was the type of guy dominated by only one agenda—his own. Men could spot the worst type of their gender immediately, and Mark considered himself an expert after fending off the sharks only out to purchase and subsequently gut his family's company. Mark inserted himself back into the conversation.

"Actually, Bradley, you're right. We were holding hands. Lisa was explaining my role in pass-the-hat and we haven't seen each other in years. Way too long."

"His sister is my best friend," Lisa added quickly. She gazed at Mark. "And long enough."

Ah, the gauntlet, Mark thought. Lisa was mad at him. But for what? He'd shown up in the ballroom to meet her and she'd been gone.

"Well, if you are such old friends, then everything is perfectly acceptable. Lisa, you know I always have your best interests at heart," Bradley said, his voice too smooth for Mark's liking.

"Mr. Smith, I'm sorry I arrived at any unnecessary conclusions," Bradley continued pleasantly, coming across to Mark as one of those disinterested customer-service representatives working at a call center. "My reaction and words were unprofessional and I apologize. My only explanation is that Lisa is my protégée. I've been training her these past two years. Now that's she's branched out on her own, I want to see her succeed. Tonight is the first major event in St. Louis whose success rests solely on her shoulders, and I want to make certain nothing goes wrong."

Bradley reached over and drew Lisa aside. "How about I take over explaining the pass-the-hat event to Mr. Smith? That way you can take care of things outside."

"That sounds fine." Lisa moved toward the door.

Mark frowned. No way. She was not going to walk away from him again. Not when she owed him an explanation at the very least. "Lisa, wait."

She stopped, turned, and Mark focused his attention on Bradley. The man shifted his weight under Mark's scrutiny. "Bradley—I hope you don't mind if I call you that—I find myself respectfully disagreeing with this current situation. I'd like to suggest that Lisa explains what I'm to do, since this is her event. It should be her call."

"I am the campaign manager," Bradley offered with a patronizing smile that didn't reach his narrowing eyes. "Herb promoted Lisa upon my advice. Lisa, Mr. and Mrs. Auble have asked to meet Herb, so be sure that happens before the end of the evening. The Aubles plan to let Herb and Bunny spend a week at their lake house."

"I'm on it." Lisa returned to pushing the door open.

"Then after the speech you, Mr. Smith, will…"

But Mark ignored him and followed Lisa to the door.

No matter how tough Lisa wanted to make this, Mark was determined to make it tougher for her to get away. He put his hand on hers and caught her in the middle of the doorway. "I asked you to wait," he said.

She shook her head, a blond tendril falling out of the updo and landing in front of her ear. She freed her hand and deliberately pushed the wayward lock back. "I have to go. Thanks for starting the hat."

"We aren't done talking," he said. "You and I have unfinished business."

Her eyes widened for a moment before she regained her composure. "Okay, perhaps we can talk for a few moments afterward," Lisa conceded. "I'm seeing my parents Saturday and I won't live it down if I don't bring news. And Joann would kill me if we don't talk."

"Still not acceptable," Mark said.

Lisa appeared startled at his firm tone, and Mark used the moment to deal with the insufferable Bradley Wayne.

"Mr. Wayne, I'm quite prepared to fulfill my father's obligations tonight. But I have a problem. I'm dateless and I dislike dining alone at a table full of strangers. I insist that Lisa be my guest. I haven't seen her for eight years and would like to catch up."

Bradley wore a stunned expression, as if someone had suggested letting beggars attend a royal ball. "She has a job to do."

"Exactly. Fund-raising," Mark inserted. "My father and Herb pledged the fraternity together and are good friends. I'd hate to go home and tell my dad about the miserable time I had and that I just couldn't, in good conscience, donate his two thousand and two of my own...." Mark purposely paused. "Anyway, I promise to look after Lisa and get that hat moving."

Bradley's upper lip curled and Mark faced Lisa. Her jaw had dropped slightly, and she quickly closed her mouth. He'd dumbfounded her. He could almost hear Joann laughing, filling the hole inside of him that she'd left when she'd moved to Springfield. Phone calls and occasional visits didn't cut it after you'd grown up sharing confidences since the womb. He turned to Lisa. "Ready? You can tell me about my important duties over our rubber chicken entrée."

Still shocked by the turn of events, Lisa said, "Huh? I sampled the food earlier. It's actually pretty good."

"Perfect." With that, Mark Smith and his Rhett Butler smile swept Lisa out of the room.

Chapter Three

She was going to kill him. The moment she got Mark Smith aside later, in private, she would rip him limb from limb. Being drawn and quartered would be too good a death for him.

Lisa tried to contain herself as the waiter set down her plate. While she'd planned on eating dinner, she hadn't planned on eating her meal out here, with all the paying guests.

Of all the infernal things… Mark Smith was impossible. First he kissed her and left with another woman, and now…could he not see that she did not need defending? She did not need him to be some pompous Sir Galahad from the Arthurian period. She did not need him to gallop to her rescue, much less misguidedly believe he should.

She had a job to do—one she was very competent at, thank you very much—and said job did not include sitting next to him, eating chicken divan and drinking the glass of white wine he'd bought for her at the cash bar.

The man had knocked her down, out and slightly sideways, but Lisa was a consummate rebounder. Always had been, always would be. No man ever got the best of her—except Mark Smith. Tonight he was two for two. Count the wedding reception and you had three times too many.

She controlled her tapping foot, lest her internal seething become too obvious to her tablemates. She'd literally been had. Shortly after their return to the ballroom, Herb had greeted Mark like a long-lost son. And when Mark had repeated his request, Herb had insisted that of course Lisa should occupy the empty seat as Mark's companion.

So here she was, enduring polite small talk with a way-too-good-looking, arrogant man who had rattled her cage. Didn't he realize she didn't want him leaning close? Didn't he understand he didn't have the right to whisper in her ear after what he'd done?

But then, wasn't he just being true to his stripes? Mark was the type of man who wouldn't even recognize his obnoxious behavior. And while tonight Lisa could watch her step and stay aloof, something inside her still wanted to flirt with danger.

For Lisa, Mark Smith had always been danger. The man was too darn sexy for his own good. His smile had always been to die for; those dark eyebrows arched perfectly over brown bedroom eyes.

But what really made matters worse was that tonight, even eight years later, Lisa couldn't say she was immune. Despite his actions following their kiss, when he turned up the charm, Mark was like a beacon in the night to which women naturally gravitated.

Part of her screamed, *Run!* while the other part claimed she was a big girl now and she should toy with Mark Smith, serve him some well-earned payback.

He had led her on, promised her things, given her momentary hope that dreams do come true. Oh, she admitted to herself at least that when she'd first met Mark eleven years ago, she'd fallen hard and fast. She'd had the biggest schoolgirl crush, which was pathetic considering that he'd only come for a weekend visit to see his sister during their freshman year of college.

For the first time in Lisa's life, the outgoing class leader had found herself tongue-tied. She'd simply been *aware* of him. When she'd managed to find her voice, their conversations would be charged and heated, often a series of put-downs. She knew her reasons—by slamming him, she could pretend she wasn't interested. That she was aloof. Unaffected.

All lies. Her crush had never waned, although she deliberately dated people just to prove her immunity to the man. Why not? Crushes were juvenile, and it was clear Mark wasn't pining for her. Lisa heard enough stories over the years from Joann to determine that Mark wasn't anywhere close to Lisa's type.

As was tradition, Mark had followed in his father and grandfather's legacy and attended the University of

Missouri–Rolla and joined the Pi Kappa Alpha fraternity. While Tori, Joann and Cecile had made the yearly pilgrimage to Rolla for St. Patrick's Day festivities, Lisa had often skipped, knowing she'd hear about the wildness anyway. The stories had often centered on Mark's exploits.

For four years Joann had described edited versions of Mark's escapades. It was obvious that Joann adored her fraternal twin brother despite what she referred to as his flagrant indiscretions. In other words, Mark Smith was a rogue playboy to the nth degree.

So Mark had reached a mythic disproportion, and his branding kiss had simply seared his reputation firmly and forever into Lisa's mind, making it ironic that she was now his "date" to her own fund-raising event.

Instead of fading into the woodwork, taking notes and drumming up potential political alliances, she was subject to Bradley's displeasure and Andrea's soon-to-occur endless questioning. The redhead's wink and thumbs-up when Mark had pushed in Lisa's chair had said volumes.

One thing certainly hadn't changed about Mark Smith. He'd been cocky and self-assured when she'd first met him and he obviously was the same now, if not even more so.

She had to admit, she'd never seen Bradley Wayne so floored as when Mark had announced his ultimatum. Perhaps there was some justice in the world. Bradley, who was hovering on the room's periphery, had been a little hard to deal with this past year after she'd left his employ and begun working for herself.

He could only be described as a micromanager and nitpicker. He would become even more impossible henceforth, that was a given. Not ever having met Bradley, and just from Lisa's conversations, Joann despised him and had railed against the man for years. She would probably pat her brother on the back for what he'd done.

"What's so funny?" Mark's whisper tickled Lisa's ear, his warm breath bringing her back to the reality that he was seated only ten tantalizing inches to her left.

And this time Lisa wasn't a silly freshman who'd lost her voice. This time she wasn't some starry-eyed bridesmaid high on wedding magic and illusions. She was all grown-up. Confident. Daring. Definitely a woman who could hold her own against the playboy whose conquests had been regaled and reviled over many cups of morning coffee.

Maybe some torture before she killed him for out-maneuvered her and probably hundreds of other women was in order.

She'd never considered herself a knockout; to be honest, she knew she was far from "ten" status. While she'd never grace the big screen or a rock video, she knew beauty was all about attitude and she'd learned to work with what she had. She angled her head and gave him a dazzling smile.

"I just find it funny that fate brought us together like

this. I'd planned on going with you that night," she admitted purposefully, lifting her wineglass to her lips and holding his gaze over the rim. "That is what you wanted to talk about, wasn't it? That night?"

But Mark Smith was suave, proving his control when the corners of his eyes crinkled and he said, "So why didn't you leave with me, then?"

She laughed and toyed with her wineglass stem as she drew on eight years of jaded political-arena experience. "Maybe you should be the politician. Turning the question around and volleying it back to me. Such ego. Joann always said you had one, but I always tried to give you the benefit of the doubt. At least I did up until that night."

"Of course you did," he said, a cheeky smile easing over his face as he played along. Her stomach did a figurative flip. He lowered his voice. "The benefit of the doubt is a very powerful thing. It's like the seat of your pants or your gut instinct. Intangible but very real. Like that kiss."

"Exactly," Lisa said, her brain racing to process the multiple innuendos. The man was good.

"So tell me, Lisa, now that fate has given us another chance, what is your gut instinct telling you tonight about me?" he queried, not giving her a chance to retrench, reload or rethink.

Oh, he was master of his game. But now so was she. While she hadn't a tenth of his sexual experience, she'd still learned to play ball and play well. "It tells me that you haven't changed a bit. You're older, certainly, but I don't know if that makes you necessarily wiser."

"I was wise enough to have you as my dinner companion." His gleam spoke volumes.

He'd left her the perfect opening and she took it. "I'm only here because it's my job."

He leaned back and studied her, and she knew she'd scored a direct hit. However, the conflicting emotions flickering in his dark eyes lasted for only a moment until he again smiled, although not as brightly as before. His words were measured yet delivered smoothly. "At least we know that you have the capacity for honesty. That's rare in the political world, isn't it?"

She had to give him credit. A compliment and a dig, both at the same time. "Perhaps," she said with a slight incline of her head. "Although, I must say that Herb is honest. He means each and every thing he says and he plans to fulfill every campaign promise he makes."

Pure skepticism crossed Mark's face, and he had the courtesy not to laugh. "Oh, they all do, Lisa. And everyone knows the road to hell is paved with good intentions and broken promises. That's the nature of the beast. Politicians have to have some sliver of raw ideology that lets them be idealistic. It lets them feel good about themselves, convinces them that they aren't addicted to the allure of wielding power. It proves to them that they have a higher calling, that they are somehow fated to save the world. Business is the same to some extent. We're all about making the world a better place for everyone, but not without padding our own pockets first. At least corporations admit that it's all about the bottom line."

"Cynical," Lisa observed.

"Always," he said, the sharpness in his tone driving his point home.

"Herb—"

Mark cut her off. "Not to be rude, but I don't want to hear about Herb's promises. I'll vote for him because he's my father's friend and because he's better than the other two candidates."

"I will personally guarantee Herb is honest."

Mark stared at her for a minute. "Sure, for as long as he can be before the job changes him."

"It won't," Lisa declared. "He's proven himself for a long time. That's why I'm working for him."

An arched eyebrow conceded that point before Mark attacked on another front. "But everyone knows Missouri politics are family affairs. The Danforths. The Blunts, the Carnahans, the Clays. In office or not, they all have a lot of influence."

"True, but Herb has a history of interactions with all of those families on both state and national levels. He's the best candidate for Missouri."

Mark took a long sip of water, his study of her never ceasing. "Do you have an answer for everything?"

Lisa didn't hesitate to nod. "It's my job. I'm sure you can understand that. After all, isn't your job important?"

"Very," Mark said with a corresponding nod.

"Then you understand what I mean. And while I thank you for this lovely meal, it wasn't at all necessary."

"It interrupted what you needed to do," he said drily.

"Honestly, yes." She almost bit her lip but stopped herself. She'd meant to chastise him, perhaps, but it hadn't come out that way. She mentally cursed herself. She'd sounded petulant.

The right corner of Mark's lip inched up and he rubbed his chin. "So I find beside me a woman who can save herself and handle sticky situations on her own. And she's riled that I stepped in."

"Absolutely," Lisa said, a prickle of wariness riveting up her spine. While he'd controlled the conversation earlier, this time he was doing more than exerting his expertise. He was leading her somewhere, readying himself to zero in on something still unknown to her.

"Although you admit that your having dinner with me did please Herb and will tickle my father and mother with delight," he pointed out.

"But my role isn't to sit here and eat with you," she countered.

"And if I asked you to another meal instead?"

Oh, he was smooth. But this time she didn't miss a beat. She said, "I'd say no."

Instead of being offended, he simply smiled, that grin of his indicating he'd been quite prepared for her rejection. "Of course you would say no. I can even list the reasons. You don't have time. You're too career-oriented. And quite frankly, despite our kiss, you've never liked me much, have you?"

She reached for her water glass, the movement allowing her needed composure. He'd turned the tables on her yet again by seeing straight through her.

"Well?" he prodded.

"No," Lisa admitted, sticking with the honesty approach. "I've heard way too many stories of your exploits over the years to believe that you're any kind of continual dinner-date material. You're a playboy, Mark. You kissed me and left me. Probably a momentary aberration, certainly a lack of common sense on my part. No, I'm sorry, but you aren't dating material, much less marriage. And with my job, I don't have time to waste."

He sat back, his expression thoughtful. "So that's it." He shook his head, more to himself than at Lisa. "My misguided-youth reputation precedes me that much. I'll have to talk to my sister about that. I can assure you that my being a rogue is extremely exaggerated."

"Right." Lisa gave a short, disbelieving laugh. "That's why you attended Joann's wedding reception with one woman and left with another after kissing me and declaring that I was the one you wanted. Can you deny that you left with someone?"

"I'm already tried and convicted. What's the point?"

Lisa pushed her dessert plate forward. Thankfully their tablemates were engaged in their own private conversations. "The point is that I'd really prefer not to discuss this, especially here. I apologize for getting us started on this topic, so let's drop it. How we feel about each other is irrelevant. You pass the hat, and I tell my parents and Joann I've seen you and that you're doing well. You do the same, and we go our separate ways and all is right with the world."

That dark eyebrow arched in skepticism. "That's it?"

"There should be more?"

"Fate reintroduced us for a reason. Are you sure you're ready to sever our newly formed alliance?"

In a show of derision, she arched her eyebrow right back. "What new alliance?"

His voice dropped a notch as he baited her again. "The one that could get you everything you need and want."

"I'm dating someone," she said, the fib automatic.

"So am I," Mark said without blinking. As for his statement, Alanna still didn't believe the relationship was over, so that certainly made his statement enough of a truth to satisfy a politician.

And as for dating Lisa, as a freshman she'd been cute: blond hair, blue eyes and a smile that, when she got just a little older, would drive all the boys wild. At the wedding reception, she'd been hot. He'd wanted her then. Heck, he remembered being just drunk enough to think that she could be the one. That's why he'd made a beeline for her at the first opportunity and worked on her all night before finally getting her alone in the hall.

Which was why this grown-up Lisa with her political

promises now annoyed him and yet still intrigued him. And he let nothing that piqued his interest simply slide by without some intervention on his part. Especially now that he understood why she hadn't met with him that night. Women. Always jumping to conclusions. Like now.

His smile faded to indicate his seriousness. "Our alliance has nothing to do with some misguided crush or some kiss or us dating—let's clear that up. However, given that you and I have Joann in common, you should consider me your ally. Despite my jaded view of politics, I have connections in this town that can get you money for Herb's campaign. I know people that you can't reach without me and I have access to even more through my mother. Do you know how thrilled Mom's going to be when I tell her I saw you? And that you're working for Herb? Herb, who was in their wedding party?"

"He was?" Lisa hadn't known that.

"Yes. And the minute I tell Joann, you know she's going to suggest that I help you, as well."

"I was already planning on calling her later this week. I also had your parents on my agenda."

"Well, plans change, don't they?"

"Obviously," Lisa said, and Mark knew she was referring to what she saw as his indiscretion at the wedding.

Mark reached forward and took a long sip of water. As he'd said, she already had him tried and convicted.

There was no point in revealing the truth now. He'd been raised that you always kept an ace in the hole. Lisa's misperception was his ace.

He could see the hypothetical wheels turning in her head as she contemplated what he'd said. For a moment he wondered if achieving her end goal ever tempted her to consort with the devil. At least he wasn't that bad, which he'd prove to her one step at a time. Then he'd reveal the truth. For suddenly Mark had clear insight into what he wanted from Lisa Meyer. He wanted the magic back. At the reception, he'd drunkenly thought she was the one. Maybe she wasn't anymore, but if nothing else, he wanted her apology and, with it, a complete surrender that she'd been wrong about him.

"You really should consider my proposition," he told her. "You know I'm right and that in reality I'm really not that bad of a guy. Let me help you."

"Why are you doing this?" she asked.

He covered her hand with his, an intense warmth fusing them together. "Because Joann would hate it if we couldn't be friends. Because it's the right thing to do." *And because I'm not finished with you yet.*

Lisa pulled her hand free as Herb reached the podium. Herb's speech gave her some time to consider Mark's outrageous proposal. The offer sounded too perfect, too ideal. And everyone knew the old adage that if something sounded too good to be true then it probably was.

But Mark held true to his word, starting Pass the Hat with the announcement he was putting four thousand into the kitty, two for him and two for his father. The female vocalist hired for the evening sang a patriotic ballad while campaign staff passed black top hats around the room. Once finished, the formal part of the evening drew to a close, replaced with dancing and mingling for those wishing to stay.

Although she was able to escape from Mark during the dancing, Lisa had to admit that his proposition bothered her. Form an alliance with him? He was on her *list,* slightly above the devil. He was a cad.

So the odds of partnering with Mark: zero. Sure, the idea held merit, but Lisa had learned early that all favors came with either price tags or strings. And he'd already deserted her once.

Being indebted to Mark Smith in any way was plain frightening, and Lisa was a woman whom little scared. But tonight, the way he'd simply taken over and gotten what he'd wanted—namely her—had been a powerful example of his gumption and guts.

He was a man who did what suited him, a man steeped in the tradition that growing up in wealth and privilege offered. Mark could have been anything, done anything. It didn't work that way for Lisa. While she would put Herb Usher into the governor's mansion, she'd never live there herself.

Seeing Herb get his governorship was her goal, an investment in achieving the political appointment she wanted.

"Herb."

"Ah, Lisa." Herb turned and faced her as she expertly extracted him from a couple with whom he'd been conversing. "Tell me, how's Bud's son treating you?"

"Very well, thank you," Lisa said as she maneuvered Herb through the crowd. Her boss was tall and thin; he'd played college basketball but hadn't been strong enough for a pro spot.

"He's a great boy," Herb said. "A good catch."

That was Herb. Having three kids of his own who had no marital prospects on the horizon, Herb was sensitive to the single status of his offspring and his staff. "You know I'm too busy to date, sir," Lisa said. "But he did offer to help with the campaign."

"Then you must take him up on it," Herb said. "We can use all the volunteers we can get, right?"

"Of course," Lisa said. She paused behind an elderly couple. "Mr. and Mrs. Auble?"

"Yes?" They turned around.

"Herb, I'd like you to meet the Aubles, Rich and Patty."

"Nice to meet you," Herb said. He extended his hand, and with that, Lisa melted into the crowd. The night marched on and the crowd divided into the dancers and the dwindlers, the latter making their way to the doors and disappearing.

She'd thought Mark was in this group until she saw him dancing with a fortysomething brunette Lisa didn't recognize. Something in her stomach churned slightly at the way his hand rested on the small of the woman's back—neither placed too low nor too high. She tore her gaze away. Who Mark entertained himself with was not her problem and shouldn't be of any interest. The man was once again showing his true colors.

"So how was dinner?" Andrea asked as she drew alongside Lisa.

"Just dinner," Lisa answered.

Andrea's expression of disappointment said volumes. "Too bad. He's got potential written all over him."

"The more accurate word is *playboy*," Lisa said. "So seriously be warned off."

"Oh, don't worry. He only had eyes for you," Andrea said.

"Clearly," Lisa said as Mark remained on the dance floor with the brunette for another song. Lisa began to circulate again, heading over to thank Beau and Tiffany Williams. The couple had been major contributors tonight.

Finally a safe time arrived that Lisa could leave, and she retreated to the smaller meeting room. Some last few diehards remained on the dance floor even though Herb and Bunny had left the event at least a half hour before. She'd lost track of Mark. For all she knew, he'd left—good riddance—and her current task was processing the checks.

After an event like tonight, rather than use campaign staff like Andrea, Lisa always preferred to count the checks and record the contributions herself. That way she knew exactly how much her efforts had brought in and could catch any discrepancies before the staff audited her work. IRS and campaign fund-raising regulations required stringent records, and Lisa went above and beyond to make sure that everything was not only legal but above reproach.

No way would she have Herb's candidacy and/or his governorship tarnished because of an error or omission on her part. Questionable dealings and donations always surfaced.

"So how did we do?"

Lisa glanced up as Bradley entered. "Is everyone gone?"

He shrugged. "Just about. A few stragglers who should make their way home after the band finishes its last number. Andrea is out there wrapping everything up. So?" Bradley crossed his arms and waited.

"I'm still recording and tabulating." Lisa moved the pad of her forefinger over the flat area of the keyboard that served as the laptop's mouse. "This new software program has really helped out. Enter a name, and it automatically finds the donor record if he's previously given. Right now I've logged in about two hundred thousand dollars as tonight's take."

"Almost halfway," Bradley said.

Lisa thumbed the list of checks she still hadn't processed. "I'm expecting to make it."

"Speaking of making it, you got through your evening with the ubiquitous Mr. Smith."

Lisa kept her gaze focused on the screen. "It wasn't that bad. He's my best friend's brother."

"He seemed like he wanted to be a little more than that when he requested to eat with you," Bradley said.

Lisa's head practically snapped as she swiveled around, the checks momentarily forgotten. "What's that supposed to mean?"

Bradley's expression revealed little and he shrugged. "You already made one mistake tonight by not realizing that you knew Mark Smith's father."

"Bud," Lisa said.

"Exactly. Luckily it worked out. I just don't want any further complications."

"I'm not planning on dating Mark. I simply made him not have to be at a full table by himself."

"Good." Bradley appeared relieved. "Herb's campaign should be your number one priority. One woman on a manhunt around here is more than enough."

Tired of straining her neck, Lisa rose to her feet, a movement that gave her equal placement in the room. "Well, don't worry. Although, he did volunteer to help out."

"Beware strings," Bradley said.

"Trust me, I know that lesson," Lisa said.

"Yes, but does he?"

Bradley's superior tone annoyed her, and she pressed save on her laptop and began collecting the checks. She'd finish sorting everything back at the hotel room in Clayton that served as her temporary home for the next seven months.

"Hey, guys." Andrea pushed open the door and entered.

"Is everyone gone?" Bradley asked.

"All but this guy here," she said as Mark Smith entered on her heels. "He said he's supposed to speak with you, Lisa."

What poor timing. Already Bradley had tensed, his lips making that "I told you so" pucker. He was smug with the satisfaction of being right. Lisa ignored him. Bradley's first nightmare was any negative press regarding Herb. His second was negative press regarding campaign staff indiscretions. As if Lisa would ever fall into that trap.

"Hey," Mark said to Lisa. His expression soured upon discovering they had an audience.

"I thought you'd left already," she said.

"Nope, we have yet to finish our conversation." Mark paused and then, ignoring the other people in the room, said, "My parents are attending a Cardinals game Thursday night. That's two days from now. There's an extra seat. Why don't you join us? They haven't seen you in forever. You can pick my mom's brain for potential donors."

She didn't hesitate. "I don't have my calendar handy."

If he was disappointed, he hid it well as he dug into his wallet. "Well, at least you didn't just say no outright. Here's my personal card printed with both my home and cell numbers. Call either at any time. If it helps, our tickets are located in section four, which are Cardinals club seats right behind home plate. It was good seeing you again, Lisa. Good night."

With that, Mark strode from the room and closed the door behind him, the latch making an audible click as it caught.

"Club seats behind home plate," Andrea said with reverent awe. "Oh, I would have gone if he'd asked me."

"Yes, you would have," Bradley said derisively. "But Lisa knows better."

"Of course I do. How kind of you to point that out," Lisa said sarcastically. Sometimes Bradley went a little too far. His superior attitude and self-assurance were the first things that had attracted her to him. But now, now that the blinders of hero-slash-mentor worship were off, those qualities annoyed her.

Andrea had simply turned her head from side to side as she'd watched the exchange. "Do we need to do anything else or can I leave?"

Lisa closed her laptop. "No. I'm taking the checks back to my hotel room and I'll bring them to the office so we can make photocopies and deposit them. I've already boxed up everything else and it'll be delivered to headquarters by noon. So I'll see you in the morning."

Andrea appeared relieved. "Thanks. I'm actually meeting a few friends for a drink, so since you don't require my services, I'm gone."

"Go have fun and be safe," Lisa said. "Call a cab if you get too wild."

"Will do," Andrea said, and within minutes Lisa and Bradley were again alone, each still standing in almost the same spot as they'd been before.

"What?" Bradley said with a gesture of his right hand.

Lisa steeled herself. "You went a little too far with your comment to Andrea. I may know better, but if I want to say yes, it's my business. My personal life and what I do with it remain apart from the campaign."

"Everyone connected with a campaign is always under a microscope. The last thing Herb needs is unsavory press regarding his employees. And you don't even like Mark Smith."

"And how do you know that?" Lisa shot back.

"Your body language," he answered. "I watched your posture, like I'm trained to do. It's screaming that he's not your type."

Finished packing her things, Lisa crossed her arms in annoyance. "He's nothing like you, that's for sure. But as for my type, I'll decide that. And, just to satisfy your curiosity, Mark Smith is very well connected. He could bring a lot of donors our way. I see this as a net-working opportunity, nothing more."

Bradley scoffed at that. "No guy gives something without strings."

"Of course not," Lisa agreed, her control solid. "But it's all about the bottom line, and you and I both know that the campaign needs money to get Herb elected. Raising money is my full-time job, and these past few years under your tutelage cannot have been for naught. I want to see a governor's mansion come November. That's the bottom line, and I'm going to uphold my end in achieving it. Mark Smith is the brother of my best friend. There are no strings I can't cut."

"I still don't like it," Bradley said. "Lisa, I'll take a liberty here since I've known you for so long. You can be emotional at times."

"Yes, I've made mistakes in the past," Lisa said, knowing Bradley meant the misguided crush she'd had on him and that he'd quickly squashed. "But I've learned when to mix business and personal and when they should be separate," Lisa said. "You taught me that and I'm quite prepared to be out there on my own. As for us, you were right—just some misguided student worship."

"I am twelve years older."

"True," Lisa said. She recognized her feelings for what they'd been. Stupid crushes. They always seemed to get her in trouble. Hindsight was always twenty-twenty, and Lisa could now be relieved that Bradley had cut their ill-suited romance short before it had had a chance to ruin their working relationship.

Although, admittedly it had hurt that he'd rebounded and married someone else so quickly. Understanding Bradley the way she did, Lisa was certain he'd married Heather Monroe Wayne, heiress and daughter of the state senate majority leader, mostly for her status and connections.

And speaking of her stupid crushes, Lisa wondered if perhaps it was time to prove that she could put Mark Smith behind her, as well. And there was one way to do that: go on the date and feel nothing for the man. She reached for her purse and dug out her BlackBerry and his card.

Bradley stared at her. "What are you doing?"

"Making some much-needed connections," Lisa said as she pressed the buttons. "If you and I can work together, Mark and I can, too. And we need his help. He knows people I can't access without him."

"Hello?" Mark's deep voice rumbled through the clear connection, and Lisa turned her back on Bradley.

"Hey, it's Lisa. Sorry for calling you so late, but I figured you were still in the car on the way home."

"Yeah, I was."

Her words rushed out quickly. "Well, I have an answer for you."

"Okay," he said, drawing the word out as if preparing himself for the ensuing rejection. "What's your decision?"

Lisa inhaled. Dealing with Mark and her residual feelings of anger and whatever else was simply the risk she was going to have to take. It was past time to prove that she could handle him—be in control—and let the whole wedding fiasco go once and for all.

Lisa expelled the breath she'd been holding. "I've decided you're right. I could use an ally. I'm in for Thursday night."

Chapter Four

"You're serious. You're not just joshing me? You really have a date with Lisa Meyer?"

Mark fidgeted slightly in his desk chair—the motion creating an audible squeak as his dress pants rubbed against the fine leather. He clutched the phone to his ear. This was not some business associate or ex-girlfriend on the line. Those callers were simpler. He could handle those types of calls with ease.

But this was his sister, and perhaps phoning her had been a mistake. He'd simply let Joann know he'd run into her best friend, explained his idea, and somehow he'd found himself on first steps to the altar. Time to clear up that misperception, fast. "It's not a date."

Joann didn't buy that. "You just told me she's going to the Cardinals game with you."

Mark twisted the spiral phone cord around his index finger. "So? That doesn't make it a date, at least not how you're thinking. Mom and Dad will be there, along with everyone else who's been sitting by us for years. She's a political fund-raiser and I'm figuring that, at the very minimum, our parents can help her find more donors for the campaign. Herb was in their wedding."

"I know what Lisa does for a living and I know you don't need to take her to a baseball game just for our parents to help her. I could have called them and asked for their assistance. Dad probably feels terrible for having to have sent you."

Mark glanced at the family photo he had of Joann and her brood. Taken last year, she and husband Kyle flanked their three young sons. "I filled Dad's role fine. As for Lisa, did she ask you to call them?"

"No," Joann answered. "I haven't talked to her since she moved to St. Louis. She probably hasn't gotten around to calling."

"Well, maybe she felt awkward," Mark said, even though he knew Lisa was planning to call. His sister could use some grief. After all, she'd been the one to cement his playboy reputation.

"I doubt that's it," Joann said. "More likely it's because she's only been in town for a week or so."

"Perhaps. Anyway, I offered my help and she took it." Mark leaned back, satisfied with the explanation.

"Then she must be desperate."

"Yeah, right." Mark joked it off, although Joann's words had a hint of truth to them. During his and Lisa's conversation at dinner the night before, she'd admitted to not liking him much. She thought the very worst of him, that he was a playboy who went through multiple women in one night. What had changed her mind and had her saying yes to the baseball game?

The money probably, Mark decided. It always boiled down to money. But in Lisa's case, Mark's normal capitalistic business attitude didn't apply.

He hated to think that Lisa had no higher calling than to bring home the Benjamins to Herb's campaign. "I think any money raised is the bottom line to Lisa's career."

"Yes and no," Joann said. "Lisa might be caught up in politics, but she remains one of the most honest and forthright people I've ever met."

Mark sat forward, the chair returning to its upright position and thumping against his back. "If you say so. Politics can change a person, and you haven't seen Lisa face-to-face for a while," he pointed out.

"True, but we talk and e-mail all the time. She's not that different from before. And when you go on your date, you'll discover that."

"It's not a date," Mark repeated.

"Fine," Joann replied, and even though he couldn't see her, Mark could picture her shrug her shoulders as was her habit when she said that one word. "So, speaking of dates," Joann said next, "whatever happened to bimbo number ten?"

Mark's brow creased. "Ten?"

"Oh, whatever number you're on now. I simply

assign them numbers each year. Makes it much easier. So what's her name? Alayna?"

"Alanna."

"Same thing," Joann said dismissively.

Mark smiled to himself. His twin sister, God love her, had considered it her role from birth to approve or criticize his women. She hated most of them and never hesitated to tell him.

"I broke it off. But she's still calling me."

Joann was immediately back on his side, but only for a moment. "Some women never learn when to give up. Which reminds me, don't you dare hurt my friend during any of this relationship stuff."

"Wait a minute. Me hurt her? How is that possible? I am not what you think I am. And this *isn't* a date. Lisa hates me. Based on information it seems you have been providing her over the years, you've already done enough damage to my reputation. She'll probably knife me in the back for no apparent reason except that she believes I'm a first-class playboy."

"Aren't you?"

"No!" Mark protested as Joann hit a sore spot. "I want to settle down as much as the next guy. I want to find the right woman, get married, have children, have that happy-ever-after love our parents and you and Kyle have. I'm not a playboy. I'm just picky. I'm not going to settle for just anyone."

And the one woman I might still crave hates my guts.

He gave himself some breathing room as he picked

up the picture. His sister had the same dark hair and eye color he did, but there the resemblance ended. She stood only five foot four while he was six foot one. She had a tiny bone structure; he'd played quarterback on St. Louis University High School's football team. She'd loved English; he'd loved math and science. He opened his mouth to speak again, but Joann beat him to it.

"Mark, do me a favor. Don't just say you aren't a playboy. Prove it. Lisa could be really good for you, and she did have a crush on you once."

A crush that had led to a very passionate kiss and then a very lonely bed.

"Trust me, sis. A lot has changed, mostly thanks to your regaling Lisa with all my exploits in a highly exaggerated style."

"So? It might do you good to actually have to woo a woman and win her back to your side. You know I'd love for you two to become friends. Lisa doesn't know a soul her age in St. Louis except for Tori, and she's always traveling somewhere with that computer job of hers and is never home. Although, the more I think about it, I bet you can't do it."

Mark fell for her bait, as he'd done since childhood. "Do what?"

"Become friends with Lisa. She's probably going to use you for your contacts and leave you out to dry. You'd deserve it."

Mark bristled. "I would not and that's rather harsh. I do happen to respect Lisa a great deal."

"Maybe, but only because Lisa's the one woman who certainly won't fall at your feet. I had eyes at my wedding, brother dear. I saw how you looked at her."

"Well, nothing happened."

"I'm sure that wasn't for your lack of trying."

"Hey," Mark said, feeling a bit awkward. He hadn't realized his sister knew anything about that evening. *What had Lisa told her?*

He didn't realize he'd spoken aloud until Joann said, "Oh, my God. Are you telling me something happened between you?"

Damn. "No. Yes. Just a kiss."

"You kissed Lisa? And neither of you told me? Spill it."

"Once. Between the cake cutting and you leaving."

Silence.

"In the hallway. No one saw us. We made some plans for after the reception, but then she saw me walk Bridget out and assumed I was leaving with her."

"I heard about Bridget. I tell you, the things that happen after the bride and groom leave. Lisa's never mentioned this."

"Well, don't bring it up."

"Okay," Joann said. "This really takes the cake. She probably thinks you're a jerk."

"That about sums it up," Mark admitted. "And it's your fault she hates me. I run into her again and she'll only give me the time of day because I have connections she needs."

"I don't believe this. I've never heard you like this. You fell for her."

"We were drunk. That allows for some license."

"You aren't now," Joann pointed out. "I think you're falling for her again. You asked her out."

Mark reached for a pencil and rolled it between his fingers. Why had he called Joann again? "Just stop right there. Who said anything about falling for each other? We just saw each other for the first time in eight years. We're not even friends. It's not a date, for the hundredth time. Do women lose brain cells with each child you have? Did you not hear me? It is not a date. Just an alliance to help her out. She can bleed me for all my contacts. I don't care."

"A hundred bucks says you do."

"A hundred bucks…" He paused. "What are you talking about?"

"A bet. I bet you'll fall in love with her long before she ever falls for you."

"I am not agreeing to a bet."

"Sure you are. It's only a hundred bucks. You can afford that. If you make her fall in love with you, I'll pay you. Just don't break her heart. Those are the conditions."

Conditions? He'd been listening, but Joann always had a way of twisting things around during an argument. Joann could jump from one place to another and know exactly how she'd gotten there, but in the process she'd leave Mark far behind and subsequently in the dark. His only solace was that her husband had once admitted to Mark that the same thing happened to him.

Born second, Joann had always maintained that her mother saved the best for last. She'd long honed and mastered the art of bamboozling her older twin brother. She'd learned to win arguments by simply being tenacious. So if she wanted to bet, it was easier to just give in, ignore her, pay up and forget the whole thing right away.

"Fine, a hundred bucks," Mark sighed. "Can I just pay you now?"

"No. You'll win if Lisa falls for you first. I win if you fall for her first. And you'll know when you should call me and concede. Just do not hurt my friend or I'll have to hurt you."

How could you hurt someone who disliked you? All Mark really wanted was for Lisa to stop thinking he was the worst sort on the planet. He wanted an apology and, okay, maybe a few more things. But he refused to tell his sister he was still attracted. "Okay. Now I do have work to do over here."

"How's the sale coming?" Joann asked, her attention now on the business she owned shares in.

"I'm down to three companies that I'd like to meet with and pursue dialogues. They should be good matches for us. Even after I find one I like, we'd still have at least a couple of months before money changes hands. I'm going to run the proposals over to Dad for his input before we leave for the game."

"Good idea. Oh, Trevor's crying. I've got to run. Great talking to you."

"Love ya," Mark said as his sister hurriedly said her goodbyes and disconnected. He gazed at the photo. Two years old in the picture, Trevor held a stuffed donkey and sat on his mom's lap.

The corner of Mark's mouth lifted wistfully. He'd always expected to have his own family by now, but he'd never found a woman who was quite right for him. He resolved to get down to Springfield and see his nephews at the next opportunity.

His secretary's voice came through on the phone's intercom. "Alanna's on line one."

Mark drummed his fingers on the desktop. His playboy reputation was exaggerated. He didn't rush into sexual encounters and had never slept with Alanna. He exhaled slowly and hoped he wouldn't sound too cruel. "Okay. Put her through."

It was time to end this once and for all.

"Alanna," he said as she came on the line. He listened to her plead for a moment, counted to ten, prayed Lisa wouldn't kill him for using her this way and then, when he could get a word in edgewise, said, "Alanna, I'm sorry, but like I told you last week, it's over. I'm already dating someone else."

ON THURSDAY LISA learned three things before the Cardinals game started. One, Mark's Porsche had every option and could weave in and out of traffic at breathtaking speed. Two, his parents had great season tickets. Mark hadn't been exaggerating. Section four was directly behind home plate, and the green theater-style seating meant that row eight had a fantastic view of the field, the scoreboard and even the top of the Gateway Arch. The seats had access to a private all-inclusive climate-controlled club and in-seat wait staff service, something Mark had instantly taken advantage of when he'd ordered them drinks and chicken strips.

All around her sat some of the biggest names in St. Louis. The last and best thing Lisa learned was that his parents were already prepared to help her—both Joann and Mark had already approached them and solicited their assistance in Lisa's endeavors.

A little into the third inning, during a break in play, Lisa finally took a sip of her beer.

"Not really a beer person?" Mark leaned over and passed her a basket of chicken.

"Not really," she said. "I outgrew drinking beer during college."

"They have wine," he offered. "I don't see the waitress right now, so would you like me to go inside and get you a glass?"

The crowd cheered as a Cardinals player hit a line drive and sprinted toward first base.

"I'm fine, really," she said, turning her attention from the infield. "They might score, and if I'd hate to miss it, I know you must."

Mark grinned and Lisa tried not to let his charm affect her. "Ah, a girl after my own heart."

She wasn't after his heart, but she did love baseball.

It was the only sport she truly followed for reasons other than being able to make polite conversation.

"I might not prefer beer, but I do love this game," Lisa told him.

"Then I'm glad you're here and could get off work."

"Herb left for Kansas City this morning. He'll be there until Tuesday. Bradley and Kelsey are running everything."

They both took a moment to watch the ensuing play. "So, is Jefferson City where you live?" Mark asked.

"I don't really live anywhere," Lisa answered. "I've been in a hotel or short-term-lease apartment for the past eight years. My mom thought I should live with her and Dad when I came back here, but I've been out since eighteen and my schedule is too erratic. A hotel is much simpler."

Mark frowned, his attention off the game and fully on her. "That's not a way to live."

How many people, including her parents, had told her they disapproved of her lifestyle? Mark Smith, of all people, had no right to judge her. Ye who are sinless cast the first stone, and all that reasoning.

"So why is it not a way to live?" Lisa retorted. "Let me guess. You have a house. It's just you living there, but I bet you have one of those huge places in Chester-field, about four thousand square feet with granite coun-tertops and the two-story great room that costs an arm and a leg to heat."

Mark had the decency to flush, turning the color of

his red Cardinals polo. "Guilty." Then he rallied. "Although, why should that be a bad thing?"

"You own a million-dollar house for one person."

"Not quite a million. And it's an investment," he countered.

Lisa warmed to the argument. The tension humming between them was close to what she'd felt that one weekend, freshman year. "It's a waste of space for one man."

"Rather odd philosophy coming from Ms. Conservative. Almost contradictory. You're all about achieving the American dream—grab that brass ring. You can't wait to get Herb into the governor's mansion."

"There is a difference between grabbing a ring and being excessive," Lisa insisted. "While I don't believe government should be redistributing wealth, explain to me how one man can live in four bedrooms. And do you have three cars for your oversize garage?"

The crowd cheered, but Mark paid no attention to the play on the field. "Ah, so this argument is more of a personal attack against me and how you perceive me as being ostentatious as well as a playboy. It doesn't matter that building the house gave some poor carpenter a job, helped him put food on the table for his family."

"He made the same union wages as he would have if he'd worked on a smaller house. And for that area of St. Louis, you overpaid. All you got was some status because of the location."

"Maybe," Mark conceded the point as he dipped a chicken strip in honey mustard. He swallowed the morsel before continuing. "I do admit that the real-estate market is a huge balloon that's been ready to burst for a while. Selling my albatross might be a little tricky, but I'm insulated. I've had it awhile."

"Then you're one of the lucky ones." Lisa leaned back, agitated.

What was her problem? She was not remaining cool and aloof, but, instead, getting into a heated argument. Why did it bug her so much that Mark had always been fortunate?

The man did have it all: good looks, good job, great car and lots of money. He was the complete package, and for some reason that irritated the hell out of her. Ever since she'd first met him, he'd rubbed her the wrong way. Worse, she'd had a crush on him!

She continued to try to pinpoint the reason for her current behavior. She had to work her fingers to the bone to achieve her dreams, whereas Mark had simply been born holding a silver spoon. Although, oddly, the fact that Joann had also been born with that spoon didn't bother Lisa in the slightest.

Maybe it was because Joann had given up her dream—she'd left her promising career to become a stay-at-home mom, and often in their conversations Lisa imagined she could hear Joann's silent lament, even though Joann never once voiced any bitter words of regret. Having been raised with siblings who simply settled, Lisa had determined long ago never to fall into that trap. Her father hadn't. While she'd grown up hardly seeing the man, he'd been the one who'd encouraged her to stay the course.

Mark finally spoke. "Okay, we need a truce. Let's not argue anymore tonight."

In the middle of moving a piece of chicken to her mouth, Lisa's fingers froze. He reached over and used three fingers to cover the top of her hand. Although the touch was brief, odd warmth remained.

"Lisa, I'm sorry if that just came out rudely, but I don't want us to fight. I want us to relax and have fun. No more politics."

"It's my job and I take what I do very seriously," she objected.

"I'm not saying you don't. But let's just enjoy ourselves. I don't think we've ever done that. And despite our checkered past, I would really like it if we could become friends. Joann also would like that."

"I'm sure she would," Lisa agreed. Joann had said as much during her phone call yesterday.

"So enjoy yourself," he said.

But how could she do that when he was seated only a few inches away? Not only had he turned the tables on her again by going from jerk to Mr. Concerned, but by doing so, he'd also exposed one of her fundamental flaws.

Aside from politics, what else did she have?

Lisa watched the game halfheartedly. Her life was

built entirely around her job. The two were one—she had no separate identity outside the political arena.

She didn't have a house and lived in furnished apartments or hotel rooms she rented. There was no husband or boyfriend to warm her bed. Her nonstop schedule meant no pets.

Basically she had nothing permanent to call her own except work. Reality was that she had nothing to discuss aside from the weather, food and pay-per-view hotel movies that, by the time she saw them, were months outdated. Lisa's life was all about current events, hot issues and solutions. Her life was about getting that political appointment.

Mark turned his body forward, his attention shifting from Lisa to the play on the infield. Lisa refocused on the game she loved, watching as the Braves shortstop threw the ball to his first baseman. Two outs for the Cardinals.

Lisa sipped her beer as the next batter walked up to home plate. Maybe Mark was right. She should relax. But that was impossible. If it hadn't been for that kiss they'd shared, Lisa would have been in heaven. She'd sit here and revel in the moment, maybe enjoy the "date," as Joann had declared the event yesterday.

Joann had been thrilled that Lisa was "seeing" Mark, and had simply sung her brother's praises. Unseen, Lisa had rolled her eyes. No, this relationship—and Lisa used that term loosely—was simply an alliance. A means to an end. Tonight was all about showing how unaffected she was.

Unfortunately tonight was proving that the joke was on her. Being next to him made her body hum. She had a heightened sense of awareness and anticipation as if fate were somehow knocking on her door. Control was slipping through her fingers as she found herself considering Mark more than just an ally.

She fidgeted as she ate the last of her chicken strips. Mark had offered to take her to dinner before the game, but she'd declined, citing work. The reality was that dinner would have made tonight's outing seem more of an official date. So now she indulged in fried food normally not allowed on her healthy diet.

But then again, neither was Mark Smith.

The man had turned her life upside down in less than three days, and she had a sneaking suspicion he wasn't finished yet.

But she wasn't going to fall for the playboy. As her relationships throughout college and even her one-sided infatuation with Bradley had shown, Lisa had a poor track record in choosing men. Heck, she'd kissed Mark Smith and he'd left with someone else. Proof positive right there.

She'd rather be by herself and put her career on a fast track than continue to fail in the relationship department. Besides, maybe after the election she'd have time to go slow—to really search for a man who might be right for her.

She definitely wanted the right man and wasn't settling for anything less. Although, Mark was tempting. He made her desire to break free and indulge. But Lisa hadn't ever been the no-strings-affair type like Tori or Cecile. So a relationship with Mark? Out. Allies only.

Loud pop music began playing, signaling the end of the inning. Lisa inhaled a deep breath and calmed her nerves. The Cardinals had stranded all players on base, without scoring any runs. Time for the top of the fifth inning in what remained a scoreless game.

Inning followed inning, and the game got interesting as runs began to be scored on both sides. During the seventh-inning stretch, she followed Mark's mom, Mary Beth, to the women's restrooms.

"I am so glad you came with us tonight," Mary Beth said as they walked back to their seats. "It is so great to see you again."

"It has been too long," Lisa admitted. "I'm glad you're feeling better."

"Just a few seasonal sniffles. Listen, I was thinking about hosting a dinner party for Herb at our home. Do you think that would work? Something for about sixty people? I've been mulling over what to do ever since Mark told me you were fund-raising for Herb."

"There are some federal fund-raising rules we'd have to follow, but a dinner is always welcome," Lisa said.

Mary Beth nodded. "Wonderful. Call me at home tomorrow about ten and we'll discuss this further."

"Thank you," Lisa replied.

Mary Beth paused as she waited for people to move

their legs aside and let her through. "Oh, no, dear, thank you. I've never seen Mark so excited about something. He's been under so much pressure lately with Bud's illness and the sale of the company. You're good for him—Joann and I both agree on that."

Great, Lisa thought as Mary Beth's words sank in. Now she was good for Mark Smith.

Mark gave her that killer smile upon her return, and Lisa wanted to melt. The man was a pied piper. He'd kissed her and left her, but seeing him sitting there suddenly made her want to consider forgiving every one of his indiscretions. It made her want to do other things, as well, stirred sexual fantasies she'd had eight years ago.

Lisa took her seat. "Your mother offered to host a dinner for Herb."

"That's great," Mark said. "And as much as I want you to tell me all about it, tonight we relax. I'll call you for all the details tomorrow."

Lisa's forehead wrinkled. "Tomorrow?"

"The day after today," Mark said with a quick rub of his fingers on the back of her hand. "After all, we're partners."

"Of course," Lisa said, sliding her hand away before he stole all her composure. "We did form an alliance."

He winked at her. "Exactly."

The game ended with a Cardinals win, and Bud and Mary Beth each gave Lisa a brief hug before departing for their car. A sea of red seeped from the stadium as fans began heading home. Time had crept close to eleven. "Let's get you to your hotel," Mark said. "You probably have a big day tomorrow."

"Always," she said. "But before I forget, thanks for taking me. I hadn't been to a game in years."

"I love baseball," Mark said. "I played in high school but wasn't good enough for college ball, let alone the majors. Those two seats we sat in are mine. As kids, they were for Joann and me, but after we graduated and she moved to Springfield, I split the season tickets with two frat brothers of mine. We rotate. Kevin brought his oldest son to the home opener…and so the next generation begins."

"You sound wistful."

"In a way, perhaps," Mark said as they reached his car. He pressed the remote key fob to unlock the car doors. "Joann has three little hellions of her own, and most of my friends are married with family. I'm about to be thirty and I have a huge house, which, as you so aptly put it, plays host to only me. I bought it hoping to fill it with a family by now."

"There's nothing wrong with not being married or having kids. It's not the be-all end-all that people say it is."

"Spoken like a woman devoted to her career."

He'd unknowingly touched a nerve and she reacted. "And is there anything wrong with that? Should I settle just to conform to someone's norm just because I'll be thirty this year?"

"Hey, hey," Mark said. "Relax. I agree with you. I'm not married because I refuse to settle. I want exactly what my parents have."

"I'm not sure I do," Lisa said honestly as she slid into the leather seat. "I mean, the love yes. But my father was often gone with the military and my mother was alone for long stretches."

"That must have been hard." Mark's car roared to life and joined the line waiting to exit the parking garage.

"It taught me I'm not doing anything long-distance, that's for sure," Lisa said. "I'm leaving in November. Maybe after I settle in Jeff City for four years I'll find a husband. I want no regrets."

"But you are planning on marriage? Kids?"

Lisa nodded, although she doubted Mark could see her since his focus was on the game traffic. "Of course. But on my timetable. People rush into things too quickly because they're under the impression that time is passing them by. I've come to peace with the fact that I may never have a permanent home or a husband. I'm not going to marry Mr. Wrong just so I'm not alone. But that's the life I've chosen and I'm comfortable with my decision. I'm in charge."

"You're in control," Mark said as they merged onto Highway 40.

"Exactly," Lisa said. "I have too many things left to do, important things. I'm not going to compromise my vision because my parents think it's past time for me to settle down."

"I'll agree to that," Mark said. "Although, since you've alluded to it, let me point out that you can't call me a playboy just because I've dated a lot of women. I just didn't find any of them right to marry."

"Men," Lisa said. "You can rationalize anything, can't you?"

"Yeah, probably," Mark said. Traffic was heavy, and Mark and Lisa's conversation shifted to other, safer topics as they passed the neon Anheuser-Busch eagle sign that was a St. Louis fixture. When they reached the hotel, a valet stood ready and he moved to open Lisa's door.

"Thanks," she said. "I appreciate everything."

Mark tilted his head slightly and a dimple formed in his right cheek. "You're welcome. I'll call you tomorrow."

She gave a shaky laugh. "Right. Partner." She accepted the doorman's assistance from the car and leaned down. Mark sat with one hand on the wheel, one on the stick shift. She was glad he hadn't gotten out; that would have made the moment somehow more awkward—more personal perhaps. "Tomorrow then," she said.

"It's a date."

And upon hearing those cryptic words, she straightened, the doorman closed the car door and the Porsche disappeared into the night with a roar. Lisa stood there for a moment before an incredulous but satisfied smile crept over her face and stayed there as she went to her room.

MARK SMITH ZIPPED through the nearly deserted Clayton streets, picking up Forest Park Parkway and taking it west to the Innerbelt and speeding down that before again catching westbound Highway 40. As much as he wanted to work out his frustrations by letting the car go full throttle, the interstate corridor all the way out to Mason Road was often one big speed trap.

He pressed the steering wheel controls, sending his radio to XM station Mix. Instantly a contemporary hit flooded the car, soon to be followed by another one. But the endless music failed to soothe his troubles. Lisa bothered him. A lot. First, her ambition and her devotion to her career seemed extremely excessive. Almost obsessive.

And then, the fact that she'd put finding a husband on a timetable, second to her career, bugged him. Like Lisa, Mark also refused to settle, but at the same time he wasn't going to stop searching for Ms. Right. She was out there. He wanted it all, too, but he'd learned that sometimes giving up control was a good thing. To Lisa, ceding control was akin to the plague. Like tonight, with her refusal to have dinner before the game.

That was her way of maintaining control of the evening. Mark admitted that Lisa's stubbornness had made him even more determined to wrestle some of that control away from her. He'd forced her to omit politics and focus on having fun. He'd deliberately upset her apple cart.

She had too many preconceived notions. She thought

him the worst playboy. False. He'd tell her the truth about that night later, when the time was right. She thought you had to control your life. False. With his father's heart attack, Mark had learned that you couldn't anticipate the course of fate. The future could change in an instant, as his and Lisa's had after their kiss.

Lisa had forgotten how to have fun. She'd become a string drawn too tight—she needed to allow herself some slack.

He'd hated being rude by not allowing her to talk about the campaign, but by doing so he'd been able to drive a few cracks into that hard shell she wore like protective armor. A powerful woman like Lisa wouldn't respect weak men, so he'd made sure to stay one step ahead of her, proving he was her mental equal. He suspected she was the type of woman who could easily chew up and spit out men who fawned over her.

He sighed and punched the gas pedal. The car jumped ten miles per hour, humming at being set free to speed.

He reached Long Road, passing the darkened storefronts before making a right turn at Wild Horse Creek and, less than two miles later, a left into his subdivision. As he parked in his three-car garage, a sudden insight hit him. Mark Smith was a firm believer in fate and divine intervention.

Lisa needed him to loosen her up, to show her that life wasn't an endless treadmill that you kept running. You could reach your goals without killing yourself in the process. Mark shut off the engine, closed the garage door and entered his house via the utility room. His dog greeted him.

Lisa needed a guy friend. Specifically someone who could show her a good time. Like him. He still had a point to prove and an apology to elicit.

He thought about that for a moment. He enjoyed Lisa's company. She was brash, bold and beautiful. Sparring with her was invigorating—she argued well. She was a woman who kept him on his toes. If only she didn't have such a stereotypical image of him. What would it take to rock her to her core? Another kiss?

That idea sounded very pleasurable. And very foolish. Lisa was leaving in November, and he wasn't going to lose a bet to Joann. Kissing Lisa would give her more evidence of his "playboy reputation." Not the direction he wanted to go. Although kissing her... His body tightened.

But since he and Lisa had already formed an alliance, becoming friends was the next logical step, which could happen as long as everyone kept his or her head clear of all romantic notions and sexual silliness. That should be easy considering Lisa's opinion of him. Despite some common ground discovered in the car, they remained oil and water. They might mix for a little while, but they couldn't gel. He preferred home and hearth; she lived in a series of hotels. She wasn't staying in St. Louis and she didn't do long-distance. Even if he'd been interested, the relationship was doomed.

So just friends. Having a woman to hang out with

would give him some breathing room before again hanging out his shingle and restarting the search for a wife. Thirty was beyond time to settle down, and Ms. Right had to be out there somewhere. Funny how he'd always expected to have found her by now. For a moment, he let himself wonder one more time about Lisa. Too committed to her career. Surely not the one. Friends. That sounded altogether win-win to him—or as politicians would call it, a certain victory. He'd prove she was wrong and be her friend. Humming to himself, Mark went to feed his dog.

Chapter Five

"So how was your date with Mark Smith?"

Lisa tried not to sputter on her sip of water and she somehow managed to put the goblet down without spilling its contents. "What?"

"Your date," her best friend Tori Adams asked between bites of salad. The two women were having a Friday night dinner at YaYa's in Chesterfield, sort of a halfway point between the Wright Solutions building in Weldon Springs, where Tori worked, and the late appointment Lisa had had in Creve Coeur.

Tori waved her fork. "I talked to Joann yesterday and she said you were going to the ballgame with her brother. So how was it?"

"The Cardinals won."

Tori rolled her brown eyes and set down her fork. She pushed her long, straight brown hair behind her ear. "Cute and glib. Ever the politician. You know I meant the hunky Smith boy."

Lisa pushed a morsel of grilled chicken around her plate to cover it with more sauce. "We are not dating. He's simply helping me out with my campaign."

"Uh-huh. Of course," Tori said as she reached forward and grabbed her glass of diet cola. The women had forgone wine since both were driving. "Your answer is akin to my saying I don't have an occasional fling with Jeff Wright. Let me guess—you and Mark just happened to reconnect and he's now your new best buddy."

Lisa nodded. "Exactly. Herb Usher was a grooms-man in Mark and Joann's parents' wedding. As for the game last night, I heard Mark broke up with his girl-friend so he had an extra ticket."

That piece of gossip had come from Andrea early this morning over Lisa's first cup of coffee. Since the fund-raiser, Andrea had been digging for information on Mark Smith. Lisa had to admit she'd underestimated the girl and her ability to sniff out juicy tidbits. She was definitely turning out to be more valuable than Lisa had originally thought.

Strange how impressions of people could change so drastically. First Andrea and now Mark. When Lisa had spoken to him on the phone earlier this afternoon, she'd found herself laughing. She'd also somehow been suckered into taking him with her to her parents' house tomorrow. Okay, so he hadn't had to press too hard for the invite. He'd offered to go with her if she wanted, and she'd said yes. Bringing Mark would make for a good buffer—with someone there, her mother wouldn't harp on Lisa's transgressions or shortcomings in the relationship department.

But for a man who she really didn't like all that much—respected maybe—Lisa was finding herself softening toward him. She still hadn't pinned down the reason for her shift of opinion. Perhaps she'd simply been so overwhelmed by his mother's thrilling ideas and Herb's enthusiasm for them. Maybe she'd simply enjoyed talking with Mark yesterday—a long and invigorating conversation with no hidden agendas. In her world, that was ultrarare.

"So there's nothing going on between you?" Tori asked.

"No," Lisa said honestly. "You've heard the stories. He hasn't changed that much. He's still love 'em and leave 'em."

Tori sat there a moment, thinking as she chewed. "You know," she said slowly, "you could just use him for sex."

"What?" The idea of using the handsome Mark Smith to slake some lust had Lisa sputtering slightly. "I… uh…"

Tori waved her fork, drawing small circles for emphasis. "If I were in your shoes, that's what I'd do. It's exactly what I do with Jeff Wright. Togetherness without strings. Caring but nothing permanent. No commitments besides an agreement to be monogamous so no one worries about sexually transmitted things. Just a whole lot of fun. And it's not like you'll be living here long. You don't need someone forever after, just here and now."

Lisa shifted uncomfortably as she considered Tori's words. Aside from her pathetic crushes, these days the only relationships Lisa involved herself in were ones she thought might last, perhaps even turn into something permanent. But most of her relationships had fizzled fast—the nomad in Lisa always interfered. Thus, Lisa had learned it was easier to have only a relationship with her career. True love was elusive and, having escaped so far, not worth chasing at this point.

"I am moving to the state capital in November no matter what," Lisa said, agreeing with Tori's assessment that Lisa's stay in St. Louis was temporary.

"Exactly." Tori nodded for emphasis. "Herb will win and you'll be a perfect addition to his gubernatorial staff. So my suggestion is that you just enjoy Mark Smith for a while. Joann wouldn't mind. Heck, she'd probably be thrilled. I'd do him—he's that hot—but I have this thing for redheads right now, so lucky for you, Mark's all yours."

Lisa knew the redhead to whom Tori was referring was her boss, Jeff Wright. "How is Jeff, by the way?"

"Oh, he's Jeff," Tori said a bit too nonchalantly to ring true. "Same old, same old, but that works for us. Neither of us wants anything more from our relationship. He's too married to his computer and I'm too committed to my career. I told you I'm up for a huge

promotion, didn't I? If I get it, I'll supervise all operations out of Kansas City. Once I move, I doubt Jeff and
I can keep something going, as I'm not doing an I-70
commute every weekend."

"So he's not worth driving across the state for?"
Lisa teased.

Tori's face flushed. "Oh, he is, but at some point a
girl has to move on, and I think we're getting to that
point. It's like a carnival ride—fun but you can't stay
on it forever. When I get promoted, it'll be a logical time
to end this. New city, new slate. And the reality is that
Jeff and I have no future beyond our romps."

Lisa's sixth sense told her something wasn't quite
right here, that maybe Tori cared way more for Jeff than
she was letting on. However, Lisa decided not to bring
up anything potentially mood busting. Not right now,
and especially since she agreed with the no-long-
distance argument.

"So are you finally getting what you want with this
promotion?" Lisa asked.

"Yes." Tori's face immediately brightened. "It's a huge
opportunity. I'll be in charge of every Wright Solutions
client service from Kansas City to the Pacific Ocean.
The entire western half of the United States. I'll oversee
systems designers, first responders, tech supporters…."

Lisa half listened as Tori began to outline her new
position. While Lisa was thrilled for her best friend, her
mind couldn't stop contemplating the bomb Tori had
dropped earlier—that Lisa use Mark for sex.

Not that the sex wouldn't be hot and phenomenal. Mark Smith was the kind of guy women fantasized about—she'd fantasized about him now and then since that kiss. Of course, she'd wanted to wring his neck, too. Bottom line, what would the night have been like if he hadn't left with someone else?

And now, eight years later? Mark had a great body, was a suave businessman and was independently wealthy. He'd matured well and become the rare type of man who was the complete package—the kind guaranteed to deliver whether in the boardroom or the bedroom.

Even the briefest touch on her arm last night at the ballpark had sent strange sensations through Lisa, indicating that the chemistry they'd had at the wedding reception bubbled beneath the surface. She hadn't been able to remain impassive. That was the thing about playboys, their reputations were usually deserved. They were men who could lift a woman up, make her feel like a princess for a while and leave her satiated.

If they didn't dump you for someone else.

Mark Smith remained on her mind like the scene of an accident—disturbing and fascinating at the same time.

"You haven't said a word in the past few minutes," Tori said, polishing off the entire entrée. "It's weird. I've been so hungry lately. Used to be that I barely ate and now I'm eating everything in sight."

"You still don't gain any weight."

"Actually, I've padded on three pounds." Tori leaned back and patted her stomach.

"Poor thing," Lisa said. "As if anyone can tell."

Having been friends forever, Tori ignored Lisa's droll sarcasm. "Maybe my metabolism's wacky since I'm turning thirty. None of us is getting any younger. So are you going to go after him or what? I mean, you always did have a thing for the guy. What's holding you back?"

Lisa took a long sip of her soda before replying. "I'm not like you or Cecile. I may be a liberated career women, but somehow it seems pretty cold-blooded to just use a man to keep the bed warm once in a while."

Tori's face scrunched in mock horror. "You need to get with the times. It's not cold-blooded. It's practical. In college we always said that guys shouldn't be the only ones getting all the great action and that women have physical needs, too. You'll be monogamous, and you and I both know you're not a tramp, so I don't see anything wrong with having a liaison like that. Beats buying the battery-operated boyfriend and using him."

"Tori!" Lisa hesitated to deliver the rest of her outraged reply, and brash Tori kept right on going.

"Oh, come on, Lisa. It's like test-driving a car. You sure like the hot-rod sports model, but it's not a practical car for long-term. But it's sure fun while the ride lasts."

Lisa tried one more argument. "This all seems so blasé. What do I do, just tell him that I want to do him?"

"Nah," Tori laughed. "Seduce him first. And then, while he's panicking afterward, tell him you just want to be friends with benefits. He'll be so relieved he'll agree. You've heard that saying about men wanting the milk without buying the cow. Tell him you're not even interested in selling the cow."

"We're cows?" Lisa asked, arching her brow as she processed Tori's suggestion and analogy.

"No, we're not," Tori said with an annoyed smirk. "You know what I mean—you'll be the one in total control the whole time."

While the whole idea was a tad too modern for the way Lisa had been raised, the idea of being the one totally in command of a relationship with Mark did have some appeal.

"I'll think about it," Lisa said, for that wasn't a lie. Now that Tori had planted the idea, Lisa's personality type wouldn't let her do anything but attack the bothersome issue from all angles until she found a solution and arrived at her own conclusion about what to do. Even if she chose to do nothing, she would still contemplate every possibility. And that meant she had to consider that Tori might be right. Maybe the best way to get him out of her system was to sleep with him.

Tori glanced at her watch. "Oh, the time. I've got to run or I'll be late to Jeff's. Be sure to tell me what you decide. I'm dying to know if the legendary Mark Smith is worth it." Tori began to dig in her wallet and Lisa waved off her efforts.

"No, I've got the bill," Lisa said. "You buy next time."

"You're on," Tori said. She stood. "You'll hear from

me later this weekend. Maybe Sunday night we can grab some wine and get together if we're both free."

"That sounds great," Lisa said. "We should see each other more while we're in the same town for a few months."

Tori smiled. "How rare is that?"

"Exactly," Lisa said. "Be good tonight."

Tori wiggled her eyebrows and shot Lisa a lascivious grin. "Trust me. I always am."

THE CALL FROM THE familiar voice came through late that night, right about bedtime, just as the previous calls a year ago always had. Lisa had let her cell phone ring twice, the contraption both vibrating and ringing in her right hand. How many nights had she spent waiting for his call, which always had come right when the political world settled down to sleep briefly. Lisa pressed talk. "Hi, Bradley."

"So how was your date?" he asked. "How was your night with Mark Smith?"

For a moment Lisa didn't answer. A year ago she would have felt a flutter upon hearing the sound of his voice. Tonight there was nothing, and now that silliness seemed ancient, like her high school pangs for the most popular guy in school. Dumb and so totally foolish. Thankfully over.

"So?" Bradley prompted.

Not in the mood to converse, Lisa sighed. "It was a ball game. The Cardinals beat the Braves, and Bud and

Mary Beth agreed to host an intimate dinner for Herb and Bunny. I'm supposed to call Mary Beth back on Monday to nail down a final date. We discussed some of her ideas this morning, and they're fabulous. This dinner could easily raise one hundred thousand hard money, which certainly wouldn't be bad for a night's work."

"So his parents came through."

The hair at Lisa's nape rose. "Of course they did. I lived with their daughter for four years and wore a lime-sherbet-colored dress at her wedding. I told you that you were making a big deal out of nothing."

"Fine, point conceded," Bradley said smoothly.

"I can handle Mark Smith," Lisa responded sharply, her statement more to convince herself now that Tori's idea of sleeping with him had taken root. On Bradley's end, Lisa could hear voices approaching. As was his habit after an event, Herb would meet with his team for a debriefing in the main suite. He and Bradley would talk for a few minutes about the upcoming events before retiring to their respective rooms. "Tell Herb I'll talk to him tomorrow and give him a complete update. His dinner go well tonight?"

"Very. You trained Kelsey well," Bradley said, offering a rare compliment. "Herb's got early-morning face time with the Boy Scouts, so call sometime before eight."

"I'll do that. Good night." Lisa disconnected. She paced her one-bedroom hotel suite. She moved the curtains and gazed out the window at the view across Forest Park Parkway. Lights from older Clayton houses were visible through the tree branches. Because it was night, she couldn't make out Meramec Elementary School, but that edifice was somewhere over there, too.

She stole a glance at her watch. Almost eleven on a Friday night. She could go downstairs, hang out in the hotel bar, drink some wine and listen to the piano player. She quickly nixed that idea. She wasn't in the mood to socialize, she rarely drank and there was work she could do. But her itch to leave the room proved that restlessness had stolen over her. Discontent had become a presence in the suite.

The room decor was a mix of soothing, calm colors, but at this moment the effect wasn't making Lisa relax. Just over Forest Park Parkway, people tucked children into bed and settled down for some late-night television. They mowed their lawns, parked their cars in their own driveways. They cleaned their houses, cooked their food. Lisa did none of those things.

In a sense she was spoiled: her every whim was taken care of. She had twenty-four-hour room service, maid and laundry service. When she ran out of something like bath soap, she simply made a phone call and whatever she wanted arrived at her door within fifteen minutes. In a sense, she lived like the rich and pampered. She was beyond those mundane daily chores.

Did that mean she'd become trapped in a lifestyle?

She bit her lower lip momentarily, curling her flesh under before releasing it. Did she exist in a false world, a reality that normal, everyday people didn't share? Even Tori had her own apartment, slept in her own bed and not a rental.

Lisa consoled herself with the fact that she'd get a permanent place all her own once Herb won the election. Although, honestly, could she handle permanence?

Perhaps she was like her father, who, before he'd retired, had always had to keep moving. While established at one military base, the job he'd chosen had kept him on the road and constantly provided new challenges. Now retired, he was often bored.

Maybe she was the same way. Maybe the melancholy she was experiencing was really only an attack of the grass-being-greener-on-the-other-side-of-the-fence syndrome. Spending four years in one place would probably feel like eternity, and Lisa predicted she'd be bored with ownership of the same old four walls before a few months transpired.

She was a drifter—always ready for the next opportunity. As for domesticity, she'd done her own laundry in college and hated it. She was a terrible housekeeper and an even lousier cook. Hotel living eliminated all of that.

Her phone shrilled, and she didn't even waste time glancing at the caller ID display. She pressed talk. "Hey, Bradley. What did you forget?"

"Not Bradley, and I forgot to ask what time we

were leaving tomorrow. I didn't wake you up, did I? If so, I'm sorry."

A tiny shiver of adrenaline shot through her and caused her toes to tingle. Mark. "Hey. No. I'm still up."

"Waiting for Bradley?"

"He called earlier," Lisa said, registering that Mark's easy tone held a tense undercurrent. Understandable since the two men hadn't gotten along at the fundraiser. "Herb had a great event today. Lots of time with some major movers and shakers in Kansas City. I trained Kelsey, so it's been great knowing that I didn't have to be jetting everywhere this weekend."

"So how'd your dinner with Tori go?"

She wants me to sleep with you.

"It went fine," Lisa said instead.

"Only fine?" Mark asked.

Lisa found herself smiling as she pictured him arching his eyebrow in silent query. "You know what I mean. She's doing well and we did have fun," Lisa admitted.

"Glad to hear it. Anything new with her?"

"Yeah. She's up for a promotion at work, and if she gets it, she'll relocate to Kansas City. She's pretty excited about her chances."

"That's great."

"It's what she's always wanted for her career. She'll be a natural boss."

"Career women since birth or at least college. She'll be Bill Gates and you're the next Condoleezza Rice."

"Only I won't be Secretary of State for the United

States," Lisa said. "I'll just be senior staff working behind the scenes for Missouri."

"I meant how you'll be moving into a more important job. Senior staff is still a terrific career," Mark said.

"It is." She thought for a moment about the people across the way, all of whom were tucked into their trendy Clayton houses, the work-free weekend having started. Senior staff members were on call 24/7.

"You sounded a little blue there for a moment," Mark said. "Do you want me to come over and cheer you up?"

"Like a booty call?" she asked, more adrenaline surging upon hearing his suggestive remark.

"Not what I was thinking, but that can be arranged. We never did have that night," Mark said. He paused, then laughed to make light of his words. "No, seriously. Scratch that. If you need me, I'm here. As a friend."

Lisa closed her eyes and counted to three before opening them again. Darn Tori for planting suggestions. Now Lisa was reading sex into everything, especially after Mark had brought up the night they'd never had. This was dangerous territory to tread across. *Remember that it was his fault nothing happened,* she told herself. Just a secret only they knew. She'd never told anyone.

"I'm all right," Lisa said. "It's just a rare moment of calm, and I find myself actually at a loss for something to do. So I'm going to go to sleep early so that I won't yawn my way through my visit with my parents tomorrow."

"I know what you mean. It's like there's nothing to do but twiddle your fingers. And then there are times when you're coming and going and you wish the day had more hours to it."

"Exactly." Lisa found herself impressed and surprised that he understood. Few men she met did.

"So what time shall I pick you up?" Mark asked.

"How about eleven? That should give us plenty of time to drive down to South County."

"Eleven it is," Mark agreed easily.

Lisa suddenly heard loud barking in the background. "You have a dog?"

"Yeah. Longman. A retired greyhound I rescued."

"Longman?" she queried.

Mark laughed. "I can tell what you're thinking. He's long and lean and a boy. Sounded good to me, and he comes running whenever I call."

"That's because you feed him," Lisa observed drily.

Mark chuckled, his voice deep and throaty. "I'd like to think it's because I'm his master."

"You would, but deep down you know better."

He groaned. "You're killing my ego. I'll see you tomorrow. Get some sleep so I don't have to poke you all day to keep you awake."

"Yes, sir," she said with mock sarcasm.

"See, I am the master," he said, smug satisfaction evident. "Remember that." Then he hung up before she could retort.

She pressed End and plugged the phone into its battery charger. The master. Unfortunately the word fit.

Mark Smith was a man who was always one step

ahead. He'd snowballed her at the dinner. He'd smoothly ingratiated himself into tomorrow's family event. As much as she'd been miffed, she'd also been flattered. Maybe a bit taken by his attention. No one would ever deny that Mark Smith was quite a dream catch.

That was, for the woman who wanted to catch him, she amended. Which she didn't, right?

Tori's prophetic words resounded in Lisa's brain. *You'll be in control of the relationship the whole time.*

Lisa sat on the king-size bed, the mattress making a muffled creak. Where Mark Smith was concerned, she had to stay in charge. He'd managed to play her correctly from the moment they'd reconnected. She'd been little challenge, simply rolling over and ignoring that he'd kissed her before deserting her for someone new. She couldn't let him sway her any further. No matter what, she had to keep a clear head. She had to remain in control.

Chapter Six

The next day dawned clear and bright, with temperatures forecasted to reach almost the eighties. St. Louis weather could be like that, from one extreme to another in twenty-four hours. Lisa chose a pair of navy slacks, a red sweater set and a gold necklace for the outing. She'd left her blond hair loose around her shoulders, and the ends curled slightly from being blown dry. After a final glance at her watch, she left the one-bedroom suite and headed to the lobby. Through the windows she could see Mark was right on time, the Porsche idling in the hotel's circular drive.

Mark stood half in, half out of the low-slung sports car, the valet holding the passenger door open for Lisa. She took a deep breath. He looked darn good and that dream she'd had last night of the two of them was still pretty vivid.

"Hey, change of plans," Lisa said as she exited the revolving doors.

"Well, good morning to you, too," Mark said cheerfully. "It's nice to see you. You are looking lovely today."

"Aren't you funny," Lisa replied, catching his condescending tone. Mark arched his eyebrow at her as if in a silent dare. She bit. "Good morning. It's nice to see you, as well," she said.

"Much better," Mark said, bestowing her with an approving nod and that irritatingly sexy grin of his. After sliding into the car at the same time as Lisa, he shut his door and leaned toward her. "I've decided that we should have more social pleasantries in our relationship."

"We don't have a relationship," Lisa pointed out as the valet closed her door.

"Of course we do," he said, reaching around to fasten his seat belt. "I thought we were friends."

Mark waited until she was safely strapped into the bucket seat before he accelerated the Porsche out of the drive and onto Bonhomme.

Lisa grimaced. If her goal was to be in control, she wasn't off to a good start. "We are friends," Lisa said.

"Exactly. And friends say good morning," he responded. And then, before she could reply to that, he said, "So what are the plans?" His words effectively changed the subject.

She stared at him for a moment. The man was infernal. Despicable. She could almost picture him saying, "You are no lady," like Rhett Butler, if it allowed him to make his point. Mark Smith took liberties with her that no other man would dare try. And even though he grated on her nerves, at the same time he stimulated her. The paradox vexed.

"My parents called this morning. Since you were coming with me, my dad saw this as an excuse to eat out."

"We're headed to South County, though, right?" Mark said as he navigated the light Saturday-morning traffic.

"Yes and no. They live in South County, but my dad decided a drive to Imperial/Kimmswick was in order."

"We're going to the Blue Owl?" Mark questioned, mentioning the Kimmswick eatery famous for its desserts and luncheon fare.

Lisa shook her head and glanced out the window as a passing car zoomed by. "No. Fancier. Their favorite restaurant, Taylor's, is hosting a special invite-only luncheon in honor of its most valued customers. Usually the place isn't open for lunch on Saturdays, but my parents are regulars, so they were included. Basically today is a fixed-price menu."

"Sounds interesting." Mark said, his attention on the road.

"Should be. They have great food and I'm hungry. All I had was half a bagel for breakfast."

"So my tagging along rates going out to lunch instead, huh?"

"Don't flatter yourself. While my mom's all about

home cooking, my dad's work history means he tries to get out of the house as much as he can. This time he claims it comes with retirement. You gave him an excuse to eat out. Although, I admit they're beside themselves with joy that they can take me *and a friend* out to lunch."

"What, don't you ever bring guys home?"

She sighed, unwilling to rise to his bait but doing so anyway. So much for control. "I don't bring anyone home," she said honestly. "I rarely go home and I haven't lived near my parents in what seems like forever. I'm at a hotel, which they hate, and frankly the fact remains that I'm much too busy."

"Ah. No breakfast, no dating."

"Stop mocking me."

"Sorry," Mark said, and she could tell by his tone he meant his apology. "It seems like you and I are so opposite. I want to settle down, you don't. I eat a good breakfast, you skimp with a bagel. I date. You don't."

They really were polar opposites, weren't they? Lisa thought. If they didn't have Joann in common, would they have even paid much attention to each other?

Oh, Lisa would have noticed him, been attracted to him. He was that sexy. But still… "As I told you Thursday night, dating is a low priority at this point in my life," she said. "It's an easy sacrifice to make while I build my career. I'll worry about finding Mr. Right once I get to Jefferson City and am settled for four years."

"I thought of that after the ball game. It sounds mercenary slotting your husband search in."

"Well, that's exactly what I plan to do, no matter how cold-blooded it may sound—which, by the way, is how my mother views it. So don't you dare bring up my dating status around her. My career always comes first."

"I still think you need to loosen up. Get out there a bit. See where fate takes you."

"Later," Lisa insisted. "You've seen those investment-account brochures that tell you it's better to invest a smaller amount early rather than a bigger amount later, right? You know, the ones that prove that, due to compounding, the initial investment is worth more at maturity? Well, that's the way my career is. I can't get where I want to be by starting late. I have to invest now."

"Yes, but there's that saying, 'All work and no play…'" Mark said.

She shifted on the leather seat. "Now you really sound like my mother. I make time for play. I'm here, aren't I?"

Mark had his sunglasses on, so she couldn't see if he rolled his eyes at her declaration. Silence fell, the only noise in the car coming from a multitude of stereo speakers. A country radio station played Kenny Chesney's latest hit.

"I wouldn't think you'd be a country fan," she observed. Talking about music might be a good way to defuse the charged atmosphere that had settled inside the car. And she liked country. Finally something they did have in common.

"There's a lot you don't know about me," Mark said, his tone serious. "I'm a man of many mysteries and hidden depths. You should dig a little deeper. You'd be amazed at what you'd find."

So much for eliminating the charged atmosphere. If nothing else, the electrons were zinging faster and further out of control. How did he do it?

"Okay. Perhaps," Lisa finally conceded in a voice that indicated she reserved the right to change her judgment.

After all, she'd never felt as competent with men as Tori or Cecile. Of the three, Lisa had often felt the most awkward, like a third wheel. Perhaps that's why she developed silly infatuations for men she couldn't have. When she did date, the men she chose were often too eager to please her. Being little challenge, they bored her quickly or smothered her with too much attention.

Mark Smith was cut from a different cloth. And as much as she hated to admit that he was her mental equal, having someone who didn't simply kowtow to her wishes and whims made for a refreshing, if uncomfortable, change.

"You seem to think the worst of me a lot," he said suddenly, nailing the problem flat out. "I'm not that same guy you remember from college or from the wedding reception. I'm different."

"What, now you won't leave me for someone else?"

"Maybe we should clear that up." Mark's words

were quiet. "Let's get one thing straight. I didn't leave you. I came back to find you and you were already gone. Tori told me you'd left with Cecile, that the two of you had gone upstairs to your hotel room to sleep."

"You left with another woman. I saw you."

Mark's fist clenched the steering wheel. "You saw me walk Caleb's girlfriend outside. She drank way too much and couldn't stand very well. Caleb told me she more or less puked all night."

"Oh."

"Oh." Mark said. "I came back and you were already gone. You let your preconceived notions of my playboy status color your perceptions. You judged me, found me lacking and didn't stick around to find out the other side of the story."

"I don't believe this," Lisa said. Her head pounded. If this were true, how could she have made such a grave mistake? But she *had* misjudged Mark. She'd been so caught up in her own excitement and then disappointment that her own alcohol-fuzzy brain hadn't let her think straight. No wonder she now avoided having more than one drink.

"I don't care if you believe me or not, Lisa, but that's the truth. I've let it go. It's past. You can't dwell on things or they drive you crazy."

Which was exactly what he was doing. Driving her crazy. Lisa hated being wrong. And she'd been wrong about Mark. Big-time.

She'd been wrong eight years ago and she'd been

wrong to paint him with that brush now. Mark wasn't similar to the men she dealt with in the political world. Mark didn't view things through the conceptual lens of "What can I personally gain from this?"

Oh, all people were self-serving in that they did things that somehow benefited themselves monetarily, physically or emotionally. To want to gain was basic human nature. But Lisa couldn't see how Mark was benefiting from hanging around her, except perhaps by earning some family brownie points.

Actually, she was the one gaining from the relationship. Her career was on a faster track and her rigid attitudes were changing—she was upsetting years of habits and behaviors. When she was around Mark, she couldn't act like her typical self, for somehow he'd become a mirror that exposed her flaws.

Like this morning.

Did she really move at such a fast pace that she skipped such things as everyday social pleasantries? Deemed them unnecessary or beneath her unless she benefited from them somehow?

Mark hadn't been afraid to call her on her rudeness. At that moment Lisa realized that perhaps their "relationship"—or whatever it was—was that of iron sharpening iron. Even though it had been years since she'd attended Sunday school, for some reason she could always remember that Proverbs 27:17 passage. The entire thing read, "As iron sharpens iron, so one man sharpens another."

The revelation that that was exactly what Mark was doing with her came as a disconcerting shock. She could learn from him, and he from her. He brought out her best—and worst.

For some reason fate had reconnected them. Maybe this was why. She chewed on her bottom lip as she thought about that for a moment. What did she want from Mark? The crystal ball wasn't clear. But one thing was.

"Perhaps we should both work on changing our be-havior toward each other," Lisa said. She hadn't been with a guy who could stimulate her for a long time. She and Mark Smith could compromise. "I guess I could…" She paused.

"Stop judging me on my past?" Mark suggested.

"Okay," Lisa agreed. She had judged him and she had treated him poorly, especially if he hadn't left her. "I could do that."

"A clean slate would be nice," Mark admitted. "I'm not a bad guy, and you and I might be able to have some fun if you stop viewing me as the world's worst playboy. Maybe we should clear something else up, as well. That night is in the past, and I simply want to be your friend."

"Uh, of course." Lisa angled her face so that she could watch the scenery speed by. Thank goodness he couldn't see the red flush that had crept over her skin. She'd agreed to be friends before she'd learned he hadn't left her for another woman. She'd agreed to be friends before Tori had suggested seducing him.

Now that she knew the truth, it changed everything. It removed the reason she held him at arm's length, decided he was off-limits. She was leaving in November, but why not try a fling with Mr. Right Now? The erotic dream she'd had of the two of them last night was proof that she was oh so tempted and that Mark would be perfect.

Already he made her step out of her world. A quick no-strings affair could be just the thing she needed. Get him out of her system by enjoying the ride until November came.

From the way his hands caressed the steering wheel, to the scent entirely his that permeated the car and her senses, the man had pure sex appeal. Mark Smith was a man's man: big, bold, solid. His physique was cut and buff. He made her nervous in an odd way. Out of control but at the same time exhilarated.

Why not reignite the spark that had consumed them that night? Why not indulge in what she'd fantasized about? Maybe Tori did have it correct. Maybe this was the way for Lisa to finally have control.

"You've grown quiet. I haven't offended you, have I?" he asked, his tone genuinely concerned. "I think I do that a lot and I'm sorry."

"No," Lisa said, resisting the urge to put a hand out and touch him reassuringly. "I'm not offended." Hot and bothered, yes.

"Honestly?" he asked, and she heard the slightest undertone of anxiety in his voice.

"Yes, honestly," she replied.

Mark stole a glance at her. "Good. 'Cause as your friend, I'm going to insist that you take some 'me' time, starting today right after lunch and shopping the streets of Kimmswick."

"Taylor's is in Imperial, right off the highway. It's not in Kimmswick," Lisa pointed out.

"I know. But it's too beautiful out to spend the day inside. For the first time all spring the temperature is finally in the high seventies, and I'd like for us to enjoy it. Do me a favor and turn your phone off."

"What?" she asked sharply. Turn off her Black-Berry? That was her lifeline. No way. "Herb has to reach me. I might get some e-mail. And…"

"Herb is in Kansas City and he's Bradley's boy this weekend, and you already talked to both of them early this morning," Mark inserted, deflating her argument.

She glanced at him, surprised. "How did you know?"

His grin inched drolly upward. "Lucky guess. So put your cell phone away. Please. It's Saturday, Brad-ley's in charge, and you can spare at least four hours without constantly worrying about life. You can check for messages later."

Her hostility ebbed slightly under the *please* and the fact that his onslaught was driven by sincerity. And he could be right. The BlackBerry was attached to her hip 24/7/365. Lisa's job did allow for her to carve out some free time, and the truth of the matter was that her mother would go ballistic if Lisa's phone went off during lunch.

Lisa removed the device from her purse and turned off the BlackBerry's ringer.

"Silent. No vibrate," she told Mark. "There, I've compromised."

"That's fine," he said, as if sensing he'd pushed her far enough. "Thanks. I really appreciate that you're doing this."

"You're welcome," she said, a funny feeling taking hold. Why was it that Mark could make her cave and somehow not see her actions as weakness? Even though technically she'd capitulated, she knew that had she refused, he wouldn't have fought her. Odd. She'd met plenty of men who'd let her win if she pressed enough but never one who made her not want to enter a battle in the first place.

They passed the sign declaring that the Imperial/Kimmswick exit was a mile ahead, and Mark eased the car into the far right lane. Mark decelerated, exited and, once off Highway 55, made a left turn. After crossing back over the highway, Taylor's was on the left, almost directly across from a gas station. Mark parked and ushered her inside.

"Lisa!" Her mother waved as they entered. Her mother was sitting on an old-fashioned velvet settee near the hostess desk and she rose to her feet. "Right on time. We're supposed to be seated next." She turned to the hostess. "The Meyer party is all here."

"Excellent," she said with a quick nod. "It'll be a moment. We're setting the table now. You're upstairs."

"That's fine," Lisa's mom said.

Located in an old house, Taylor's main dining room was two stories high. A long exposed staircase led to the upstairs, which was, in essence, an L-shaped balcony at least twenty feet from rail to wall. The place was done in reds and gold—the wallpaper red with a gold floral motif pattern, the curtains red satin with gold tassels. White moldings accented the interior walls, and everything from the chair rail to the floor was painted white, as was the crown molding.

"Nice place," Mark remarked as he and Lisa approached her mother. "I didn't realize a restaurant of this caliber was down this way."

"It's a hidden gem. Elegant yet casual. My mother loves this type of decor. Victorian, I think, but don't quote me. The reality is that I've got no clue whether I'm right or not. Architecture and design are not my thing." They'd reached Louise Meyer. "Mom, you remember Mark, don't you? Joann's brother?"

Louise extended her hand, which Mark clasped firmly. "Mark, it's nice to see you again."

"The pleasure's all mine, Mrs. Meyer," Mark said.

Her mother's smile widened. "Call me Louise. Joann is practically family, so by extension that makes you family, too. Oh, here's Mike."

Lisa's dad returned from the bar carrying a glass of white soda for Lisa's mom. He passed it over and shook Mark's hand. "Nice to see you again."

"Thanks," Mark said. The hostess picked up four

menus and the group followed her up the staircase. Their table was next to the railing and the location gave them a prime view of the dining area below, where, in one corner, a woman played a baby grand piano. A waiter approached and took their order.

Because she usually avoided red meat, Lisa had a chicken salad club. Her mother had cider-lime chicken with a mango tomato salsa. The men opted for the grilled steak sandwich with chips. Lunch was surprisingly pleasant. Bringing Mark had been a wise idea, Lisa thought. Not only was the food delicious but Lisa also discovered quite a few things about both her parents and Mark that she didn't know. For one, both Mark and her father loved NASCAR and followed drivers for both the Busch and the Nextel Cup series. Lisa had a hard time picturing her father at a speedway, only to discover that he and her brother Andy had watched a race at Gateway International just last week.

After the complimentary crème brûlée dessert, the foursome drove their respective cars the few miles down to Kimmswick for some shopping. While no one bought anything, the day was warm and the walk welcome, and around four-thirty the group finally decided to head home.

"Don't forget daylight saving time begins tonight," Louise said. "Spring those clocks forward."

"Will do," Lisa said. She gave her mother and father each a hug. "It was wonderful spending time with you."

"Then let's do it more often," Louise said, her expression serious. "Mark, see to it, will you? You're more than welcome to join her."

"I'll make sure it happens as long as you take me up on my offer for those Cardinals tickets. Lisa can attest that they're great seats, and I'd rather you use them than see them wasted if I can't go. My treat."

"You are too generous," Louise said. "Lisa, don't run this one off." And then, with one more kiss, Louise and Mike drove away.

"You have great parents," Mark said as they walked the short distance to the Porsche, which was parked a few car lengths away.

"Thanks," Lisa said. "I have to admit, today was good. I was rather nervous."

Mark arched an eyebrow as he opened her door for her. "You didn't think it would be?"

"No, but since I had you with me, my mom wasn't able to do her typical 'Why haven't you settled down?' speech. Of course, she's now hoping that I'll do just that with you."

"Poor thing. We all know you aren't the settling type," Mark said wryly. He closed her door, walked around and slid into the driver's seat.

"I want to settle. Just on my timetable," Lisa said.

Mark sat there for a second, as if he had something to add. Had she offended him? Before she could ask, he shrugged and said, "So what shall we do next? The day's still young."

Lisa shrugged. "I'm not sure. I have to tell you, I'm finding being with you nerve-racking."

"Why? I offered you my friendship expecting nothing in return. My eyes are open. I know you're leaving in November."

She blinked. Joann had once mentioned that Mark was a planner. "Have you really thought this thing through?"

He nodded. "Of course I have. I'm a businessman by trade and that's what I do. I know you're only here because of my connections. Trust me, I'm not going to get hurt, so use me until you use me up. There's an old song that goes something like that. I'll download it and burn it to a CD for you."

She stared at him almost as if seeing him for the first time. Oh, he looked the same—dark hair, dark brown eyes, dark blue tailored button-down and fitted dark blue jeans. But he wasn't the playboy she'd always considered him to be. Far from it. "You are truly different from any man I've ever known."

"I don't play games," Mark said, his tone sharp and serious. "I have no need or use for them. I'm a very straightforward person, always have been. If I want something, I go after it and get it."

He had once wanted her. The fact that he didn't now rankled. A lot.

"I don't like manipulative people and conspiracies," Mark continued. "I like things at face value. That doesn't mean I can't be ruthless when the time warrants, but I'd rather not be an ass if I can avoid being one."

"I'm a little overwhelmed."

"No reason to be. What you see is exactly what you get," Mark said. He raised his hand as if he was making a pledge. "You want to know something about me or need something from me, just ask."

"So I just tell you what I want and you'll give it to me?" He was making her want him.

The idea seemed ludicrous, but he nodded. "Yeah, I suppose so. If I can help you get something, as long as it doesn't ask me to compromise my values, I'll do everything in my power to see that you have it."

"You are…"

He arched an eyebrow. "Amazing? Nothing like you expected? Strange? Different?"

"All of the above," Lisa said. And he hadn't left her that night of Joann's wedding. He had wanted her. It had all been one big misunderstanding. The thought spread warmth through her. "You know, all this doesn't seem fair. You aren't some well I should be able to drain dry between now and November."

"I can take care of myself," Mark said. "Always have, always will."

She still didn't believe he was serious. "And what do you get out of this if there aren't strings? What's in this for you?"

He reached forward and pushed a strand of her hair behind her ear. The intimate movement brought his face closer to hers. "I get nothing that you should have to worry your pretty little head about. Once in a while you just have to go with the flow, and this, Lisa, is one of those times."

They sat in silence for a few moments as Lisa absorbed all of what he'd said. Mark Smith was truly amazing. Some woman should have snagged him a long time ago.

"I'm sorry," Lisa said suddenly.

"For what?" Mark asked.

"For misjudging you."

"Thanks." He turned the ignition key and the sports car roared to life. He lowered the radio volume. "Although I like what you're wearing, I was thinking we'd go back by your hotel and pick up some fancier clothes. How about we take in an early movie and then go by my place and change? We'll do a late dinner and some dancing afterward. How does that sound?"

So blown away by what Mark had said a few minutes earlier, Lisa simply nodded. She'd always thought to end the date here, but instead she wanted more. She just had to remain in control. "Dinner and dancing sounds good."

Mark put the car in Drive and eased it slowly forward, a man in total control of the powerful machine. He gave her a wink. "Great. Then let our evening begin."

Chapter Seven

"Nice place," Mark said as he and Lisa entered her twelfth-floor suite. He surveyed the living area. TV. Sofa. Desk with laptop that was attached to the room's Internet connection. Small refrigerator and microwave. Two side chairs and a square table covered with piles of file folders. Exactly like every other hotel room except for its choice of colors.

"This suite is actually one of the better ones I've lived in," Lisa said, not noticing his frown as she closed the door behind him.

"It's not bad."

"No, it's not. One nice thing about a full-service hotel is that they offer it all—why else would all those people live at the Plaza in New York?"

She sounded nervous, as if somehow worried about his approval of her living arrangements. Mark winked at her. "Okay, even I have to agree that there is something to be said for not doing your own laundry or cleaning up after yourself."

"I should go get out of these clothes," she said. "The TV remote is on that table, so make yourself at home. There's some soda in the fridge."

As Lisa entered her bedroom and shut the door, Mark had to admit he was anticipating the evening. What he wasn't looking forward to was the phone call he knew he'd eventually have to make. Darn Joann. She just might be right. Lisa, who he'd craved heart and soul at the wedding reception, could loosen up and be a woman he could fall for.

She'd impressed him by not checking her phone once that day. Furthermore, he'd had a great time touring Kimmswick's antique and specialty shops with her. She'd even indulged when they'd gotten cookies and brownies at the Blue Owl's bakery. He'd noticed that Lisa was very particular about her food, especially the portions she consumed, not that she had anything to worry about.

Her body was perfect. Delectable. Definitely off-limits. He sighed once. He was an idiot.

Where had that "just friends" crap come from? He didn't want to be friends with Lisa. He wanted her. He wanted to kiss her, to press his body next to hers. He was intrigued by the grown-up Lisa Meyer. He wanted to dig below her surface, but she was leaving in November, so there was really was no point in investing a lot of emotional energy.

Unfortunately he wanted to do just that. She'd even apologized. His victory had been bittersweet, as it had proved how different she was from women like Alanna.

Money didn't mean much to Lisa, unless it was heading into the political coffers she loved so much. Lisa also didn't care that Mark drove a Porsche, and after her lecture the other night about his house being too big, he could tell she didn't care much about keeping up with the Joneses.

Sure, she moved at light speed and seemed morbidly overobsessed with her career, but despite those things, Lisa was a breath of fresh spring air. Invigorating. Challenging. Her mind was sharp. She cared little for his "stuff" and more about his brain. She didn't like admitting her flaws—who did?—but she'd agreed to work on their friendship. He had been amazed at that.

His twin sister knew him way too well. Although, because he was a guy, he refused to let himself contemplate exactly why he'd offered Lisa friendship without asking anything in return. Everyone knew being just friends couldn't be done—just watch the movie *When Harry Met Sally.*

Damn the bet. He didn't want to fall in love with a woman who wasn't going to be in his life past November. He certainly didn't want to have Lisa fall in love with him.

So why had he bet Joann that she would? Maybe to prove to his sister that he could resist the lure of a pretty woman. For Lisa was beautiful. He liked her eyes and he loved her smile. She'd been blessed with kissable lips—occasionally he thought he could still remember their taste. Mark shook his head.

He'd said back in January that this would be his year. He was turning thirty, so this year had to set the tone for the rest of the decade before he hit forty. But this year was becoming one of change, not of settling down as he'd hoped. No one had foreseen his father's heart attack or that he would have to sell the family company before becoming a private consultant as planned.

While he would end up with time to offer Lisa more than friendship, the fact that she lived in a hotel and was satisfied with her nomadic existence made his decision crystal clear. Mark wanted permanence from his Ms. Right, and Lisa couldn't be her.

LISA SCRUNCHED HER FACE in thought as she thumbed through her garments on the clothing rack. She glanced down at the slacks and sweater set she was wearing. They were okay for a movie but not for dinner and dancing.

Sudden stubbornness had Lisa jutting out her chin as Tori's words came back to haunt her. *Friends with benefits. You're the one in control.* Right now Mark held all the cards. Not that they were playing a game. Wrong choice of words. But in essence, at this point in her life, having control mattered. Having passion, if even for a short time, mattered. But he'd withdrawn that part of himself.

Lisa had to admit she'd always wanted him, despite what had happened at Joann's wedding. No man had ever gotten under her skin as Mark had. She wanted the night she'd been denied, especially now that she knew the truth. She wanted to be the one he cared about, if only for a few months.

Minus her infatuations, she went into every relationship, even with the wrong guy, hoping that it would last. Maybe it was time to try one that she knew wouldn't. She bit her lip. She was known to make the world's worst decisions because of her stubbornness and usually chose terrible men. But there was nothing wrong with Mark, and he had said she could ask him anything. As much as he had changed, he was still a man. And one thing never changed about men. They rarely said no.

He'd wanted her eight years ago, and she had a sneaking suspicion that despite his "friends" attitude, deep down he still wanted her. Maybe he was only subduing sex because he thought she only needed his connections. He'd said something similar today in the car.

She walked to the door and hesitated, her hand inches from the handle. Her awareness heightened and her nerves tightened. She curled her fingers around the cold metal and pushed downward. The door swung inward with the smooth motion of her arm.

She strode forward, out into the living area. Mark had propped his feet up on the coffee table, the TV tuned to some late-eighties movie rerun. He glanced up and frowned as he saw that she hadn't changed.

"What's wrong?" he said.

Lisa's chest heaved. "I need to clear the air."

"Okay," he said slowly, as if quite lost. "About what?"

"About this. Us. Our motivations."

"I thought we'd done that already," Mark said, frowning as he tried to comprehend the situation. "Today's simply about having fun. I've got some great places in mind for tonight."

She crossed her arms over her chest. They couldn't afford any miscommunication here. She inhaled a deep breath. "Before I can go anywhere with you, I have to know how tonight is going to end."

Mark shifted, planting his feet on the floor. He straightened but remained seated. The dark blue shirt set off his deep brown eyes, and his troubled gaze locked onto hers. Each of the words leaving his mouth was precise and deliberate. "Tonight ends like any other night. I've already told you to stop worrying. We're friends. I'm not going to seduce you."

Adrenaline unlike any she'd ever experienced before pulsed through Lisa's veins. "That's the problem," she said, somehow keeping the quaking out of her voice. "I really think you should."

Chapter Eight

Mark sat there in the hotel room with what he knew had to be a dumbfounded expression on his face. Had he just heard what he thought he'd heard? Had Lisa Meyer just propositioned him? Asked him to seduce her? The very Lisa Meyer who'd always insinuated how much she hated his guts? The very Lisa Meyer who had kissed him and then run away, thinking he'd left her? The woman who had only agreed to a date because he had connections?

At that moment all Mark could do was make sure his mouth was closed—the last thing he needed was to look like a shocked and drooling idiotic fool.

Score one for Lisa, he mused as his frantic mind raced though every possible answer—and its consequence—to her offer. With her bombshell, she'd definitely regained control of the current Mark and Lisa push-pull relationship that they seemed to be in. One step forward still equaled two steps back—or in this case maybe an exponential jump forward. Of course, he didn't understand why there was such a massive tug-of-war between them anyway, but that was irrelevant.

Right now what mattered was giving her an answer, especially if she was serious. And from her unsmiling, staid expression, he could tell she meant every loaded word.

"Why?" Mark finally asked, for responding to her question with another question seemed the best way to go. The technique had worked well with her in the past, after all.

"Why?" she parroted, her nostrils flaring slightly with annoyance. Since her nervousness hadn't subsided, Lisa made a fist behind her back. She relaxed all five fingers slowly in an attempt to defuse some of the stress consuming her. Why couldn't Mark have been like most men and simply said yes? How difficult was it to say, "Okay, I'll sleep with you" or, "No, I won't"? She'd been prepared for either of those answers, but once again he'd done the unpredictable.

For a moment Lisa wished she were more like Tori. Bold and brash, Tori would be prepared with what to say, what to do in this situation. Even Cecile knew how to take decisive, immediate action when the moment called for it.

Lisa was different. Out of the four Rose sisters, she was the thinker, the politician. She considered circumstances from all angles. She analyzed dreams. But now, she had to depend on her wit. Hopefully it wouldn't fail her here.

"You asked me why?" she repeated, buying herself a second or two. This time her voice squeaked out a bit higher, so even though *why* came out sounding incredulous, her tone also chastised. Not the effect she'd wanted, but she would work with it.

"Perhaps 'Why *not* sleep with me?' is the better question," Lisa continued. "We wanted to once, and now that we've cleared the air about why we didn't, I'm still very interested. As I'm leaving, our relationship would be only temporary. We'd get the sex thing out of the way once and for all."

Politicians were experts at finding common ground and using it to create understanding. She could do this. "I'm thinking that we should simply indulge all our whims. Not hold back. Not pretend to be friends when we both just want to jump each other's bones like we did that night. Especially now that we're sober."

"You'd like to jump my bones?" Mark stared at her. Lisa was certainly full of surprises today. He wasn't quite sure how to handle this change.

She crossed her arms again, clearly disgruntled. "You sure know how to make a girl feel low. I'm sure you've been propositioned before. Do you give all of them the third degree?"

"Most of them aren't my sister's best friend," Mark said. Her eyebrows drew close together, a sure sign that she was angry now. He began to open his mouth, but she cut him off.

"So much for you telling me I could ask you anything. Well, let me tell you that standing here isn't very comfortable. I mean, please. It's not as if we'll see each other much, if at all, after November, so what's the big deal? We didn't see each other for eight years. We're not going to develop silly emotions for each other and we wouldn't have that night, either. No strings. You go your way and I go mine without hysterics. Unless you're not interested in me."

Not interested in her? Shock must have registered on his face, for her eyes widened. "You are?" she said.

He nodded. "Of course, I'm very interested in you. I always have been."

And therein lay the problem, Mark realized. He wanted her long-term. Yet Lisa Meyer was one of those women you couldn't keep, the dream you couldn't reach. All she wanted was a fling.

Eight years ago, that might have been enough. Now it wasn't.

Mark winced. Parts of him were already hard with anticipation of how she'd feel writhing beneath him. That male devil—that joke of thinking with the little head—wanted her now, wanted relief that sliding into her would provide. The bedroom was just through the doorway behind her. Their lovemaking would be fireworks and could start quickly.

But unfortunately Mark Smith didn't play the field. He wanted happily ever after. He'd matured, and by god, Lisa was either going to kill him or make him a saint before she returned to Jefferson City in November. He took a moment to compose himself.

"I believe the current vogue term is 'friends with benefits,'" Mark finally said when he regained his voice.

"That's what Tori called it."

Figured she'd talked to Tori. Lisa's proposition made a little more sense now; it was something Tori would do.

"Thanks for clarifying," Mark said. "We do seem to misunderstand each other often, and I don't think either you or I want that right now."

"No, I don't want that. And, yes, that's what I meant."

Lisa's breath caught on the word *yes,* and Mark couldn't take his gaze off the long expanse of her creamy neck. For a second he wondered how she would taste when he placed his lips there. He'd only kissed her mouth that night. "I understand all but one thing. Why this sudden change?"

"Because I know the truth. Because you told me to tell you what I wanted," Lisa continued, sounding a little desperate. "That night I wanted you. I still do."

Mark wished he could ease her tension, but he couldn't. He knew Lisa, at least through Joann's stories. For Lisa to proposition him—sober—meant her action was out of character. She wasn't the fling type. She was the type a man married. A man like him.

He blinked. Had he really just thought that? He

focused on the task at hand. "So this is what you want? Sleeping with me, a man you consider a playboy? A man that you disliked at the fund-raising dinner four days ago and couldn't wait to get rid of?"

Lisa somehow managed a nonchalant shrug as she said, "I made some mistakes. Okay, a lot. And you know what they say. When a woman is overwhelmed with newly discovered feelings she doesn't understand, often the easiest thing to do is lash out and retreat. That's what I did."

"I've never heard of that, but the explanation makes sense," he said. "So what was the feeling you were fighting?"

"Lust," Lisa managed. "A remembrance of what we should have shared eight years ago. A need to get you out of my system."

"Oh. I see."

Damn, Lisa thought as Mark simply stared at her. Did he have to suddenly go speechless? He sat there on her couch, an immovable object who still had not told her yes or no.

As the pause got to the awkward stage, Lisa figured that since she'd started the conversation, she should be the one to end it. Obviously he wasn't going to give her a straight answer, at least not at this time. Maybe never.

"I'll go get my things and we can leave for dinner and dancing." There. That sounded good. Then she frowned. "That is, if you still want to go."

"I do," he said, the husky undertone obvious. "Very

much." His brown eyes darkened with something, and Lisa's body experienced a hopeful surge.

He laced his fingers together. "How about we let the night lead us as to what happens next? Now that nothing's off-limits we'll see where we end up," he suggested.

"Probably a good idea to let nature take its course," Lisa admitted, the tension draining from her now that the conversation was coming to a close. "I'm just a believer in talking things out and I think I needed to clear the air."

"I'm glad you did. I don't want misunderstandings like what happened before at the reception. And just so you know, I'm not a cold-blooded guy, Lisa. You've thrown me for a loop. I was sitting here thinking you hated me, and instead you tell me you want to jump my bones. Not that I'm not attracted to you. I've been attracted to you for years and I could drag you into that bedroom and show you exactly how much. But that wouldn't be wise. Not yet."

A thrill raced through her, but Lisa managed to keep her excitement hidden. "Right. Good." She coughed. "This has been rather surreal, so no matter what, let's promise each other no awkwardness at any time from here on out. If the night's going to get weird, I'd rather retreat now and just call it a day."

"No awkwardness," Mark promised, for he could at least try to make sure of that. Although how he'd deliver on that promise, he had no idea. Since Lisa had disappeared to get clothes, he dropped his head onto his hands. Eventually there would be uncomfortable moments. Whether they were when she realized during the morning after that she'd made a terrible mistake or when the awfulness of saying goodbye came in November, eventually harsh reality would creep in and one of them would succumb to its bad influence.

He hadn't lied when he told her she'd thrown him. Just what did a man do when the woman he wanted long-term proposed only a temporary fling? Mark heard Lisa return and stood. He was about to find out.

THERE'S AN OLD SAYING—or at least Lisa thought there was—that dancing was the way to get to know someone before you took him or her to bed.

Certainly dancing said a lot about a man. Whether he was suave. Silly. Flamboyant. Classy. Or simply sexy as all get-out when you held him close.

Having never danced with him before, Lisa was about to find out Mark's type.

Admittedly the evening had gone well. Once they'd left the hotel suite after their charged conversation, they'd defused the tension by choosing to see the latest dramatic offering from Hollywood. With nary a love scene in sight and enough room for thought after the movie's open-ended conclusion, Mark and Lisa's dinner conversation had centered on solving the moral dilemmas the film had raised.

They stayed in St. Louis's central corridor—the

movie at the theater off Old Olive Street in Creve Coeur and dinner at Dierdorf & Hart's in West Port Plaza. Lisa succumbed, avoided her usual chicken, and had one of their famous and irresistible steaks.

Afterward, the warm spring night had people outside on the plaza even at a late hour, and Lisa and Mark had walked side by side and done some people watching. Then they'd entered one of the plaza's clubs for some dancing.

The place was packed but not jammed so much that they had to elbow their way through. Mark located a circular table with two chairs a bit away from the dance floor, and he and Lisa took a seat. He ordered her a glass of white wine from the roving waitress.

"You've grown quiet," Mark said. The lights from the dance floor created patterns of color against his dark hair. After the movie, they'd stopped by his house and he'd changed into a casual navy sport coat, matching slacks and a white button-down.

When they'd reached his house, she'd opted to change into her black sequined jacket, slinky black cami top and dress pants.

His house had been huge, his dog the same. Despite its size, the place had reeked of home and hearth and personal touches. Although she hadn't explored more than the kitchen, half bath and hearth room, Mark's influence was evident in the antiques and the classic decor he'd chosen, something he told her he'd done all by himself. Lisa had few gifts in the decorating area, which made hotel living a palatable solution. Or so she tried to convince herself. Without even deliberately trying, Mark had tilted her world on its axis. He'd created more of a home than she could create, even if she had a home. By age thirty, he'd managed to have it all, while she was still working toward the goal.

But she didn't feel comfortable telling him this real reason she'd grown quiet, so she said, "I'm just soaking in the atmosphere. It's been a long time since I danced. Joann's wedding, I think."

"We never did dance together," Mark said.

"No."

"Joann said you loved to dance," Mark said. "You all were out partying every weekend."

"I was just dancing," she said. "I was always the group's designated driver."

"That doesn't sound like much fun," Mark observed.

She shrugged. "I'm in politics, so appearances count. My older sister got a DWI at twenty-two. Routine sobriety checkpoint. She had to pay higher insurance rates, attend special classes and do community service in addition to paying her fine. So I taught myself how to have fun and not drink to excess unless I wasn't driving, like at Joann's wedding."

"Sounds very wise," Mark commented.

"I never wanted to be caught in any uncompromising situation. And frankly being a designated driver provides a valid excuse out of participating in college stupidity."

"Sometimes you sound so cynical," Mark observed.

"No, just practical," Lisa said as she fingered her wine-glass. "I was born with the practicality curse. My siblings are all dynamic. They'd jump in a pool or lake without even testing the water or worrying about having a towel. Not me. I first spread out my towel. Then I slather on the sunscreen and do all sorts of preparations before I even get around to testing the water temperature."

Mark's fingers played with the condensation on his water glass, absently tracing a pattern on the side. "So you're an ease-into-it type of person."

She nodded. "Absolutely. Although, once I'm up to my waist, I'll dive under and get myself totally wet. At that point, you might as well. Half of you is already cold and you'll warm up once you're all wet."

"Well, you dived into the question you asked me earlier at your place." Mark lifted the glass and sipped his water. He'd forgone alcohol since he'd had a glass of wine with dinner.

"For some reason you've always made me jump in and lose control. Although, I do admit that I'd been thinking about what I was going to say ever since Tori and I talked. And you promised me no awkwardness."

"Then it's time to dance." He stood, reached out, and Lisa put her hand in his. Just like that, the chemistry roared back to life faster than embers lighting paper.

The feelings between them were powerful, more than she'd ever experienced. For Lisa, the sensation of his skin touching hers sent shivers down her back and curled her toes which were wedged in one-inch pumps.

She thought Mark's eyes darkened, but that might have been a trick of the ever-changing club lights. He led her toward the dance floor, her hand tight in his grip as he wove them through the crowd. They stepped onto the floor, finding space between some other couples and a bachelorette party.

She was not surprised to discover that Mark Smith could dance and that, like everything else, dancing was something he did well. Unlike guys who simply did the Weeble and wobbled from side to side or guys who did the Hamster by balling their fists up and holding them close to the chest, Mark had real moves.

"What?" He leaned forward and spoke into her ear during a transition in songs.

"I'm just impressed," she said, placing her hand around his ear. Other women were, too; quite a few had looked at him wistfully.

Mark cupped his hand around her ear and his breath tickled. "We did a lot of dancing in the frat house basement. One of the guys grew up dancing and he taught us a bunch of moves."

"He was at an engineering school?" The University of Missouri at Rolla wasn't necessarily the place one chose for an artsy education.

"His parents told him he had to get a degree. The moment he graduated, he hightailed it to Hollywood. I've heard he's been in a few music videos." Mark grinned. "You're not too bad yourself."

"Thanks." They danced a few more numbers, each

song getting progressively sexier and becoming a form of foreplay. She wove her legs between his; he ran his fingertips down the insides of her arms. When a slow song arrived, Mark held his hands out and drew her close.

That she'd had an effect on him was obvious. It was there in the way he held her, his hand resting on the small of her back. Five fingers spread wide lightly caressed her skin through the jacket and cami top. She rested her head against his chest, breathing in the essence uniquely his.

He drew her tighter and she intertwined her limbs with his, following his lead. One step, then another. Their hands fused. The music faded into the background and she lost herself in the moment. As they danced, neither could deny what existed between them. He was her man, at least until November.

The song ended, replaced by a faster number that had some couples on the dance floor blinking and going their separate ways. Some simply danced on. Mark leaned forward so she could hear him. "Let's take a break," he suggested.

Lisa followed him off the dance floor. This time her hands remained by her sides as she followed him through the crowd. Suddenly she almost crashed into his backside as he stopped abruptly. Stepping to his left, Lisa craned her neck to see what—or rather who—had him pausing. A pretty brunette, much younger than Mark or Lisa, had moved off her bar stool into his path.

The conversation didn't last long before Mark was ushering Lisa past the table without introduction.

"Who was that?" Lisa asked when they returned to their seats.

"A friend," Mark said simply, reaching for his water and draining the remnants in a long swallow.

"Mark," Lisa said, taking a sip of wine. She set the glass aside and, when the waitress stopped by, ordered two more waters. "We said no awkwardness. And after that long conversation we once had about how men and women can't be friends, do you really think I'm going to believe that?"

"And your prying will make you feel better?" Mark asked.

"One thing the wedding reception proved is that if we want this to work, we have to be honest. An ex?" Lisa guessed.

He gave a curt nod. "Alanna. The one that I was dating right before you."

"We're not dating," Lisa responded immediately, before saying, "Oh. Sorry. I guess we are dating." She forced herself not to swivel around and turn to look at the girl.

"We never slept together, so stop pretending that you don't want to take a good look at her."

Lisa blushed. "That's not what I was—"

"Yes, it was," Mark said simply. The waitress returned with their water and he drank half the glass. "Quite simply, she and I didn't fit. We had fun in the beginning, but overall we weren't really compatible to go to the next level. And I don't go for casual sex just to have sex."

"Did seeing her make you uncomfortable?" Lisa asked.

Mark shook his head, causing his hair to fall across his forehead. He brushed it back. "No, and she told me she's already dating someone else. That was a very brief how-are-you-no-hard-feelings-sorry-I-was-silly conversation."

"Ah." Lisa drank her own water. She sensed that this was something important, somehow an insight into a side of Mark she hadn't been privy to before. "So it was always pretty low-key."

He wasn't looking at her but rather watching two lovebirds a few tables over. "Despite Joann's overzealous exaggerations, I'm not one to get deeply involved unless I think it might have potential to go the distance."

But if so, why had he agreed to let nature take its course where Lisa was concerned, especially when he knew they would never become serious? She swallowed. "So perhaps I shouldn't have made my offer tonight," Lisa said.

He swung around to face her then, his expression more intense than Lisa had ever seen. "No. I told you that you could ask me anything and I meant it. Just because you took me by surprise—"

"But you don't go for casual," Lisa interrupted. "If I'd known…"

"No. Don't second-guess yourself. With you, nothing is casual. It never has been." Mark stood abruptly and reached for her hand. "Let's go. Let's discuss this somewhere more private."

Lisa didn't quite know what to think. Her career had always taken all of her time, which was probably why she'd never dated the right men. She hadn't had time to search for them, which meant she had little experience reading situations like this. "Is it a bad thing we're leaving?"

"It might be if we don't leave now," Mark said.

She heard the concentration in his voice and knew he wasn't angry. But he'd reached his breaking point. So had she. "I'm ready," she told him, the words loaded with meaning.

They left the club and walked toward the car. The temperature had dropped and Mark put his arm around her. They'd parked in the covered garage, and Mark unlocked the doors and helped Lisa inside.

Suddenly a question crept into her head that she knew she had to ask. "So did I make things worse by not being a challenge?" she said as he climbed in and shut his door. The last thing she wanted was for him to be bored or smothered, as she often had been in the past. He angled his body toward her.

"You are the biggest challenge I've ever faced." He moved closer and reached forward so that he could tuck a blond strand behind her ear. His fingertips lingered at the end of her jawbone, his touch tender. "I have no idea what to do with you."

"I'm sorry," she said.

The moment softened as he traced her jaw and then pressed his forefinger against her lips. "Don't ever be sorry for that."

"Why not?" she asked as his face inched closer to hers. He cupped her chin and tilted her head slightly. Lisa's breath caught in her throat. Never had a moment been so tender yet so passionate.

"You have nothing to be sorry for," Mark said. "Nothing."

He studied her, those beautiful brown eyes moving back and forth as if committing her face to memory. "And I'm great at improvising," he said. And with that, he leaned over and finally kissed her.

HE SHOULDN'T BE KISSING her—not here. Not like this. Those were his first coherent thoughts when time began moving again. Kissing Lisa Meyer was a mind-numbing drug. Addicting. His lips couldn't break free from hers no matter how wrong—or right—it was.

During the slow dance with Lisa, Mark had realized something, acknowledged the truth. Holding Lisa had been heaven. He wanted her, but not for one night or a temporary fling. He wanted forever. Seeing Alanna had only served to confirm how different the two women were and how Lisa was the perfect woman for him. She fit him as if preordained to do so, as if all the roads he'd taken had led to her.

She was his sister's friend, and his sister had bet him

one hundred dollars that he'd fall in love. He had Joann's approval; his sister knew him too well.

The money he'd lose was irrelevant. It was his heart he now had to protect. For as much as Lisa was his perfect mate, the realist in Mark knew she was also the totally wrong woman for him. She would never be home and hearth. She'd always be a workaholic devoted to her career. At Joann's wedding reception, Mark hadn't been concerned about tomorrow. Now that he cared, Lisa didn't want anything except a casual relationship and a nonawkward goodbye in November. The irony irked.

But kissing her like this, with his tongue tickling hers, made him realize something else. Any type of affair with Lisa would be like a forest fire. He'd burn for her with white-hot passion as long as the conditions were right. But fires eventually faded, leaving nothing but devastation in their wake. No matter how good he could make the sex between them, no matter how much he changed and proved himself worthy, come November she'd still be moving on, leaving him behind.

If she'd been any other woman, maybe he could readjust his plans to allow for something hot and temporary. But Lisa was more than his sister's best friend. She was the woman to whom he'd lost his heart. Mark could end his search for happiness right here, right now. He'd rediscovered his Ms. Right, as his drunken stupid self had somehow known eight years ago.

Even that kiss eight years ago wasn't like this one.

Oh, sure, he'd gotten rock-hard as he was now. His body strained against his slacks, craving Lisa and her touch. Desperate recklessness consumed him and he deepened the kiss. He could taste promise. He could taste the future. The trouble was that they were both smoke and mirrors. Illusions. Tricks designed to fool a man into thinking he was happy.

If Mark were honest with himself, he'd label this kiss for exactly what it was—some lust unlike any other he'd experienced before.

But to call the kiss that would cheapen Lisa, and the man Mark had grown to become couldn't allow that. He also couldn't allow this to continue. He couldn't let this moment lead to anything further, no matter how much he desired to slide his hand underneath her cami top and find the smooth flesh that eagerly awaited his touch.

She scraped her teeth along his tongue and he lost control, moving both hands behind her head so that he could draw her closer. He ravaged her mouth, plundering her sweetness like a bee seeking nectar. He could kiss her forever. At this moment, that was all he wanted.

He heard laughing voices approaching in the distance and used the distraction as an opportunity to grasp his last shred of sanity and lift his mouth from hers. Lisa's eyes were closed, and he took a moment to study her before he turned away. He couldn't risk gazing into her eyes or he'd come undone. She already had one hand on his thigh.

"Strap in," he told her gruffly as the voices neared.

Mark started the car and secured his seat belt. Lisa's hand lifted off his leg and she worked to fasten her belt.

His leg registered the removal of her hand's heat, and he shivered as if his whole body had chilled. She had too much of an effect on him. He reached for the gearshift and put the car into Reverse. Taking a quick glance behind him, he eased the car out of the parking space and soon they were headed south on Highway 270.

"You like highway driving, don't you?" Lisa said to make idle conversation as they passed the Olive Street exit.

"Yeah," Mark said, glad for something about which to make small talk. He'd never experienced a situation like this and he knew what he had to do. "Page east to the Innerbelt has too many stoplights for my taste," he told her.

"Understandable. This way is probably faster anyway."

Probably too fast, Mark thought as within five minutes they'd turned east onto Highway 40. Clayton and her hotel were just minutes away. Lisa's hands remained clenched in her lap, and silence had fallen in the car, the only sound the song playing on the pop radio station.

He'd promised her no awkwardness, yet here it was. He reached over with his right hand and grasped her left. He pulled her fingers apart and laced his in between. As he did, some of the tension ebbed from her. "I do want you," he said bluntly as they went under the Spoede overpass.

"That makes me breathe easier," Lisa said. She'd turned her face so that she was staring out the passenger window. "This whole night has had way too much of a surreal tint to it. Even though I know you aren't going to, for some reason I'm sitting over here waiting for you to simply leave and dump me."

Mark winced. "Ouch. That's certainly not going to make what I have to say easy. This is not a rejection, so please don't take my words the wrong way. But I'm not going to come in or stay with you tonight."

He gripped her hand tightly as she tried to withdraw and pull away. "After that wonderful kiss between us, there's nothing I want more than to follow you upstairs to your room and make love to you all night."

They were at McKnight, meaning their exit was less than a mile away. She still hadn't turned so that he could see her face. "Then why are you saying no?" she asked quietly.

He took a breath. "Because I've waited eight years and I know that tomorrow will be awkward and I promised it wouldn't."

"I don't understand."

"Remember how I told you about the sale of the company and what I'd do afterward?"

"Yes," she said.

"My father made his choice late last night, and because of that I'm leaving town Monday to finish the sale. I've been meaning to find the perfect time all day to tell you that I'll be gone for at least a week, maybe two. We've already had one night that ended badly, and I don't want this to be the same. I don't wish to make love to you all night, get up in the morning and go. Besides, while I'm gone, you can use the time to consider if you really want this. Because when I make love to you, I can tell you one thing—it's not going to be casual and it's not going to be just once."

"Not casual?" she echoed. "More than once?"

Mark loosened his grip on her hand now that she'd relaxed somewhat and turned to face him. "Not casual," Mark confirmed. "We won't be getting sex out of the way. Our relationship will become physical and maybe something more. Once I'm inside you, I doubt I'm going to want to leave. I doubt once will ever be enough."

The song playing on the radio was appropriately belting out a line about "I'm just being honest." Mark hit the button and changed the radio station as he exited and then pulled into the Galleria parking lot. The engine still running, he put the car in park and turned her so that he could fully see her face.

"Lisa." He reached forward and gently caressed her cheeks with the backs of his fingertips. "Look at me."

She did and he groaned. He'd pulled into the darkened mall parking lot because he didn't want the valets hovering when he kissed her goodbye. But that might have been safer. For the night's shadows were flickering across her beautiful countenance, making her even more of a siren he couldn't resist.

He lowered his mouth to hers. Again she tasted divine. He heard her whimper and hoped security wouldn't pick this moment to do a parking-lot sweep. If he ached—and oh, how he did—he knew she must also. He could at least give her some much-needed release. But first…

"You and I will talk when I get back," Mark said. "While I'm gone, ask yourself if making love to me is what you really want. Because when I make love with you, you will surrender part of yourself."

"I want—" she began.

"And I want you," Mark said before he kissed the rest of her words away. "And I want to touch you."

He slid his hand between her legs, which parted automatically, and moved it under her waistband and into her panties. Keeping some semblance of time was difficult, but they couldn't stay parked here.

He longed to be where his hand was when she gasped. He moved his fingers over her, rubbing in a circular motion and making her slick. He kissed her throughout, catching her cries of release. He resisted his own desire to enter her; focusing only on her pleasure and on bringing her to climax before he took her back to her hotel.

Her body quivered and shook, and he held her tightly afterward as her body returned to normal.

"I…" she said, her breath ragged from the release that had consumed her body.

"Shh," Mark said. He kissed her again, his lips lingering before he drew away. "You aren't thinking clearly right now."

"I can't think of anything," Lisa said as Mark put the car in Drive and headed north toward Clayton. "You've ruined me."

"I haven't even begun to do that. What just happened is nothing compared to what I'll do to you if you decide I'm really what you want." Mark made a right turn and a few minutes later pulled into the hotel drive. "I'll call you tomorrow."

"Okay." Lisa remained a bit dazed, but the valet was already opening her door and reaching for her hand. She stepped out and then, as if remembering something she'd forgotten, leaned back to glance at him one last time. "Where are you going?"

"Boston. I'm on the noon flight. Talk to you tomorrow…well, later today."

"Okay. I'll talk to you then," Lisa said. The valet closed the door, and Mark waited until she was through the revolving glass doors before driving away.

Chapter Nine

The ringing of the hotel phone woke up Lisa. She rubbed the sleep from her eyes and glanced at the clock. Ten o'clock. She'd overslept.

The curtains were closed, and she fumbled in the darkened room until she found the phone receiver and lifted it to her ear. "Hello?"

"Good morning," a ticked-off voice said.

Lisa grimaced. Bradley. She'd forgotten to call him yesterday afternoon. "Hi," she managed.

"Where have you been?" he asked. "I've been trying to reach you. You've got Herb all worried that something bad has happened to you. Obviously I can reassure him that you're fine now that I've talked to you."

"My BlackBerry battery is dead," Lisa lied, shifting to a seated position as she shook off the last vestiges of sleep and became fully awake. She clicked on the bedside lamp. The real truth was that she'd never turned her phone's ringer back on. In fact, she'd never removed the device from the bottom of her purse, as was her habit.

"It's charging." Or it would be in a few minutes.

"And you never thought to check your voice mail from your hotel phone? I also sent you an e-mail. You have a laptop. Did that die, too?" Bradley chastised from Kansas City.

"No, it didn't. I was out with friends until late," Lisa said. The sheet fell to her waist, revealing the boring flannel sleepwear she'd changed into upon entering her hotel room last night. With Mark deciding not to stay, wearing something sexy had been pointless. Her body had been satisfied, so she'd gone for practical. As always.

"So you went out partying and were fine. Lisa, you know how Herb is. You told us you were going to call. He worried and you were on the town."

Lisa winced. She'd been irresponsible. No matter how much she'd like to throttle Bradley, the fact remained that she'd let herself become swept up in the whirlwind that was Mark Smith. She hadn't remembered to check her phone—or that she even had a phone—until now. With the ringer off, the device had been out of sight and out of mind.

She chastised herself for her stupidity. Just because she'd had a fun night and slept soundly because of a great orgasm didn't mean she could forsake her duties. Yesterday, being with Mark had made her totally forget everything.

"Are you just getting up?" Bradley asked suddenly.

"As a matter of fact, yes, because for once I had nothing on my agenda that had to be done before noon," Lisa retorted. "Don't you dare even begin to question my dedication to the campaign. I had two glasses of wine the entire night. That cannot be mistaken for partying. Tell Herb I'll call him in an hour."

There was silence for a brief moment, and Lisa loosened her grip on the receiver. She'd been clutching it so tightly her knuckles had whitened.

"Okay, one hour," Bradley said after a moment of ominous silence. "Be sure to catch up on your messages and e-mail so you can report if anything's new. Herb is leaving at eleven-fifteen for a Daughters of the American Revolution lunch."

"I'll call at eleven," Lisa said and, without adding goodbye, hung up.

Damn. Damn. Damn. She flew out of bed and grabbed the BlackBerry from her purse to charge it. She opened up her laptop and immediately her computer sprang to life. She knew she'd be even angrier with herself as soon as she listened to her voice mail, so she took a moment to tromp over to her bathroom, use the facilities and brush her teeth. She'd shower after her phone call to Herb, after she'd sorted through the moderate disaster she was certain awaited her after forsaking her duties.

What had she been thinking? Okay, she hadn't been thinking. Yesterday she'd let Mark become a huge distraction. Just being with him had made her forget all that she held important and dear. Political novices made the mistake of thinking that their jobs had start and end times. Lisa knew better.

She clicked on her e-mail icon and the display told her she had fifty-nine messages. Yuck. Half of those would be something legitimate and thus needed to be addressed immediately.

As the e-mail downloaded, she bypassed the "missed calls" display on her phone, instead holding down the number one key so that she could retrieve her voice mail. She had fourteen messages. Lisa winced and grabbed a sheet of hotel stationery to jot names, numbers and call topics as the recordings began.

Only two of the calls were from her friends. One was from Tori wondering if they were still doing wine and movies Sunday night. Highly doubtful at this moment, Lisa thought. Visiting with Tori depended on how the afternoon went and how much work Lisa had to get done.

The other call was from Cecile; she announced that she had great news and that Lisa needed to call her back at her first opportunity. The rest of the calls were all campaign-related, which Lisa should have dealt with yesterday. But she'd switched her phone to silent.

She was an idiot. Like an emergency-response worker, her job was to be there when the 911 calls occurred. Instead she'd been seeing a movie, having dinner, dancing and getting fondled like a teenager in a car.

Got to love her dumb ideas. All last night had proved was that Mark Smith had great fingers and the ability to make her forget her priorities and throw her practicality to the wind. Instead of controlling the evening, she'd let him sweep her away. She'd wanted temporary escape and zing, and he'd provided the perfect opportunity and outlet. But life wasn't like that. You couldn't just turn and walk away from your responsibilities.

Her career—being someone who mattered in the political arena—was Lisa's dream. November was around the corner. She couldn't let an affair knock her off the path she'd set for herself. She couldn't let temporary pleasure sway her from her course.

Maybe Cecile and Tori could handle friends-with-benefits relationships. As for Lisa, she'd been wildly out of control. Spending time with Mark wasn't getting him out of her system. If anything, he was digging further beneath her skin. She was acting out of character. He was a flame she couldn't put out.

Thank goodness *he*'d had the sanity to stop. If Mark had been here when Bradley had called, it would have been indeed an awkward moment.

Lisa closed her eyes and, for a second, let herself remember. Then she opened her eyes and focused on the mound of work she had ahead of her. Mark had told her to ask herself if making love to him was what she really wanted. He'd warned her that when he made love to her, she'd surrender a part of herself. Lisa bit her lip. She couldn't take that risk.

"I LOVE EVERYTHING YOU'VE done," Lisa said. A little more than two weeks after that fateful night of dinner and dancing with Mark, she was sitting with his mother, making final arrangements for Herb's fund-raising dinner that upcoming Friday night. "This is all so fantastic. I can't tell you how much Herb and Bunny appreciate this."

"Oh, we're happy to do it," Mary Beth said modestly. "I love hosting parties, especially ones where I can pull out all the stops. Herb's always been such a great friend. Doing this has allowed us to reconnect with him and Bunny."

Mary Beth frowned slightly. "Just between us girls, as you get older, you start to drift apart from your friends. Once you saw them all the time. Then you have children and careers, and the next thing you know five years have gone by with only some of those silly forwarded chain e-mails and printed Christmas letters as your only real connection."

"I already understand that," Lisa said. "I don't see Joann like I used to. And Cecile called me two weeks ago telling me she had news, and I still haven't caught up with her. Her sister is getting married soon, but none of us know the sister well enough to be invited. With the campaign in full gear, I wouldn't have had time to go to Chicago anyway."

"Chicago's Cecile's hometown?"

"Yes. She's a die-hard sports fan of any Chicago

team," Lisa said. "You should have seen her after the White Sox won the World Series in 2005."

"You sound like you miss her."

"I miss all my friends. Cecile did live with me in Columbia for a few months following college graduation, but for the past few years she's been in New York working on one of the early-morning news and talk shows. I'm not sure exactly what she does. She claims it's a stepping stone."

"That's great. I'm glad she's doing well. I always liked Cecile. Actually, I liked all of you girls. You were such great friends to Joann."

"Thank you," Lisa said. "We were a tight group, and even though we're miles apart, we still are. Despite the distance, I know I can count on any of them to be there in a heartbeat if I needed them."

"Those are your forever friends," Mary Beth said. "The ones you can count on no matter what. You four will always have a bond. Now you just need some events to bring you together. A wedding maybe."

"We're all too committed to our careers," Lisa said.

"You never know," Mary Beth said sagely. "But speaking of your career, I'm very impressed by how well you have Herb's campaign running. He'll be a great governor."

They glanced up as Mary Beth's housekeeper entered the room. "I've set up a light lunch in the four-season room," she said.

"Thank you. Let's take a break, shall we?" Mary Beth

led Lisa to a glass room addition just off the great room. The May day was warm and some of the indoor plants had bloomed. The Smith house was located on five acres in the city of Town & Country.

Lunch had been set on a white wicker dining table. Blue-checkered cloth napkins, white china with a blue border and matching coffee cups completed the table arrangement. Martha Stewart would have been proud of Mary Beth's presentation and that she'd influenced her son. Having been in his house, if only to briefly change for dinner and dancing, Lisa had been impressed with Mark's decor. He'd made his four thousand square feet into a warm and welcoming home. She took a seat, which gave her a great view of the inground pool that was already open and ready for use.

"We always open the pool no later than Mother's Day. It's heated, and Bud loves to swim, so we open it early and close it late. The doctor said swimming is good for Bud's heart."

"He's doing better?" Lisa asked.

"Much. A full recovery so long as he slows down and eats properly."

"That's good news," Lisa said. "And your pool is very pretty."

She suddenly shifted. Now that the focus was off the campaign, she found herself in uncharted territory. She'd never been uncomfortable with Joann's parents, but that had been before the "thing" with Mark.

"I like your snow globe," Lisa said, making conversation as the housekeeper rolled lunch out on a wicker cart.

"Thanks. I collect them and this is my newest addition." Mary Beth reached forward and picked up the eight-inch-high globe. "Mark express couriered it from Boston for Mother's Day." She passed it over so that Lisa could get a better look. "That's the statehouse that sits on Beacon Hill."

Mother's Day had been yesterday, and Lisa had managed to spend time with her parents. Her brother Andy and his brood had been there, as well, so the house had been full.

"How's the sale going?" Lisa asked casually as she studied the ornate globe. Since that morning after, she'd been sending his calls to voice mail and hadn't responded except for sending him one or two quick text messages saying that she'd been extremely busy.

"Fine. Mark's wrapping things up and hopes to return home tomorrow or Wednesday," Mary Beth said. "He'll definitely be back for the party. Why, haven't you talked with him? He mentioned he called you."

"We've been playing phone tag," Lisa replied. "Herb has had at least one event per day scheduled in the eastern part of the state since his return. I've been on the go nonstop. By the time I'd be able to call Mark, it would be one in the morning my time." That much wasn't a lie.

"Don't work yourself to death, dear. I know how all you girls are, just like Joann. She always had to have fifty things going at once. Now she's got those boys to run her ragged."

"True," Lisa said.

"You know, Joann and I were talking about you this week. I know it's probably not my place to meddle in my son's life, but both Joann and I still think you're the right woman for Mark."

"I, uh…" Lisa reminded herself to kill Joann later.

Mary Beth pretended not to notice her stammer. "Mark's been pretty wrapped up in the sale of the company. The job was to be Bud's, but his doctor forbid him to take on more stress after his heart attack. This dinner and Herb's campaign have been a good distraction for my son. You've been an even better diversion. You challenge him. It's always best to keep a man on his toes."

Lisa didn't know quite how to respond to that so she said, "Could I be rude and ask why you're selling the family company? Mark's turning thirty. He's in charge now and has years ahead of him."

"Oh, I don't mind, dear. Mark's very open. You can ask him anything. The answer is that at this point, with Bud wanting to retire, the best decision was to sell. Mark's a great boss, but the company must grow to stay competitive, and really, he's just not that interested being a slave to his job and investing the hours it's going to take."

Like her. Lisa sipped on her iced tea, contemplating how different she and Mark were. Probably best that she hadn't called him back. Her idea to sleep with him to get him out of her system was stupid. The events in the parking lot had added only more fuel to the fire.

Mary Beth must have noticed her silence, for she said, "So, Lisa, do you remember the time when you and Joann…"

As the two women ate lunch, their conversation shifted to college reminiscences and then back to Herb's dinner party. Later, after a few more hours of work, they'd accomplished all they could for the day.

"Now, you will be there, won't you?" Mary Beth asked.

"Yes, but I'll stay in the background," Lisa said. "Andrea and I will be in the kitchen while everyone eats."

"Oh, no. That won't do," Mary Beth said as she held the front door open. "I can't have Mark eating alone when everyone else is part of a couple. I've penciled you in as his date. Do I need to find one for Andrea?"

"No. Andrea needs to remain in the background. She'll have way too much to do."

"But you don't. You have to eat with Mark. I won't take no for an answer."

Lisa plastered a smile on her face. This had to be the work of Joann the matchmaker. Once again Lisa would be Mark's date to Herb's event. "Okay."

"Good," Mary Beth said, satisfied. "I'll be in touch this week and definitely see you Friday. Don't worry, Lisa, everything's going to work out fine."

"So HOW ARE YOU AND Lisa doing?" Joann asked.

"We aren't doing anything," Mark said. He held his phone to his ear. He was at Boston's Logan Airport waiting to board his flight and had taken one last call. His sister had zeroed in on Lisa within seconds of saying hello.

"Did the sale go through?" Joann asked.

"Everything's in the hands of the lawyers, who will pore over the papers endlessly for a few weeks. But yes, it's done and I'm very relieved. We should be able to make an official announcement soon."

"The fund-raising dinner is tonight," Joann said. "Mom said Lisa will be there and that she's your date."

Back to Lisa. Joann wasn't even trying to be subtle. "I heard that, too," Mark said simply.

"So what is going on between you two?" Joann demanded. "Have I won the bet yet?"

"You haven't won anything. We're just friends." *With benefits,* Mark didn't add. He checked his frustration. He'd given up trying to reach Lisa.

From her actions, he could easily tell that she'd changed her mind. He'd figured she would. An affair wasn't something you could control. Affairs took on lives of their own. She couldn't stand being out of control. And she had been. Having gotten only two quick text messages saying she was too busy to talk, Mark assumed she was currently ignoring him, if only to put herself in the driver's seat.

"Did you ever think that you might have to chase her?" Joann asked.

"What? Chase who?" Mark had been glancing at the monitor in the corner. Tuned to ESPN, the commentators were currently analyzing the Boston Red Sox's chances this season, including how the team would fare in the game that night.

"Chase Lisa," Joann said. "You might need to chase her," she repeated, just in case the line had been crackly.

"Why would I want to do that?" Mark asked.

He heard Joann's sigh of exasperation. "Because you like her? Because she's fun? Because she's probably the woman you've been looking for all your life?"

"She's too married to her career," Mark said. "She has to be in charge constantly and…"

"Aha!"

"Aha what?" The commentators were showing a clip from one of the World Series games against the Cardinals in 2004. It didn't matter which game, the Cardinals, the best team statistically in baseball that year, had lost to the Red Sox in four straight, ending what Boston considered its curse.

"Stop watching TV," Joann commanded. "And aha, you didn't deny that you like her. You gave an excuse as to why a relationship isn't possible. Not an excuse as to why you don't want the relationship."

"You know," Mark said with a hint of irritation, "I'm really going to stop calling you or answering your calls."

"No, you won't," Joann said matter-of-factly. "And I'm right. You've fallen for her."

"How can I fall for someone I've only really known for about a week or two?"

"You just can," Joann said. "Heck, you had a thing for her in college. She's the one you always asked me about. Not Cecile. Not Tori. Those two were afterthoughts. It was Lisa who interested you."

"Okay," he said slowly, buying time.

"Now that both of you are older and wiser, maybe it's time to act like an adult. The clock's ticking."

"Mom's already planning our birthday bash next month," Mark said. "Don't remind me."

"Sorry, but that's somewhere in the small print declaring me your twin. Chase Lisa. Make her settle down."

"Wait a minute." Mark paused. "Settle down? That'd be like trying to catch the wind. Lisa doesn't even have a permanent address."

"Irrelevant. What I mean is that she won't settle down with just any man. He has to be Mr. Right."

"That's not me," Mark protested. An announcement came that boarding was going to be delayed by twenty minutes. Irritated, he said, "She just wants me for sex."

"What?" Joann gasped. "Did you just say what I think you did?"

Mark rolled his eyes. He probably shouldn't have said anything, but now that he'd opened his mouth… "You heard me correctly." He apprised his sister of the whole situation and finished by saying, "Don't you dare say anything to her."

"I won't," Joann promised. "But, Mark, that doesn't sound anything like her. That sounds like Tori or Cecile talking."

"It's Tori, which is why I haven't taken her up on it," he added grumpily. "I don't want casual and I want her to be sure. But she's not answering my calls."

"Ouch. Maybe I should head up there for the weekend. Bring the brat pack for Mom to play with. It's only noon and it's a four-hour drive."

"Mom would not appreciate small children at her elegant affair for Herb and Bunny. She's got a tent set up in the yard and real china."

"True. I'll come alone. Kyle can watch the kids."

"Not necessary," Mark said quickly. "Everyone is going to be coupled up. Besides, I can handle this on my own."

"How?" Joann asked.

"I don't know," Mark said. "But I'm working on it."

"LISA!" THE MOMENT LISA opened the door, an unexpected female voice greeted her and she was immediately enveloped in a huge hug.

"Cecile! Oh, my God! What are you doing in St. Louis? How did you get up to my room?"

"I have a way with front desk guys," Cecile said.

She disengaged from the hug and stepped into Lisa's hotel suite. A stunning five-foot-ten-inch redhead with green eyes, Cecile could easily be the one in front of the camera instead of behind one.

"This is such a great surprise. So the front desk guys gave you my room number?"

Cecile winked. "Men just can't resist telling me information that I'm not supposed to know. That's why I work in television. Anyway, I only have about an hour before I have to catch a cab back to the airport and be on my way home. For some reason, they just don't have direct flights to New York from Hannibal, and so I decided to use my layover to come see you."

"What were you doing in Hannibal?"

"We were filming an upcoming segment on famous small towns—which you would have known had you ever called me—and what town in Missouri is more famous than the birthplace of both Mark Twain and the Unsinkable Molly Brown?"

"I did call you," Lisa pointed out.

"Yeah, I'm just giving you grief," Cecile said with a grin. "You wouldn't have gotten ahold of me anyway. We wrapped this morning with a sunrise shot over the river and here I am. I didn't know if I'd catch you, but even a drive through St. Louis in the back of a cab is far better than sitting in an airport club with my crew for four straight hours. You know me—I can only read book after book for so long."

Lisa glanced at the clock. It was a little after three. The fund-raising dinner began at six-thirty and she planned to leave the hotel at five. Amazingly she was ahead of schedule, and Cecile's sudden appearance wouldn't put a dent in her timing. Fate was being kind.

"I'm really glad you're here," Lisa said. Seeing Cecile proved how much she'd missed her friend. How long had it been since they'd actually seen each other face-to-face? Mary Beth had been correct about friends drifting apart. No one planned it; life just got in the way. But best friends for life could just pick up right where they left off. "So aside from being in Hannibal, what's new? You said you had news."

"This was my last segment. I'm leaving New York."

"You're quitting?" Lisa did a double take, but Cecile was smiling.

"Yep. I chose not to renew my contract, which expires at the end of June. I turned in my notice and they let me escape early. I'm heading home for my sister's wedding in June and I'm staying. As of July third, I'm one of the new segment producers for the Allegra Montana Show."

Lisa's mouth dropped open. "Fantastic! Congrats. She's practically the next Oprah!"

Cecile nodded, her excitement evident. "Exactly. I was aiming to be the show runner, which is the person who oversees every show and its producer, but a few months ago Allegra hired someone with a little more experience. That's okay, though. I'm getting a fantastic salary increase and it's a super opportunity. I'll be in charge of an entire episode start to finish, two to three times a week. I haven't met the new show runner yet. His name's Morgan, but I'm not sure if that's first or last. I do remember that Allegra told me he used to be with one of the competing talk shows."

Lisa reached into the refrigerator and removed two bottled waters. She handed one to Cecile and took a seat on the sofa. "Tell me more about the new job."

"Oh, I can't wait to get started. I took two weeks off in between so I could pacify my mother—she's been a beast now that the wedding is getting close."

Lisa uncapped her water and took a drink. While both mothers were wealthy, Joann's mother was subdued. A former actress, Cecile's mom had a flair for the dramatic. "I do remember her as being pretty intense."

"That's putting it mildly. This wedding is a family drama all by itself. Almost worthy of being a tawdry talk-show episode. Speaking of, Allegra's not interested in having her talk show be anything like 'my mother stole my boyfriend.' I'm looking forward to working with her."

"It sounds like a fascinating opportunity."

Cecile took a sip of water. "I'm really excited to be producing quality segments that make a difference. I'll be back in Chicago for the first time in forever. I love New York, but I'm ready to go home. Besides, Oprah and a few other talk shows are there. I also get to root for my beloved teams. I just couldn't ever cheer for the Yankees or Mets."

"I like the Midwest," Lisa said. "There's something about it that's just, well, home."

They sat and contemplated that a second before Cecile said, "So Tori and Joann both tell me you're seeing Mark Smith."

Here we go, thought Lisa. "I'm not seeing him."

"Using him for sex?" Cecile prodded with a sly grin.

Lisa sighed. No secrets had ever existed between the four friends. Tell one and assume they all knew. "So Tori told you that?"

"Well, yeah. That's what friends are for, sweetie. We gossip about you so that you know someone has your back at all times. Did you proposition him yet?"

"I…" Lisa began.

Cecile frowned. Even though years might have passed, she could still read her old roommate. "You did and it didn't go well?"

"That's not it," Lisa said, a blush spreading. "He's infuriating and makes me forget myself." She sipped her water and found her resolve. "I have to keep my priorities straight. Work comes first. I don't have time to have a fling with him."

Cecile stared, her green eyes unblinking. "Wait a second. How can you not have time for a big hunky guy like that? Wasn't the sex good?"

Lisa blushed again. "We haven't had sex."

"But you've done something."

"And it was good. And now we're at TMI." *TMI* meant *too much information*.

"Okay, fine," Cecile conceded. "But if he's interested in you, you should go for it. I used to flirt with him all the time, but he was always the perfect gentleman. He wasn't interested in me, which was a bummer as he's very attractive. But you…he's just your type."

"I don't have a type," Lisa said.

Cecile scowled. "Well, if you did, he's it. You are so stubborn."

"My career has to come first. I'm so close to getting what I've worked for all these years. I refuse to risk messing it up."

Cecile leaned back against the couch. "Don't. Have both. That's what we always said we were going to do."

"It doesn't work that way. When I'm with Mark, I lose focus. I make mistakes and forget things that are important, like answering my phone. So maybe once Herb's in the governor's seat, then I'll find Mr. Right. And as for Mark being that guy, there's no way."

"Why not? He's gorgeous. He's rich. He's also a nice guy. Do you know how rare that is?"

"Mark is Mr. Domestic. Guys like him are the settling-down kind. I can't even manage to rent an apartment or cook anything besides toast."

"That doesn't mean you can't get something started with him. If you like someone, you have to go for him. You can't miss an opportunity."

"Not possible. I'll be in Jeff City and he'll be here. That's like Tori trying to maintain her relationship with Jeff Wright once she moves to Kansas City. Absurd. Remember that guy you dated? He was in Jeff City and you in Columbia? Finally you both just had to admit that you were too geographically challenged and that there wasn't a way to overcome the distance."

"He just hated to make the forty-five-minute trip, and I got tired of being the one always doing the driving."

"Exactly. As much as you cared, it wasn't going to work. And I refuse to end up like my parents, caring for someone but never seeing each other until retirement."

"When do you see Mark next?" Cecile asked.

"Tonight," Lisa said. "Thanks to matchmaking Joann, I'm his date to the fund-raising event his parents are hosting. No odd numbers allowed at these type of things because it makes for an unbalanced table."

"So what about that other date? The one with the TMI you refuse to tell me about? How did that night go?"

"It went fine. Dinner. Movie. Dancing. Nothing interesting." *Mind-blowing* was a better word.

Cecile arched a brow. "Have you talked to him since?"

"He's been in Boston and I've been busy. I sent him two text messages."

Cecile shook her head in exasperation. "You always were the worst at dating. You're too practical. You have to be emotional once in a while."

"No, I don't," Lisa insisted. "Look at that silliness with Bradley. Talk about emotional. I get these stupid crushes on people that always land me in hot water. Being practical is much better. And I have nothing in common with Mark except some blatant chemistry. A little lust."

"Some relationships don't even have that," Cecile pointed out. "I'm a firm believer that if you can't be interested in the person in bed, you can't have a good long-term relationship. You're just two people tied together by a legal piece of paper, like my parents. They sleep in separate rooms. One thing being a talk-show producer has taught me is that you should never settle and be unhappy."

"I don't plan to settle, which is why I'll probably be the last one married out of all of us. I'm okay with that. There's someone out there for me, but I don't have time to search. If I'm supposed to find him, fate will drop him in my lap."

"Maybe fate already has."

"Ha," Lisa said. "All this talk is depressing. Tell me more about this job of yours. We don't have much time and I don't want to talk about my messy life anymore."

Cecile finished her water and set the bottle on the table. "Fine. I'll change topics. Even though I'm not officially starting for a few weeks, I can give you a hint at what comes next. We're going to be having the Nextel NASCAR guys on at the end of July. Tony Stewart, Jeff Gordon, Elliott Sadler and Dale Earnhardt Junior."

"My dad would love to see that show. He's into NASCAR."

"I'll e-mail you the exact dates. Get him to Chicago and I'll make sure he's in the audience for the taping. Of course, don't breathe a word of this to anyone or I'll have to kill you."

Lisa and Cecile laughed and they talked for a while longer, until Cecile finally stood up. The clock flickered and changed to four o'clock. "That's my cue. I've got to get out of here or I risk missing my flight. As it is, I won't be back in New York until a little after eight. I want to sleep in my own bed."

"I'm so glad you popped in," Lisa said. "I've missed our chats."

Cecile appeared wistful. "I know. Distance is a really lousy thing. You put it on your to-do list to call your friends and somehow never get around to it. Maybe when I'm at least back in this part of the country we can see each other more often."

"Hopefully," Lisa said. "I like Chicago, and your being there will give me an excuse to come up there and shop once this election's over."

"Then call me. Listen, you hang in there with Mark. He's sexy as hell. Give your relationship a chance."

"Maybe," Lisa said noncommittally. There was a knock at Lisa's door and both women glanced at each other. "I'm not expecting anyone," Lisa said. "In fact, I've got to leave in an hour for the party and I still have to get ready."

"Want me to send whoever it is on their way?" Shoes back on, Cecile was already headed toward the door.

"Really, it's no big deal…." Lisa began as she followed Cecile, but she'd already tossed open the door. "Lisa's not available. Can I help…" Her *you* faded off and her tall figure froze.

Lisa pushed her way to Cecile's left. "Who is it?" she asked. She didn't have a direct view of the hallway and she couldn't see anyone in the doorway.

"It's fate," Cecile said, finding her voice. She giggled. "And as much as I'd love to see how this next scene plays out, I'm going to miss my flight if I do. Darn. See ya, sweetie. I love ya. Good luck."

And with that Cecile escaped out into the hall. Lisa heard voices and grabbed the door. Cecile was at the end of the hall. And closer, Mark.

"Hey," he said, stepping forward so that his body was mere inches from hers. "It's time we talk."

Chapter Ten

"Talk?" Lisa said. Now? She had to get ready.

And how was she supposed to talk when she was dumbfounded and speechless from his unexpected arrival? Here he was on her doorstep, and darn if he wasn't a sight for sore eyes. His brown hair had grown a little longer in the past two-plus weeks and several strands dropped almost to his left eyebrow. He hadn't shaved since this morning; a five-o'clock shadow graced his face. He sported leather boat shoes, dark blue jeans, a casual sport coat and a white button-down that had the first few buttons unfastened.

"Talk?" Lisa repeated. "We can't right now. I don't have time." She saw his scowl and corrected herself. "*We* don't have time. *You* have to be cleaned up for a dinner at your parents at six-thirty."

He stared at her, his intense gaze not shifting. "Takes me ten minutes to shower and shave, and my parents' house is twenty minutes from mine, giving me plenty of time."

The man was infuriating. "But then I'll be running late. I have to leave at five—that's in less than an hour—and I'm not dressed."

Mark strode into the hotel room. "I'll make sure you're ready on time. But we're going to talk."

Lisa stepped aside and let him pass into the living area. Gosh, he was tall. Over six feet of pure muscle. Barefoot as she was, he had half a foot on her.

Instead of settling onto the couch, he turned back to face her. "Answer a question. Are you paying me back for that night?"

"Paying you back?"

"Yes. Lead me on and then drop me like lead, like you thought I'd done to you after the wedding reception. Because if so, then let's be honest and end this now. I don't want games. And you don't come apart in my arms and then refuse to answer any of my calls."

The hotel door clicked closed, a jarring sound. "I sent you text messages," Lisa said, her body humming at the mention of his touch. She fought for control. "I was trying to be cool. Letting you know it was no big deal."

"No big deal?" Mark questioned, his expression serious. "I don't have casual sex, especially with my sister's best friend. When I gave you time to think, I at least expected you to call."

"I just reconsidered," Lisa said. "I can't lose focus on my priorities."

"What happened between us was a big deal to me. I had hoped…"

"Please understand," Lisa said. "I wasn't trying to get revenge. When Tori suggested I use you for sex while I was here, I had to admit the idea had some appeal. I mean, you're hot. Who wouldn't want to have sex with you? Even Cecile said that she flirted shamelessly with you during college."

"And I ignored her," Mark pointed out.

"She did say you didn't pay her any attention," Lisa admitted. Cecile had also told Lisa to go for Mark. "And that proves my point. Women lust after you. I have since college. So I figured, hey, why not? Just have some fun until November, experience what I'd only sampled at Joann's wedding."

He shook his head vehemently. "You're not that kind of girl. Never have been. You started kicking yourself the next morning after our date for propositioning me."

"I did not," she protested.

"Liar," Mark declared with a force that had Lisa's eyes widening. She'd never seen him so riled up, and about her of all things. She wasn't scared but oddly excited. Foreplay, she realized. This moment was raw and real. He was breaking down her barriers, washing them away like a flash flood.

He shook his head again, sending another lock of hair into his face. He harshly brushed back the strand. "If you hadn't been kicking yourself for your outrageousness you would have called me. You realized you'd lost yourself that night with me and couldn't handle it."

"I can handle being out of control." Her lip quivered as he moved closer and invaded her space. He reached his forefinger forward, traced a circle pattern on her cheek. Her breathing stopped.

"No, you can't. Stop playing games with me, Lisa. I don't play them, especially now. I'm no longer that man you pegged me for being long ago."

"A cad, a playboy," she whispered.

"Yeah, those and the guy who left you for someone else, which you now know didn't happen. I'm turning thirty. I'm not into flings. I want substance. So what is it going to be? We're supposed to be friends, then friends with benefits, then not friends at all? You're hot one minute, cold the next. Which is it? What do you really want?"

He'd short-circuited her. All she could think about was one thing—the mouth that was inches from hers. "I don't know," she said honestly.

"Then let's find out," Mark said. And with that he hauled her in his arms and kissed her.

She opened to him as he deepened the kiss. Chemistry. Pheromones. Lust. Whatever. Only Mark had ever generated this primal of a response from her. Only Mark made her want to toss all caution to the wind, strip herself bare and bury him inside her up to the hilt. Then just maybe she'd be satisfied. Then she might find what she'd been missing, the part of her that, no matter how fulfilling her career, was somehow not whole.

He framed her face with his hands, turning the onslaught more sweet and seductive. She melted against him, clutching his sport coat as if the fabric were some sort of life preserver. Her phone alarm beeped, reminding her that she had forty-five minutes before she had to leave for the Smith residence.

"Ignore it," he commanded.

"I can't," Lisa said, her logical brain overriding her physical need. Her breath came out in gasps as he kissed the side of her neck. "That's my cue. I have to leave for your parents' house at five and I'm not ready."

"And Lisa Meyer is never late." Mark was already distancing himself from her, giving her space.

"Never," Lisa admitted.

As she stood there, a visible wall descended over Mark. He dropped his arms to his sides. "I could call my mother and ask her if she really needed you before six-thirty. My mother would say no. But I know you, and you have to be early to make sure that everything is perfect. It's your job."

"It's my job," Lisa repeated.

His rueful smile said volumes. "I can't compete with your career, Lisa. Your body wants me. Your mind, somewhere deep, does, too. The practical part of you devoted to being in control and to your career is keeping you from something that might be special. I don't want you for just sex, Lisa."

She stared at him.

"Casual isn't in your nature any more than it is in mine. We have something here, something that has massive potential. We have to decide what to do with it. You have a choice to make, for I can't be casual with you."

No! She was losing him and at the worst moment, when her career literally had to come first. "I…" She glanced at the clock, praying it would slow.

"I know. You don't have time." He ran a finger down her cheek, his touch tender. "I'll see you tonight."

WHEN INCLUDING LISA and Mark, Herb and Bunny and Bud and Mary Beth into the head count, there were sixty-six diners at the Smith estate. Mary Beth knew how to throw a party, Lisa thought as she mingled with the guests a few moments before dinner started. Mark's mom had pulled out all the stops, including renting a huge carnival-type tent.

The tent had been installed in the yard directly behind the great room and four-season room. Tall outdoor-variety propane heaters kept the temperature perfect, and dozens of floating candles shimmered in the pool. Tiny strands of white Christmas lights were woven through the tent trusses and provided a subtle enough glow to illuminate the area. Lanterns hung from the joists provided the rest.

A professional party company had set up eleven round tables for six that had been covered with crisp white linen and bone china, crystal glassware and silver-plated flatware. No disposable plastic or paper here.

Sequins in one form or another dominated the

women's attire; men wore black tuxedos. Once Lisa became a member of Herb's gubernatorial staff, she would have to mingle more with this set. Of course, then she'd be in a position of power, a mover and shaker out to better the world. Herb and Bunny were making their rounds, and even Bradley and his wife, Heather, were present and meeting various potential donors.

Lisa double-checked that her sleeveless black linen sheath was wrinkle-free. When competing with the moneyed set and their designer duds, Lisa had learned that you couldn't go wrong with a simple, understated classic. She'd topped the fitted dress with a multicolored tapestry bolero jacket she'd found in a vintage shop. At this moment her jacket was draped over her chair, which was next to Mark's. Mark, who hadn't yet put in an appearance although the cocktail portion had begun ten minutes ago. He was late. Probably deliberately so, Lisa thought.

"Nervous?"

Upon hearing his voice, Lisa started, the movement causing her water goblet to slosh and fling a few drops over her hand.

"I guess you are," Mark said.

"I had everything under control," Lisa said, shaking her hand to remove the excess water. Her annoyance at his tardiness, mixed with her relief that he'd shown up after the scene in her hotel room, had her saying a biting, "I was fine until you arrived."

But as soon as she turned around to face him, she gulped. The man wore a black tux. It fit. Way too well.

As she faced Mark, she had sudden insight that everything was about to change. No more games. Stopping what was inevitable between them would be like trying to stop the sun. Impossible. Even if she tried to ignore him, sometimes in life, risks were necessary. Lisa knew the consequences might be immense, but Mark was right. This relationship was anything but casual, and she could not shut it—him—out. She had to override her practical nature, put down her crystal ball and worry only about the moment. Tonight she needed to make love to him, not to get him out of her system but because he had become like breathing. Something she couldn't be without. A shiver of anticipation ran up her spine and she trembled slightly.

"Are you cold?" he asked.

If anything, she was way too hot. She shook her head, her shoulder-length blond hair skimming the edges of her shoulders. "No."

It was then that he must have seen the emotion in her blue eyes, for his own eyes darkened and he reached forward to cup her elbow. Heat from his touch warmed her flesh, provided a promise of even better things to come once they were alone. "Yes," Mark said as if reading her inner thoughts. "No more wasted time."

"I can't be casual," Lisa admitted. "Not with you."

"And I can't be that way with you, either," Mark said.

He gave her a tender smile. "And I'm very glad of it." His expression turned wicked then. "Although, I don't want to wait. Want to disappear for a while? Check out my old bedroom?"

Now here was the old Mark, the tempting rogue she could control. "Down," she commanded, although part of her admittedly would love to sneak off.

"You're the one who's always impatient," Mark teased, his fingers deliberately tickling the skin on her forearm. "I'm just giving you some options. Slip upstairs real quick and—"

"Lisa." Bradley's approach had Mark immediately stopping his sexual innuendo. Although Lisa knew there would be no way that her and Mark's first time would be a quickie during appetizers, the charged banter had still caused her skin to flush.

"Lisa, you're looking well tonight," Bradley said, his gaze speculative. He reached behind him, and the woman following him caught up. "You remember my wife, Heather."

Heather Monroe Wayne was a slip of a thing. Her silk dress was classic, nothing overtly fancy. She wore an air of charming plainness that had its roots in a private-school upbringing.

"Of course I remember her. Heather, it's a pleasure to see you again. May I introduce you to Mark Smith, son of our gracious hosts."

"Nice to meet you," Heather said. She smiled pleasantly, the practiced expression of one whose manners had been groomed by years of attending political functions.

"Hi, I'm Mark. I'm escorting Lisa tonight," Mark added helpfully, as if explaining why he still had his hand on Lisa's arm.

Lisa disengaged from Mark's touch. She, Bradley and Andrea had to iron out a few last-minute details, so she and Bradley moved toward the house, leaving Mark and Heather to socialize.

A little while later, Lisa rejoined Mark. They were sitting with two other couples, both about ten years older. They all made conversation as the wait staff began to pass out the first course, a chilled soup. Salad followed, and during the main course, Mark and Lisa had a moment for a private chat.

"So the sale's done?" she asked as she cut her salmon.

"Pretty much," Mark said with a shrug. "It's all in the hands of the lawyers."

"Good."

"How about you? Are you still good with this? Us?"

"Yes," Lisa said. She was. "I don't want to be miserable for the rest of my life," she told Mark. "All this time my job has been my number one priority. All these years I've been searching for political connections. But real relationships should be about feelings. I've decided to stop trying to fight what's going on between us. I'm ceding some control. I want you in my life."

"You're sure?" he said, leaning closer.

"As sure as I've ever been," she whispered. "You're right. We may have something here."

"We do. And it's more than the state I'm in, which I'd whisper into your ear, but then I would have to take you upstairs and ravage you. You have to work later, don't you?"

"I'll be helping Andrea collect checks," Lisa said.

"Exactly," he said with a wry grin. "You're going to make me wait."

"I'm waiting, too," Lisa reminded him.

"But I'm a guy. That means I have a one-track mind when it comes to you. Especially now that you've told me where it's going to end up."

He left the word *bed* unsaid, but Lisa blushed anyway. The woman to Mark's left leaned forward. "How long have you two been dating?" she asked.

"Oh, we're—" Lisa said.

"Two weeks," Mark inserted smoothly.

"Ah. Young love."

"We're only forty-three," the man next to her said.

"Yes, but we've been married for twenty years. Can you believe it?" his wife asked Lisa.

"Must be wonderful," Lisa said.

"It is," she said.

"Feels like yesterday," her husband said, making his wife blush.

"And you two," his wife said. "Anyone can see you're already in love."

Mark reached under the table and squeezed Lisa's hand. At that moment the waiter arrived with key lime pie for dessert, and the table's conversation topic switched to Herb's agenda, something Lisa easily addressed.

Mark found himself quite proud of her as she explained Herb's positions and key points. Not that Mark wasn't always impressed with Lisa. Even when she was driving him crazy.

He loved being with her.

He froze for a second as the revelation hit. He was, just as the woman said, in love with Lisa. Aside from her leaving in November, Lisa was everything he'd ever wanted. He had months before Lisa left. Months to change her mind, months to find a solution. He lifted her hand to his lips and kissed it. Her eyes darkened and she blushed. His body hummed. He would finally have her…tonight.

"THIS WAS JUST WONDERFUL," Bunny said to Lisa hours later. Most of the guests had departed and the remaining ones had moved into the great room. It was almost ten, and she and Herb would depart soon. "I'm extremely impressed. Thanks so much. I knew we could count on you."

"I appreciate the compliment," Lisa said. She and Andrea had finished with the checks about fifteen minutes ago, and Lisa had Andrea take them with her when she left. Tonight's total was well over one hundred thousand dollars, and many had pledged to donate to the political party, as well. "Anything we can do," one couple had said.

The offer had been genuine, and Lisa had made plans to call the couple later next week to discuss some ideas.

Herb approached, circling his arm around his wife. She turned and gazed up at him, the love evident. "Thanks, Lisa," he said.

"You're welcome," she replied. She curled her toes inside her pumps. Herb's compliment felt good— kudos for a job well done.

"Where's that young man of yours? We haven't seen him for a while," Herb asked.

Lisa glanced around the great room. Mark was nowhere in sight. "I'm really not sure," Lisa said.

"I thought I saw him leave," Bunny offered, "but I'm probably mistaken."

Lisa's stomach clenched, a gut reaction based on having lost him years ago at Joann's reception. Mark could not have left without a goodbye, not tonight. Not after what she'd told him. "I'm sure he'll turn up," Lisa said.

"If he's wise, he will," Herb joked. "And as he's Bud's son and wise enough to catch you, I'm sure he's around here somewhere. Hang on to this one."

"I plan on it," Lisa said.

"If only we could get ours married," Bunny said, her focus momentarily on her own clan. "Two children in their late twenties and one in her early twenties and nary a prospect in sight."

"It means you're still young," Herb teased.

Bunny smiled at Lisa. "My greatest fear? Growing old and not having made a mark on this world, not having made it a better place. At least you don't have to worry about that yet. Always live life on your terms."

"I will," Lisa said, sensing Bunny was somehow trying to tell her something. Perhaps the campaign was taking a toll on Bunny. Unlike previous races Herb had entered and won, this campaign was an intense whirlwind with no guaranteed victory.

"Be sure you do that," Bunny said. "We'll see you Sunday morning for church. Tomorrow at least is a quiet day. Nothing scheduled except some downtime at home."

"Studying political briefs," Herb said. "Bradley is coming over to work on issue statements."

"Oh, I forgot about that. At least I can sleep in. Speaking of…good night, Lisa. Thanks again. I'm really glad you're part of our staff."

"See you Sunday," Lisa said. She would escort Herb and Bunny to the church service and afterward to the homeless shelter where Herb would serve lunch. It was the perfect opportunity to outline his plan to deal with the state's homeless problem. After that he would head to Springfield on Monday for a week of campaigning. Lisa almost wanted to travel with him so she could see Joann, but Springfield was Drew's territory and while she oversaw his work, she didn't want to micromanage.

Bradley did that enough for everyone. Besides, Lisa had some groundwork to do in St. Louis and Kirksville. She headed into the hallway.

"I've been looking for you."

The familiar voice washed over her and Lisa's body instantly warmed. "You have?" she said, her voice playfully dubious. "I heard you'd left."

"Lies. I learned my lesson eight years ago," Mark said, his tone one of mock shock. He eased his arms around her waist, drawing her so that her backside spooned into his front. "I've been hiding in the kitchen while you do your work. I knew where to find the extra slices of key lime pie, which were able to satisfy my craving until I could taste something a little sweeter."

Lisa flushed. "Shh."

"What?" Mark feigned innocence as he pulled her closer to him. Her shoulders scrunched up and a delightful shiver shot through her as his breath tickled her ear. "No one can overhear me. No one can hear me tell you what I'm going to do to you later tonight."

"Stop," Lisa said, his teasing turning her on.

"Oh, that's not a word you'll be using tonight," Mark said. "*More* maybe. But not *stop*."

Whoa. If Mark Smith could make her want with only some suggestive talk, it was definitely time to leave, Lisa thought. After all, Herb and Bunny had. So had Bradley and Heather. Every one of the guests who planned on donating had already written checks, and

Mary Beth knew how to take care of the stragglers and get them to the door. Most of the diehards still in the great room were close personal friends of Bud and Mary Beth who showed little intent on calling it a night and instead were enjoying talking to their hosts. And no one was paying Mark and Lisa much attention.

"Let's go," Lisa said.

"You'll get no argument from me." Mark released her but kept a grasp of her hand. He led her to the front foyer, where he removed her coat from the closet. He assisted her into the garment, his fingers lingering at the base of her neck. Then, because he couldn't wait any longer, he turned her around and kissed her. Hard.

"Someone might see," Lisa protested, but he swallowed her words and drove all rational thought from her mind as he continued his masterful onslaught. She snaked her arms around his neck. She needed this man. He breathed life into her, called forth something that she'd never experienced.

He tore his lips from hers and groaned. "My place is closer," he told her, and the butterflies in her stomach danced.

As his mouth made magic with hers, Lisa couldn't think straight, couldn't remember what she was trying to fight for. She was tired of worrying, tired of control. Just let nature take its course. Let fate lead you....

And fate was leading her out the door. "We'll get your car tomorrow," Mark said.

"I don't have any clothes or any…"

"You don't need anything but me," Mark said, his cryptic words sending another shiver of anticipation through her. "No more wasted time. I have everything you need."

He was right. Always right. As she'd done with Herb, Lisa was a woman who only attached her star to a winner. Had there ever been any question that that man was Mark?

Could she have it all? If only for tonight, she was going to try.

Chapter Eleven

When you're hot for someone, a fifteen-minute drive can seem like forever. Mark's right hand, except when shifting, remained on Lisa's leg, burning a heated impression through the linen fabric. "You have too many clothes on," he said. "Panty hose should be outlawed."

"I agree," Lisa said, "but not for the reason you're suggesting."

"I'm taking them off you the minute we get in the door."

They were almost to his house and she found herself shaking. How long had it been since she'd made love to someone? Sudden fears consumed her. Would he even find all this emotional buildup worth the act itself? Would she at least be adequate?

"It'll be awesome," Mark said.

"Do you always have to read my mind?" Lisa said.

"Yes," Mark said, his expression smug.

"How do you do it, anyway?"

"Lucky guess."

"I'm that predictable?"

"You are in no way predictable," Mark answered as he parked the Porsche in its spot.

"Good," Lisa said. "Then you'd have no idea I was going to do this."

This time she was the leader, unhooking her seat belt and twisting around so that she faced him. She brought her lips down on his, initiating a kiss that sent them both spiraling. She tasted everything that was him and she deepened the kiss, this time treating herself to a thorough exploration of his mouth. She darted her tongue in and out until he threaded his hands through her blond hair and pushed her head away gently.

"Inside," he said, his breath ragged. His dark eyes had glazed over and she knew he walked a precarious line. He wanted her—bad.

She smiled to herself. For that moment she'd had control. One last bit of defiance before she totally surrendered herself. They kissed their way into the laundry room, and who had control became irrelevant.

Tonight was about letting go, and Mark scooped Lisa into his arms and carried her upstairs to his bedroom. She lost a shoe as he made his way to the king-size four-poster bed. He set her down beside it, not on it, and Lisa took a moment to assess her surroundings while Mark shed his tuxedo jacket and tugged off his bow tie.

The decorating fairy had worked her magic here, for

every portion of Mark's bedroom coordinated. He flipped a switch and recessed lights glowed in the coffered ceiling. He flipped another switch, sending the room into darkness except for that indirect light.

"Wow," she breathed at the subtle beauty of it. "And you never broke this room in?"

"Never wanted to until now," Mark said. "I refused to share my bedroom until the right woman came along."

He'd unfastened the top two buttons of his shirt and undone his cuffs. She watched him in the muted light, each of his movements heightening her awareness of what came next. Tonight was the night she'd know this man in all ways possible.

He lowered his mouth to hers.

With his kiss, the tempo changed. Tonight wasn't about possession or dominance but mutual pleasure. Mark took his time undressing her, the zip of her dress clicking as each of the teeth separated. He slid the dress down, exposing her black satin bra, the texture smooth so as not to show through her dress.

She shivered, her white skin a contrast to the black fabric, and he warmed her by moving his mouth over her jaw and down her neck. He bent, kissed the exposed top of each breast before he tugged the satin down, lifting her soft flesh to his seeking mouth.

A shudder of pleasure racked her body, and his arm kept her supported when her knees threatened to cave under his delicious onslaught. He laved each peak before raising his mouth back to hers for a deep and mind-spiraling kiss. He then fingered her bra straps, sliding them down her shoulders and leaving them midbicep. She whimpered as he caressed her softly and lowered his mouth to again bring her to ecstasy.

It was only then, after she'd been satiated, that he peeled away her outer clothing, leaving her standing only in pumps, thigh-high panty hose and a black G-string.

"Beautiful," he told her. She shivered as the air hit her exposed flesh, and he eased her down so she was seated on the bed. Heat pooled lower as desire flared, and Mark kneeled to remove her shoes and the nylon stockings that kept her semicovered.

As these items slipped to the floor, he kept his lips in motion, first kissing the arch of her foot, next the inside of her knee and then planting more kisses as his mouth traveled up her left thigh. Only a tiny slip of fabric kept him from his quest, and he kissed her through the silk, heating her. He used his tongue to move the barrier aside, and she leaned back on her arms, her head falling sideways to rest on her left shoulder, as the next wave of bliss began and he brought her over the edge.

She reached for him afterward as he kissed his way up her stomach, but Mark avoided her grasp with gentle admonishment. "Let me savor you," he said as he began to touch her all over.

Lisa, her body quaking with passion yet to be totally quenched, could only nod and let him bring her to another peak. Only then did Mark finally remove his clothes, moving onto the bed beside her. He cradled her in his arms and kissed her. Lisa ran her palms over his skin, delighting in its fine texture. When she found that part of him that strained for her attention, she stroked him gently and he groaned.

After he sheathed himself, he drove her wild by teasing her with his fingers. Then he filled her completely.

Her eyes widened at the welcome intrusion, and Mark stroked gently at first as if understanding she had not done this for a while.

It's like riding a bike, Lisa thought before she couldn't comprehend anything but the pleasure crashing over her in waves. *You just got back in bed and did it. But better. Especially with the right man.*

And he was the right man for her. Never had she made love like this, as if she were home, really "home."

He increased his pace, and she cried out, her body needing release only he could give. He was perfectly in sync with her biorhythms and he matched them, shattering both of them when their mutual moment of freedom came.

He held her tightly afterward. They were on top of his quilt, and he moved her underneath, covering her carefully as he rose and disappeared into the en suite bathroom. Then he returned, slid underneath the covers and drew her close to his side. Safe and secure. Those two words flitted through her mind as their breathing slowed.

At this moment she was at peace with herself and her world. She sighed and let sleep overtake her, her body satisfied and resplendent in his arms.

SHE AWOKE TO THE frantic shrilling of her cell phone. She'd left the thing in her purse, but even upstairs in Mark's bedroom she could hear the blasted device ringing. Whoever was calling wasn't leaving a message, just hanging up and dialing again the minute voice mail kicked on. Lisa raised her head, the bedside clock showing the time as barely seven. Figured. Fate's way of making her pay for a night spent making love, with a few hours of sleep tossed in. In fact, she was still naked. Mark wore boxers; when had he put those on? He cuddled her to his bare chest. "Good morning."

"My phone's ringing," Lisa said.

"Wrong," Mark said. "The correct answer is to also reply 'good morning.'"

"Something's wrong," she said, ignoring his urging for social pleasantries. "I have to deal with this." She sat up, the sheet falling to expose her torso. Where were her clothes? Underwear? Bra? Sensing her determination, Mark rose and handed her his bathrobe. "Stay here. I'll go get your purse."

"Thanks," she said, quickly wrapping the terry cloth around her like a shield.

He disappeared, returning with her purse. "I have to feed the dog. Just come downstairs when you're done."

The phone began to ring again. She knew he wasn't pleased and gave him a tentative smile before he strode out.

"Lisa Meyer," she said, even though she already knew who the caller was.

"We've got problems," Bradley announced.

"What's going on?" Lisa asked.

"Drew ran into a major snag, and when he couldn't reach you a few minutes ago, he called me."

"Start talking." Lisa listened for a while as Bradley outlined the issue. Springfield, Missouri, was often considered the gateway to the Bible Belt. One of the local papers with a very conservative stance had pulled its support of Herb, citing him as a modern-day Judas to conservative issues. While the paper hadn't officially endorsed Anson Farmer, having Herb labeled the lesser of two evils was not the image his campaign was trying to portray, especially with the August primary still months away.

"The local party is freaking out. This is way over Drew's head," Bradley said, and Lisa knew he was right. She and Bradley were the two who were experts at smoothing ruffled feathers. Like a horse doomed by not getting out of the starting gate fast enough, Herb could not afford to lose potential donors or political support this early.

"I want us in Springfield by tonight," Bradley said. "I've already had meetings scheduled with leaders of the far right moved forward. I've also begun setting up meetings with the local party leaders across the entire southwestern portion of the state."

"We can't promise things we aren't planning on delivering," Lisa said. "Herb doesn't want to enter office beholden to a bunch of special-interest factions."

"I agree, but we must make sure those factions aren't stabbing him in the back, either. I've readjusted his Springfield schedule since this is going to require all of us. Be here by eight tonight, as I've called a meeting with Drew for eight-thirty. I've got rooms blocked for us at…"

Bradley named the hotel the campaign staff usually stayed at. "Andrea can handle the fort in St. Louis for the next week or two. Have her accompany Herb and Bunny tomorrow. The experience will be good for her and I think she's ready to handle the responsibility."

"You're right. It will be. I'll see you tonight." Lisa hung up and called Andrea, taking a few minutes to outline what the girl needed to do. Then Lisa hopped out of bed and tightened the belt on her robe. She found Mark in the kitchen.

"What's going on?" he asked.

"That was Bradley. We've got a major problem to deal with in Springfield. It's bad." She gave him the information. "I need to be there by eight tonight."

"I see." Mark had made coffee and he poured her a cup. The ceramic mug warmed her hands.

"I might be gone a week, maybe two," Lisa said, adding fuel to the rising tension.

Silenced stretched as she stood there dressed only in his robe. The coffee was hot enough to burn her tongue, and she caught herself before taking a huge swallow. She set the mug on the granite countertop. Then Mark did the absolute unexpected. He set down his own mug, walked around the center island and pulled her into his arms, where he held her tight.

"I'd be lying if I said I liked this situation one bit," he said. "But I've resigned myself to the fact that your career will call you away. I refuse to waste any more time on small things. I want you, Lisa, for as long as you're going to give me. Right now you don't have to leave for several hours."

"I have to get my car and—"

Mark silenced her with a long kiss. "Priorities," he said when they parted for a moment. "Give me a proper goodbye. Please. You have the time."

As he kissed the last of her weak defenses away, Lisa simply nodded. It only took four hours at the most to drive west down Highway 44 to Springfield. "I have the time," she said and led the way back upstairs.

Two weeks later Lisa finally caught her first break. The pace had been insane, meeting after meeting. She'd wrangled with local political party leaders, trying to reach consensus and drum up support.

She'd talked to Mark several times, usually late at night, holding long conversations into the wee hours of the morning. Somehow, despite surviving on little sleep, she'd still been in top form.

That hadn't been easy. Missouri was often a very conservative state, regardless of political party. Trying to find some common ground without making dangerous promises had been difficult.

She and Bradley had had to remake Herb's image slightly, making him more aggressive in some areas while tamping down his beliefs in others. Herb had hated removing the focus from several of his preferred issues, but as he could do nothing if not in office, the overall focus had to be on winning in November.

Mark had understood these things and had brainstormed with Lisa. He'd been invaluable help. If you'd asked her at the first fund-raising dinner, never in a million years would she have guessed that she and Mark would have ended up like this, as lovers and confidants. Definitely more than friends and something beyond that casual "with benefits" moniker.

Which was why Lisa found herself very nervous as she drove her used Lexus onto Joann's street. She was finally visiting Joann, who probably already knew the status of things from her brother.

Joann's street, built before the subdivision craze, was typical of the older, more established part of Springfield and consisted of one- and two-story houses, each with unique architecture. Mature trees shaded lush green landscaped yards.

Lisa withdrew the keys from the engine as a group of boys ran out the front door at full tilt. Kyle followed, diaper bag tossed easily over his arm. "Hi, Lisa. Great to see you. You two have fun," he said as he ushered the boys into the minivan parked at the curb. "I'm off to Chuck E. Cheese."

"Don't pretend you mind," Joann called from the doorway. "You play all the games, too."

Kyle grinned, blew his wife a kiss, strapped the younger two into their car seats and was soon on his way.

"Hey, stranger! It's so good to see you finally!" Joann gave Lisa a huge hug when she reached the doorway. "Come in. Welcome to Chez Messina, which I somehow managed to get slightly cleaned up before your arrival. I've got a stew in the Crock-Pot. Is that okay? We can always go out or I can order in."

"Stew sounds perfect," Lisa said. "I am so tired of eating restaurant food that a home-cooked meal sounds great. Kyle didn't have to leave."

"He didn't care. He loves Skee-Ball. He's hit three-fifty a few times." Joann described the game where you rolled the ball up a ramp and tried to get it through the rings. The higher up, the higher the score. "Besides, the boys would much rather eat there and run and play than hang here and go, 'ew stew.'"

"I just hope I'm not an inconvenience."

"You? Never," Joann reassured.

"Good," Lisa said with genuine relief. She hadn't

known when she'd finally be free to visit, so she'd only been able to give Joann about eight hours' notice.

"Would you like something to drink? We do have wine, soda, and I'm sure there's something stronger around here, although Kyle and I probably haven't touched any hard alcohol in years."

"Some iced tea would be great if you have that," Lisa said. "I don't really drink alcohol and I'm not in the mood for soda."

"You never did drink much. It's good some things never change. And of course I have tea. Kyle drinks it by the gallon. Follow me into the kitchen. You haven't toured this house, have you?"

"You were in the other one the last time I was in town."

"That was three years ago. We really haven't seen each other in that long?"

"No, I guess not. Time flies, doesn't it?"

"It does. My oldest is almost eight." Joann poured Lisa a glass of tea and returned the pitcher to the refrigerator. "So what's new?"

"I saw Cecile," Lisa said. "She showed up unannounced while she was in between plane flights."

"I haven't seen her in ages. We talk a lot, and last time she was bragging about her new job."

"She looked great. Still tall and thin and drop-dead gorgeous. Not one gray hair."

"Oh, I have those already. Kids," Joann said.

"I'm dreading the day. I also had dinner with Tori. She's concerned that she's gained three pounds."

"Oh, please. Tell her I've gained ten. That's motherhood for you. What else is up with her?" Joann began to serve two plates of stew. During dinner, the two women gossiped about their mutual friends. Afterward Joann gave Lisa a tour of the house and then they settled into the family room.

"This TV is always on," Joann complained, pressing the remote and silencing the set. The children's programming went black. "I swear, kids thrive on noise. You think they're watching TV when really they're on another floor entirely and the TV is just blaring to an empty room. Just wait, you'll find out once you have your own."

Lisa shifted uncomfortably. "I'd say it's a little too early for that. As much as I'm all for women's empowerment and single parenting, that's not me. I'm doing the child thing the old-fashioned way. And since everyone claims I'll be the last one of our foursome to wed, I'd say I've got some time."

"I wouldn't count on that," Joann said. She kicked off her shoes and wiggled her toes. "I think my brother might have other ideas. In fact, I'd bet you money on it."

"Still gambling?" Joann had always loved to bet on anything.

"Only when I can't lose," Joann said with a smirk.

Lisa arched her eyebrow. "So are you privy to something that I'm not?"

"Maybe," Joann said.

Lisa sighed. "I know Mark tells you just about everything, but I'd hate to take your money. I mean, don't get me wrong, but Mark and I only started whatever this relationship thing is between us. We've decided we're exclusive, but neither of us has mentioned that L-word, much less anything about marriage."

"My brother's the marrying type. He's always liked you and he's ready to settle."

"Well, I'm not," Lisa said, although deep inside her the idea of being with Mark long-term had appeal. But that wasn't possible, so she fought the notion. "And tell me how we're going to be married anyway, with me in Jeff City and him in St. Louis. Like that would work. All you have to do is look at my parents. My mom practically raised me alone. I can't imagine starting something like that. So unless you know something I don't, I wouldn't get your hopes up. Mark and I might both be besotted with each other, but that means nothing."

"I think you're wrong. I know my brother. He's taken. You might not be thinking ahead, but I'm absolutely positive that he is."

"Mark and I talked about this last night on the phone," Lisa said. "Since I'm more committed timewise to the campaign than ever, we agreed to take our relationship one day at a time."

Joann spread her hands wide and rubbed them on the tops of her thighs. "And when did my brother never have his days mapped out? Mark's a planner, like you. College in four years, start work and then go to night school for his MBA after that. Just as you have Herb organized, Mark's organized, too. Where you're concerned, the only difference is that he's got a marriage campaign to run."

Lisa rolled her eyes. "Joann, really, that's not the case. This relationship is destined to be as much as it is now. I had enough of a long-distance relationship with my dad. I won't do it with a man, even one I might be able to fall in love with."

"Even if the man has something to say about it?"

"Like what?"

"Like the fact that he sent me a check for a hundred dollars?"

"One hundred dollars? What does that prove?" Lisa asked, her eyes narrowed.

Joann winced. "He didn't tell you?"

"No," Lisa said slowly. "Did you two make one of your wagers and make me part of it?" Mark and his sister were always betting on something.

"Yes," Joann said. She sighed. "I know my brother. He called me—or maybe I called him. Anyway, he was in quite a huff over you. He told me about your newly formed alliance. I told him not to hurt you. I told him to prove he wasn't a playboy and that he'd deserve it if you took him for his contacts and dumped him afterward. I bet him that he'd fall in love with you long before you'd ever fall for him."

"And he paid." Lisa felt as if she'd been doused with cold water. Mark Smith had bet his sister that he wouldn't fall in love with Lisa. He'd conceded. The thought weighed so heavy that she repeated it just to make sure. "He paid."

"Yes. He sent a note saying I was right. My brother has lost to me before, but this is the first time he's ever gladly paid me. That can only mean one thing. He loves you."

"Oh, please," Lisa said, the revelation very unsettling. "I'm sure he mailed you the money for the other reasons you stated."

Joann crossed her arms. "Can you sit there and tell me you don't love him?"

Lisa sat there a long moment. Had she fallen for Mark? Certainly. Now that she'd given up fighting her need to be in control of the relationship, she thought about him constantly. She loved hearing his voice on the other end of the phone. She craved being in his arms, feeling him inside her as he sent them both over the edge during lovemaking. But love didn't mean happy ever after. She refused to be in a relationship she couldn't commit to one hundred percent. She would not wait until she retired to have her husband full-time.

"Joann, how I might feel is irrelevant. I have a career that's moving me to Jeff City. I do not have what it takes to do a long-distance relationship. Mark already muddles my thoughts enough that I forget things. Love shouldn't be about sacrifice but about sharing. We promised each other on graduation we'd have it all, remember?"

"And you will," Joann said as if sensing that somehow she'd made things worse. "Things always work out somehow."

How wonderful that would be if it were true! But Lisa didn't have the heart to tell her friend that she was a prime example. Joann had never had that promising broadcast career she'd dreamed of, giving it up so that she could get married and stay home to raise three boys.

Paths and dreams changed, and as much as Lisa might want things to work out with Mark, she was the practical one. You didn't always get what you wanted. Things didn't always work out. Lisa shook her head. "I wish they did," she told Joann, "but they don't."

Before Joann could reply, both women heard the sound of an opening door, which was followed by the running of little feet. Three children bounded into the room and bounced into their mother's arms.

"Trevor went potty in his pants," Tommy, the oldest, announced.

"In my Pull-Up," Trevor said matter-of-factly. "Daddy changed me."

"And Timmy threw up," Tommy continued regally, the bearer of all bad news. "He ate too much pizza and then *blat*."

Joann grimaced. "Where's your dad?"

"Upstairs with Timmy," Tommy said. "He ruined his clothes."

"Lovely," Joann said. She gave Lisa an apologetic

smile. "It appears as if we're going to be interrupted. Wait here a few minutes, will you?"

"I'm hungry," Trevor announced. He put his forefinger into his mouth.

"Stop that," Joann said. Trevor lowered his hand, and Joann rose to her feet.

Lisa stood, as well. "You seem like you have your hands full, and I have a busy day tomorrow, including driving back to St. Louis. I'm going to get out of your hair."

"Really, you don't need to..." Joann began. She stopped as the running of feet was heard.

A few seconds later Kyle's voice boomed down the stairs. "Hey, honey? I think Timmy might really be sick. He's back in the bathroom with the heaves and his forehead is warm."

"I'm hungry," Trevor repeated. He tugged on the hem of Joann's shirt. "Want peanut butter 'n' jelly."

"I'm going to go," Lisa said, surveying the scene and deciding that escape was the best course of action, as she could be of little help. Lisa gave Joann a quick hug. "You take care of yourself and I promise that we'll have a longer visit sometime in the future."

"Definitely," Joann said. Tommy had turned the television on, the sound of a cartoon flooding the room. "Turn that down," Joann ordered. "Let me at least walk you to the door. I'll fix you a sandwich in a minute," she told Trevor.

"Thanks for coming over," Joann said as she gave

Lisa one last hug. "I'm glad to have seen you for at least a little bit."

"Me, too," Lisa said. The minivan was in the driveway, next to Lisa's Lexus. "You go and take care of your sons. It sounds like they need you."

"They always do," Joann said. She seemed melancholy for a moment and then she brightened. "And you take care of my brother. If he's fallen for you, give him a chance. He could be very good for you. He might just be exactly what you need. You know I'd love for you to be my sister-in-law. So you'll see. Everything will work out."

Lisa nodded noncommittally and was soon in her car, backing out of the driveway. As she drove off, she knew things wouldn't work out. Just as one candidate wouldn't win the November election, not all people who fell in love could stay that way.

As for her relationship with Mark, if he'd already fallen for her, then they'd passed a danger point. Love was a string. And as Bradley had been right in teaching her, sometimes strings had to be cut early. Bradley had recognized Lisa's attentions as hero worship and not real love. He'd been wise to break things off.

Lisa knew that she'd have to do the same thing with Mark, especially as his emotions ran much deeper. She wasn't ready for permanent commitment or long-distance, and the unknown brought her need for control rushing back. Mark already had her turning off her phone and forgetting her campaign duties. The risks were too great that by falling for Mark Smith she'd have to sacrifice a very important part of herself. And that was her greatest fear. She could not take the risk.

She reached the hotel, parked her car and entered the building. To reach the elevators for her room, she had to go partway through the lobby and then make a left. Before she made the turn, she heard a voice call her name. She stopped and looked around. She didn't know anyone in Springfield aside from Joann, and anyone who might know her was at a fund-raising dinner she didn't have to be at. She frowned and took a step forward.

"Lisa."

She spun around. She knew that voice.

Mark stepped forward and dragged her into his arms. "I missed you," he said in answer to her unasked question of what he was doing here. "I couldn't wait until tomorrow night."

Lisa froze. This was a man she cared a great deal about. He'd driven four hours to surprise her. She had to be the greatest fool in the entire world for what she was about to do. She was about to send away Mr. Right. The risk was too great if she let him stay. She could not lose her heart. "Mark," she said, "we have to talk."

Chapter Twelve

Mark's feet felt like heavy leaden weights as he followed Lisa into the elevator. He knew exactly what *We need to talk* meant. Lisa was freaking out.

He sighed, already knowing tonight was not going to end up like the night of his parents' party. Sure, by some rules, guys weren't supposed to just show up on their women's doorsteps. But that hadn't mattered last time. And Mark didn't play by the rules, nor did he play games. He'd missed Lisa. He'd had business in Springfield—some legal paperwork related to the sale that he'd needed Joann to sign—and had planned to meet with Lisa tomorrow. So what if he'd shown up early and decided to surprise her? He'd done it successfully before. And after all the wonderful conversations they'd shared these past few days, the Lisa he'd come to love should have been fine with his actions.

But the Lisa stalking toward her hotel room had obviously changed since last night, and he was about to find out why. His phone began to shrill.

"Shouldn't you get that?" Lisa asked as she inserted her passkey.

"I..." Irritated at the interruption, Mark reached into his pocket and withdrew his cell phone. Unlike Lisa, he hadn't upgraded to a BlackBerry. Intent on getting rid of the caller, he flipped open the phone without checking the display. "Hello?"

"Lisa knows about the bet," his sister said without preamble. "I thought you'd told her and I let it slip when she was here earlier."

Mark bit back the expletive that threatened to explode from his mouth. So that was the problem. Lisa had discovered how he felt. He'd meant to prepare her, to ease her into his declaration of love. Her practical nature would have her panicking otherwise. He glanced at her. She was staring at the painting above the bed. Wonderful. She already had lost her nerve.

"I'm in Springfield," Mark told Joann simply. She would understand the rest. "I'll bring the papers by tomorrow."

"You're in Springfield. Oh, good grief! Goodbye!" Joann hung up.

Lisa had her back to Mark, as if trying to give him some privacy. He sighed. "That was Joann. Is that what you want to talk about? The bet?"

"I don't care that you made one," Lisa said. Tension had made her posture rigid. "You paid."

Mark knew he had to tread carefully here, so he made his tone light. "So? Why is that a problem? I always bet my sister and usually end up paying her, even if I win."

"She said you volunteered the money," Lisa said, turning around to face him. She studied a fingernail. "By doing that, you told her you loved me."

"And what if I do love you?" Mark said. His voicing the words aloud only confirmed them. "Lisa, being in love with someone isn't a crime."

She picked at her cuticle and his stomach clenched. He was losing her. Her stubbornness meant she'd dig in, refuse to budge from her point.

"But you're having difficulty with me loving you, aren't you?" He paused and she glanced at her feet. "That's what this is all about, isn't it? Why you want to talk?"

She raised her head, finally facing him. Her blue eyes contained immeasurable sorrow, which only fueled Mark's concern that nothing was going to end well tonight.

"Yes. Mark, you're in too deep. We can't do this. Us."

For once, he had no idea what to say to her, no clue how to sway her. "You mean *you* can't do this, be in our relationship, because you're afraid of what's going to happen in November when you move."

She nodded. "Exactly. I have to be realistic and I'm not the type of person who can invest the energy when I know it's not going to work out."

Mark tried to keep his growing anger in check.

"Realistic? Not work out? Lisa, when two people care about each other like we do, that's what's real. The rest is just details."

"No." He could hear the anguish in her voice. "Those details can't be left out. They're important, especially to me. This is my life, and I want it all. I want to make an impact on the world and the only way I can do it is through my career. That means I'll be moving in a few months to Jefferson City. You live in Chesterfield. Long-distance never works."

"It will," Mark said stubbornly. He could literally see her slipping away, withdrawing as she protected herself. What was in Lisa's psyche that kept her so focused on her career that she feared everything that might cause her to digress or detour? She was throwing away the perfect chance.

"We can be happy, Lisa," Mark tried.

Those words only made her shake her head. "How? I grew up never seeing my dad. My mom never saw her husband. I don't want that. We cannot have a relationship and be in two different cities, which is exactly what's going to happen. It's best to end this now, for if we stay together, by November it'll be unbearable. We'll care too much and I can't set myself up for that. This is painful enough."

"Lisa, in November, if we want it to work out, it will. I, for one, can do anything I set my mind to doing."

She'd dropped her hands to her sides, her posture resigned. "No. I'm so sorry."

At that moment Mark knew that showing up in Springfield really hadn't been an issue at all, his actions serving only as an earlier impetus for this conversation. Even if he'd waited to come see her or waited until she returned to St. Louis, all that would have been different was the timing of this "talk." Whether a week from now or a month, Lisa had made up her mind and stubbornly refused to budge from the course she'd charted.

Mark had to try one last time. Loving someone was a weight. You carried that person's heart. But the responsibility wasn't a millstone but rather a joyous burden, one he was ready to carry.

Lisa wasn't. And tonight she was telling him she might never be ready. He reached forward and ran a finger down her cheek. She closed her eyes, the movement allowing one tiny tear to escape.

"I'm going to leave," Mark said, because he knew that at this moment his staying would only strengthen her resolve to push him further away. He had to remove that control from her if they ever stood a chance at all of surviving tonight's setback. While the relationship might fizzle out, he couldn't kill its only hope. He had to walk out on his own before she asked him. "I'm guessing you have a lot of work to do."

"Yes," Lisa said. "Always."

"Yeah, I know," Mark said. He smiled wistfully, the best he could do at the moment.

He'd made many tough decisions in his life, and this one was going to rank up there. But a man had to know when to fold his cards and throw down the hand. Right now Lisa had to fight the battle within herself. He couldn't rescue someone who didn't want to be rescued.

"Goodbye," he said and he turned and left. He closed his eyes for a brief moment as the hotel door clicked shut behind him. The blackness did nothing to soothe him. Then he glanced about and drew out his phone. "Hey, it's me," he told his sister. "No, it didn't go well. Yeah, I'm coming over."

Mark pocketed the phone and walked away without looking back.

BREAKUPS SUCKED, LISA thought a week later. They were like funerals. Both were extremely difficult and both ripped out your heart. And with each, the wound took a long time to heal.

She hadn't spoken to Mark in a week, not since that fateful Friday night. Just because time was passing, it didn't mean that Lisa found getting over him any easier. If anything, the pain that raced through her on a daily basis increased instead of ebbed. She'd done the unspeakable. She'd destroyed the one thing that had the possibility of being perfect for her.

She'd endured the week as if she were an automaton. She'd processed campaign checks. She'd made phone calls. She'd organized dinners. She'd buried herself in work.

But the solace she usually found in her beloved tasks had disappeared. Satisfaction in a job well done had vanished. Dissatisfaction with her life had reared its ugly head.

The worst part of the situation was that with each subsequent day, the realization that she'd probably just made the worst mistake of her life increased exponentially. She'd hurt the perfect man. She'd sent him away.

She could still picture his face, the pained expression he'd masked quickly. She hated herself for hurting him.

Worse, she hadn't made herself feel better by doing so. She hadn't rid herself of her insecurities or solved her problems. If anything, she'd compounded them. She'd refused to take Joann's calls this week, lest Lisa somehow lose that friendship, too. Although, Joann's life was so different from Lisa's that, really, while they'd be lifelong friends, they had little in common anymore except some shared glory days.

Joann's life was her boys. Lisa's life was her career. Don Henley's "Heart of the Matter" song had become Lisa's current mantra. It was about forgiveness, and the person she had to forgive was herself.

She'd been the one to ruin everything, to tear apart the relationship so that she could prove to herself that she had control over her life.

But love wasn't about control. Love was about trust. Lisa didn't trust herself and she hadn't trusted Mark enough to cede control, to become a partner with someone. Although Herb had compromised to save his campaign, Lisa had refused to do the same to save her love life. The result was that she'd just destroyed the best thing that ever happened to her.

Hindsight was twenty-twenty and she was an idiot. The question was what to do about it.

No matter what, she had to do something, and stop being a chicken was step one. Lisa reached forward and retrieved the printed invitation off the hotel desk. She was back in her hotel suite in St. Louis. She read the front of the card: *You're invited.* The inside text announced a thirtieth birthday party for Mark and Joann to be held at the Smith estate. Casual dress. Lisa hadn't RSVP'd yet and the event was tomorrow night.

Sighing, she reached for the hotel phone and dialed the number. Expecting the Smith's housekeeper to answer, Lisa found herself momentarily speechless when Mary Beth picked up on the third ring.

"Lisa! I'm so glad it's you. You are coming, right?"

"I—" Lisa began the excuse she'd rehearsed.

Mary Beth interrupted quickly. "Great. I'm so glad you'll be here. Tori's out of town unexpectedly on an emergency and she's not sure if she'll make it back. Cecile's sister's bachelorette party is tomorrow night, so Cecile has to be in Chicago. But you'll be here. You're one of Joann's oldest friends, and I'd hate for all of her bridesmaids to have missed this party."

"She's the first of us to turn thirty," Lisa said. Despite her hesitation about running into Mark, Lisa knew she couldn't hide out from Joann. Not on a special night like this. She took a deep breath. "I'll be there."

"Thanks, Lisa." Both women heard a click. "That's my other line. I'm glad you're coming. See you tomorrow."

Lisa hung up the phone. Twenty-four hours from now she'd be in the same house with Mark. Thirty hours from now the night would be over and she'd probably never see him again. One last meeting.

She could manage. Would manage. Somehow.

"LISA, IT'S WONDERFUL to see you!" Mary Beth gave Lisa a warm hug the moment she stepped through the front door. Since the June night was warm, Lisa hadn't worn a coat. While the invitation read casual, Lisa knew that still meant upscale dress. She'd chosen basic black—a soft knit pants set with a matching lace jacket. She'd left her purse in the car, slipping her car key inside a pocket.

"Here, let me get those." Mary Beth removed the two gift bags from Lisa's hands. "I'll put these in the dining room. Joann is in the great room. Go on in."

"Thanks," Lisa said, noticing Mary Beth's delicate omission of Mark's whereabouts. A little tension eased from her. Perhaps the Smith family simply planned on ignoring what had occurred between Mark and Lisa. That's what Lisa knew she would prefer.

She wandered into the great room, which was full of people. The crowd spilled out into the four-season room and onto the patio surrounding the pool. Lisa recognized some faces but not others.

"Lisa." Joann rose from her seat on the couch.

Dressed in something glittery, she gave Lisa a quick hug. "I'm so glad to see you. I was worried you weren't coming, especially since you haven't been returning my calls."

"Of course I'd be here," Lisa said. Joann was one of her oldest and dearest friends. No matter what, Lisa had done the right thing by attending. "I wouldn't let you down."

"Thanks. I just wish Tori and Cecile could be here. But work and family came first. I was so hoping we'd all be together again, if only for tonight. It's been forever."

"I've been really busy with work, not one spare moment," Lisa said. "Sorry if I've been ignoring you."

"At least you are here, and I will bestow some brownie points. The other two will have to beg my forgiveness." Joann laughed at her joke. "By the way, I saw that Herb is again the toast of southwest Missouri, so congrats on that. Now what?"

"Dinners, photo ops, et cetera. Same old, same old," Lisa said. "Different day."

"Ah, politics." Joann led Lisa over to where a portable bar had been set up. "What do you want?"

"Soda's fine," Lisa said, watching as Joann gave the bartender her order. Just as she had for Herb's party, Mary Beth had hired a catering firm. A waiter offered a tray of appetizers, but Lisa declined.

Joann handed Lisa a clear plastic cup full of soda. Joann had chosen white wine and took a drink before saying, "Can you believe it? I don't feel thirty, although I swear I found another gray hair today."

"You're fine," Lisa said.

"You don't have dark hair like mine," Joann said. "Your blond hides the gray."

"Which I don't have," Lisa added quickly.

"Yet," Joann said knowingly as they stepped away from the bar.

"So where is the brat pack?" Lisa asked. She hadn't seen any children running about.

"The kids are upstairs with a babysitter. They went to Six Flags all day so they're beat. Only Tommy's still awake, and he's watching a movie." Joann led Lisa outside. The garden and pool were again lit with dozens of little white Christmas lights strung through the trees. "That's the great thing about my mom's house. Somehow they always fall asleep early and sleep late."

"Sounds perfect," Lisa said.

"You know, since my dad got sick, my parents have talked about selling the house, but then they wouldn't have the space for events like this. Speaking of…my mom raved about how wonderful you were to work with for the party. I never did get to hear much about it that night Timmy got sick." Joann gestured to a wicker table with two chairs.

"I don't want to keep you from your party," Lisa said.

"You're not. Most of those people in there are my parents' friends. Once they say happy birthday, their job is done. I'd rather hang with you. You're the one I never get to spend any time with anymore."

"As long as we don't talk about Mark," Lisa said. "That's too awkward."

"Okay," Joann said with a nod. "I know I'd like to, but we don't have to. I mean, remember our freshman year when I dated that guy you liked? You know, before I met Kyle? We survived that, didn't we?"

"Yeah, we did," Lisa said. She relaxed a little now that Mark was off-limits, and within minutes she and Joann were catching up and having a great conversation.

"Hey, Joann." A slim twentysomething woman wearing a floral sundress approached the table.

"Hi, Rhonda."

"Sorry to interrupt, but have you seen your brother? This is his." Rhonda held a legal-size envelope in her left hand, and Lisa found herself automatically glancing for a wedding ring. The woman wore a massive diamond, and relief stole over Lisa. Then she chastised herself for being so pathetic. Mark could date. She'd ended their exclusivity.

"I haven't seen him," Joann said. "He was in the basement rec room playing pool. Have you tried there?"

The woman frowned. "These are his copies of the paperwork, and unfortunately Josh and I have to cut out now. Sorry we'll miss your cake cutting."

"Don't worry about it," Joann said with a dismissive wave. "I'm just grateful you stopped by. Why don't you leave that envelope with me? I'll get it to him."

"Thanks. That'll save me from having to mail it. Tell him that the Realtor open house is Tuesday at eleven and we'll open to the public at two next Sunday."

"Will do. Good to see you again," Joann said. She placed the packet on the table, the dull brown a marked contrast to the white wicker.

Lisa stared at the envelope. Aside from Mark's name scrawled in the center, the only other printing on the envelope was a label for a local real-estate firm.

"He's selling his house?" Lisa asked.

"You made Mark off-limits," Joann said, arching her eyebrow as if to say *Remember?*

"Forget that," Lisa said. "Is he selling his house or not?"

"Yes," Joann admitted. "Rhonda's been a friend since high school and she's a great agent."

"Why?" Lisa demanded. She didn't care about Rhonda's abilities. "He loves that house."

"No, he doesn't," Joann said. She sighed. "Lisa, Mark grew up with a lot of stuff. But stuff is just that— stuff. He's decided that one man puttering around that huge house is just a waste. He's searching for something smaller, more appropriate. Said he'd finally realized someone was correct in calling his home excessive."

Lisa sank her teeth into her lower lip. She'd been that someone. She'd criticized him for having four thousand square feet. Mark could not sell his house just because of her. She'd been wrong to criticize its size. Heck, she'd been wrong about so many things, and this proved it. She had to at least set this right.

She rose to her feet and grabbed her cup. "I'll be back," she said.

"Want me to go with you?" Joann offered.

"To the bathroom?" Lisa asked. A strange expression crossed her face. "This isn't college."

As Lisa wove her way through the crowd, Joann tapped the envelope on the table in front of her and chuckled. Twenty bucks said Lisa was off to find her brother, not the ladies' room.

Fate sure had a strange way of working where matters of the heart were concerned. Joann couldn't have set this current situation up any better had she tried. Just as when she'd gotten pregnant. She'd had the hugest decision of her life to make regarding her career—did she really want to move halfway across the country, away from Kyle, so she could take that news anchor job? But then fate had intervened and Joann had become a wife and mother instead. Through the glass patio doors Joann watched Lisa bypass the half bath and slip through the basement door. Mentally paying herself twenty dollars, Joann grabbed the envelope and went back inside.

LISA FOUND MARK IN THE finished basement, playing pool with some man she didn't recognize. The basement had nine-foot ceilings, making the space seem less crowded, but Lisa still had to weave her way through several groups of people before she reached the edge of the pool table.

Mark sank two solid balls, and as he straightened, Lisa looked him directly in the eye and said, "We need to talk."

"Again?" Mark asked. He missed the next shot, and his competitor chalked his cue and leaned over the felt.

Lisa clenched her fists slightly. Although she deserved it, let him not be difficult here! "Please."

Her voice had dropped on that last word, and Mark glanced around the room. He placed his cue stick back into a holder. "Sorry," he told his competitor, "but I'm going to have to forfeit."

"No problem," the guy said, proceeding to sink three striped balls. "I was about to clear off the table, anyway."

"Yeah, right," Mark said about the game. His grin faded as he moved past Lisa. "Follow me."

At the top of stairs Mark made a left into the kitchen. The catering staff glanced up at him and then went immediately back to their business as Mark passed through and began to ascend the back stairs.

"Where are we going?" Lisa asked. It had been over ten years since she'd been on the second floor of the Smith home.

"To talk," Mark said. Unlike the front stairs, which ended at a wide landing, the back stairs led to a narrow hallway. He passed several doors before tossing one open. "In here," Mark said.

Lisa stepped into the room. Decorated in muted blues and grays, the room looked like a study. Many of Mark's high school mementos—trophies, certificates and photos—still lined the walls.

"I never saw fit to take any of this stuff down when I moved," Mark said. "Usually Tommy stays in here, but tonight he's bunking with Timmy in another room. But that's not why you're here. I'm listening. What do you have to say?"

Her chest heaved. "Some woman gave your sister a package for you. Your real-estate papers."

"So?" Mark frowned. "Joann will get it to me."

"You can't sell your house," Lisa blurted out. "I…"

She faltered under his intense scrutiny. Finally he said, "You of all people should understand why I'm selling. The house is too big, a fact you made plain several times."

"Yes, but—" she paused to inhale a calming breath "—I've been wrong about a lot of things. You shouldn't be listening to me, especially when I don't make sense. Which has been a lot lately. My world is different from yours and I shouldn't try to impose my moral code on you."

He shrugged, and a longing to touch him and make him understand began to build.

"Really, Lisa, you don't have to feel guilty about my decisions. The market is a balloon and selling now will ensure I don't lose any money."

He hadn't comprehended her point. "But you have

no reason to move. Your house is perfect and you've worked so hard decorating it. You love that house."

"I don't love that house," Mark said. His expression turned pained. "Not like I love you."

"You don't love me," Lisa said. "It was just some lust. It was just—"

"No," he said. "Don't shortchange what we had. I was never casual with you." The tone of his voice changed, became contemplative, as if he'd figured out something important. "Wait. You wouldn't be up here having a fit about my house if you didn't care."

Lisa resisted the urge to stomp her foot. "Of course I care. I don't want you to give up something because of me. I've already hurt you enough. You should be happy. I want that for you. I…"

Love you.

Silence descended in the room as Lisa finally admitted the full truth to herself. She loved this man more than anything.

"I know," Mark said gently, as if reading her mind. His tender demeanor was reassuring. "And it scares the hell out of you, doesn't it? Love is something you can't control and—admit it—you've fallen for me right back."

Lisa nodded, her voice mute. Here was a man who understood her. Loved her without smothering. He was her other half.

They both stood there a moment, simply drinking each other in. Her gaze swept over his blue Dockers slacks, red polo shirt and loafers. She'd missed him terribly. When she'd been in his arms, she'd been happy. Complete. But there were still issues, barriers in the way of long-term bliss.

"But I'm moving," she said. "I can't do long-distance."

He smiled. "Then aren't you glad that I've just removed your biggest hurdle? I'm about to be home-less. And as I can run my consulting company from anywhere that has a fax machine and an Internet con-nection, I don't see any reason why we can't be together. I'll move where you do."

"This is all so sudden," she said as panic edged back in. She'd been in sole control for so long that the idea of a mutual partnership still scared her slightly.

But Mark wasn't afraid. He was assured, deter-mined. He stepped forward into her space, and she let him.

"Nothing with us has been sudden. It's been almost twelve years in the making," Mark said. "Each road we've taken in our life, including that kiss at Joann's reception, has led us to this moment. The question we have to ask ourselves now is, where are we going from here?"

He was mere inches from her, and she trembled, not from fear but from desire. She'd always wanted him. She now had that chance to have it all; her physical, mental and emotional needs could all be met by loving this man.

"You know," Mark said suddenly, "my sister's been correct about us all along. So if chasing you is what it's going to take to prove myself and my love to you, then you best get ready to run."

"Run where?" Lisa said. She frowned for a moment until she realized he meant that he'd come after her. He'd sold his house so that he could be with her. "Oh…"

He was making her believe.

"Is Herb going to win?" Mark asked, the question seemingly out of the blue.

"Yes," Lisa said, wondering where he was leading her with this new vein.

"And at this time he's deep in his campaign," Mark added.

"Yes," Lisa said.

"Although I'm not running for office, I'm the exact same way," Mark said. "You see, he's not settling for anything less than the governor's mansion and I'm not settling for anyone but you. Since I'm a straight shooter, I'll be very up front and tell you that means marriage. A marriage campaign, if you will. And, Lisa, no matter how much you fight me, I'm going to win. And I don't think anyone will bet against me."

"This is too much," Lisa said, but as she voiced the words, she knew how false they were. All her hopes and dreams were found here, with him. He loved her. She loved him. Maybe it really was that simple when she stripped away all the insecurities that kept her from grasping the brass ring. Maybe that's why Lisa's mother, despite having missed Lisa's father, stayed with him and loved him greatly to this day.

"Am I really too much?" Mark asked.

"No," Lisa said. She shook her head and became bolder. "You are exactly what I want, and for the long-term. But we have to have parameters. My career is important to me. I want to work and—"

"And that's fine," Mark interrupted quickly. "I can work anywhere. So I'm going to be with you no matter what. Whether we live in St. Louis or Jeff City or Washington, D.C., location doesn't matter, Lisa. I will be with you."

And with that, Lisa began to cry. Mark drew her into his arms, sheltering her.

"You've overwhelmed me," she said.

"I intend to," he admitted. "I love you. I'm not going to lose you ever again."

"I've been miserable without you. But you really were going to chase me? I mean, you didn't know I'd come find you to talk," Lisa said between sniffles.

"No, but I'd planned on finding you. I've spent this whole week moving everything into place and freeing myself up so I could woo you properly. I made myself a vow to settle down at thirty but only if I found the right woman. I did. You. And unlike the reception, I won't ever let you get away again."

"You are such a terrific man," she said. "I can't believe I sent you away. I'm so sorry. I try to be so tough and…"

"Hush," Mark said. "None of that matters. You can be tough. I won't tell anyone you have a sensitive side."

She heard the teasing in his tone and that stopped the flow of her tears. "You are always going to be one step ahead of me, aren't you?"

"Probably," Mark said. "That's just my nature. But I don't think that's a bad thing, do you?"

"I used to," Lisa admitted. "But I'm having second thoughts."

"Good," Mark said. He touched her cheek, and the gesture conveyed more than words how much he loved her. "So are we straight on the plan?"

He was ahead of her again. "Plan?" she asked.

"Dating. Career. Marriage. Kids. Happily ever after in whatever town we settle in."

"Oh," Lisa said. Joy had her hugging him tight. "That plan."

"Yeah. That one," Mark said with a loving grin. He rubbed his hands on her lower back. "It doesn't have to all happen overnight, so long as you know that it will happen. You know I'm a planner. So what do you say?"

"Yes," Lisa said. "I say yes."

And with that, Mark lowered his mouth to hers and kissed her. The kiss promised that all would be okay. His lips moved over hers, washing away her fears and sealing their commitment to each other.

"This way," he said, leading her to his former bedroom. Once there, Lisa molded herself to him. "I think you should show the birthday boy how much you love him," Mark said.

Lisa raised her lips for a long kiss. "A very, very good idea."

Epilogue

One thing could be said for Mark, Lisa thought a week later. If he ever did want to go into politics, he'd win hands down. His marriage campaign had required only one week before she'd put both feet totally in his camp and said yes.

They'd been at a baseball game, scene of their first date, when he'd gotten down on one knee and proposed to her during the seventh-inning stretch. The game had already been special, Herb having thrown out the ceremonial first pitch.

"Happy?" Mark asked Lisa later the next afternoon around four. They'd spent a leisurely Saturday making love.

"Very," Lisa said. Herb had given her the weekend off, and until Mark's house sold, they would live there. "I've got some work I must do," she said.

"I'm going to mow the grass for tomorrow's open house," Mark said. He leaned down and kissed her.

"No," he said, drawing away with a regretful groan. "I cannot kiss you more. I must mow and you must work."

"Okay." Lisa giggled. As he left the room, Lisa studied the way the diamond engagement ring on her finger sparkled in the sunlight. News like this had to be shared. She reached for the phone. As Tori was still out of town, Lisa decided to start with Cecile.

Once it had become apparent Mr. Right wasn't going to reveal himself, the former roommates had joked often about how they'd probably go into their thirties together as single career women. Until now. That was all about to change. The phone connected.

"Cecile! You won't believe it! Mark and I are getting married!"

"Congrats," Cecile said. Lisa could tell she was stunned. After all, the last time they'd talked Mark and Lisa hadn't even begun a relationship.

"And no, I'm not pregnant," Lisa said, laughing as she pictured Cecile's expression. "I'm in love."

"Wow. That was fast."

"It happens that way," Lisa said. "You know what this means, don't you? I'm not going to be the last one married anymore. And since Tori's too busy with Jeff, that means one thing. Cecile, the order's changed. You, my friend, are next."

* * * * *

Watch for Cecile's story, THE WEDDING SECRET, the next AMERICAN BEAUTIES release coming December 2006 from Michele Dunaway and Harlequin American Romance.

*Experience the anticipation, the thrill of the chase
and the sheer rush of falling in love!
Turn the page for a sneak preview of a new book from
Harlequin Romance
THE REBEL PRINCE by Raye Morgan
On sale August 29th wherever books are sold*

"OH, NO!"

The reaction slipped out before Emma Valentine could stop it, for there stood the very man she most wanted to avoid seeing again.

He didn't look any happier to see her.

"Well, come on, get on board," he said gruffly. "I won't bite." One eyebrow rose. "Though I might nibble a little," he added, mostly to amuse himself.

But she wasn't paying any attention to what he was saying. She was staring at him, taking in the royal blue uniform he was wearing, with gold braid and glistening badges decorating the sleeves, epaulettes and an upright collar. Ribbons and medals covered the breast of the short, fitted jacket. A gold-encrusted sabre hung at his side. And suddenly it was clear to her who this man really was.

She gulped wordlessly. Reaching out, he took her elbow and pulled her aboard. The doors slid closed. And finally she found her tongue.

"You...you're the prince."

He nodded, barely glancing at her. "Yes. Of course."

She raised a hand and covered her mouth for a moment. "I should have known."

"Of course you should have. I don't know why you didn't." He punched the ground-floor button to get the elevator moving again, then turned to look down at her. "A relatively bright five-year-old child would have tumbled to the truth right away."

Her shock faded as her indignation at his tone asserted itself. He might be the prince, but he was still just as annoying as he had been earlier that day.

"A relatively bright five-year-old child without a bump on the head from a badly thrown water polo ball, maybe," she said defensively. She wasn't feeling woozy any longer and she wasn't about to let him bully her, no matter how royal he was. "I was unconscious half the time."

"And just clueless the other half, I guess," he said, looking bemused.

The arrogance of the man was really galling.

"I suppose you think your 'royalness' is so obvious it sort of shimmers around you for all to see?" she challenged. "Or better yet, oozes from your pores like...like sweat on a hot day?"

"Something like that," he acknowledged calmly. "Most people tumble to it pretty quickly. In fact, it's hard to hide even when I want to avoid dealing with it."

"Poor baby," she said, still resenting his manner. "I guess that works better with injured people who are half asleep." Looking at him, she felt a strange emotion she couldn't identify. It was as though she wanted to prove something to him, but she wasn't sure what. "And anyway, you know you did your best to fool me," she added.

His brows knit together as though he really didn't know what she was talking about. "I didn't do a thing."

"You told me your name was Monty."

"It is." He shrugged. "I have a lot of names. Some of them are too rude to be spoken to my face, I'm sure." He glanced at her sideways, his hand on the hilt of his sabre. "Perhaps you're contemplating one of those right now."

You bet I am.

That was what she would like to say. But it suddenly occurred to her that she was supposed to be working for this man. If she wanted to keep the job of coronation chef, maybe she'd better keep her opinions to herself. So she clamped her mouth shut, took a deep breath and looked away, trying hard to calm down.

The elevator ground to a halt and the doors slid open laboriously. She moved to step forward, hoping to make her escape, but his hand shot out again and caught her elbow.

"Wait a minute. *You're* a woman," he said, as though that thought had just presented itself to him.

"That's a rare ability for insight you have there, Your Highness," she snapped before she could stop herself. And then she winced. She was going to have to do better than that if she was going to keep this relationship on an even keel.

But he was ignoring her dig. Nodding, he stared at her with a speculative gleam in his golden eyes. "I've been looking for a woman, but you'll do."

She blanched, stiffening. "I'll do for what?"

He made a head gesture in a direction she knew was opposite of where she was going and his grip tightened on her elbow.

"Come with me," he said abruptly, making it an order.

She dug in her heels, thinking fast. She didn't much like orders. "Wait! I can't. I have to get to the kitchen."

"Not yet. I need you."

"You what?" Her breathless gasp of surprise was soft, but she knew he'd heard it.

"I need you," he said firmly. "Oh, don't look so shocked. I'm not planning to throw you into the hay and have my way with you. I need you for something a bit more mundane than that."

She felt color rushing into her cheeks and she silently begged it to stop. Here she was, formless and stodgy in her chef's whites. No makeup, no stiletto heels. Hardly the picture of the femmes fatales he was undoubtedly used to. The likelihood that he would have any carnal interest in her was remote at best. To have him think she was hysterically defending her virtue was humiliating.

"Well, what if I don't want to go with you?" she said in hopes of deflecting his attention from her blush.

"Too bad."

"What?"

Amusement sparkled in his eyes. He was certainly enjoying this. And that only made her more determined to resist him.

"I'm the prince, remember? And we're in the castle. My orders take precedence. It's that old pesky divine rights thing."

Her jaw jutted out. Despite her embarrassment, she couldn't let that pass.

"Over my free will? Never!"

Exasperation filled his face.

"Hey, call out the historians. Someone will write a book about you and your courageous principles." His eyes glittered sardonically. "But in the meantime, Emma Valentine, you're coming with me."

SAVE UP TO $30! SIGN UP TODAY!

INSIDE *Romance*

The complete guide to your favorite
Harlequin®, Silhouette® and Love Inspired® books.

✓ Newsletter ABSOLUTELY FREE! No purchase necessary.

✓ Valuable coupons for future purchases of Harlequin,
  Silhouette and Love Inspired books in every issue!

✓ Special excerpts & previews in each issue. Learn about all
  the hottest titles before they arrive in stores.

✓ No hassle—mailed directly to your door!

✓ Comes complete with a handy shopping checklist
  so you won't miss out on any titles.

- -

SIGN ME UP TO RECEIVE INSIDE ROMANCE ABSOLUTELY FREE

(Please print clearly)

Name

Address

City/Town   State/Province   Zip/Postal Code

(098 KKM EJL9)

Please mail this form to:
In the U.S.A.: Inside Romance, P.O. Box 9057, Buffalo, NY 14269-9057
In Canada: Inside Romance, P.O. Box 622, Fort Erie, ON L2A 5X3
OR visit http://www.eHarlequin.com/insideromance

IRNBPA06R   ® and ™ are trademarks owned and used by the trademark owner and/or its licensee.

ANGELS OF THE BIG SKY
by Roz Denny Fox

(#1368)

Widow Marlee Stein returns to Montana with her
young daughter, ready to help out with Cloud Chasers,
the flying service owned by her brother. When Marlee
takes over piloting duties, she finds herself in conflict
with a client, ranger Wylie Ames. Too bad Marlee's
attracted to a man she doesn't even want to like!

On sale September 2006!

THE CLOUD CHASERS—
Life is looking up.

Watch for the second story in Roz Denny Fox's two-
book series THE CLOUD CHASERS, available in
December 2006.

*Available wherever books are sold, including most
bookstores, supermarkets, discount stores and drugstores.*

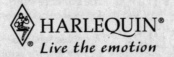

HARLEQUIN®
Live the emotion

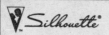

INTIMATE MOMENTS™

Don't miss the next exciting romantic-suspense
novel from *USA TODAY* bestselling author

**Risking his life was part of the job.
Risking his heart was another matter...**

Detective Sawyer Boone had better things to do
with his time than babysit the fiercely independent
daughter of the chief of detectives. But when
Janelle's world came crashing around her, Sawyer
found himself wanting to protect her heart, as well.

CAVANAUGH WATCH

Silhouette Intimate Moments #1431

When the law and passion
collide, this family learns
the ultimate truth—that
love takes no prisoners!

*Available September 2006
at your favorite retail outlet.*

Visit Silhouette Books at www.eHarlequin.com   SIMCW

If you enjoyed what you just read,
then we've got an offer you can't resist!

Take 2 bestselling
love stories FREE!

Plus get a FREE surprise gift!

Clip this page and mail it to Harlequin Reader Service®

IN U.S.A.	**IN CANADA**
3010 Walden Ave.	P.O. Box 609
P.O. Box 1867	Fort Erie, Ontario
Buffalo, N.Y. 14240-1867	L2A 5X3

YES! Please send me 2 free Harlequin American Romance® novels and my free surprise gift. After receiving them, if I don't wish to receive anymore, I can return the shipping statement marked cancel. If I don't cancel, I will receive 4 brand-new novels every month, before they're available in stores! In the U.S.A., bill me at the bargain price of $4.24 plus 25¢ shipping & handling per book and applicable sales tax, if any*. In Canada, bill me at the bargain price of $4.99 plus 25¢ shipping & handling per book and applicable taxes**. That's the complete price and a savings of at least 10% off the cover prices—what a great deal! I understand that accepting the 2 free books and gift places me under no obligation ever to buy any books. I can always return a shipment and cancel at any time. Even if I never buy another book from Harlequin, the 2 free books and gift are mine to keep forever.

154 HDN DZ7S
354 HDN DZ7T

Name	(PLEASE PRINT)	
Address	Apt.#	
City	State/Prov.	Zip/Postal Code

Not valid to current Harlequin American Romance® subscribers.

Want to try two free books from another series?
Call 1-800-873-8635 or visit www.morefreebooks.com.

* Terms and prices subject to change without notice. Sales tax applicable in N.Y.
** Canadian residents will be charged applicable provincial taxes and GST.
  All orders subject to approval. Offer limited to one per household.
  ® are registered trademarks owned and used by the trademark owner and or its licensee.

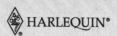